"FEEL FREE TO TAKE WHATEVER YOU LIKE, MAEVE."

"Thank ye . . . *you*, Charles. I'll be readin' any book you care to bring home."

"Even if they're only manuscripts I'm considering publishing?"

"Aye, I'll read your market list if ye wish!"

He laughed out loud, then turned to leave before Maeve asked, "Have ye talked to the police about your stolen sketch?"

"Yes." His jaw clenched as he opened the door. "They gave me little hope of recovery. But I will find it. I must. I've taken an advertisement offering a reward."

Maeve smiled gravely. "I'll be askin' the Lhiannon Sidhe to look out for your sketch, Charles."

"Aaah . . . thank you, Maeve."

Charles retreated to his study, feeling edgy. Pouring himself a brandy, he stretched in the leather wingback chair by the fireplace.

So his wife believed in fairy folk and adored books . . . and liked wearing men's nightclothes. Charles smiled to himself. He had never guessed how alluring a woman could look in an oversized shirt. No matter how he attempted to keep his attention on their conversation, his mind conjured tantalizing images of a petite, voluptuous body hidden beneath all that red flannel. The desire to rip away the concealing nightshirt very nearly overwhelmed him.

But a Rycroft always did the right thing.

Didn't he?

BOOK YOUR PLACE ON OUR WEBSITE AND MAKE THE READING CONNECTION!

We've created a customized website just for our very special readers, where you can get the inside scoop on everything that's going on with Zebra, Pinnacle and Kensington books.

When you come online, you'll have the exciting opportunity to:

- View covers of upcoming books
- Read sample chapters
- Learn about our future publishing schedule (listed by publication month *and author*)
- Find out when your favorite authors will be visiting a city near you
- Search for and order backlist books from our online catalog
- Check out author bios and background information
- Send e-mail to your favorite authors
- Meet the Kensington staff online
- Join us in weekly chats with authors, readers and other guests
- Get writing guidelines
- AND MUCH MORE!

**Visit our website at
http://www.zebrabooks.com**

COMFORT AND JOY

Sandra Madden

ZEBRA BOOKS
KENSINGTON PUBLISHING CORP.

http://www.zebrabooks.com

ZEBRA BOOKS are published by

Kensington Publishing Corp.
850 Third Avenue
New York, NY 10022

All Kensington titles, imprints and distributed lines are available at special quantity discounts for bulk purchases for sales promotion, premiums, fund-raising, educational or institutional use.

Special book excerpts or customized printings can also be created to fit specific needs. For details, write or phone the office of the Kensington Special Sales Manager: Kensington Publishing Corp., 850 Third Avenue, New York, NY 10022. Attn. Special Sales Department. Phone: 1-800-221-2647.

Zebra and the Z logo Reg. U.S. Pat. & TM Off.

First Printing: October 2001
10 9 8 7 6 5 4 3 2 1

Printed in the United States of America

*Nollaig agus Athbhliain faoi shéan
is faoi mhaise dhuit & emdash*

*Wishing you peace and happiness
for Christmas and the New Year*
—A Gaelic Greeting

Chapter One

Boston 1873

Dear God! He was in bed with an unfamiliar woman. A beautiful woman, indisputably—but nevertheless a stranger.

While it wasn't the first time Charles Ashton Rycroft had awakened to find himself in bed with a pretty female companion, it had been several years since. At thirty years of age, he'd put those days of reckless youth behind him. But even then, on the morning after a frolic he'd almost always recognized the lady in his bed and most of the time remembered her name as well.

Unlike the present.

The woman snuggled familiarly against him, the bare flesh of her silky, warm back pressed to his chest. Charles's cheek nestled in a thick mane of shining sloe-black hair that smelled of sweet spring violets. His arms wrapped around her small body intimately as if he were in the habit of sleeping this way.

His head ached, an ache so fierce he feared it might split. Obviously, he'd had far too much to drink the night before.

Unwilling to wake the sleeping woman before taking stock of his predicament, Charles lay quite still. For a moment he listened to the ringing in his ears, willing the annoying sound away. Only his eyes moved as he scanned the foyer-sized room searching for something that might trigger a memory of what had occurred the night before. Nothing.

The barren chamber held only one rickety chair, a spindle-legged table with a washbasin, and a faded print on one wall, the subject of which appeared to be fairies romping among the stars. The narrow mattress beneath him felt lumpy and rough as if it were made from straw.

Outside, through the cold room's single window, flurries of snow danced in the gray winter dawn. Charles had never been in such humble surroundings and for the life of him could not fathom how he happened here.

"Good morning, me love."

The nameless stranger spoke!

Charles stiffened.

Awakening slowly, the woman stretched and wiggled deeper into his arms. Her body, warm and velvety soft as a rose petal, rubbed against him, arousing Charles in a swift, shameful way. Stifling a groan, he gritted his teeth. He did not even know this woman. How could she do this to him?

She rubbed her eyes. He carefully withdrew one arm; the other remained pinned beneath her. Charles squirmed in a backward movement, intent on preventing any further embarrassing contact with the stranger's body. In the nick of time he realized that he would fall from the bed if he moved an inch more. He froze.

She sighed. A deep, contented sound.

Charles cleared his throat. "Good morning."

She purred again. Her lustrous blue-black curls tickled his nose. He gingerly swept the silky wayward strands away.

"I think we should lie abed all day," she murmured. A melodic Irish lilt laced her speech.

He knew no Irish women.

Charles looked wildly around the room for his clothes. "Ah, but I'm afraid I must be going now."

"And where would ye be going? You're not strong enough for work yet." She yawned loudly, not bothering to cover her mouth. "But I must be off to the Deakinses, I suppose."

That said, she rolled over. With no place to run, no clothes in sight, Charles held his breath and closed his eyes. A disturbing thought flashed across his mind. What did she mean, he wasn't strong enough to work? Had they spent an especially vigorous evening together?

Not wishing to appear at a loss, he replied, "I suppose you must."

Before he could say more, she moved. Soft, generous breasts brushed, then pressed, against his chest. A searing heat shot through Charles.

He opened his eyes, attempting to ignore the tightening in his lower regions, the sweet leaden ache her body ignited in him. "Before I get up, what do ye say to a mornin' kiss?" she teased in a low, throaty tone.

Dear God, the woman had no mercy.

Charles closed his eyes again and held his breath, hoping the gripping heat would pass.

Her arms curled around his neck.

He opened his eyes. His throat went dry. Large, twinkling, lapis-blue eyes fringed by long, dark lashes gazed up at him. Full ruby lips smiled in a coquettish fashion. "One kiss?"

What kind of cad would he be to deny such a lovely wench?

But as he dipped his head to comply with her request, she gave another little sigh and shook her head. A shadow of regret darkened her extraordinary eyes. "I suppose we should not start what there is no time to finish."

Damn.

"I . . . I suppose not."

"Will you miss me, me love?"

How could he possibly miss a woman he could not recall? Granted, she was a beauty. Still, Charles must nip what could only be called a careless misadventure in the bud.

"Miss you?" He took a deep breath. "I'm afraid I do not know you, Miss. One night of passion is hardly—"

The smile slipped from her lips and her deep blue eyes went even wider—if it was possible. "One night of passion?" she cried, unquestionably incensed.

Apparently the tart angered quickly.

But Charles refused to retreat. "I daresay, I cannot seem to recall your name."

"Ye can't recall me name!" she cried. Quite loudly.

"Forgive me."

To his surprise, her anger melted away as quickly as it had come. A frown wrinkled the smooth alabaster plane of her brow. She really was quite breathtaking. Although it had been years since he had turned to a strumpet for physical release, it was not difficult to understand why he hadn't been able to resist this woman. Actually, a man would not have to be in his cups to want her. Her silky, fair complexion and the natural blush of her cheeks put him in mind of sweet peaches and cream—indubitably a delicious dish.

However, any association with an Irish woman, ravishing or not, was unthinkable for a man of his social status.

"Me name is Maeve. Maeve O'Malley."

"Maeve. A pleasant name."

"I am your wife."

"My wife!"

Shock, as a descriptive term, did not come close to capturing the cold, immobilizing force that took hold of Charles. He couldn't be certain his heart was still beating. It felt as if the blood drained from his body, his stiff, numb body. He could not seem to draw a breath of air, much less swallow one.

"We were wed five days ago by Father Thom," she added quietly.

"You could not possibly be my wife!"

A loud rapping on the door served to silence Charles. He jerked his head toward the door. What new horror lay behind it?

A deep, graveled voice hollered from the other side. "What's goin' on in there?"

"That would be me dad," Maeve said.

"I warned ye about this," her father bellowed in a thick Irish brogue. "I didn't mind ye bringin' home the stray cats and the dogs, but a man is altogether another matter."

She shot Charles an impish grin. "Sure'n it is."

"Nothin' but trouble."

"And wouldn't ye be knowin', Dad?"

"Are ye all right in there?"

"I'll be out in a moment and puttin' on the tea. Go away now and give us some privacy."

Charles heard Maeve's father mutter and shuffle away.

"You brought me home like a stray dog?" he asked, confused.

"Me brother Shea and I found you in an alley on the way home a week ago now. In the true spirit of the Christmas season I thought to bring ye home to give ye a wash and a bowl of champ." She lowered her eyes. "I believed ye to be a bummer."

"A bummer?" Mightily offended, Charles bristled at the insult. How could anyone believe the heir to the Rycroft fortune—and the president of the prestigious Rycroft Publishing firm of Boston—to be a bummer?

"Ye were unconscious when we found you. It appeared as if ye had a wee too much ale and had passed out as me dear dad sometimes does."

"I see." But he did not. Such a mistake seemed inconceivable no matter what the circumstances.

"When I wiped away the dirt, I discovered ye had been beaten. Can ye not feel the bruise here?" Maeve took his hand in hers and moved it to a sore spot on the left side of his jaw and then to a lump on his right temple. "And here?"

"Beaten?" Her story became more mysterious. He could not think how he would come to such a state. Charles had no enemies—that he knew.

"Ye were dealt a heavy blow to your head and to your jaw and ye were kicked about the ribs as well."

He couldn't be sure if his now-throbbing head was from the lingering effects of the blow Maeve described, or from the news he'd married an unknown Irish woman.

"How does it happen that you . . . that you and I are married? I am quite certain that I do not know you."

"Me brother Shea insisted."

"Why?"

She lowered her eyes and gave him a shy, whispered explanation. "When ye weren't quite yourself, he saw ye pull me down to the bed and kiss me full on the lips. Ye were bare as a newborn babe at the time. 'Twas only the second day ye were here. Myself? I took it as a favorable sign that ye were regaining your strength."

"Dear God."

"But me brother convinced me dad that ye'd compromised me. A wee bit angry he was for the liberty you took. I tried to tell him you were out of your head at the time."

"Dear . . . dear God."

"But Shea argued he, bein' a man, knew the truth about what ye were thinkin'. He said just because I was sleepin' on the pallet beside the bed, didn't mean ye didn't lure me into your bed after he and my dad were asleep. Besides, he said I'd seen your private parts and only a wife should do that."

His private parts. She'd become familiar with his private parts? Charles thought his head might explode with the pounding.

"But I was nursin' ye. What would ye have me do?"

Charles shook his head. A small ray of hope blossomed in his heart. He would seek an annulment immediately.

"I didn't think it right to wed, myself. But I had no choice."

The girl had been forced to marry him. More than likely Maeve O'Malley would be as happy as he to have the union quickly dissolved. His first matter of business this morning would be a visit to his lawyer and friend, Spencer Wellington.

He glanced at her hands—small, chapped, working hands. Maeve dropped them under the covers as if she were ashamed.

"You have no wedding ring," he pointed out, as if the lack of the symbol might prove no marriage had taken place.

She pulled on a chain around her neck. It held a narrow gold band of clasping hands and a crown. "It was me mother's. But I do not need a ring to know I have a husband. I vowed to be loyal to ye and stay the course through sickness and health."

Charles wondered if the law would hold him to a vow he had no memory of taking. He thought not.

Maeve smiled then, a radiant smile that swept through the chilly room like a warm summer breeze. " 'Twas a sweet, simple affair at the church," she said, "with just Father Thom, Shea, and your new father-in-law."

"What name did you call me for the ceremony?"

"Charles Rycroft. The name sewed into your jacket. But I've been calling ye Charlie."

"Charlie? How curious." How common.

"Aye. 'Tis a strong-sounding name, befitting a man with broad shoulders and the strong-muscled arms of a boxer. Ye are not a boxer, are ye?"

Charles could not help but feel flattered at her assessment of his physique. "No. I fence and row," he told her. He'd engaged in gentlemen's sports all of his life. "And my name *is* Charles Rycroft."

"Fancy that, now. I thought the name might be that of the tailor's who made your fine jacket."

Looking around the room once again in search of his clothes, Charles saw rough woolen trousers and a flannel shirt hanging from a corner peg. "Do you know where my jacket might be? And my trousers?"

"Aye," she nodded. "We burned them. They were of no use to anyone, torn and covered with blood as they were."

The information made no sense. Bloody clothes. A beaten body left to die in an alley. Charles tried to think back to what might have happened to him, but it seemed the harder he attempted to recall the events, the more his head throbbed.

He started as Maeve whisked the top cover off the bed and wrapped the wooly blanket around herself as she stood. "I have a job that I must be off to now."

Charles pulled the old down coverlet she'd left for him up over his chest. "What sort of position do you hold?" he asked with a fair amount of trepidation.

"Parlor maid to the Deakinses on Beacon Hill," she replied proudly.

Dear God, an Irish maid! Worse than he feared.

He'd been wed to an Irish maid! The throbbing in his head intensified to an unholy roar. It simply wasn't done. Charles had to extricate himself from this marriage as quickly and quietly as possible. A Rycroft did the right thing which meant—among other interests—preventing a scandal on Beacon Hill. And there would certainly be a scandal if it was known he'd married an Irish serving woman.

His diminutive wife stood above him, her head held high, her raven curls tumbling in provocative disarray about delicate, creamy shoulders. A sweet, captivating smile parted her lips, and for a fleeting moment Charles thought her the most ravishing creature he'd ever seen. A powerful silence fell across the room as his eyes met hers.

Maeve forced her gaze away. Suddenly shy, she pulled her dress from the peg, a dark-blue silk hand-me-down from the Deakinses' daughter, Pansy.

"Would ye be turnin' your head for the sake of me modesty?"

"You were just lying in bed naked with me."

"That was when ye were Charlie."

Maeve had fallen in love with the man she called Charlie the moment she saw him wiped clean of blood and dirt. It was love at first sight and she knew it to be foolish. She thought him a gift from above, from her sweet mother who promised always to watch over Maeve.

From the moment Charlie regained consciousness he'd been a sweet and gentle man, a curious blend of vulnerability and strength. But Maeve knew amnesia to be a temporary condition, more than likely brought about by the beating. She understood that when his memory returned, the man she called Charlie might not be to her liking, or that he might reject her out of hand. From the time he first spoke, Maeve realized her Charlie wasn't Irish, which might be a problem. Irish immigrants were not welcomed or accepted by many of Boston's long-time residents. But Maeve chose to believe all would be well. It was the season of love, after all. She'd even speculated that the striking man she'd found might never regain his memory.

So much for that shamrock wish.

Dressing hurriedly, Maeve splashed cold water on her face from the basin and quickly swept her hair up to the top of her head. She fastened a bright red grosgrain bow in the center of her dark curls, paying no heed to the untamed locks that tumbled from their pins. She could not see them so they mattered not. The small wall mirror had fallen and broken several months ago and Maeve could ill afford to replace it.

"Tea will be ready in just a few minutes," Maeve told her plainly disturbed husband. "Best be dressing now. Ye'll find your clothes on the peg."

She scurried from the room without a backward glance. Charles Rycroft was a stiff sort. But she knew beneath his starch lay a more affable man.

"What was all the shoutin' about?" asked her irascible father, who slouched at the small table in the center of the room.

"Never you mind. 'Tis none of your affair." Maeve set the kettle on to boil.

"As long as yer livin' under my roof, all that happens here is my affair," he insisted.

The O'Malleys lived in a three-room tenement flat on the first floor of a dilapidated brick building in South Boston. Her father and brother shared one room, she another, and the cramped kitchen served as their living area. A table with four spindly chairs, small bookshelf, and a worn gold velvet sofa discarded by the Deakinses were the only furnishings.

The halls of the building smelled of cabbage and onions. The odor seeped under the doors, permeating every room and seemingly every pore of the tenement residents. Maeve imagined the awful aroma clung to her hair and adhered to her skin. She constantly sprinkled herself with her favorite violet fragrance, the only luxury she allowed herself.

"Me husband has remembered his name." Maeve set a chipped cup and saucer before her father.

Mick O'Malley looked up at her. His vivid blue eyes held the mischievousness of a leprechaun but the fringe of snowy white hair around the bald dome of his head was all his own.

"Aye? And has the fellow remembered what he did for a livin'? We could use another paycheck, me darlin'."

Maeve's father worked a block away at Rosie Grady's Saloon. Often as not, he drank away most of his salary.

"Saints above! How could I ask such a thing when he does not even remember marrying me?"

"Did he try to disavow ye?" The red-bulb tip of the old man's nose deepened to a fiery shade.

"No. But . . ."

The door of her room opened then and Charles's towering form filled the frame—she must become accustomed to calling him Charles. He regarded them silently—a bit warily, she thought. As Maeve gazed up at him, her heart fluttered like the wing of a startled bird on the branch . . . that commanding he was. A restless, raw energy flowed from Charles Rycroft like sizzling lava from a volcano, stirring an ancient heat deep inside of her.

The teakettle whistled.

"Good morning," he said, barely moving his lips.

From the start, Maeve suspected her husband might be a wee bit priggish, an endearing trait she nevertheless meant to help him overcome. His refined way of speaking and poker-stiff posture spoke of good breeding. The man she'd rescued came from a different world, one of privilege.

He stood well over six feet and exuded an air of authority no one could deny. His dark good looks radiated a power and masculinity Maeve found riveting. Clean shaven—she had taken the liberty of trimming his abundant side whiskers while he was still unconscious—his strong, square jaw revealed a man of power and potency.

Tearing her gaze away, Maeve motioned to the nearest chair. "Sit ye down. I'll have tea in—"

"Regrettably, I cannot stay."

"Just where do ye think ye be goin'?" Mick growled.

Charles arched an eyebrow. "Sir? I don't believe we've met."

Maeve raised a hand to cover her racing heart. Her father could be a hard man.

"Me name is Mick O'Malley, as well ye know." The old man's eyes narrowed. "Me bein' the daddy of yer bride."

Charles did not blink, although from Maeve's viewpoint, his jaw appeared to tighten. He extended his hand. "How do you do? I am Charles Rycroft."

Only five feet four, Maeve's father was strong for his limited stature. She knew he could crush a man's hand. Eyeing the tight clasp and the squeeze he gave Charles's hand, she held her breath.

Her husband didn't flinch. Maeve felt a gentle heart swell, a surge of respect for him.

"Where are ye from, Charles Rycroft?" Mick asked.

"My family has lived in Boston for years," Charles replied.

The old leprechaun's blue eyes lost their luster as they narrowed once again. "Ye one of those?"

Charles glanced at Maeve. All she could do was lower her head, shaking it slightly in warning.

"I beg your pardon?"

"Look." Mick turned to Maeve. "Ye can tell by the new way he's carryin' himself. By the mask he wears and the dull color of his eyes."

"What is that you can tell, my good sir?" Charles lifted his head and drew himself up to his full height.

Maeve knew Charlie was a proud man despite the lowly workingman's clothes he wore. He must be ill at ease and uncomfortable in her brother's worn garments. More than that, he was at a dreadful disadvantage, finding himself in strange surroundings with a cranky old man and a wife he did not know.

Her father, however, had no concern about Charles's discomfort. "I can tell by the looks of ye that you're one of those blueblood swells who have no use for little people like me. Ye make yer fortunes off the backs of poor immigrants like us who—"

"Dad!"

"Quiet, lass. I'm speakin'."

"Ye don't know what you're saying."

"Ye be mindin' my words or it's sorry ye'll be."

Charles Rycroft cleared his throat. "I shall take my leave now, but I will be contacting you—"

"Do ye be thinkin' to leave without your bride?" Mick growled.

Charles turned his attention to Maeve. Silver-gray eyes, the shade of fine pewter, met hers. He raked a hand through his hair, straight and thick; the rich, dark-walnut strands fell to the nape of his neck in helmet fashion. Maeve had taken her scissors to her husband's head as well as his whiskers, and so much the better he looked for her efforts. If she didn't say so herself.

Rycroft stood with his shoulders squared regarding Maeve as if she were a dilemma he must resolve. Although he might not be handsome in the chiseled manner some women preferred, with his aquiline nose and deep-set eyes Charles Rycroft made Maeve's heart feel a bit lighter, beat a bit faster.

"Come, then." Rycroft took her arm and hustled her to the door.

She snatched her worn woolen coat from the peg.

Once out on the street, Charles reacted with annoyance when she told him carriages for hire did not abound in South Boston. Maeve patiently explained they must walk to the horse-drawn trolley stop. Every day save Sunday, Maeve took the trolley to Boston and then walked across the Common to the Deakinses' brownstone residence.

The early morning air encouraged a swift pace to keep warm. Boston winters were long and brutal. The city was regularly beset by violent northeast storms. Between nor'easters, the sky seemed to remain a permanent grizzly gray and the temperature rarely rose above a piercing, arctic cold. Like today.

Puffs of white smoke rose from the three-story brick

dwellings into the somber gray sky. Predominately Irish, the South Boston streets bustled with activity as the residents left the area to fill their positions as servants and street mongers in Boston proper. Dressed in poorly fitting and worn layers of clothing, men, women, and children greeted each other in their musical accents.

An accent Charles found pleasing to his ear although he knew it to be a lower-class distinction. He'd been raised with a mind to class, schooled to treasure his heritage and uphold the tradition of the class to which he'd been born. As his mother often reminded him, his ancestors came to America aboard the *Mayflower*.

"Maeve, I want you to show me where you found me."

"Aye, but first I must let Mrs. Deakins know why I will not be workin' today."

No one ever objected to Charles's orders for any reason. "I will take care of the Deakinses. Now, do you remember where you found me?"

If he was not mistaken, Maeve slanted an irritated frown his way before hurrying on. "Aye. We found ye not far from here. Follow me."

Charles allowed her to take the lead, wondering fleetingly if she was warm enough in the thin wool coat she wore. His own unfamiliar garments did not protect him from the chill. They had only gone two blocks when he noticed Maeve's ears and the tip of her nose were red. Her slender fingers extended bare beyond the scratchy mittens that reached only to her knuckles. His heart went out to her, his wife . . . a poor Irish immigrant. A woman who'd taken him in and shared what little her family had with a stranger. Charles had never met such a woman and he admired the courage she showed in taking in a man she thought to be a "bummer."

Maeve stopped and looked up at him.

Charles sucked in his breath. Her blue eyes were as deep and sparkling as the sun-swept sea. Arresting. He was momentarily blind to anything else but those startling blue orbs fixed on him.

"In there." She pointed to an alley filled with rotting trash. "Ye were propped against the wall midway."

"Why were you in this alley?" he asked, suddenly suspicious.

"Me brother Shea meets me at the Boston side and walks me home every night when 'tis dark. Shea's a boxer, you know, and is not afraid to take shortcuts when it will take us out of the cold sooner."

Charles nodded and moved into the alley. He searched, kicking through unidentifiable trash, not quite knowing what he expected to find. Maeve O'Malley hummed.

"Is this the spot?" he asked.

"Aye, more or less."

"And you took me home from here?"

"You would have frozen to death if we hadn't. And 'twas Thanksgiving eve, a day we are happy to observe, countin' our blessings an' all. With a roof over my head, and food left over from the Deakins table, it was only right we should take ye home and share our bounty."

Bounty? Charles found Maeve's outlook plainly astonishing. While he wished to explore her intriguing thought process further, he concentrated on the subject at hand. "When you found me, I had nothing? No money? Not even a pocket watch?"

She shook her head. "Nothing. Shea said you looked as if you were done over by a professional, a boxer like himself."

"I know no boxers, and I have never been to this part of town."

"Where was the last place you remember being?"

"If I knew that—" A memory, a fuzzy picture, floated up from the depths of Charles's subconscious. He recalled leaving Edgar Dines's gallery on Warren Street in the heart of Boston proper. Slowly the picture in his mind cleared. He carried a painting beneath his arm wrapped in brown paper. It was a valuable sketch, an irreplaceable rendering of St. Nick by an artist no longer living.

Dear God, he'd been robbed of his most precious possession.

A flood of pictures flashed through his mind in lightning-like fashion as the memory of the attack on him returned full force. Charles had been heading toward his carriage, which waited half a block away in front of his tailor's shoppe. Previous to his appointment with Edgar Dines, he had been fitted for a new suit and several other garments for the upcoming holiday festivities. But he'd not gone more than six feet from the art dealer's gallery when a blow to the head from behind felled him. All was blank after that.

For five days he'd existed without memory or will, doing whatever he was bid including marrying the girl by his side, whose head barely topped his shoulder. Surely he'd been missed by someone. A man of his standing didn't simply disappear.

"Were there no posted notices that I was missing?"

"Perhaps. I hardly ever read notices."

"You *do* read," he intoned.

Maeve reacted with an angry stomp of her foot. Her eyes sparked with indignation. "Of course I know how to read! What do ye take me for? Do ye think me dumb because me name is O'Malley and I'm Irish? And a woman?" Her fists dug into her hips and her midnight curls bounced atop her hatless head. "I'll have ye know—"

"Shhh," Charles raised a finger over his lips to still her. "You're creating a scene."

"Ye insulted me, ye arrogant man!"

"Must you be so loud?"

"Don't be thinkin' ye are better than me because—"

"I don't. I don't think such a thing."

She appeared somewhat mollified, but a suspicious glint remained in her eyes. She tilted her chin, meeting his gaze. Charles looked away, away from the unspoken accusation, the pain in her eyes. He turned back to the spot in the alley where she'd found him.

"Obviously, I was moved from the scene of the attack."

"I wouldn't be knowin'," she snipped.

"Was there . . . did you find a package here?"

" 'Twas no package, only you."

"I was carrying a package which means a great deal to me. It was wrapped in brown paper and about this size." Charles described the two-feet-by-four-feet package with his hands.

"We found no package," she repeated, shifting from one foot to the other.

He thought she might be lying. The Irish were known to have liars and thieves among them. But then again, how would a young, uneducated immigrant and her boxer brother have any idea of the painting's value?

Only the most knowledgeable art collectors would know the piece was the only one of its kind. Charles had searched long and hard for this particular sketch of St. Nick. While he enjoyed collecting art, this acquisition had meant more than any of the others.

Staring at the cold, hard ground where he'd been discarded, Charles bit down on his lip. A searing mix of frustration and anger shot through him.

"Could we be movin' on then?" the little bit by his side demanded. "Me feet is colder than a frost fairy's toes."

"A what?"

"Never ye mind," she said with a roll of her eyes and a rueful sigh.

Charles nodded. He didn't want to know about frost fairies—whatever the hell they were. Recovering his sketch was a primary concern, where to take Maeve another. Until he resolved the awkward dilemma of their marriage, he couldn't possibly let his friends and family know he'd wed an Irish maid. The whole town would be talking.

Maeve O'Malley gazed up at him, waiting impatiently. Her long lashes and jewel-like eyes, innocent and trusting, reached deep inside him and touched his unguarded heart.

She had saved his life. He must do something for her. Charles decided to take Maeve home with him if only for a day or two. He would have her fitted with a warm new wardrobe and offer a generous settlement. It was the least he could do.

Before he divorced her.

Chapter Two

Charles breathed a bit easier when the hired carriage pulled up to the stately Rycroft residence. The six-story Federal style brownstone was located on Louisburg Square in the exclusive Beacon Hill section of Boston. Although the trees were bare and the square's lush park greenery had given way weeks ago to the muffled sepia color of winter, the affluent neighborhood retained its charm. Situated in the center of the square, the Rycrofts' venerable town house, embellished with black wrought iron gates and grillwork at the purple paned windows, had been Charles's home for most of his life.

Eight servants worked to keep the twelve-room house—and Charles—comfortable. Upon his father's death three years ago, Charles inherited both the brownstone and the family publishing business.

His mother, Beatrice, resided with him when the mood suited her. But she preferred New York, where she shared her sister's home on the Hudson. Beatrice enjoyed the more glorious social season and the abundance of spiritualists and mediums offered in the city. She'd been seeking to contact her late husband, Conrad

Rycroft, in the great beyond ever since his abrupt departure.

Each year, Beatrice returned to Boston for a few months to visit with old friends. Her visits usually occurred in the summer, when she removed to one of the north shore resorts to take advantage of the cooling ocean breezes. This year, however, Beatrice had sent a message announcing she would join Charles for the holiday season. She'd neglected to mention an arrival date but he'd immediately put the household on full alert and preparedness.

Charles hardly knew his mother. Tall and elegant, Beatrice had always been a social butterfly, flapping about in bright, beaded evening dresses with wide satin skirts. Owing to Beatrice's lack of maternal instincts, a succession of nannies raised Charles. His favorite, Lizzie, served as mother and father to him for the longest period of time. He'd been twelve years old when Lizzie's gout got to be too much and she retired. His heart had broken. Even though Charles was off to boarding school, knowing Lizzie would not be there when he returned home for holidays saddened him. His loneliness intensified when Lizzie left.

He conspired to stay in touch with his beloved nanny, sending her funds regularly, disguised as birthday and holiday gifts. A wizened old woman now, she lived with her daughter in the mill town of Lowell. Charles stopped to call whenever he was in the area.

"Is this where ye be livin' then?"

Dear God, she was still with him.

Charles had momentarily forgotten the little bit of a woman who sat at his side. All hope that he might soon waken from an especially grievous nightmare vanished.

"Yes. This is my home. Come." He helped Maeve from the carriage. Her mitten scratched against his palm as he took her hand. But the sweet violet scent of her somehow contrived to soothe and warm him in the frosty morning air.

Maeve O'Malley's eyes grew wider as Charles escorted her up the steep steps of the brownstone.

"I've lived here ever since I was a boy," he said, releasing her hand. Charles knew he must be careful not to give the diminutive creature any reason to think he might continue their unsuitable marriage. He'd married under duress, married in the only way conceivable to a confirmed bachelor. He'd been quite out of his mind at the time. Literally.

"The Deakins house is not near so grand as this," Maeve whispered. "And sure'n I've never walked in through the front door. Aye, and just look at the polished brass nameplate ye have here!"

"My grandfather built the original house," Charles told her. "And later my father added two floors."

Charles loved his home. The high-ceilinged, paneled rooms smelled of beeswax, lemon, and leather—constant, comforting aromas. He took solace in the evenings reading manuscripts in his study. Bolstered by a fine cigar and brandy, Charles found contentment surrounded by his favorite leather-bound books and treasured art collection. By nature he was a quiet, solitary man.

Maeve did not move when he opened the door.

"What is it?" he asked.

"After you," she deferred in a hushed tone.

"No, after you. Ladies before gentlemen."

She inclined her head.

Charles leaned to whisper in her ear. "I'm not going to carry you over the threshold."

Maeve's hands went to her hips and her lovely lapis eyes darkened to a deep, stormy indigo. " 'Tis not what—"

"Please," he begged, raising his hands in front of his chest as if he expected to ward off a blow. "No public scenes."

With a sniff and a tilt of her chin, she marched before him into the foyer.

Inexplicably amused, he followed.

A scream went out from the top of the stairs. The upstairs maid, who had been polishing the bannister, stood stock still, her hand clapped over her mouth.

Responding to her cry, Dolly, the housekeeper, and Stuart, the butler, rushed to the foyer, each coming to an abrupt halt. Charles's servants were clearly shocked to see him.

"Mr. Rycroft, we'd given you up for dead!" exclaimed Dolly, the ruddy-faced housekeeper.

"Did you contact the police?"

"Yes, sir. And we contacted Mr. Martin, who did so as well, sir." Round and stout as a stump, the housekeeper referred to Martin Rycroft, Charles's cousin and second in command at the publishing house.

"Well done. Have the police reported their findings as yet?" Charles asked drolly. The Boston authorities were used to young men from well-heeled families disappearing for days at a time. Sowing wild oats with women, gambling, and whatever other mischief available was expected and quite acceptable.

"No, sir. Though they've questioned us all several times." Dolly regarded his clothes in silent horror. Instinctively, he pulled at the hem of the flannel shirt to straighten it as he would one of his tailor-made jackets. "What's happened to you, sir? If I may ask," she added quickly.

"I met with an unfortunate accident and this brave young woman saved me."

All eyes flew to the petite woman at his side, who blushed and angled her chin a degree higher. She was humming, so softly he could barely hear, but it was a definite hum—and a familiar tune. A Christmas carol, he thought.

"This is Maeve." Charles rested a hand on Maeve's shoulder and, to his surprise, felt her trembling. He'd assumed a woman who took home a man she believed to be a bummer must be a woman who feared nothing. Apparently not.

In an awkward attempt to ease Maeve's anxiety, Charles patted her shoulder as he spoke to his curious household help. "Maeve will be staying on the sixth floor temporarily."

Maeve nodded and bobbed a clumsy curtsey simultaneously. Plainly, she did not know how to acknowledge his vague introduction. But to introduce her as his wife would be a disservice to the Irish beauty in the end. They would not be married long.

Charles pretended not to notice her uncertainty.

Dolly had yet to remove her startled gaze from his shirt.

"You will afford Maeve every courtesy and provide her with anything she desires. I will show her upstairs personally."

Stuart, who served as both Charles's valet and butler, pressed his lips together in silent evidence of his disapproval. "Yes, sir."

Charles did not miss the exchange of alarmed glances between Stuart and Dolly. They obviously thought he'd lost his mind during his absence. And of course, he had. Indisputably.

"Come with me, Maeve," Charles ordered. "I shall require a bath and fresh suit," he called over his shoulder to Stuart as he marched ahead of Maeve up the stairs.

The sixth floor consisted of two guest suites, known as the rose room and the blue room. Charles led Maeve to the rose room, a spacious bedchamber complete with marble fireplace and an adjoining sitting room. Thick Oriental carpets were spread over the polished wood floors and heavy claret velvet drapes framed the floor-to-ceiling windows.

As she inspected her splendid rooms, Maeve's eyes felt as big as the cream cabbage roses in the floral-patterned wallpaper. She could barely conceal her awe.

Even the Deakins house where she was in service had no room that could compare to this one. The flat she shared with her dear father and Shea could be placed twice over in these rooms. She felt an overpowering urge to spread her arms and spin—or do a jig of joy. But she knew instinctively that such a spontaneous display of delight might unduly disturb Charles.

Instead, humming softly, Maeve ran her hand over the rosewood armoire, feeling the smooth, cool wood beneath her fingertips. Beneath the watchful eye of her taciturn husband, she gingerly tested the large, cream-satin-canopied four-poster bed.

She'd never dreamed of living in such luxury. Her dreams had always been simple. Maeve wished for a loving husband, several babes hanging about her skirts, and a full pot of stew every night.

"Do you think you can be comfortable here?" Charles asked.

"Saints above, I'm certain of it, me love."

His jaw dropped and his light ash eyes widened. "Charles. Under the circumstances, I believe you should consider calling me Charles."

"I've been used to calling ye Charlie." And how she adored her Charlie.

He frowned. His dark brows knit together at the bridge of his nose, making him appear a bit fearsome. "Charlie definitely won't do."

"Then Charles it shall be," Maeve assured him, rising from the bed to examine the corner dressing table. "Ye'll find me as easy to be gettin' on with as the mornin' sun."

Charles did not appear convinced. The quirk of his lips might have been a nervous tic.

Maeve didn't know what to do, what more to say. She who had nothing, suddenly seemed to have everything. She could not quell the unsettling roil of her stomach, nor could she keep her knees from knocking. Truth be told, she felt so lightheaded that she feared she would collapse any minute at her husband's feet.

The little Irish immigrant who had never even owned a rag doll had suddenly been set down in splendor. Surely, one of the wee people, a fairy princess perhaps, was looking out for her just as her dear mother had promised. Life would be different now and so much better.

Charles cleared his throat. "This is a . . . difficult situation we find ourselves in."

"Aye."

"But we shall deal with it like the adults we are."

Something in his tone made Maeve leery. "Aye? And how would that be?"

He shoved his hands into the pockets of Shea's denim trousers and studied the tips of his shoes. "I would like you to place yourself in my position, Maeve. Can you imagine how extremely discomfiting it might be to go to sleep and wake up to find yourself married?"

"To the likes of me?"

His head shot up. "To anyone."

Maeve knew Charles was not used to plain talking. In his world, the world she'd glimpsed as a servant in the Deakins household, the truth was hardly ever spoken. And if it was, the words were couched in terms to render it almost unrecognizable. Polite society wrapped the truth in sugar like bitter medicine to make it palatable. Maeve did not see the sense in such behavior. She had always spoken her mind and had no intention of changing.

Obviously disturbed, Charles Rycroft paced the room.

Just the sight of him, tall and solid and darkly masculine, ignited a sweet heat within her. She felt a sadness, too. When the man she'd married regained his memory, he'd lost his easy smile and become a somber man. Charles took himself much too seriously.

"Ye were a confirmed bachelor, then?" she asked. "Is that what you're sayin'?"

"Marriage has been the last thing on my mind."

"If you don't mind me sayin' so, 'twas time ye thought of it. Love can sneak right by ye."

"I thought to arrange a marriage when the time was right."

"More's the pity." But she knew that's what his upper-crust class did. A body would have to look long and hard to find kindling and fire in a blue blood's cool veins—unless they forgot who they were. When Charles believed himself to be a man called Charlie, he had enough fire in him to light the city of Boston.

"I beg your pardon?"

"Look on the bright side, me love. Now ye won't have to worry about any arrangin'. 'Tis taken care of, you're a married man."

"Our marriage . . ." Charles's voice trailed off and he swiped a hand through his hair, the rich dark brown of fertile earth. For a well-spoken man, Charles appeared to be having a difficult time.

" 'Twas a stroke of luck, to be sure. Do ye not remember how well suited we are in . . . in bed?"

"Maeve!" A flash of bright silver light sparked in his eyes as they locked on hers.

She'd shocked him. She'd stirred genuine, unmasked emotion from her stoic husband. Unfortunately, it wasn't the emotion she'd hoped for. "Do ye not remember?" she repeated softly.

"No. I . . . I don't." For a moment he looked remorseful. His gray eyes reflected a gentleness and concern. But the moment swiftly passed.

" 'Tis your loss!" Exasperated and angry that he could not remember the most wonderful moments in her life, Maeve turned on her heel.

Charles seized her forearm and turned her back to him. The intensity of his gaze caused her stomach to somersault. "Maeve, is there any chance . . . do you suppose we could have our marriage annulled?"

He sorely wounded her.

"Over me dead body!" she bristled. "Saints above. Ye took my maidenhood, and that's a fact."

"Shhh." He hastily placed a finger over her lips.

Which didn't stop Maeve. "I did not hear ye complain at the time!"

"The servants will hear you," he warned.

She jerked out of his grasp. "And so?"

"My business is not theirs to know."

"The servants know your business before ye do."

"What?"

" 'Twas my experience at the Deakinses."

"Dear God."

"Sure'n I know what's whispered behind the stairs. Have ye forgotten? Ye married a maid."

"I have not forgotten."

"Let's hear no more talk about annulment," Maeve muttered, straightening her shoulders and marching toward the sitting room. She'd had enough of this conversation. A terrible foreboding settled in the pit of her stomach like a ten-pound stone. Tears gathered behind her eyes. "You're stirrin' me temper."

Charles followed, letting out what could only be interpreted as the sigh of a persecuted man. "Maeve, we must consider what to do about the predicament we find ourselves in."

Maeve perched on the edge of the serpentine-backed sofa. "What predicament would that be?" she asked with a haughty hike of her chin.

"You were forced into this marriage as much as I."

"True, but I did not mind it. Ye are a good man. I could not do better."

"Well . . . well, of course you couldn't!"

"Aye."

"But that's not the point."

"And ye'll be tellin' me what the point is," she smiled, hoping to charm him.

"You are impossible!" Rubbing his brow as if he had the headache, Charles turned away.

"My dear dad and Shea have claimed the same about me on occasion. But ye shall grow used to me ways in time."

Charles spun back to face Maeve with a glower that would have turned a timid woman to dust.

"Or perhaps you mightn't," she added quietly.

"Tomorrow, you will pay a visit to my doctor so that he may verify your—"

Maeve leaped from the sofa. Waving a finger, she advanced on him. For every step she took forward, Charles took one back. "Ye arrogant man! Do ye take me for a fool? Just what would a visit to your doctor prove? Soon ye'd be claiming there was some man before ye. No. No, there was no man before ye— although there were plenty hanging round me skirts."

"I . . . I apologize. I didn't mean to imply you were a—"

"A strumpet, sir?"

"Yes. No!"

"I've been a good girl, like me dear mother made me promise before she died."

"Forgive me."

The words were spoken so softly, Maeve almost missed them. While she'd had days to grow used to the idea, her husband had not.

"I shall do me best to make ye happy . . . and proud of me," she said, offering what she knew to be only a thread of comfort. "Ye won't regret this marriage, Charles Rycroft. That's me promise to ye."

Once again, he rubbed his brow, dark and wide. "Yes. Well, ah, we shall continue this discussion later."

"Are ye leavin' me then?"

He strode toward the door. "I must see to the recovery of my sketch and pay a visit to the publishing house."

"What am I to do while ye are away?"

"I shall arrange for Mrs. Potts, my mother's seamstress, to look in on you and fit you for a new wardrobe."

"A new wardrobe?"

"Certainly there will be Christmas festivities where you will want to look your best?"

Before this moment Maeve hadn't thought about a future that included anyone but Charles. She wasn't prepared to assume a role in society. Awash with uncertainty, she nodded. "Aye."

Maeve knew what to expect in her world. On Christmas Eve she would bake Christmas cakes and prepare Black Fast for her father and Shea. On Christmas Day she would go off to the Deakinses as usual. Midday, she would join with the other servants to celebrate Christmas with a feast of their own.

In the spirit of the season the Deakinses would dismiss their help early and Maeve would return home to join her family at Rosie's saloon where they would dance until their feet grew numb.

But here in Charles Rycroft's world, Maeve had no idea what Christmas festivities meant. She feared she could not become a part of Charles's world, that she would be held in contempt, rebuffed at every turn. Charles's family and friends might never accept her.

Charles opened the door, avoiding eye contact with Maeve. "Mrs. Potts will be here before noon and more than likely will keep you busy for most of the day. Pull this bell rope should you need anything. Dolly will see that you have a light luncheon."

"Aye." He was leaving Maeve alone in a strange place. Her brash, brave front evaporated.

"Have I forgotten anything?"

"Deakins. Ye won't forget about informing the Deakinses of my whereabouts? I've never missed a day of work nor been late. About now the Mrs. might be gettin' upset."

"No. No, I won't forget the Deakinses," he assured her, and hurriedly closed the door behind him without so much as a smile.

"Good-bye then," Maeve whispered, alone in the

large, empty room. The spaciousness made her feel even smaller than she was.

She did not care for her new husband's high-handed manner. She liked him much better when he was a quiet, genial man unashamed of the vulnerability visited upon him by his amnesia. As Charlie, he'd depended upon Maeve for guidance without ever displaying pride or malice. And yet in bed, his masculine instincts proved to be remarkable.

On their wedding night Maeve had gladly given the gift of her virginity to Charles. With infinite patience and sensitivity, Charles taught her the ways of love between a man and woman. His touch and his kiss were like heaven on earth, transporting Maeve to a wondrous place far beyond the leprechaun's rainbow. She became lighter than air, lighter than a fairy's wing. And to her great delight, Charles had seemed unable to get enough of her. He fired Maeve's desire and satisfied her passion with astounding eagerness. For almost five days, he'd been the perfect man.

How could he forget?

But he had. And he had already asked about an annulment. Maeve worried that Charles meant to divorce her or lock her away up here in this suite of rooms. Her father would never countenance divorce. Besides, she'd grown attached to her husband. She did not want to part from him. She would not.

But soon Charles would discover Maeve's pitiful lack of education and be mortified. She would rather die than disgrace her husband. Whatever she needed to do to keep Charles wed to her, she must do it quickly.

Maeve knew of only one person who could help her. Although her husband had ordered her to stay in her rooms, she could not obey him. She must seek Pansy Deakins's counsel immediately.

* * *

Maeve slipped into the Deakins household in her usual manner—by the rear door. Using the back steps, she managed to make her way to Pansy's bedchamber without running into any of the other servants. She knocked softly on the door.

"Come in."

Maeve slipped quickly into the room. Pansy sat at the vanity brushing her long, rust-colored hair. When she saw Maeve's form reflected in the mirror, she turned with a great, broad smile. "There you are at last! I had given up hope."

Unbuttoning her coat, Maeve stepped forward. "I cannot stay."

"What do you mean? Mother is furious." Pansy always added more drama to a situation. She longed to be an actress although such a profession was not at all suitable for one of her class.

"Sure'n I'm sorry, Miss."

Maeve was uncertain how it had happened but she and Pansy had become more than servant and mistress. They were friends. She suspected it had something to do with the fact they were only two years apart in age. Maeve was nineteen and Pansy twenty-one. The free-spirited redhead constantly rebelled against the strictures that her parents and society presented her.

Pansy rose and crossed the room to where Maeve stood in anxious indecision. Slender and of average height, the only Deakins child possessed remarkable hazel eyes. The changing colors made Maeve think the good Lord could not make up his mind whether Pansy's eyes should be green or brown.

The light of curiosity danced in them now. "What happened to delay you?"

Shaking her head, Maeve hurried to the window and swept back the lace curtains. "Has Mr. Charles Rycroft been here yet?"

"Rycroft? Heavens, no! What would he be doing here?"

"He was supposed to tell ye that I wasn't coming to work today . . . or tomorrow . . . or . . ." Maeve could not finish. Her throat closed as unbidden tears streamed down her cheeks.

"Rycroft was to deliver this message?"

Swiping at her tears, Maeve nodded to Pansy. "Yes."

Her socialite friend seized her hands. "Why are you crying?"

"My hu . . . hu . . . husband has regained his memory."

"Maeve! What secrets have you been keeping from me? I didn't know you were married."

"Several days ago. It . . . it was quite sudden." Fresh tears spilled from her eyes.

"Oh, my." Much to Maeve's chagrin, Pansy didn't believe in marriage. She advocated free love since forming an admiration for Victoria Woodhull.

"And now my hu . . . hu . . . husband doesn't remember marrying me."

"Oh, dear!"

"Ye haven't heard the worst."

Pansy's lips rounded and her eyes brightened. "Come sit with me." After leading Maeve to the striped satin chaise, she sat down and patted the spot beside her. "Tell me everything."

"He's . . . one of you."

"One of me? You are not making sense, Maeve."

"Charles Rycroft. That's me husband."

"Charles Rycroft!" Pansy repeated in astonishment.

"What am I to do?"

"Charles Rycroft?" Pansy asked in disbelief. "No!"

"Yes."

To Maeve's surprise, her friend giggled. "The mothers of Boston's finest young ladies have been after Rycroft for at least a half dozen years. Including my own dear mama."

Maeve readily understood. "Charles is exceedingly handsome in his own way."

Pansy did not comment, she only grinned. "How did you manage it? To marry him?"

"Me brother Shea accused him of compromising me when Mr. Rycroft wasn't quite himself. Shea forced me upon him when Charles could not say nay."

Pansy could barely contain herself. "This is famous!"

"Charles is wanting to annul the marriage but it's been—"

"Oh, don't tell me!"

"Consummated."

"Consummated!" Pansy repeated, jumping up with a clap of her hands. She regarded Maeve fondly. "Who but you would ever say the word aloud?"

"I'm only sayin' what is true."

Pansy's eyes twinkled with unabashed glee. "You will never have to work again. You will never have to tie my corset nor pack my trunks."

"Ye are a good mistress—I do not mind—"

"If Charles Rycroft wants an annulment he will be willing to settle on you," Pansy interrupted.

Maeve stood. "But I do not want his money."

"Of course you do. You and your father and brother will be able to move to a sweet little cottage by the shore and you will have nothing to do all day but brush your hair and sew samplers."

"I want me husband," Maeve declared, digging her hands into her hips.

"Who?"

"Me husband. I'm thinkin' I love him. Loved him at first sight of him . . . cleaned up."

"Cleaned up?"

"He'd had an accident."

Pansy raised her rust-brown eyebrows, but went on with what she obviously considered a more important question. "Just how long have you been married?"

"Five days."

"It's infatuation."

Although Maeve didn't like to disagree with Pansy,

she did. "Sure'n I think it's more, but I'll never know unless I stay married to the man for a time."

"Have you considered that you will most likely be ostracized by society?"

While Maeve never cared what others thought, she cared for what they might say or do to Charles. "I am not frightened," she bluffed.

"Good. You will need your courage." Pansy slanted her a wide smile. "You have always been my friend and will remain so. We shall go about together as equals. What fun we shall have!"

"But I am not of your class. Nor have I your education, or fancy manners. Me husband thinks me too loud. And he's been after me for creatin' a scene. I'm not even sure what he means by that. Worse, I've lost my temper with him a time or two already this morning ... and it's not even midday." Maeve's shoulders slouched as she lowered her head and sank to the chaise once again. "I'm an embarrassment to him."

Pansy pulled her up. "Maeve, do not think yourself an embarrassment to anyone. You are most intelligent. How long have you been borrowing books from me? Three years? Four? You have learned more than I know."

"I've had no fancy schoolin'."

"Where you learn makes no difference."

"I don't know. There's so much about me that needs fixin'. In case ye haven't noticed, I've a hint of an Irish brogue that marks me as an immigrant. What am I goin' to do about that?"

"Let me teach you elocution! I can teach you to talk softly and lose your accent. All great actresses excel in these matters."

"I cannot ask you—"

"Yes, you can. Please let me help. You know how bored I am. There is nothing for me to do until my parents relent and let me pursue a stage career. I cannot possibly play the piano for twelve hours a day."

"Ye would do this for me?"

"You are my friend, Maeve. And now you are Mrs. Charles Rycroft, who must travel in the same social circle."

Maeve's heart pounded a bit faster, a bit harder. Her eyes teared up again. "I'll be obliged to ye for the rest of my life. I do not care to be hidden away on the sixth floor like some mad, ranting wife."

"Charles wouldn't dare hide you away or divorce you if you were the Belle of Boston," Pansy offered with a sly smile.

"The Belle of Boston?"

"We haven't much time. The round of Christmas parties is about to begin." Pansy stopped and clapped her hands, her eyes sparkling with delight. "We shall create a new you in time for the Cabots' Snow Ball. Everyone who is anyone in Boston attends their ball."

"It would be a magnificent adventure," Maeve allowed, although she felt a bit lightheaded. Dizzy with trepidation rather than pleasure. "And I must do me best to keep my hus . . . hus . . ."

A heavy pounding on the front door knocker interrupted Maeve. Her head snapped round to the sound. Her heart nearly stopped.

With a mischievous grin and a finger to her lips, Pansy snatched Maeve's hand and pulled her from the room. Although Maeve resisted, she could not dissuade the impulsive Pansy. They reached the landing on tiptoe and hunkered down. Peering over the bannister, they watched as Charles Rycroft strode into the small foyer.

As Maeve watched her dour husband address the Deakinses' housekeeper, she wished she could shrink to leprechaun size and disappear into the Land of the Ever-Young, the home of Irish fairies.

She wished to be anywhere but here.

"I wish a moment with Mrs. Deakins," Charles informed the butler. "Tell her Charles Rycroft has come with a message."

"One moment, sir."

Pansy grinned, apparently enjoying the little drama immensely.

Maeve held her breath. Before she could gather her wits and flee the landing, Harriet Deakins emerged from the parlor. The large-bosomed matron glided toward Charles like a schooner at full sail.

"My dear Charles, to what do we owe this great honor?"

"Harriet, how good to see you." He tipped his head and gave her a polite smile. "Regrettably, I cannot stay. I've merely come with a message."

"Oh?"

"Miss O'Malley will not be able to serve you this week."

Harriet Deakins did her best to disguise her displeasure but her tight-lipped smile held little warmth. "Really? How do you know this? You are not in the habit of stealing servants, are you?"

If possible, Charles's already rigid figure appeared to stiffen several degrees. "No, not at all. If you will—"

Pansy sneezed.

Maeve sucked in what she thought might be her last breath.

Charles's head jerked up. His steely gaze took in Pansy crouched by the rail with Maeve just behind her.

"Maeve?"

She moved her hand in greeting, a hapless little flick of her wrist.

Harriet Deakins glared up at her daughter and maid. "What is the meaning of this?"

"It's all right, Mama." Pansy took Maeve's hand and led her down the stairs. "Maeve and I are friends, Charles."

Feeling dreadfully faint, Maeve forced a weak smile.

"Friends?" Harriet Deakins echoed in unconcealed horror.

Charles glared at Maeve. "My carriage is waiting. You will return to Rycroft House with me immediately."

Weak-kneed, Maeve turned to Pansy for support. The improper Miss Deakins fairly beamed with pleasure. But of course, what did Pansy have to fear?

Chapter Three

"No one disobeys me!" Furious, Charles ground the words through his teeth.

Once inside the confines of the luxurious Rycroft town coach, he felt free at last to release his anger. From the time he had awakened this morning to find himself wed to the petite, dark-haired creature beside him, nothing . . . absolutely nothing, had gone his way. His world had been turned upside down.

Instead of searching for his missing sketch as he meant to be doing, Charles was forced to deal with a headstrong bride who paid no heed to him.

Dear God. How could someone so small cause so much trouble?

Maeve's chin tilted defiantly. "I could not have Pansy and Mrs. Deakins thinkin' I'd just disappeared into thin air like one of the wee fairy folk, could I now? I am a responsible woman."

A responsible woman who assumed the impervious attitude of England's Queen Victoria and believed in fairies. Pausing to summon patience from his now considerably shallow well, Charles regarded Maeve from the corner of his eye. Her lips were deep red like the juiciest apple on the tree. He wondered how it had felt to kiss those full, currently petulant, lips. For a moment he longed to remember the taste of her.

Damn. Once again he'd allowed Maeve to become a distraction.

But Charles refused to be deterred from his message. The stubborn little creature must realize her duty to obey him. In his circle of civilized society, wives unquestionably obeyed their husbands' bidding. And, for the moment, she was his wife.

"Maeve, I told you I would deliver the message to the Deakinses and I distinctly asked you to stay in your rooms. Did I not make myself clear?"

"Aye, ye did indeed. You're not talkin' to an Irish feather-brain, ye know."

"I did not mean to imply—"

"There are folks who depend upon me like Pansy and me dad and Shea," she interrupted indignantly. "I cannot just disappear—"

"Allow me to remind you once again, you have not disappeared."

"Ye took me straight off to your attic!" Plainly agitated, Maeve's dark blue eyes flashed with anger and her head bobbed sharply to emphasize her words.

"Guest apartment," Charles countered. "You are *not* in the attic."

"Are ye thinkin' to hide me away now?"

In hopes of restoring peace between them, as imperfect as it might be, Charles proceeded with caution. "You and I need time alone," he explained in a conciliatory tone. "Time to get to know one another. For the present, I think it's best to keep our marriage to ourselves. We do not need interference from others, including Pansy and Harriet Deakins."

A gleam of suspicion burned in Maeve's steadfast gaze. "Aye, and your wish to keep me hidden would not be because ye are ashamed of me? Ye wouldn't be fearin' the gossips?"

Gossip. The words of his father rose from his subconscious. Conrad Rycroft's many admonitions lurked within Charles, always close to the surface of his awareness. Too close.

A Rycroft is above reproach in all matters, personal and professional. A Rycroft does nothing which would incite gossip or condemnation. A Rycroft can be counted on to do the right thing. Charles did not have to think twice; marrying an Irish maid was definitely not the right thing. He had no doubt that at this very moment his father was rolling over in his grave.

Conrad Rycroft had demanded much from his son. From the time Charles could walk, he was striving to please his father and meet seemingly impossible expectations for a boy his age. His father was a strict disciplinarian, an unforgiving authoritarian intent on building a legacy. Like the Scribners, his New York rivals, he meant to build a family publishing dynasty known round the world. Sometimes of late, in the deep of night, Charles feared he was becoming his father.

With Maeve's dark, intense gaze upon him, Charles chose his words carefully. "There will be gossip when our marriage is made known," he acknowledged. "Indisputably. It's unlikely that we will be able to escape the wagging tongues."

"I am not afraid." She raised her head in a show of eloquent defiance that served to lengthen her long, porcelain neck. The graceful arch struck Charles as lovely, but unusual in a small person.

"The gossips will be unkind," he warned.

She stared straight ahead into some unknown abyss. "Sure'n mere words cannot hurt me."

The girl had spunk. Charles had to give her that, spunk and a fine, fair beauty. "Maeve, let me speak plainly. I don't know you. And you only think that you know me. For only a handful of days you were married to a shadow of a man—a man without a past or future. The man you wed doesn't exist."

"I married a man with a gentle soul and loving nature."

"Which anyone will tell you is not me."

"Aye? And my Charlie might be the real you. The soul of you."

"Maeve, my instincts tell me you've endured a difficult life and I'll wager you've suffered a great deal for one so young."

"Saints above, I'm not so young. I shall be twenty years in just a matter of months."

She was an innocent.

"I intend to do everything in my power to ensure your future happiness, Maeve, but—"

"Ye are not speaking plainly as ye promised! What are ye meanin' by 'your future happiness?' Will ye be packin' me off with a pocket full of shamrocks for good luck?"

Dear God, she could read his mind.

"Damn it, woman, no!" Charles quickly denied his plan. Unaccustomed to being challenged, he also disliked the fact that Maeve's mind seemed to be running ahead of his. In the future he would be more careful when engaged in conversation with her. "But I . . . I have a business to run. A business neglected for over a week. I cannot be constantly at your side."

"Has your business fallen on hard times in a week?"

Charles cocked his head and shot Maeve a look meant to quell her impertinence. Both the effrontery of her question and the sarcasm with which it was delivered annoyed him. "Not that it matters to you—nor that you should care, but in my absence, Martin—"

"And who would Martin be?"

"My cousin. My cousin acted on his own to take over the helm while I was among the missing. He implemented several policies we recently have been in disagreement about. I stayed longer in my office than I assumed would be needed in order to set right the wreckage."

In fact, Charles spent most of the time at the office searching through piles of mail and messages. Against hope, he sought to find a ransom note for the priceless sketch of St. Nick stolen from him seven days ago. In truth he was more upset and angry about the loss of his prized art than about Martin's impropriety.

"And that is your excuse for not delivering my message to the Deakinses promptly?"

"I am not obliged to offer excuses to you," Charles replied tersely. The Irish harridan relentlessly ruffled his feathers. Who did she think she was talking with?

Her husband. *Dear God.*

Maeve turned her head away, silently gazing out of the window, ostensibly engrossed in the passing scenery.

Charles could think of no other woman in his acquaintance who had ever exasperated him so. Yet, he took an odd comfort in her presence. An amazing abundance of warmth emanated from her small, round body, a warmth that eased the chill of the coach and thawed the icy marrow of his bones. Maeve's violet scent spilled through the coach like a spring mist, mingling with the leather fragrance, softening the masculine edges and colors of his elegant conveyance.

Charles heaved an audible sigh of relief when his driver pulled the town coach up to the family brownstone. He jumped down quickly and was about to help Maeve from the carriage when he noticed two other coaches. Saratoga trunks, satchels, and hatboxes were being unloaded from the closest coach.

His mother had arrived. Earlier than expected. Much earlier.

Maeve vigorously protested at being driven to the back of the brownstone and hustled up the back stairs like so much contraband. She had been mistaken; this new man who was her husband did possess emotions—anger and impatience. His anger operated at various levels from brooding to barely controlled, between-the-teeth anger. If Maeve didn't know better, she would have suspected Charles of having a bit of the Irish in him.

He was quite unlike Charlie, the easygoing, thoughtful man she'd married. In the short time they had spent together in happily wedded bliss, Charlie displayed a wide range of emotions. Maeve found it difficult to believe that two such different men dwelled beneath the same skin. She wanted Charlie back.

Abruptly deposited inside her guest apartment with hasty orders to stay put, her anger flared. Two buttons went flying as Maeve removed her old woolen coat with more strength than required.

"Would you be Maeve O'Malley?"

The rather shrill voice that startled Maeve came from the sitting room. Throwing her coat on the bed, she marched into the room.

"Ilona Potts. Howja do?"

The unsmiling woman gave a curt nod. Taller than Maeve, the seamstress wore a black silk dress accentuated with a high white collar and white cuffs. One of the new small, round bustles graced her rear. Mrs. Potts presented a striking but inflexible figure with high, rouged cheekbones and silver hair swept into a sleek chignon. Her young assistant slept in a corner and was not introduced.

"Have ye been waitin' long, Mrs. Potts?"

The woman who Maeve judged to be in her late fifties folded one hand over another at her waist. "Over an hour."

"Sure'n I'm sorry."

"Dolly gave me tea and brown bread."

"Dolly is a good-hearted woman."

"I was asked to bring some ready-made clothes, but your size was unknown. Mr. Rycroft said small."

"Aye, I am small," Maeve replied with a melancholy smile. And too round as well, she added to herself. Her next thought held a ray of hope. Perhaps the dressmaker could make her appear slender.

"I shall do my best to make you presentable in spite of your . . . size."

"Thank you." Hope slid away.

"If it pleases you, I shall fit the store dresses and take measurements for the others."

"What others?"

"Mr. Rycroft has ordered a complete wardrobe. You shall have walking dresses, day dresses, and ball gowns."

"Ball gowns?"

"Yes, Miss O'Malley, ball gowns."

Apparently Charles hadn't told her this wardrobe was for his wife. He'd meant what he said about keeping their marriage a secret. Though she might not betray her feelings with words, the disdain Mrs. Potts felt for Maeve showed in her drawn blue lips and sharp countenance. Her frosty manner left no doubt that Ilona assumed Maeve to be Charles's mistress, a wanton Irish mistress to boot.

Determined to win the resolute woman over, Maeve gave her a grand, shameless grin. "Now fancy that. A complete wardrobe. Aye, the luck of the Irish is smilin' on me today."

Mrs. Potts turned her back on Maeve. "Step up on the platform, please. We will begin."

Apparently it would take more than a smile and a dash of charm to win over the sour dressmaker.

Maeve had never owned but two dresses to her name at one time, and those had either been sewn by her mam or later by herself. When she went to work for the Deakinses, she wore silk for the first time. Ever-generous Pansy gave Maeve her cast-off dresses. With a few adjustments Maeve made the castoffs her own.

To have dresses made just for her and to own new ready-made store dresses seemed a dream come true.

If only her dear mother could see her now, how happy she would be. The thought of her mother brought a wave of sadness over Maeve. A sadness that settled directly behind her eyes. Was her sweet mam up there, perched on a silver cloud, watching over Maeve as she'd promised?

Famine and fever had combined to be the death of Kathleen O'Malley. Maeve remembered her mother before the ravages of ill health. She'd been the most beautiful woman in all of County Armagh. Her eyes were a bright blue and her voice as soft as an angel's breath. Maeve loved to stroke her mother's long black hair, a mass of silky waves and curls that tumbled to her waist like a midnight sea.

Even as Kathleen lay on her deathbed, she'd remained strong of spirit. She gathered Maeve to her and held her through the long nights. Maeve tried to stay awake through those nights, desperately memorizing the faint chamomile smell of her mam and the smoothness of Kathleen's fair skin. Even on the nights when the sick woman's body burned with fever, Maeve refused to leave Kathleen's side. Young as she was, Maeve thought that by sleeping close, her life force would transfer itself to her mother. It was a futile attempt to save her mother, by an innocent child who believed in miracles.

When the end grew near, Kathleen promised Maeve that she would always be with her, watching over her. She would live the rest of her days in Maeve's heart. And the good fairy queen, Rane, would always be near to protect her dear, sweet girl and bring her good fortune. A prophesy that Maeve had good reason to doubt—until now.

"Turn around, Miss O'Malley. Just a tuck or two more and this dress will be ready to wear."

"Yes, ma'am."

Maeve could not remember her mother as possessing the same hot temper as she did. There was no denying

Maeve had inherited that unfortunate part of her disposition from her dad. One day she meant to take hold and learn to control her temper. Her rush to anger was forever getting her into trouble.

Kathleen O'Malley, on the other hand, had been everything good in this world. Despite her hard and hungry life, she loved her husband and she took great pride and delight in her children.

More than anything, Maeve wanted to be like her mother. But she feared she did not have the goodness of heart nor the courage to be content with her lot.

Maeve had always wanted more.

"Ouch!" The pin pricked her hip, stirring Maeve from her reverie with a start.

"Sorry." Mrs. Potts did not sound sorry.

Maeve hadn't realized fittings could be so tiring. A wave of relief lightened her weary body when Dolly appeared with the late-afternoon tea tray and a small package. After insisting Mrs. Potts and her assistant have tea and rest, Maeve retreated from the sitting room to open the package in her bedchamber.

The unexpected gift had been sent by Pansy. Maeve began to read the small leather-bound guide at once. 'Twas the perfect gift: *Miss Hastings' Etiquette for Young Ladies.* She took the book with her when she returned to the sitting room and resumed her pose on the platform.

Miss Potts pretended not to notice.

Engrossed in her reading, Maeve paid slight attention to the remainder of the fitting, simply obeying commands to step in or step out of the dress. Only when corseted and strapped into a wire cage-like contrivance did she look up from her reading to wonder at it all.

When at last Mrs. Potts put an end to the pinching, turning, pricking, and pinning, the November sky had darkened and lacy flakes of bright, white snow drifted past the windows.

"You now have two fine dresses to wear immediately."

"I'll be thankin' ye, Mrs. Potts—"

"Now, we must choose the fabric for the other gowns."

"Aye?" Maeve did not realize looking grand took so much work.

An hour later, at last alone, she approached the mirror wearing the latest style for the first time in her life. The azure blue silk store dress was draped with a striped overskirt that swept up to the back and gathered in a tidy bustle. Tiny mother-of-pearl buttons marched from the waist straight up the tight-fitting bodice and stopped where the ruching of the low, square-cut neckline began. The same ruching trimmed the sleeves, which stopped at Maeve's wrists. A double row of ruching hemmed the dress.

Maeve was astounded to see the extraordinary difference a proper dress could make. Her eyes sparkled bluer than before and her cheeks appeared to be rosier. Buoyed by her new look, she took the brush to her hair. Instead of sweeping the whole mane to the top of her head, she pulled the front to her crown, pinned it with a comb of faux pearls left by Ilona Potts, and let the rest cascade in glossy, blue-black glory past her shoulders. If she only knew how to fashion ringlets like Pansy. She had so much to learn. And she would learn. Maeve was determined to be a wife Charles could take pride in, a wife he would adore.

A tingle of hope skipped down her spine and Maeve pirouetted before the cheval mirror wishing someone could see her . . . wishing Charles could see her now.

Charles greeted his mother in her sitting room where she was resting from her journey. Streaks of silver threaded through Beatrice's dulling chestnut-brown hair, reminding Charles how his mother aged between visits home, how long she'd been gone. Beatrice took great pains with her appearance. She wore the latest fashions, the most expensive jewels, and rouged her lips and cheeks. Not so much as a hair upon her head was ever out of place. He'd always thought his mother most intimidating. Only his father had been more threatening.

Beatrice made a great show of being happy to see him again, insisting Charles have dinner with her and their houseguest that evening. And by houseguest, he knew his mother did not mean Maeve.

Charles had no opportunity to tell Beatrice about Maeve as she waxed poetic—and at length—over her friend Stella Hampton. Within minutes Charles feared the worse. It became all too clear that Beatrice had decided to fill her empty hours by becoming a matchmaker. She had brought Stella Hampton home to dangle before him as a potential mate.

Dear God. Was he destined to have one torment follow another?

Charles had no choice but to accept his mother's invitation to dinner. So much for his plan to dine with Maeve in her sitting room tonight. He felt certain that by spending as much time with his Irish bride as possible, the strong-willed beauty would quickly understand they were ill-suited. She would agree to the dissolution of their marriage. But he would spend no time with her tonight.

Charles rubbed his brow. His headache had begun when he started thinking of how to break the news of his ill-gotten, exceedingly unsuitable marriage to his mother. He'd earlier sworn the servants to silence about Maeve's presence in the house until he devised a satisfactory explanation. A cowardly avoidance, he admitted to himself, and definitely not the right thing for a Rycroft. In all likelihood, the thunder Charles imagined he heard was the sound of his father attempting to rise from the dead.

At the appointed dinner hour Charles gamely strode into the spacious dining room. Beneath his feet, a magnificent Aubusson carpet overlaid the new parquet

flooring and cushioned each step. The walls were paneled with dark mahogany reaching to the dado rail.
Gaslight sconces mounted against the gold-and-ivory
damask wallpaper added to the glittering light from the
enormous crystal chandelier bright with candles.

Charles felt comfortable among the heavy, masculine-
style Renaissance Revival furnishings: the long dining
table, the intricately carved chairs, the massive side-
board. And he needed to feel as comfortable as possible
on this particular evening.

A fire blazed in the handsome marble fireplace at
one end of the room. At the opposite end, two floor-
to-ceiling windows were draped with burgundy velvet
curtains pulled back and looped with golden tassels.

Charles's mother and an attractive young woman
waited at the table. A small golden dog slept on the
young woman's lap. He could hardly believe his mother
had allowed a dog at table. Seated opposite one another,
the women fell silent as he approached.

Smiling, Charles attempted to loosen his collar—
which at once felt a bit too tight. He was late and he
was in trouble.

Dipping his head in greeting, he took his place at
the head of the table between the two ladies. "Good
evening, Mother."

Beatrice bestowed a warm smile in return. Her gray
eyes—he'd inherited his eyes from his mother—shone
round and soft like smoky pearls. While once her slender figure complemented her height, his mother now
appeared bony. Tall and bony. All angles and knobs.
Charles tried to remember when this evolution had
happened.

"Charles, I should like to present Miss Stella Hampton. She is the daughter of Elsie, one of my dearest New
York friends."

Charles turned to the woman on his left. "It's a pleasure to meet you."

The little dog woke and yapped at him in a high, irritating pitch.

"The pleasure is mine," Stella said, stroking her pointy-nosed pet into silence. "Your mother has told me how wonderful you are."

"My mother exaggerates."

Charles's first impression was of excessive paleness. Stella Hampton possessed a pale complexion, a pale smile, and pale blond hair gathered high on her head, where it fell in thick sausage curls to her shoulders. She reminded him of a faded canvas.

Her emerald green dress dipped deep to reveal most of her generous breasts. Pale satin breasts, with pale blue lines mapping a labyrinth trail to what barely lay hidden beneath her gown.

Stella's little dog stared at Charles, growling low. Neither his mother nor Stella seemed to be aware the dog had taken a dislike to him. He made a mental note to watch his ankles if the dog should leap from Stella's lap.

Beatrice arched her brows. "You are much too modest, Charles. Stella has been looking forward to meeting you."

"I can only hope my mother has not created false expectations."

"Not at all." Stella's pale pink lips curved in an enigmatic smile and for the first time Charles noticed the small black mole at the right corner of her mouth. "I regret that I had already retired to my rooms when you arrived home this afternoon," she said. "Our journey exhausted me."

"I understand." Charles's mother had lectured him early on how women were frail creatures to be cosseted. "Are you staying in the blue rooms?"

"Yes." Her cocoa brown eyes locked on his.

"I hope you are comfortable."

"Exceedingly."

Charles had the unpleasant feeling Stella was sending

him some sort of message. He couldn't be sure if it was the tone of her voice or the look in her eyes. At least her little dog had gone back to sleep. Ignoring his momentary confusion, Charles turned to his mother.

The tiny lines fanning Beatrice's nose and eyes had deepened since last he saw her. Although she held her head high and her neck stretched to a certain tautness, Charles could detect the small beginnings of jowls puffed at either side of her chin.

"Have you rested well, Mother?"

Instead of replying, Beatrice gave Stella a knowing smile. "Did I not tell you? Charles is the most considerate son a mother could have." She leaned toward him then, lowering her voice. "Dolly insisted the blue rooms were best for Stella. She's convinced it is the quietest of the two guest suites. Do you agree?"

"Quiet? Definitely. Most assuredly, I agree."

But for how long? Maeve had not proven to be an especially quiet woman. A shudder swept through Charles. Maeve and Stella were installed across the corridor from one another—his wife and the woman his mother would have as his wife.

He had no illusions as to why Beatrice had brought Stella home for the holidays.

"The rooms are so comfortable and well appointed, I shouldn't care if they were quiet or not," Stella demurred.

Beatrice's smile never wavered. "You are too kind, my dear. You know, I worked with Mr. Ward, Boston's finest designer, on our guest rooms. During the next few weeks, I am certain that you shall discover many splendid aspects of Boston."

Charles had never known his mother to smile so much.

Stella matched her, smile for smile. "I do not doubt it for a moment."

"There are all sorts of holiday festivities." Beatrice adjusted the ruby-and-diamond necklace that adorned her thin chest, though Charles hadn't noticed it move. "Isn't that so, Charles?"

"Yes." He nodded. "Yes, many events."

"We shall host a party immediately for Stella," his mother announced. "She shall meet your friends within the week."

"A party?" Charles felt a terrible gnawing in the pit of his stomach, the pointed teeth of trouble.

"I made the plans and sent invitations from New York. It shall be the very first Christmas party of the season."

"You are a wonder, Beatrice dear," Stella marveled.

His mother acknowledged Stella's compliment with another bright smile and dismissive wave of her hand. "Undoubtedly we will be invited to attend a round of parties. We shall visit our country house and, of course, we must be at the Cabots' Snow Ball."

"I look forward to all of the Christmas festivities."

"You will be the star of every gathering. Won't she, Charles?"

Charles shifted in his chair. He grew more uncomfortable by the minute. "Most certainly."

"Stella is just coming out of mourning, you know. She's a widow."

The pale woman by his side gave him a doleful smile. "My condolences."

"Thank you." Stella inclined her head. Her brown eyes regarded him with a melting sweetness. "I hope my visit won't interfere with any plans you've already made. I should dislike being a bother."

"Tish!" Beatrice rocked back. "You could not be a bother if you tried. Could she, Charles?"

"No, Mother. No bother." Charles felt like a man caught in a cage and the bars were closing in on him, preparing to squeeze the very life from him. "Ah, how long do you plan to stay in Boston, Stella?"

She smiled . . . of course. No offense, that he could detect, taken. "I've not restricted myself with a return date."

"How . . . wise of you."

"On the other hand, I promise not to wear out my welcome."

The dog opened one eye and, growling softly, leveled a hostile gaze at Charles.

Beatrice took up the dinner conversation, going on about the excellent meal the cook had prepared while Charles wondered if Maeve, alone in her rooms, was enjoying the roast and Yorkshire pudding as well. Had she been served wine? Did she enjoy French burgundy? Were the apple dumplings to her liking?

He decided to find out for himself. Dabbing at his mouth with the linen napkin, he prepared to make his getaway. "I beg your forgiveness, but I don't seem to be feeling well at all tonight. Will you excuse me?"

Stella's mouth turned down. Her dog looked up.

A suspicious light sparked in Beatrice's eyes. "Of course, son. I will look in on you later."

Charles almost made his getaway; he'd reached the stairs when there came a loud knocking at the door. Not expecting a visitor and fearing yet another disaster, he waited in the foyer while Stuart the butler opened the door.

Two men, one big and the other small, stood on the small stoop. A surge of excitement shot through Charles's veins. These might be the thieves who stole his sketch of St. Nick come to demand a ransom. Charles stepped closer but stopped when he recognized the voice.

"Me name is O'Malley and this here is me boy, Shea. I'm wantin' to see me Maeve."

"Daddy!"

Charles turned from the male O'Malleys to Maeve, who stood midway on the staircase behind him. His anger at her for once again disobeying his orders dissolved in a heartbeat.

Dear God. She was stunning.

A striking vision in blue silk, Charles regarded Maeve

as if he were seeing her for the first time. The pleated ruching about the gown's low neck could not hide an abundant and delicious display of creamy cleavage. A natural deep blush colored Maeve's cheeks and her midnight mane cascaded in an enchanting tumble of curls. Her large jewel eyes sparkled in the gaslight.

Time and place ceased to exist. For the first time in his life Charles was mesmerized.

"Dad, what are ye doin' here?"

Before Mick could answer, Charles heard a rustle of skirts and looked to see Beatrice scurry to his side.

"Do we have visitors?" His mother looked from the men outside to Maeve still poised on the steps. "Who are you, young lady?"

Maeve lifted her chin. "I am Mrs. Charles Ashton Rycroft."

Beatrice's gasp was quite audible.

Chapter Four

"Smelling salts! I need my smelling salts!" Beatrice cried, sinking against her son.

"We brought ye yer things, me cailin," Mick barked to Maeve, ignoring Beatrice Rycroft's distress. Waving a paper sack in the air, his mouth turned up in a silly, broad grin.

Maeve's gaze flashed from her father to Charles. Her eyes narrowed on him as her little hands balled to fists at her hips and her fair complexion took on an ominous crimson flush.

"Ye haven't even told yer own mother!" she bristled. Her dark, arched brows burrowed into a furious frown.

Dear God, what next?

A single man living alone was unused to this . . . this pandemonium. Up until the moment he'd awakened to find himself in bed with Maeve O'Malley, Charles had lived in quiet contentment. He'd been satisfied with his well-ordered life and the gracious predictability of his days. From dawn until dusk he'd known exactly what to expect.

Although little more than skin and bones, Beatrice

weighed heavily against him. Charles eased his mother into the only vestibule chair just as Stella Hampton rushed in to join the melee. She carried her poor excuse for a dog under one arm. The miniature canine's high-pitched yapping proved immensely irritating.

The last drop of color drained from Stella's face as her gaze flitted from one person to the next. "What's happened? Who screamed?"

"That was Mother."

"Oh, dear!"

Charles felt Maeve's blistering gaze upon him as he turned to Stella. But the young widow had become an innocent victim of this disturbance and she deserved an explanation. A Rycroft always did the right thing—even when in danger of losing his life, as Charles was now if the look in Maeve's eyes was any indication.

"There's been a misunderstanding," he told Stella with a forced, but hopefully reassuring, smile.

"What 'ave ye done to me girl?" Mick O'Malley growled, attempting to brush by the butler.

Beatrice reared back as if she were being attacked by a mad dog. "Who is this man?"

"Me name is Mick O'Malley an' who would ye be?"

"Oh!" Beatrice gasped.

Unaccustomed to rudeness of any kind, Charles's mother appeared to be on the verge of swooning.

"Hush, Baby, hush," Stella crooned to her detestable, pointy little dog as she hurried to Beatrice's side.

Charles drew in a deep breath. *Dear God, let this madness end.*

Stuart remained at the door, steadfast and stoic, blocking the O'Malley men from entering. The cold winter wind swept in like an uninvited caller, but the group gathered in the gleaming marble foyer took no heed.

"Close the door," Dolly ordered as she bustled into the increasingly crowded entryway. After one bewildered look, the housekeeper made her way to Charles's mother.

"Have you brought my smelling salts?" Beatrice asked in a small, pathetic voice.

"In my pocket, Mrs. Rycroft. Don't you worry."

As Dolly gathered up Beatrice, Stella slanted a distrustful glance toward Mick and Shea before turning her attention to Maeve. The Irish beauty stood as still and proud as a Michelangelo sculpture while Stella blatantly scrutinized her from head to toe. At length the chalky widow raised an eyebrow and lifted her chin in a haughty cut. Without a word, she turned on her heel to follow Dolly and Beatrice up the stairs, cradling her bared-teeth, growling dog.

Charles felt as if he were locked in a nightmare from which there was no escape.

Scowling impatiently, Mick O'Malley pushed Stuart aside. Nonplussed, Charles's butler simply stared as Mick strode through the door, trailed by his son.

With a curt nod, Charles dismissed Stuart. Obviously vexed, the tight-lipped butler took his leave.

Old man O'Malley smelled faintly of whisky as he took another menacing step toward Charles. "What 'ave ye done to me Maeve?"

"I have done nothing to hurt your daughter. As you can see, she looks . . ." Charles dared another glance to where Maeve stood on the stairs.

His heart lurched, a soft leap that took him by surprise.

Maeve looked like a princess stepped from the pages of a fairy tale. She was the same girl she had been moments ago but somehow not the same. With head held high, she clutched the bannister with one hand. Despite the murderous look still flashing in her eyes, she was startlingly beautiful. The flush of her cheeks contrasted against her delicate porcelain complexion put Charles in mind of rose blossoms drifting on a blanket of snow.

His rather uncommon poetic thought was quickly followed by another. Her soft colors were in marked contrast to Maeve's headstrong nature. And she was humming, a characteristic Charles had come to recognize as manifesting itself when she was nervous. And when Maeve was nervous, anything could happen.

"She looks . . . splendid in her new dress, don't you agree?"

Maeve's father grunted.

"He is ashamed of me, Dad!"

"No!"

"Aye."

"I am not—"

But Mick O'Malley cut Charles off, speaking about him as if he were invisible. "The man's damn lucky to have ye!"

"Damn right," Shea agreed.

Charles rubbed his forehead. Torture was too good for the culprit who robbed and beat him and left him at the mercy of the O'Malleys. The villain should be forced to spend eternity with Mick O'Malley in particular. Nothing seemed cruel enough for the thief or thieves who had stolen his prized sketch and left him with an Irish shrew and her contentious family.

Nevertheless, a Rycroft must do the right thing. If only he knew what that might be in a situation like this.

Shea stepped forward to stand beside Mick. Maeve's brother was a big, broad man, almost as tall as Charles. His shabby jacket did nothing to hide his brawn. The young, handsome Irishman possessed the same coal black curls as Maeve's but his eyes were a blue-gray shade.

"Me sister is a good woman and deserves the best," Shea said, aiming a cool gaze at Charles. "If ye don't treat her with respect, sir, ye'll be answerin' to me."

"I assure you, Maeve will be accorded all due respect," Charles replied. To his relief, Shea spoke softly and appeared more levelheaded than either his cantankerous father or spirited sister.

A movement above shifted Charles's attention.

Holding her dress up so that her ankles showed in a most indecent manner—Charles overlooked her breach of etiquette to admire their slim turn—Maeve skipped down the steps to join the small circle of men.

She lashed into her father and brother.

"Saints above! Now tell me true, what are ye doin' here?"

"We wanted to make sure ye were all right," Shea replied.

Mick held up the sack he carried. "And we brought some things ye might be needin'."

"Like what?" Her hands went to her hips.

"Yer knittin' an' nightshirt, most important."

Maeve's stomach knotted with an unpleasant blend of tension and frustration. Her father would be her undoing yet. Maeve slept in a man's nightshirt, a secret she did not take kindly to having shared with her high society husband.

In the hopes Charles hadn't heard the nightshirt announcement, she took up another evil. "Me knittin'?"

Blue-blooded Boston ladies did not knit.

"The cranberries and ribbon, too." Mick lowered his voice. "Ye'll still make the decorations for our Christmas, won't ye?"

Her father was in his cups. Maeve turned on Shea. "What was ye thinkin', bringing his own here after he's been drinkin'?"

"I thought it was better than him comin' without me."

Swallowing her embarrassment, Maeve looked to Charles for his reaction, knowing she would be mortified if she found disdain in his expression.

But her taciturn husband did not evidence displeasure, nor hesitate. "I'll have Stuart take Maeve's things to her rooms."

Lowering her voice, Maeve spoke to her father in soft, gentle tones. "Dad, go now. I'll come by and visit with ye soon."

"Yer a good cailin."

She turned to Shea then. "Are you stayin' out of the ring?"

Her brother gave a wag of his head. "There's a big bout bein' scheduled. The pot is growin' so heavy that it might make a man rich enough to buy his own boat."

"My brother wants to get off the docks and become a fisherman," Maeve explained to Charles. "He yearns to work for himself."

"Someday I'll have me own fleet," Shea declared with a confident grin.

"If ye live," Maeve scoffed. "I'm not one for grown men fightin' in the ring—or anywhere else."

"I have never met a lady yet who is fond of the sport," Charles said.

Maeve embraced her father. She worried at being away from him. She loved him dearly, this small curmudgeon of a man who was both her father and her child.

Although Maeve had only been a ten-year-old lass when her mam died, Dad and Shea depended on her to take care of them. She'd done the mending and cooking, the cleaning and all that needed doing. For the past four years she'd brought home a steady income as well.

"I'll be callin' on ye before the week is out, Dad," Maeve promised.

Holding her father close, she kissed him lightly on the cheek, wishing he did not smell like Jamison's. Essence of alcohol had clung to him for years. He wore it like some men wore cologne. While her father had always raised a few in celebration, the serious drinking began after Maeve's mother died. Kathleen O'Malley's death changed her dad forever and had everything to do with his decision to take his children to America

before they starved. To this day, Maeve knew her father
pined for his darlin' Kathleen something fierce.

On long, lonely nights, Maeve had yearned for a man
to love her in the way Mick loved his Kathleen. Now
she meant for that man to be Charles.

Reluctantly releasing her father, she turned to Shea.
Standing on tiptoe, she wrapped her arms around him.
A strong and gentle giant, her older brother had always
offered protection and comfort. To the end of her life,
Maeve knew she would do anything in the world for
him.

The first time she'd seen Shea bruised, with his knuckles swollen following one of his professional boxing
matches, she'd cried. Although Shea won more bouts
than he lost, the results of his time in the ring always
showed. As she wondered who would soak her brother's
big hands and rub ointment on his bruises now that
she would not be there to do it, a lump as large as
Faneuil Hall lodged in her throat. Maeve would sell her
soul not to have Shea box again.

"Thank you for bringin' me things. If you need me,
ye know where to find me now you've been here. And
feel free to knock on Mrs. Gilhooly's door. She'll help
you with Dad if I cannot be there," Maeve added to
Shea quietly. Mrs. Gilhooly lived in the rear of their
South Boston building.

"If yer fancy husband does anything to make ye
unhappy, just say the word," Shea whispered gruffly in
her ear. "And I'll be takin' care of him for ye."

"Ye'll be the first to know," Maeve said with a wink
as she stepped out of his arms.

Taking each in hand, Maeve walked her father and
brother to the door. She tugged at her father's worn
jacket and buttoned him up snugly against the cold.
He'd gained weight round the middle and needed a
new jacket.

Mick pulled his knit cap down over his ears as Maeve

gave a yank to Shea's bright red scarf. She would miss her O'Malley men dearly, every day.

"Stay safe," she said, blinking back tears as she pushed her family closer to the door.

"Make sure ye keep yer promise, me darlin'. I expect to see ye before the week is out," her father called over his shoulder as he and Shea started down the steps toward the street.

Maeve watched silently until the figures of her father and brother disappeared into the silent, icy night.

A shiver tore through her as she stood in the open door. Maeve felt rather than saw Charles move up to stand beside her. The heat of his body warmed her. The masculine, woodsy scent of him eased her emptiness.

"I'll be apologizin' for the interruption," she said, still gazing into the black night.

"There's no need to apologize. They were worried about you. It's a blessing to have a family who cares so much about you," he said with what sounded to be a wistful tone. He closed the door.

" 'Tis indeed," she said quietly.

"And now I must face Beatrice." Charles straightened his shoulders and shot Maeve a wry smile. "I expect with the aid of her smelling salts that my mother has fully recovered. And I am certain she is waiting with great anticipation for a full explanation."

The unexpected, and quite enticing, twist of his mouth might have charmed Maeve at another time. But not at the moment. "And me as well," she asserted. "Do ye not think I deserve an explanation? I did not even know your mother lived in your home!"

"It seems I have much to answer for." His eyes met hers, soft and silvery and sincere. "Can you forgive me?"

How could she not, when with just one look, he'd managed to melt her heart?

* * *

The fourth floor corridor of the Rycroft brownstone featured gilt portraits of deceased ancestors. The painting of Charles's father, Conrad B. Rycroft, was by far the largest and most prominent. In the gallery of rogues, as Charles thought of this display, the flattering portrait was mounted at the end of the long, narrow hall. From this particular spot it seemed the elder Rycroft's eyes followed every move. Charles felt his father's critical gaze upon him now as he approached his mother's bedchamber and sitting room.

Beatrice's suite was on the same floor as Charles's. Since she was rarely in residence, he thought himself the beneficiary of the utmost privacy, a privacy he'd enjoyed. Up until now.

Every muscle in his body felt as tightly wound as a mainspring of a clock run amuck. For the first time in memory, he experienced the angst of a tormented man, a man caught in the grip of circumstances quickly spiraling out of his control. As he walked the chilled corridor, beads of sweat broke out on Charles's forehead. Clearing his throat, he knocked on his mother's door.

Beatrice answered with a faint bid to enter. Alone in her sitting room, she reclined on a pink-and-white striped satin chaise. Only the ornately carved rosewood furniture offered the eye a respite from the many shades of pink used with abandon in his mother's rooms. Wall and bed coverings, drapes, and upholstered furniture had been swathed in varying shades of Beatrice's favorite color. She made no secret of feeling that pink was the only color that truly flattered an aging woman.

Charles pulled one of the uncomfortable, dusty-rose, tufted chairs close to his mother's chaise and sat gingerly on the edge of the seat. He always expected the balloon-back gilt chairs to give way under his weight.

"How are you feeling, Mother?"

"What has happened? What have you done?" Beatrice snapped, holding her head in an anguished fashion.

"I am afraid it is a long—"

"Surely you make some cruel jest," she interrupted impatiently.

"No, Mother, it's no joke."

"But you cannot be married."

"My thought exactly, when I was first informed."

"How could you let such a dreadful thing happen?" Beatrice wailed, more dramatically than necessary, Charles thought.

"I was under the impression that you wanted me to marry, Mother."

"To a suitable woman . . . like Stella."

"Of course."

Tears brimmed in Beatrice's eyes as she extended a limp hand toward him. "Did the vixen hoax you, son?"

Charles took his mother's cool hand. "No. Not really." He could think of no easy way to explain. "It's, it's an . . . extraordinary situation."

"I don't think I can bear to hear it." Beatrice closed her eyes, in a bid Charles supposed to shut out reality. "But do go on."

What choice did he have? "Last week, I paid a call to Edgar Dines's establishment in order to purchase a sketch I'd heard—"

"Oh, no. Another?"

His mother's disapproval did not trouble Charles. Someday, he would bring Beatrice around to his way of thinking. Someday she would understand. "The sketch of St. Nick is the best of the lot, I believe."

"Go on."

"On my way to the carriage, I was accosted. Attacked. The sketch was stolen."

Dropping his hand, Beatrice bolted upright. "My dear boy! Were you hurt?"

"Yes. As a matter of fact, I was."

"Oh!" She reached for her smelling salts.

"Maeve—"

"Maeve?"

"Maeve O'Malley. The young woman you met earlier."

"Oh Lord, is she Irish?"

He nodded slowly. "Yes."

"Oh, no." Beatrice rapidly fanned the bottle of smelling salts under her nose.

Charles continued. "Maeve found me bruised and incoherent. A blow to the head had left me with a temporary loss of memory. During the time when I was not quite myself, we were forced to wed."

Beatrice threw her head back and moaned.

"As Maeve nursed me back to health, there were . . ." He faltered here, letting his thought go, envisioning others.

His mother's frosty frown demanded that Charles finish.

"Evidently there were some compromising moments."

"Have mercy!" Beatrice's outcry startled Charles. He was unaccustomed to hearing such an epitaph from his proper mother.

"I didn't mean to shock you, Mother."

Upright on the chaise once again, Beatrice's angry frown involved every line, fold, and wrinkle in her face. "Did the Civil War nurses marry all their patients?"

"Hardly."

"And certainly, they faced compromising situations and awkward moments."

"More than likely those angels of mercy did not have Maeve's father and brother standing over them," Charles pointed out.

"It is a ruse to use you and gain your fortune!" Beatrice declared.

"Perhaps." Charles had entertained the same thought and could not deny the likelihood.

"Annul—"

"Impossible."

"You've engaged in . . . ?"

"So I've been told."

"Why are you not outraged?"

"I am outraged, Mother, but I must proceed with reason."

"Charles, you behave the same whether you are outraged or pleased," she huffed. "I have never known whether you were happy or sad, angry or joyful."

"Father taught me long ago that wise men do not reveal their emotions."

She arched a dubious brow. "Perhaps in business, but if you are to have a proper wife, you must display a bit of emotion."

"I shall endeavor in the future to make my feelings known," Charles hedged. He had no intention of leaving himself vulnerable in such a way.

"As much as I hate the scandal of it, you must obtain a divorce at once," his mother pronounced. "It's long past the time when you should have made a proper marriage and produced an heir. You have neglected your duty to the family and your father's publishing company for far too long."

"Yes, Mother." A blueness settled into his bones. As much as he'd declared himself a confirmed bachelor— before Maeve—he knew it to be impossible. A Rycroft did the right thing, and the right thing for Charles was to produce heirs.

"The sooner you are rid of this Irish woman, the sooner you can make a suitable marriage."

Charles stood, preparing to make his escape. "I quite agree."

"I brought Stella home with me especially for that purpose. She is from a fine family with impeccable breeding—"

"Yes, but—"

"Is she not attractive?"

"Extremely attractive, Mother."

"And being a widow, she is eager to marry again and

start a family. Stella has been so looking forward to meeting you."

"At present I am not in a position—"

"You soon shall be," his mother assured him with some asperity. "Make arrangements at once."

"Mother—"

"You cannot continue another day with a marriage so ill-suited. A marriage foisted upon you by shifty, greedy Irishmen cannot be considered a true marriage."

"No, and I—"

"Why did you not put an end to it immediately after you came to your senses?"

"Because Maeve saved my life," Charles said, biting back the unexpected anger swirling like a tainted meal in the pit of his stomach. "I brought her home so that by spending time with me, she will see firsthand that we come from far different backgrounds. Maeve will quickly come to understand that she and I are too dissimilar to make a success of our marriage."

"You give her much credit," Beatrice sulked.

"I intend to reward Maeve for taking my life into her hands. Mrs. Potts has been instructed to provide a proper wardrobe and after the holiday I will settle with my . . . Maeve."

"What do you mean?" His mother frowned as she inclined her head.

"Maeve will have enough funds so that she will never have to work again. In return she will give me a divorce."

"Work?" An even deeper frown drove Beatrice's eyebrows dangerously near to the bridge of her nose. "What sort of work does the woman do?"

"She is in service," Charles said quietly.

"I beg your pardon?"

"Maeve's a maid . . . or was, in service to Harriet Deakins."

"Oh Lord, save me!" Beatrice closed her eyes and moaned. The Deakinses! Does Harriet know about your marriage?"

"I don't believe so." Charles rose. This interview had gone badly. He attempted to reassure his prostrate parent as he ambled to the door. "Mother, this will all be over soon. In the meantime, please be kind to Maeve. Remember, she saved my life."

"I cannot promise," Beatrice replied faintly, lifting the smelling salts to her nose once again.

Charles reached the door and was about to say good night when his mother spoke again. "Be warned. I shall speak to your father about this."

His hand froze on the polished brass handle. "I beg your pardon?"

"There's a new medium in Boston, Mrs. Helen Foster. I have been corresponding with her and she promises contact with the spiritual world and most especially your dear departed father."

A man Beatrice avoided as much as possible during his lifetime had been relegated to sainthood shortly after his death.

"Mother, no one talks to the dead."

"I shall, through Helen."

Heaving a resigned sigh, Charles turned the handle. "Very well. Give father my best."

He brushed his fingertips over the sketch, soft strokes of admiration for the art. His hands trembled from the chill of the damp, cold room.

He gazed with reverence at the picture: St. Nick sketched in black and white. Not a drop of color on the canvas and yet every fine line evoked a feeling. Love and whimsy were portrayed in the curl of the old man's beard, the twinkle in his eyes and even the very girth of him. His generosity was depicted by the sack across his back that overflowed with toys: dolls, wooden soldiers, trains, and tops.

The artist had only produced a dozen sketches before his untimely death. Each was valuable, but this sketch of St. Nick was the only known piece by the artist showing joy. The difference made it especially valuable.

The sketch promised to bring a great deal of money when he sold it in London. And he needed money desperately. Things had gone badly for him most of his life. He was due a stroke of luck, even if he had engineered it himself.

When he'd tried to break off with his mistress recently, Lydia had balked. The tart threatened to expose him to his wife—who was not an understanding woman.

Using his forefinger, he stroked the bristly corner of his mustache. From the first, Lydia had been expensive. Over the course of a year, she'd driven him deeply into debt. Now she'd turned to blackmailing him. Blackmailing her Samson! He still thought of himself as Samson. He liked the image the name conjured. But unfortunately, if he did not placate the harlot, he knew well enough what the consequences would be. He stood to lose his business and his family. With the price this sketch would bring, he could pay off Lydia and move his business and family to another city.

But he could not make the sale yet. He could not leave the country until a decent time had elapsed from the theft of the sketch. He would not risk being caught. He wasn't an evil or greedy man, just a man forced to do what he must when life conspired against him, as it seemed to do time and again.

Exercising great care, he slowly and carefully wrapped a brown paper covering around the sketch. He carried the small piece of art to the safe in the darkest corner of his office and placed it gently inside. The covered sketch rested alone, the only item in the safe. And he, Samson, was the only one who knew the combination.

No one would ever find the only sketch of St. Nick by Barnabas.

Chapter Five

Maeve had given up on Charles. He wasn't coming. He had no intention of offering any explanations. Why should he? She'd lost her temper and lit into him like some demented druid.

She changed her nightdress. Instead of the lacy gown Mrs. Potts had left for her, Maeve slipped into the comfortable flannel nightshirt her dad had brought. The scarlet garment had been a gift to Shea by an admiring but rather tarty lass. Maeve's mountain of a brother preferred to sleep in the altogether. Being the good brother he was, Shea passed on the bright nightshirt to her. Although its fiery color screamed alarm and its size enveloped her as if she were a bee in a blanket, Maeve loved its warmth and comfort.

She extinguished the gaslights, leaving only the bedside candle aflame. Maeve was afraid of the dark. She'd feared the dark since the morning she'd awakened beside the still, cold body of her mother. Kathleen O'Malley's life had been stolen during the silent blackness of night.

The fireplace gave off a golden glow and a waning

heat from the smoldering fire. Soon the small fire and its light would go out. As Maeve pulled back the billowing down comforter, she heard a soft rap on the door.

Her heart thrummed in an unnatural rhythm as she caught up the candleholder and hurried to answer. Although expecting Charles, she rather feared finding herself face-to-face with Beatrice Rycroft. With only a glance at Maeve, the woman had required smelling salts. The matriarch had come close to fainting dead away. Maeve dreaded the moment Mrs. Rycroft's strength returned.

She opened the door a crack and peeked.

"Good evening, Maeve."

'Twas Charles, as tall and magnificent as a man could be and still be mortal. The first time she'd seen Charles in his natural state, Maeve thought of Lug, the legendary Celtic God of Fertility. Should Lug ever appear in human form, she felt certain he would take Charles's body.

Though her heart fluttered with unnatural agitation, as if it had sprouted wings of its own, Maeve coolly dipped her head in greeting. No man had ever set her blood to tingling the way Charles did with just the merest shadow of a smile. Hard pressed to contain her excitement, she bit down hard on the soft inner side of her lip. Charles had come to her rooms. He hadn't dismissed her from mind.

"Come in."

Charles followed Maeve into the sitting room and stood before the chair she'd presumed he'd chosen to take. But he did not sit. He stared—at her.

His perplexed examination traveled the length of Maeve, from the too-long column of her neck to the folds of the scarlet shirt dragging on the floor.

The scarlet shirt. She'd forgotten!

"What is that you're wearing?" he asked.

Maeve expected she looked to Charles as if she'd

been swallowed whole by a red flannel monster. Heat flooded her cheeks.

" 'Tis a nightshirt," she replied with great dignity.

"A man's nightshirt?"

"Aye." Embarrassed to be caught in men's clothing and blushing to boot, she shifted her weight uneasily.

"How interesting." Charles cocked his head, slowly perusing the length of her once again. The corner of his mouth turned up in a lopsided grin. "Do women wear men's nightshirts as a rule or is it a custom from your mother country?"

She briefly thought about claiming her garb as a cultural phenomenon but decided on the truth. "Sure'n I do not be knowin' about other women, but a man's nightshirt is most comfortable."

"And colorful." Charles grinned. A glint of amusement sparkled in his eyes.

" 'Tis me brother's shirt. Shea's," she explained.

"Aaah." Charles sank to the tufted velvet sofa. With trembling hands, Maeve lit the group of candles set on the marble-topped table between them.

Charles looked so fine. He filled a room with a subtle male magnetism that sparked a heat in Maeve from the tips of her toes to her hammering heart. The moment she came upon him more than a week ago, she'd found his dark, brooding features intriguing. She thought him handsome in a rough-hewn way. And she knew that beneath his elegant suit, white linen shirt, and striking silk vest lay the body of a lusty man. Maeve knew Charles intimately. Craved him desperately.

She had spent their wedding night in wondrous exploration, delighted to discover Charles's well-honed, muscular form. On that night of all nights, her bridegroom's tender touch ignited a firestorm of passion Maeve never guessed she possessed.

Now, as the silence between them deepened, the memory of the sensuality simmering just beneath Charles's placid exterior sent wave upon wave of tingling warmth shooting down Maeve's spine. Fearing her wobbly knees might not hold her another moment longer, she sank to the chair opposite him. Marveling.

Even as he contemplated the crease in his trousers, Charles exuded a powerful, masculine presence. His deep pine woods scent filled Maeve's senses, leaving her as woozy as an Irish boxer who'd taken too many blows to the head.

She had slept beside this man, nestled against his warmth. And despite his cool indifference, Maeve yearned to do so again. Aye, even though he wasn't an Irishman, Charles Rycroft was a grand specimen of a man. If only he didn't hold his thoughts and feelings so close.

He raised his eyes to rest on the tray of untouched food gone cold.

"Have you not eaten anything tonight?" he asked.

"I've not been hungry. Besides, I do not need any more food settlin' on my hips."

With a twitch of his lips, Charles quickly lowered his head again.

Why had she said such a thing? A lady did not discuss such concerns with a man. But she was still learning to be a lady. With an agitated intake of breath, Maeve pulled her clasped hands against her roiling stomach. She must do better.

Charles lifted his head again. He gave Maeve a crooked smile as he met her gaze. "I hadn't noticed anything amiss with your hips, Maeve."

"You're a fine gentleman to be sayin' so."

He tipped his head as if her compliment was debatable and swiftly moved onto another subject. "How did your fittings go today?"

"Sure'n more dresses and coats and gowns will be delivered to this house soon than a body can ever find time to wear."

"A woman can never have too many gowns."

Maeve did not agree, but she did not disagree, for

once managing to keep her thoughts to herself and any argument at bay. In the ensuing silence, she gazed down at her hands—familiar, working hands. Hands almost as red and rough as her nightshirt. But she had no place to hide them.

Charles seemed to be having difficulty making conversation and Maeve had little heart for confronting her husband. But 'twas best to clear the air. A man and wife should have no secrets between them.

"Ye . . . ye did not tell me your mother lived with you."

"As a rule she prefers to live in New York City," he said, leaning back. The slight slump of his shoulders gave visible proof of his weariness. "Beatrice has come for a holiday visit and arrived earlier than I expected."

"Did ye tell her about me . . . about us?"

"I did."

"And did she require more smelling salts?"

Charles chuckled. "She did, indeed."

"She cannot like me for your wife."

"Mother cannot dislike you, for she doesn't know you."

"Are ye sayin' that if she'd had a choice, your own mother would have picked an Irish maid to be your bride?"

"Ah . . ." Charles exhaled the sound on a sigh. "Mother might have chosen what she would call a more suitable match."

"A society woman, the likes of Stella Hampton?"

He shrugged. "Perhaps."

"Did ye not notice how pale this Stella is? Are ye thinkin' like me the woman is sickly?"

Again Charles's lips twitched and he lowered his gaze to what he must have considered a bewitching crease of his trousers. "I cannot give you a reason why my mother has taken to Stella. Perhaps she feels sympathy. Stella is from a notable New York banking family, but she is also a widow . . . like Mother."

Maeve felt no sympathy for the young widow. "I do not think ye are suited to Stella. An' I would think the same even if I were not your wife."

"Of course."

His condescending smile told Maeve Charles didn't believe her. "Stella is like the first ice of winter and ye are a passionate man."

Charles bolted upright, his body stiff as a spike.

She'd done it again. Maeve's hands flew to her offending mouth.

Reflecting shock and surprise, Charles's smoky eyes locked on hers. "Maeve."

It was a whispered remonstrative.

Maeve had read enough in her new etiquette book to know that it was exceedingly impolite for a woman— or man—to speak his or her mind. Worse, what took place between a man and woman in the bedroom was never discussed aloud by the lovers.

"Saints above!" she breathed. Placing a protective hand over her racing heart, she pleaded forgiveness. "Sure'n I'm beggin' ye pardon. I do not know what made me say that. It must have been the wicked fairy."

"A fairy?"

"Oooooh, such an evil fairy, she is."

If it were possible, Charles's body appeared more rigid than before. One dark brow arched in astonishment. "Do I understand correctly? Do you believe in fairies?"

Certainly she did! Did he not?

Maeve could not deny the heritage she'd learned from her mother, the legends kept alive and passed on by her father and the rest of the Irish community. Fairies, leprechauns, and druids were as much a part of her as her own Gaelic language.

She looked Charles straight in the eye. He simply needed to be enlightened. "Aye. Now, ye be understandin' that there are good fairies and evil fairies, and they all live in the land of the Tir Nan Og . . . the Land of the Ever-Young. The Lhiannon Sidhe is the most famous, most powerful fairy of all. She can be both goodness itself or evil incarnate. But 'tis the Goddess Danu who protects the fairy folk, for they are all her children.''

Charles nodded, but his eyes had glazed over. Clearly, he thought her daft.

"Sometimes a mischievous fairy will put words in the mouth of an innocent Irish woman," she added, determined to convince him of her truth.

Charles nodded once more and stood. "I should like to learn more about the Land of the Ever-Young . . . at another time. Obviously, I interrupted you as you were about to retire."

Maeve rose. She'd frightened her husband off. Her heart wilted like a thirsty flower. "If you believe in St. Nicholas, then why not believe in the fairy folk?" she asked softly.

"Only children believe in Santa Claus," he said. "I haven't believed in St. Nick for years."

"More's the shame. We must believe."

"I confess I haven't believed in anything or anyone but myself in years," Charles said as he crossed to the door.

Maeve followed.

He held his hand poised over the doorknob. 'Twas clear, he couldn't wait to leave her. "Maeve, Mr. Raymond, an excellent dance teacher, will come to your rooms tomorrow afternoon to give you a lesson."

"A lesson?" She danced the reels and jigs better than any woman in South Boston.

"He will be teaching you the waltz and others you might need to know."

"Aye." To dance in Charles's arms would be splendid.

"My mother plans to hold a small Christmas party the day after tomorrow."

"To introduce me?"

Charles looked away, over her shoulder. "Ah, well . . ."

His voice trailed off, his hand dropped from the door-knob to sweep through his dark hair in an agitated fashion. "Well, it's actually a small holiday party to introduce Stella to our friends. It seems Beatrice sent the invitations while she was still in New York. At the time, Mother didn't know we were married."

"I understand." Hope and spirit seeped from Maeve at once.

"Do not feel slighted—you are most welcome at the party and I promise it will be festive with all the holiday trimmings. My mother is a skilled hostess."

Maeve's heart felt as heavy as the Blarney stone. She raised her eyes to his. "I will not know anyone."

"Neither will Stella, but I assure you she will attend."

"But I do not like parties."

"Neither do I." He smiled then, a small, gentle smile, and his eyes grew warm and soft. "But my presence is mandatory as well."

For a fleeting moment Charles had become Charlie again, the sweet, sensitive man Maeve loved and could never deny. "All right, then. I shall be dancin' at your mother's party."

Charles did the unexpected then. He tweaked her nose playfully. "Just make sure the wicked fairy doesn't get hold of your tongue."

Maeve grinned. "I'll do my best."

Charles's hand went to the doorknob again. "One more thing. We must keep our marriage a secret for a little longer. It would be most impolite to steal the spotlight from Stella as she makes her debut here in Boston. To say nothing of how it would anger my mother," he added. "Beatrice insists on being the first to make the grand announcement."

Maeve experienced a sour feeling in the pit of her stomach, a wary tightening. "And how shall ye be introducin' me then?"

He replied cheerfully. "As Maeve O'Malley, of course."

She nodded.

"Now, is there anything you need? I'll be away at the office most of the day tomorrow."

There was something Maeve needed, wanted. She wanted to make Charles stay, to lure him to her bed. But what sort of male would be attracted to a wife wearing a scarlet nightshirt that mopped up the floor behind her?

"And what'll ye be doin' at your office?" she asked in a feeble attempt to delay his departure.

"I'll be convincing my thickheaded cousin that coming out with a monthly magazine in direct competition with our rival is a bad idea."

"Will ye compete in some other way?"

"Yes. By publishing good, exciting books."

"I love books."

"You do?"

"Aye. Pansy Deakins has lent me many a book and I'm a regular at the public library."

Once again, Charles's hand fell from the doorknob. "What sort of books do you like to read?"

"My favorites are history books, but I'm fond indeed of the Brontes, Dickens, and Eliot."

"You'll find history books and more that might interest you in my study. Feel free to take whatever you like . . . whenever you like."

"Thank ye . . . *you*, Charles. You're a good man and I know you'll be successful in persuadin' your cousin. I'll be readin' any book you care to bring home."

"Even if they're only manuscripts I'm considering publishing?"

"Aye, I'll read your market list if ye wish!"

He laughed out loud. It was the first time Maeve had heard Charles give out with more than a chuckle since his memory had been restored. A bubble of pleasure bounced from her heart to the tips of her toes. She'd made Charles laugh!

"I'll bring manuscripts home for you tomorrow,

Maeve." Once again he grasped the doorknob and this time he turned it.

What could she do to make him stay?

"Have ye talked to the police about your stolen sketch?"

"Yes." His jaw clenched as he opened the door. "They gave me little hope of its recovery. But I will find it. I must. I've taken an ad offering a reward."

"I'll be askin' the Lhiannon Sidhe to look out for your sketch, Charles Rycroft."

"Aaah . . . thank you, Maeve."

Charles retreated to his study, feeling edgy. It was a different restlessness than he'd experienced before his visit with Maeve. Pouring himself a brandy, he stretched in the leather wingback chair by the fireplace.

So she believed in fairy folk and liked books . . . and men's nightclothes. Charles smiled to himself. He had never guessed how alluring a woman could be in over-sized clothing. If he hadn't known better, he might have accused her of teasing him. No matter how he attempted to keep his attention on their conversation, his mind kept conjuring tantalizing images of a petite, voluptuous body hidden beneath all that red flannel material. The desire to rip away the concealing nightshirt very nearly overwhelmed Charles.

But a Rycroft always did the right thing.

Didn't he?

Dear God. He was hot.

Through pure force of will, Charles turned to less dangerous thoughts. He admired Maeve's independent mind and spirit. But she also believed in fairies, which put her intelligence, and perhaps her sanity, in question.

On a positive note, earlier in the evening when she had been fully dressed Charles had seen nothing amiss with Maeve's hips. Softly rounded, they promised sweet haven. The fact that he'd experienced the pleasures of her curvaceous body firsthand and had no memory of it unduly disturbed him. He felt cheated.

He'd made love to an undeniably beautiful woman at a moment in time when he suffered from amnesia. He'd recovered from the amnesia but he could not recall the touch nor the taste of Maeve. Gross injustice is what he called it.

If Charles could only remember the events of their wedding night, he might be free of the curiosity that possessed him, the insistent need to know more about her. Once satisfied, Charles felt certain he could banish Maeve from his mind and concentrate on finding his missing sketch.

Of course, such carnal knowledge might also put a stop to the troublesome ache in his loins.

Early the next morning, Charles entered the Washington Street building of Rycroft Publishing. Located in the financial and publishing district of Boston, the Rycroft offices had been spared during the great fire of the previous year. Sixty-five acres had been leveled and thousands were left without jobs.

For some reason he felt more of a sense of purpose today than he had in a long time. Before doing anything else, Charles set aside a few manuscripts to bring home for Maeve. If he kept her busy reading, he hoped she would not feel so confined to her rooms. He had little desire to hold her prisoner.

Martin sauntered into Charles's office two hours later. Tall and thickly constructed, his cousin ate well and often. Unlike Charles, he had no athletic interests outside of watching an occasional baseball game at the park. The result was a stout body on a young man. Three years younger than Charles, Martin had suffered from chicken pox as a child. A once-attractive countenance had been left scarred. Martin disguised the disfiguring effects with a plethora of fashionable facial hair. He sported a full brown beard, side whiskers, and mustache. But his overweight cousin had a more difficult time masking his resentment of Charles.

"Good morning, Charles."

"Good morning, Martin." Whatever Charles did for Martin, it still was never enough to suit his cousin. But he could hardly turn out a family member, especially one who tried so hard to succeed. A Rycroft did the right thing.

Martin dropped down into the sturdy Sheraton chair in front of Charles's desk. "Have you reconsidered our discussion of yesterday?"

"No, Martin. I feel certain that competing with a monthly will not profit us."

"It will if we hire the finest writers and illustrators. We could steal Thomas Nast away for the right sum. I am certain the Rycroft treasury holds enough money to ensure his defection as well as the cream of the writing crop."

"I prefer to create a new market rather than go head-to-head. Rycroft Publishing will succeed by moving away from publishing the usual text and religious books. We'll concentrate on fiction."

"Who will buy fiction?" Angered, Martin's arms flailed above his head. He often talked with his hands as well as his mouth. "Would you ruin our reputation with dime novel publications, Charles?"

"Rest assured, we will not be publishing dime novels."

"As vice president, do I not have any say?"

"I always listen to you."

Charles knew Martin intended to be president of Rycroft Publishing one day. His cousin's ambition made Charles a bit nervous. He could only hope that if something should happen to him, Martin would have learned enough to keep the publishing house solvent.

"Charles, can't you see? I need to make my own mark on the company. I deserve my own . . . project."

"Then come up with one that I can approve. A monthly magazine will not win my approval."

"Monthly magazines are the wave of the future. Why do you suppose the rest of the publishing houses—"

"Magazines will never replace books. Rycroft Publishing will continue to focus on books."

Martin's eyes seemed to shrink, growing smaller as he glared at Charles. "You are making a grave mistake."

"I regret that you believe so."

Martin pushed himself out of the chair and headed toward the door.

"By the way, how is Sally?" Charles asked.

"Most days she is ill."

Martin's wife was expecting their first child. "Give her my best. I hope she will be able to attend Mother's little gathering tomorrow evening."

"Not to worry. We shall be there."

As soon as Martin left his office, Charles wrote a hasty message to Boston's most renowned private investigator, Herbert Lynch, asking for a meeting at the investigator's earliest convenience.

Mr. Raymond proved more pompous than any blue blood on Beacon Hill. Maeve's headache started the moment Stuart ushered the tall, lean dance instructor into the drawing room.

Mrs. Rycroft and Stella Hampton had gone out earlier in the day without a word to Maeve. She told herself their snub did not matter. All that mattered was pleasing Charles.

In preparation for her dance lesson the carpet had been rolled back and the piano tuned. Maeve, however, wasn't entirely certain that she was ready.

The dance teacher wore his curly, sandy-colored hair parted in the middle. His side whiskers boasted curls as well and ended where his mustache began. Impeccably dressed, Mr. Raymond appeared to be bound up tighter than Harriet Deakins's corset.

He offhandedly introduced the accompanist who

would play the piano during Maeve's lessons. His son, Robert, who resembled Mr. Raymond in stature and coloring, smiled shyly.

When Robert began to play, Mr. Raymond's starch dissolved in a puddle of liquid grace. In a swift, introductory demonstration, he danced for his skeptical pupil. Each effortless step he took became a lesson in artistry. Maeve had never known a man who possessed such grace.

After successfully dazzling her, the dance instructor announced he would teach Maeve the basic steps of the waltz. Before much time had passed, the dance seemed slow to Maeve and she attempted to increase the pace.

"Please," her instructor remonstrated. "You cannot lead. A lady does not lead."

"Aye? Was I leadin' now?"

"Just relax and follow *my* lead, Miss O'Malley."

No one called her Mrs. Rycroft. That was a secret she shared with Charles. A secret she did not care to hold. No matter how gracious he appeared, Maeve realized Charles could not bring himself to think of her as his wife. Somehow, she must change his way of thinking.

Prevailing etiquette mavens specifically instructed wives to defer to their husbands in all matters and never to bring up unpleasant subjects. But Charles must face the truth. Maeve was his wife and deserved to be accorded every respect.

Oh, Saints in Heaven, who did she think she was?

Maeve had no business being Mrs. Charles Rycroft! She did not speak properly, she could not even dance properly. Charles Rycroft's family and friends would never accept her. She stood out like a brittle stick of straw among smooth strands of silk.

"Must you step on my feet?" Mr. Raymond asked tersely. His patience apparently had run its course.

"I lost my concentration. Aye, an' I'm not used to dancin' with a partner."

"Do you dance alone?"

"In a manner of speakin'."

Mr. Raymond raised his eyes to heaven, as if requesting help, and then halted the dance abruptly. "My dear woman, we've accomplished enough for the first lesson."

The piano music stopped. The cover thumped down over the keys.

A sense of doom—and failure—descended on Maeve. "I'll be doin' better the next time."

"I shall return tomorrow and give Mr. Rycroft a full report. I know he has high expectations, but one man can only do so much."

"Are you thinkin' I can't dance?"

"No, no. Not at all. In due time. Anything is possible."

She pulled him to a chair and pushed him down. "Just you watch!"

Picking up her skirts with both hands so Mr. Raymond could clearly see her feet, Maeve launched into a lively jig. She accompanied herself. "Da da da da, da da. Da da da da da."

His brows arched in surprise—or horror. His eyes reflected alarm and finally his face folded in a thunderstruck frown. Mr. Raymond's appalled gaze locked on Maeve's feet.

It took skill not to entangle her new high-button shoes in the thick folds of the lavender silk dress. The Irish jig required intricate, swift steps.

Moments later, Maeve surrendered entirely to her music. She was not even aware the young man at the piano had picked up the melody and accompanied her.

Soon even Mr. Raymond let himself go, clapping his hands in time to the joyous Irish jig. Maeve's heart beat faster and faster. Her spirits soared as she kicked up her heels and danced round the room to the music. Laughing and lost in memories of merrier times, she did not hear the door open. She did not look up until the music stopped.

"Maeve."

Out of breath, she managed half a gasp. "Hell ... hello, Charles."

"What are you doing?"

"An Irish jig."

"We had finished for the day. Miss O'Malley was simply demonstrating the steps to me as I requested," Mr. Raymond explained, winning Maeve's heart forever. "You see, I have never seen a jig danced before."

Charles dismissed him curtly. "Thank you, Mr. Raymond."

"I will return tomorrow with Robert."

"Yes. Please do. But no more jigs," Charles warned.

Maeve turned on Charles as soon as the Raymonds left the room. "Is there somethin' wrong with an Irish jig now? Is Irish dancin' outlawed in the home of a Beacon Hill aristocrat?"

"Certainly not."

"Are ye certain?" she asked, advancing on him with blood boiling.

Frowning, Charles cleared his throat. "I am certain your ankles were showing. *And,* you were holding your skirts up for all the world to see."

"Aye, and do ye think Mr. Raymond and Robert took a shine to me ankles?" she bristled.

"Maeve, do you know anything about propriety?"

"Aye. I know to respect my elders and to be kind to those about me."

"There are rules of behavior—"

"I don't believe in rules."

"That's abundantly clear."

"And I would like to be introduced as your wife from now on. Mrs. Charles Rycroft is my name now, not Maeve O'Malley."

"I have already explained why we needed to keep our marriage a secret just now."

Maeve dug her fists into her hips. "Explain it again."

Charles appeared to have been brought up short.

"We must wait until Stella has returned to New York and the Christmas holiday has passed."

"Christmas is the season of love, ye know."

"Yes. Well. You must have realized there would be complications arise from marrying a man you picked up off the street."

"Aye. I suppose I did now."

"How did your dance lesson go before the jig?"

"Mr. Raymond taught me the steps to the waltz. But I do not care for the waltz—'tis too slow a dance."

"The waltz is considered by some to be a rather risqué dance."

She inclined her head in disbelief. "No. Why?"

"When a man takes a woman in his arms like this . . ."

Maeve caught her breath as Charles's arm wrapped around her waist and drew her against the solid steel of his chest.

"And takes her hand like this . . ."

She could no longer feel her heart beating as Charles's hand enveloped hers.

"It is a rather intimate position," he continued. "Especially when a couple is moving and their bodies brush against one another. Like this."

"Mr. Raymond did not hold me like ye are doin'."

Before Maeve could tell Charles exactly how Mr. Raymond held her, her husband's mouth came down on hers.

Charles kissed her fiercely, crushing her against him.

As if she'd been sleeping for centuries, Maeve suddenly came alive, sparks of delight prickling her flesh as she savored his kiss . . . wet, warm, and delicious.

A flood of feelings old and new spiraled through her at a dizzying speed. Her blood ran sweet and warm like the wildflower nectar fairy folk sipped as wine. Trembling within and without, Maeve did not think she could stand alone should Charles release her.

Saints above! She prayed he wouldn't release her.

Charles lifted his head slowly. A wry smile played on his lips. "Do you now understand the danger in the waltz?"

Chapter Six

"Do ye like me new gown?"

"Not me ... *my*," Pansy corrected Maeve patiently. "*My* new gown."

Maeve repeated Pansy's example. "Do ye like *my* new gown?"

"Do *you* like my new gown?"

"Sure'n I'll never get this right!" Maeve cried out in frustration.

"Yes, you will. You're an intelligent woman. We all are, actually. Victoria Woodhull promises women shall go far once we gain the right to vote."

Maeve learned all she knew about the Woodhull woman from Pansy. The shocking, one-time clairvoyant was divorced and an advocate of free love. Pansy revered the women's rights advocate and recited her virtues frequently to Maeve—who could not condone either free love or divorce.

"Sure'n I'm not lookin' to go anywhere. I'm only interested in keepin' me husband."

And keeping his kisses. Unconsciously, Maeve raised

her fingertips to her lips, lips that still tingled from Charles's unexpected and wondrous kiss yesterday.

"*My* husband," Pansy echoed.

Pansy had been invited to Beatrice Rycroft's holiday party. As soon as Maeve learned of it, she beseeched her friend to come early. Pansy happily complied and now busied herself perfecting Maeve's appearance.

"When Charles sees you tonight you shall not have to speak a word. He will find you utterly irresistible."

Maeve's nerves had been on edge since dawn. It felt as if a toy top spun continually in the center of her stomach. Except for a spot of tea, she'd been unable to eat all day.

Late this afternoon Ilona Potts had delivered the dress she wore. Maeve approached the beveled mirror tentatively. She had never looked irresistible in her life.

She gasped at the girl reflected in the mirror.

Trimmed with handmade lace, Maeve's holly green velvet and silk dress swept back gracefully to a small bustle. The lush color complimented Maeve's fair skin and rose-petal cheeks in a captivating contrast. The sleeveless gown's snug bodice crisscrossed in front, plunging into a deep vee that revealed a generous display of cleavage. She felt quite immodest, never having worn such a daring gown. If he could see Maeve now her dad would be cursin' to all the saints in heaven and drainin' his bottle of Jamison's.

For some unknown reason, with the arrival of Stella Hampton and Beatrice Rycroft, Charles's housekeeper had become sympathetic to Maeve. Dolly had helped with her hair this evening, sweeping the sides back but allowing a mass of glossy raven curls to spill in a shining cascade from the crown of Maeve's head to the middle of her back. Pansy completed the arrangement by artfully arranging silky tendrils to frame Maeve's face.

Unnerved by the stranger in the mirror, Maeve turned away and crossed to the window. A light snow fell, a glistening tumble of crystal flakes beneath the gaslights.

It was a beautiful sight but instead of soothing Maeve, her nervousness grew as she gazed down at the street below. A stream of carriages waited to discharge their passengers.

Wily in her way, Beatrice Rycroft had seen to it that Stella's introduction to Boston society was the first, and possibly the foremost, party of the holiday season.

"Sure'n I cannot go downstairs."

"You need not say 'sure'n,' " Pansy corrected.

"But I am sure that I cannot."

"But of course you can—and will."

"Saints above! Do ye not understand? I've never been to a party like this. I do not know what to say or do."

Pansy wrapped an arm around Maeve and spoke in a soft, comforting voice—unusual for her. "Maeve, you will be introduced to any number of people whom you may never see again. All you need do is smile and say how pleased you are to make their acquaintance."

"Aye?"

"Most likely there shall be parlor games—"

Maeve spun away. "Aye!"

"What's wrong?"

"Sure . . . I *do not* know any parlor games!"

"Silly! The rules of each game are repeated at the start. Do you think the rest of the guests will know every game?"

Maeve gave a hapless shrug. "Oh, Pansy. I do not wish to shame Charles. Make my excuses. Say I have the headache. No one will be missin' me. They don't even know I exist."

"But I do know and I will miss you," Pansy declared. Fire danced in her wide-set hazel eyes. "I only agreed to attend Beatrice's party because of you. You can't imagine how bored I would be otherwise. I meet these same people at every occasion, you know."

Maeve cast a suspicious glance at her friend. "Bored?"

Pansy grinned. Despite the freckles that Maeve knew she hated, Pansy looked quite pretty in her simple white satin dress. With her flaming red hair and ready smile, she would surely stand apart in this evening's crowd.

"Exceedingly bored." Pansy repeated. "Now, following the games, supper will be served. It's always the same."

"What if I take up the wrong spoon during supper?" Maeve had studied the sketch of a proper place setting in *Beadle's Dime Book of Etiquette* but feared she was so nervous she would forget what she'd learned.

"The world will end, surely!" Pansy teased, taking Maeve's hands in both of her own. "If you feel unsure, watch what I do and follow my lead."

But Maeve was awash with fears. She could not be comforted. "What if I forget mese . . . *myself* and speak too loudly?"

"You won't. But if you should, I will signal you."

"Ye know Mrs. Rycroft and Stella have avoided me. They may cut me."

"At Beatrice's own party?"

Because Pansy chose to answer Maeve's question with a question, Maeve interpreted her friend's reply as meaning yes, Beatrice Rycroft just might cut her. Maeve debated: should she flee now, before the party, or after when the whole town was talking about her social blunders?

"Come, let's go down and join the party else they think you are frightened of them," Pansy urged, guiding Maeve to the door.

"And that I am! Frightened. What if they don't like me?"

"You are bound to be the Belle of Boston. It's just a matter of time. And this is where you start."

Maeve had little choice but to brazen it out. She pinned a sprig of holly in her hair.

Charles stood apart, observing with his childhood friend, Spencer Wellington. Spencer enjoyed these gatherings more than he, taking particular delight in lampooning selected guests.

Beatrice Rycroft had managed to invite a lively group of sons and daughters from Boston's finest families to the first holiday party of the season. Her intimate gathering peaked at thirty guests.

The parlor, drawing room, and study were opened and the servants had decorated the public rooms gaily with garlands of holly and pine, scarlet ribbons, and bowls of fruit. Juicy red apples and great round oranges stuck with cloves testified to the wealth and plenty of the household. The scent of cinnamon and warm mulled cider filled the festive air.

Beatrice and Stella received their guests at the door. Always elegant, Charles's mother wore gray satin bedecked with berry-red velvet ribbons carefully designed to conceal the sharper angles of her thin body.

But he wondered at how Stella managed to breathe. The tight bodice of her scarlet gown pushed her breasts up and over the squared fringe neckline. Charles feared the pale woman might spill out before the night was over. But most of the male guests seemed quite taken with Stella's clearly visible charms.

Charles glanced at his pocket watch, wondering why Maeve had not yet joined the party. If he didn't miss his guess, she had already begun to understand how different his world was from hers, how difficult it would be for her ever to fit in. She could never truly feel comfortable in Boston society.

But dear God, the taste of her fired his imagination and brought his blood to the boil.

The kiss he'd stolen yesterday afternoon had not served to satisfy Charles in any way. He wanted more, more of her.

Tonight he resolved to stay close by Maeve's side to make certain she would not be slighted. He didn't wish to see the girl hurt, especially by the sometimes wicked tongue of his mother. He only wanted her to understand. This evening Maeve would gain firsthand knowledge of the world into which he was born. A world she was ill-suited to, a world he often disliked.

Stella sidled up to Charles as he pondered the evening ahead. Her overpowering spicy perfume forced him to step back. "Good evening, Charles."

"Good evening, Stella." He turned to introduce Spencer, but his friend had wandered off. Spencer's timing was impeccable.

"It's a marvelous party. Christmas is in the air," she gushed.

"Yes, well . . . it is." And then Charles said what he was expected to say. "You look lovely, Stella. I daresay every male at the party will soon be under your spell."

"Thank you. You are so sweet." She wrinkled her nose.

Charles just stared for a moment. He supposed the wrinkling of her nose to be a failed attempt at girlish coyness. "You are the first to think so," he finally replied.

Apparently believing him to be teasing, Stella smiled broadly. "You are too modest, Charles." Before he knew it, she'd tucked her hand beneath his arm. "Your mother tells me that following supper, the carpets will be rolled up in the drawing room for dancing. May I be so bold as to hope I shall have the opportunity to dance with you?"

"I shall be delighted to have the first dance with the guest of honor."

"Your wife will not be jealous?"

"My wife?"

His wife.

Charles had not used the term before nor spoken it aloud. It sounded odd to him. My wife.

"Your mother confided in me concerning your unfortunate entrapment. But do not worry, I shall keep your secret."

"I appreciate your discretion." Would Maeve be jealous of Stella? He had no idea. "Maeve really does not care for parties."

"I see. Poor thing."

"She will probably retire before the dancing begins." Stella tipped her head and gave him a coy smile. "How convenient for you."

"My wife knows I would never do anything to injure her," Charles blurted, purely in a burst of self-protection. He had no idea what seeds his mother might have planted in the mind of Stella Hampton. He had enough to worry about at the present without dodging a husband-hunting widow.

"I shall look forward to the dancing," Stella said. With another plainly seductive smile, she glided away.

Charles was surprised but pleased that Stella had not brought her sharp-snouted, snarling dog to the party. He considered the widow attractive in a pale sort of way, but not his type. Although on further examination, he wasn't at all certain what his type was.

Having been a firsthand observer during his parents' marriage, Charles had not developed the highest regard or hope for the institution. He thought love a much too intangible emotion and certainly no reason for marrying. A marriage arrangement made more sense and left less chance of expectations being dashed.

Since he'd come of age, Charles had enjoyed the company of any number of women—some quite ineligible. He'd been exceedingly grateful the Boston beauties found him attractive, even though he understood the attraction might be to his wealth and social standing.

Over the course of time, Charles chose his entanglements carefully, refusing any situation which might put his heart in danger. He'd been safely involved with a sassy courtesan for several years, an opera singer he supported until her marriage over seven months ago.

Charles had not had a woman since.

His deprivation had left him especially vulnerable to temptation. It was the reason he gave himself for having taken Maeve into his arms yesterday afternoon and kissing her. His self-imposed abstinence also explained why her lips tasted like spun sugar, why they felt as warm and soft as berries ripening in the sun. After being deprived of a woman for so long, it only stood to reason he'd want more of Maeve's kisses.

But Charles refused to take advantage of the situation. Even though Maeve was presently his wife, he'd soon be seeking a divorce.

Unused to being kept waiting, and impatient for her appearance, Charles made his way from the parlor. It occurred to him she might have cold feet and had barred her door. If necessary, Charles intended to carry her down to the party.

A group had gathered round the piano to sing a lively rendition of "We Wish You a Merry Christmas." He stopped for a moment, envying their good spirits. It was, after all, the season of love and joy.

Waving to Martin, who had just arrived without his wife, he turned to the stairs. Charles stopped. His breathing stopped, his heart may even have stopped. He did not know, could not think. He could only stare.

Maeve stood at the top of the landing. The instant their eyes met she sent him a brilliant smile, a smile that made him feel as if he were the only man in the room, a god of a man at that. Jarring bolts of white heat shot through his veins. He felt himself grow hard.

Oh, dear God.

Maeve descended the stairs slowly, a luminous vision in rich green velvet. Her sparkling lapis gaze never left his. Pansy Deakins followed with what appeared to be an annoyingly smug smile on her lips.

Charles clasped Maeve's hand as she reached the bottom of the stairs.

"You outshine the stars tonight."

Damn. What made him say that!

Maeve responded with an even more radiant smile. "And ye are looking very handsome, yourself."

Her saucy gaze swept from his head to his feet, lingering a moment near his ... his crotch! He had to sit quickly.

He led Maeve away, heading for a corner of the room. Unfortunately, Martin intervened. He held an unlit cigar in one hand and slapped Charles on the back with the other.

"My aunt has done it again," he said, looking about the room filled with beautiful young men and women. Everyone who is anyone is here ... another Beatrice Rycroft success. And a fitting way to start the season."

"Yes, Mother has outdone herself." Charles quickly scanned the foyer entrance and then the parlor. "Where's Sally?"

"Sally's not well. She suffers from morning sickness morning, noon, and night." Martin's gaze fixed on Maeve's decolletage. "She couldn't be with me tonight."

"I'm sorry. Give her my best wishes." Unreasonably irritated by his cousin's rude ogling, Charles started to lead Maeve away.

"And who is this enchanting woman on your arm?"

"Did I not introduce you? Forgive me. This is ... Maeve."

Maeve inclined her head and smiled sweetly.

Martin appeared enthralled.

Charles decided to finish the introduction quickly and whisk his wife away. He didn't trust his cousin—never had, really. Just because Martin was married did not mean he would behave honorably toward Maeve—or any woman, for that matter. Martin loved women—as a whole. What's more, he made no secret of the fact that he preferred variety in his life. Charles suspected his cousin kept a mistress.

"Maeve, this is my cousin, Martin Rycroft."

"Charmed, my dear. Absolutely charmed."

Maeve blushed.

"Where did you meet?" Martin blurted, turning to Charles. "I have—"

"We met last week . . . by chance," Charles said, tugging at Maeve's hand.

Martin grasped Maeve's free hand, preventing Charles's flight. "My dear, you've managed what no other woman has been able to do for months. You've captured my cousin's eye."

"As he has captured mine."

"The lady came to my rescue one snowy day."

"She rescued you?"

"I shall be glad to tell you the whole of it later. We must not ignore our other guests."

"No, no. Beatrice would be quite upset."

Without giving Martin the opportunity to prolong the conversation, Charles pulled Maeve from his cousin's grasp and strode into the crowded parlor where the games had begun.

A rousing rendition of Hunt the Slipper was followed by a round of Charades. Maeve managed to sit quietly in a corner with Pansy, Charles, and his best friend, Spencer Wellington. Though many inquiring glances were thrown her way, Charles had only introduced Maeve to a few select friends.

An hour into the party, she'd yet to speak a word. With each introduction, Maeve merely bowed her head and smiled. And hoped she would not be sick to her stomach. Her tossing stomach threatened to send her from the party at any moment.

Charles looked extraordinarily handsome dressed in formal attire. His dark velvet jacket eloquently defined the broad expanse of his shoulders. Maeve noted the rich fabric of his waistcoat, the precise fold of his tie. He cut a dashing figure, one that could never be overlooked. Towering over the rest of the guests, Charles moved with animal grace, compelling and powerful. He exuded subtle signals of strength and a keen intelligence.

A tumble of warm, prickly needles and pins raced down Maeve's spine. Her heart leaped like some wild thing locked within her chest. She wanted him. Alone. Now.

Impossible.

Throughout the games an enigmatic smile lurked about his sensuous mouth. The desire to taste Charles's lips again and warm his cool smile filled Maeve to an aching point.

But she was not the only woman in the room drawn to him. Stella appeared unable to tear her gaze away from Charles. The merry widow flirted openly with Maeve's husband from beneath pale, hooded eyes.

Maeve concentrated on the games, learning and memorizing so that she might play with abandon at the next party. Even now she still possessed the heart of a child. Perhaps because there had been no time for games in her childhood. Each day had been a new struggle for survival.

"You are about to play Blindman's Bluff," Pansy whispered. "It's time to take part and no skill is required for this game."

Maeve looked to Charles. "Would it be proper?"

He gave her a smile of encouragement. A true smile. "Yes, of course, Maeve. Join in."

Her heart skipped several beats and landed with a thud.

"I'll play, too," Pansy declared.

"Dear God. I fear my cousin has been chosen as blindman," Charles remarked drolly.

"Is that bad?" Maeve asked.

"In this game the blindman must identify a person by touch alone. It's the only game I know Martin to play. Keep your distance," he warned.

Once Martin was blindfolded and a circle of participants formed, Pansy snatched Maeve's hand. "We must change our seat, he knows where we are."

Maeve did not like leaving Charles's side but giggled

as Martin stumbled toward Stella and patted her hair before stepping back.

"A woman with lovely, silk hair . . . but I do not know who. And I dare not touch again, I fear."

The room broke out into laughter.

As Martin turned in place like a drunken sailor, Pansy led Maeve to a spot on the other side of the room where they could observe—and dodge the blindman if it became necessary.

Martin reached out and patted the shoulders and chest of the young man standing next to Stella. "I don't believe I know you." As an afterthought, Charles's cousin ran his fingers lightly over the man's face. "No, no, I don't know you. But I should like to become acquainted!"

Again, the room filled with laughter. When it became quiet again the blindman lurched in the direction of Maeve and Pansy.

Maeve froze in place, barely breathing. Even if Martin touched her, he would never guess who she was. They'd only just met. She hoped he didn't touch her.

With his arms outstretched, the heavily bearded young man moved slowly toward her. Maeve had seen photographs of grizzly bears that were not much more fearsome than he. It was almost as if Charles's cousin could see exactly where she stood. Maeve's feet felt rooted to the floor. She could only stare at Martin Rycroft's approaching bulk.

He stumbled.

She turned just in time. His outstretched palm missed her cleavage and clutched her bare arm. A unified gasp went up.

"You are a bit off the mark, old boy." Charles appeared at Maeve's side before she took her next breath. His gray eyes, dark as ash, glinted with anger.

Martin's hand dropped away.

Maeve straightened her shoulders and lifted her chin,

but beneath her gown, her knocking knees felt as unsteady and runny as morning mush.

Beatrice rushed into the brink. "Ladies and gentlemen, supper is about to be served. Let us remove to the dining room."

Charles roughly removed Martin's blindfold.

"My humblest apologies, Maeve . . . Charles."

"Accepted," Charles snapped. He turned to leave the room but Martin refused to stifle his curiosity.

"You know the whole room is abuzz, wondering about the identity of the beauty at your side. I simply sought to break the ice . . . as the saying goes."

"Maeve, you and Pansy go in to supper. I wish to speak with Martin for a moment."

"It was an accident," Martin insisted as soon as the ladies were gone.

"I don't believe you. Your blindfold was placed so that you could see."

"Have you proof?"

"No." The anger churning inside Charles was out of proportion to his cousin's latest misdeed. He knew it, but could not overcome his simmering rage.

"How can I convince you?"

"You can't." Charles could never believe Martin. He'd been dishonest since he was a boy, mastering the art of lies and subterfuge from an early age. Yet no one, even within the family, seemed the wiser. A testimony, Charles supposed, to his cousin's expertise.

"It's just a game," Martin scoffed. "No need to get so riled."

"Keep your distance from Maeve. She is an innocent young woman."

In rapid, agitated movements, Martin jerked at the purple scarf used to blindfold him. "Who are you to tell me?"

"The cousin who has kept you out of trouble all these years."

What flesh that showed behind Martin's beard, mustache, and side whiskers deepened to a ruddy shade of anger. He spoke quietly and distinctly. "You are a very fortunate man, cousin. You have inherited a publishing empire—you have more money than Midas and more women to choose from than any man I know."

"But I am burdened with a cousin who resents me."

"Why shouldn't I? You give nothing to me!"

"Which doesn't stop you from taking," Charles bit out, hardly able to restrain his mounting fury.

Martin narrowed his eyes, his mouth turned down in surly arrogance. "Taking?"

"You have just recited all the things I have. Well, there is something I don't have that was in my possession a week ago."

"Are you accusing me—?"

Releasing his anger, Charles launched into a verbal attack. Although his mother's guests had gone up to the dining room, he dared not be overheard. Instead of bellowing at his cousin as he wished to do, Charles ground the words between his teeth. "I didn't just disappear from the city, from the publishing house. I did not abandon my responsibilities to embark on a sudden holiday. I was robbed, beaten, and left for dead."

Martin's mouth dropped in apparent shock. "No!"

"It was a robbery and the sketch taken from me at the time is extremely valuable in more ways than one."

"You think I had something to do—?"

"I was left for dead," Charles repeated. "If I had been killed, you would have inherited Rycroft Publishing."

Martin stiffened. His lips drew into a thin, tight line before he shook his head slowly and emphatically. "My only crime is envy. I envy you Charles, I always have." Stepping back, he scanned the richly appointed parlor. "While I have had to struggle for everything I own, you take all of this, your golden life, for granted."

"Do I?"

"Yes." Martin made a move to leave the room, but stopped. "Perhaps you'll find the men who beat you.

You may even recover your missing sketch. But do not insult me further."

Charles met his cousin's gaze. "The stolen sketch was of St. Nick . . . by Barnabas."

A dark stillness fell over the room. In the silence Charles heard his heart beat in a slow, thudding rhythm.

"You have my condolences," Martin said at last.

"I have hired a private investigator. The sketch will be recovered and my attackers found."

"Naturally. You have always enjoyed the best of luck, Charles." Casting his cousin a sardonic smile, Martin turned on his heel and strode from the room without even a nod to the figure he passed.

Maeve stood in the doorway, her curious gaze locked on Charles. He wondered how much she had overheard.

Chapter Seven

"An' is yer husband doin' right by ye, me cailin?"

Maeve had returned to her father's South Boston flat to pay the call she'd promised. Before leaving, she'd made a detour through the Rycroft kitchen where the cook helped her fill a basket with potatoes, cream, flour, bacon, lamb, eggs, oranges, and apples. Shea and her father would feast for days on these simple pleasures.

"Sure'n he is, Dad." Maeve stood at the old iron stove stirring a steaming pot of potato-and-leek soup, her father's favorite.

Mick sat at the small, chipped, and faded wooden table watching her cook. Shea was at work on the docks, but the elder O'Malley didn't have to be serving the ale at Rosie's until late afternoon. Before he left for the saloon today, Maeve meant for her dear dad to have a good, hot meal. Lord only knew what he did for meals now that she wasn't around to cook.

The flat felt twice as cold as Maeve remembered. Even wearing her new leather high-button shoes and warm stockings, her feet were cold. There were no roaring fireplaces to warm each room as there were at the

Rycroft residence. During the winter months the O'Malleys depended on the iron stove to provide heat.

Determined to leave her father and brother well stocked with food, Maeve had spent the better part of the morning mixing, boiling, and baking.

She'd brought decorations as well as food, "borrowing" two fragrant green garlands from last night's party. Now draped over the flat's two windows, the garlands added a bit of color and life to the drab atmosphere. It didn't seem right that Maeve should be living in such splendor while her father and brother remained trapped in the cold, smelly tenement.

While she didn't expect Charles to take her father and Shea into his Beacon Hill brownstone, he could afford to see them situated under a far better roof. Maeve hoped she could persuade him.

"Society stiffs like the Rycrofts don't hold with little people like us," Mick O'Malley grumbled, scratching a snowy, three-day growth of beard. His fringe of uncombed, wispy hair shot off in several directions. "Don't let 'im hold his station over ye."

"There are no little people, Dad. Unless by little people you're meaning the leprechauns," Maeve replied. "Charles can certainly see that I'm not a leprechaun."

"If he does anything to harm me girl, I'll send Shea's boxer friends after him."

"Please, Dad. Charles is a good man."

"If I'd known he lived on Louisburg Square, I might not 'ave been so quick to see ye married to 'im."

"But ye did and it's done."

"The air we breathe, 'tis not good enough for the likes of him."

"Nonsense."

"Sean Casey is still askin' about you."

Maeve never cared for Sean although he'd courted her stubbornly for the past three years. He'd fancied himself a gift to ladies, but the young Irish lad had never inspired any fire in Maeve. "Have ye told him I'm a married woman?"

When Mick did not answer, she knew her father had not broken the news to the man he'd long hoped would be his son-in-law one day. "Sean's a policeman now, you know. The whole neighborhood is lookin' up to him."

"I'm happy for him, Dad. Tell him Mrs. Charles Rycroft sends her best wishes."

Except for the faint bubbling of the soup, the flat fell silent.

"Yer losin' your brogue, me cailin." Her father's soft comment was laced with the unshed tears of an expatriate's regrets.

"Saints above!" Maeve dropped the spoon and whirled around in a swish of silk to face her father. "I'm not."

Mick woefully disagreed. "Yer soundin' more like one of them."

"Dad, I'll always be one with you," she insisted. Kneeling by his side, she took one of his heavily veined hands in both of hers. Maeve loved her father too much to hear the pain in his voice without aching for him. "You're me own dear Dad and I'm proud of bein' an Irish lass."

After working so hard to lose her Gaelic accent, it had never occurred to Maeve that her more proper speech would be cause for criticism. She would rather be mute than hurt her father.

"Yer frownin', lass."

"Do not ever think I'm not proud to be an O'Malley."

He squeezed her hand. "Mind yer husband knows it as well."

With a wry smile, Maeve pushed herself up. "Sure'n I'm convinced there's not a minute goes by that Charles doesn't remember who he is married to."

After serving Mick soup and soda bread fresh from the oven, Maeve watched with satisfaction as he attacked his meal like a starving man. After filling his bowl a second time, she reached for her coat.

"Where are ye goin'?" Mick barked.

"Oh, Dad, I must be on my way. There's much to do."

The old man's eyes almost disappeared beneath the weight of his dark scowl. "Like what?"

"For one, I haven't finished my knitting for the Essex Orphanage."

Located on Essex Street, the orphanage housed over fifty immigrant children from several European countries. Some had lost their parents on the crossing to America; others had been abandoned by mothers and fathers who could not afford to feed and clothe them. Every year, all year, Maeve knitted mittens and caps for the children at Essex. Not only was she behind this year, but Elsie Dunn, who ran the shelter, must think she'd fallen off the face of the earth. Used to helping at the orphanage at least twice a week on her way home from work, Maeve hadn't visited in more than ten days.

"Ye don't have to knit for 'em now. Charles Rycroft is a rich stiff. He can buy mittens for the whole of New England. Let yer husband take care of the matter."

"It wouldn't be the same, Dad. If it comes from me hands, it comes from me heart. It's about more than just mittens. Besides, there are Christmas cakes to bake and berries to string for the tree."

Year after year Maeve stretched her imagination to brighten up the cramped, barren flat and to bestow a sense of cheer. Last Christmas Shea brought home a small, broken pine tree he'd found on his way from the docks. Despite its dry, prickly branches and scraggly appearance, Maeve had been overjoyed with the sad little tree.

She'd always taken great pleasure in the Christmas season and the spirit of good will that prevailed for however short a period of time. Maeve loved the Yuletide music, the carols, the festive decorations, and colorful ornaments. The shades of the holiday, warm holly and gold, bright scarlet and silver-capped snow. The mistletoe. Santa Claus. Though the jolly fellow had never yet paid her a personal visit, she knew that someday he would.

Nothing gave Maeve more happiness than giving gifts she'd made either in the kitchen or with her knitting needles. Invigorated by the icy bite in the air and dazzled by the beauty of ice needles dangling from the eaves, Maeve even enjoyed the cold and snow during the holiday. Nothing had ever managed to dampen her spirits for long during the month of December.

Mick O'Malley screwed up his face. "Christmas will be different this year," he said, as if he was in mourning.

"It shall be better."

"I remember ye put one candle atop our tree last year. 'Twas all the poor dead fir could hold. And ye sang all day about figgy pudding."

" 'Twas wonderful!" Maeve agreed enthusiastically. "But this year you and Shea shall have a tree ablaze with candles and a feast to celebrate."

She would make certain of it.

"We'll see," he said, sounding doubtful.

"Dad, what do ye suppose you give a man like Charles for Christmas?" Maeve asked, seeking to turn her father's thoughts in a different direction. "A man who has everything."

"And how would I be knowin'?" he asked peevishly. "Yer askin' a man who never had anything."

Maeve slanted her father a teasing smile. "What are ye talkin' about? Ye have always had the best. Ye have Shea and me."

After a moment Mick's surly frown collapsed into a grin. "Aye. That I have."

"I know what I would like to give Charles for Christmas," she said, warming to the idea as she shrugged on her new winter coat.

"You wouldn't be knittin' Rycroft mittens, would ye?"

"No, Dad."

"Ye still know how to cook a good soup," he said, turning back to his meal. He slurped as if to emphasize the fact.

"I've not been gone but a few days. Why would I be forgettin' how to cook?"

"Seems longer."

Maeve's heart blossomed tightly against her chest. Though he never said the words, Maeve knew her Dad loved her. His way of saying he missed her was indeed roundabout. Still, she knew since her mother died, no one had ever loved her more.

"I know, Dad. It seems longer for me, too."

Batting back tears, she looked up at the only picture on the wall, a print of Currier and Ives that Pansy had given her the year before.

"That's it," she breathed.

"What?" Soup dripped from her father's spoon as he held it midway to his mouth.

"When Charles was robbed and beaten, the thieves took a sketch he holds dear. A sketch of St. Nick."

"St. Nick? Santa Claus?"

"Aye. 'Twas a sketch he'd just purchased."

"Sure'n you can tell me what a full-grown man wants with a drawing of St. Nick?"

"I don't know. But I would like to find it for him. What a grand gift that would be!" And surely, if Maeve recovered Charles's stolen treasure, he would understand how much she cared for him, how her heart beat only for him. In time he might even come to love her.

"And how are ye thinkin' to track down hooligans?" her father demanded.

"I'm not certain. But at the time, I remember Shea sayin' Charles appeared to have been beaten by a professional. It's a boxer I'd be lookin' for."

"An' what would a boxer want with a picture of St. Nick?"

Maeve shook her head. "I don't know."

"Boxers don't believe in Santa Claus. That much I'll be knowin'."

But Maeve had a thought. "Maybe the thief took the sketch just because it was there. Maybe he robbed Charles out of desperation. If a man is out of work and has a family to feed, he often resorts to criminal ways. Perhaps this thief took the sketch only because he thought it a pretty gift to give to his woman or a child."

"Ye don't know any of that. Where do ye come by yer imagination, Maeve? From the Red Man?"

Legend had it that the Red Man was a creative fairy fond of playing practical jokes.

"It's possible," Maeve grinned.

"Get any idea of findin' the hooligan who done it out of yer head. Yer just a lass. I don't want me cailin to get hurt over some St. Nick foolishness."

Once an idea took hold, Maeve didn't give up on it easily. "Don't worry, Dad. I'll be careful."

"Ye'd best be thinkin' of somethin' else to give yer upper-crust husband."

But she refused to consider anything else until she'd made every effort to find the only thing Charles wanted. Shea would help her. He knew and had fought most of the boxers in the area. While Maeve understood Shea might have been wrong and the man who attacked Charles wasn't a boxer, she had to start somewhere. There wasn't much time.

Dinner promised to be a trial, but one Charles could hardly avoid. His mother insisted this might be the only evening to become acquainted with Maeve. The holiday social season—which is what she and Stella had come to Boston to enjoy—was about to launch into full swing.

Charles experienced an especially deep sense of foreboding when Beatrice lamented the fact that she'd been unable to greet Maeve properly. The girl *had* saved her son's life. If dinner could not be managed, his mother suggested she might enjoy a woman-to-woman talk with Maeve over tea.

Chills ran down his spine just thinking about Maeve and Beatrice alone, an innocent lamb devoured by a lioness. He had not the heart to embroil Maeve in such a situation.

Resolute, Charles approached Maeve's rooms, prepared to coax her to dinner. At least he would be at the table to protect her and his presence might subdue his mother.

When Maeve didn't answer his knock, Charles hesitated only a moment before entering the apartment. He was her husband, after all. He found her in the sitting room. A pile of pale blue yarn and knitting needles heaped upon the upholstered rococo side chair nearest the secretary had been abandoned.

Maeve stood before the mirror with a book precariously balanced upon her head. Her small, lushly curved body listed at a rather ungraceful angle. Holding another book in her hand, she attempted to read from its open page without lowering her head. Apparently frustrated by this effort, she looked up and addressed the mirror.

"How do you do, Mr. Smith? I am sooooo pleased to make your acquaintance."

Charles could not help but grin. Maeve's exaggerated demeanor might have offended his mother if she'd witnessed this scene, but he found it amusing.

"Is there a foul fragrance in the air, Mr. Smith?" she asked the mirror. "Is that why you hold your nose so high?"

Swallowing a chuckle, Charles knew he should make his presence known, but he rather enjoyed eavesdropping. Obviously, Maeve had learned a thing or two about Boston society while employed by the Deakinses. Just as obviously, she didn't like what she'd learned.

Charles leaned back on the door frame, folded his arms, and studied his wife. The stubborn tilt of Maeve's chin reflected a strong will and saucy attitude . . . traits he found challenging and rather captivating. It might be wit, or intelligence—or the devil—behind the sparkle in her remarkable eyes. A man could lose himself in those deep blue depths before realizing the danger. When Charles looked into Maeve's eyes, he saw the enticing shade of a siren sea.

And he could not deny that her softly rounded figure, displayed so neatly in a dark blue day gown, would turn any man's head, shanty Irish or Beacon Hill bred. Silky tendrils of shining onyx hair had escaped from her thick topknot to fall in charming disarray, framing her fair, heart-shaped face. The face of an angel.

An untoward impulse to loosen the pins of Maeve's topknot took hold of Charles. At the moment he would give his publishing empire just to run his fingers through the temptress's glossy mane. Temptress?

Dear God, she was his wife!

But he never bowed to impulse.

Charles was entitled to do much more than run his fingers through Maeve's hair, but he refused to take advantage of a woman he would soon part from. No matter how much she made him ache. A Rycroft always did the right thing.

"Oh, sir, no." Maeve declared to the mirror. "I could not possibly flee to the garden with you! Whatever would my husband say? Yes, I know 'tis done. Affairs are common, but not by a woman who fancies her husband. Not I. Not me."

Biting her lip, Maeve fell silent, apparently deep in thought. "I? Me?"

The knowledge that she "fancied" him warmed Charles, caused an unexpected spurt in the beat of his pulse. Smiling, he watched in silent fascination as his Irish wife's softly arched brows bunched in an irritated frown.

"Oh! What is it?" she cried in frustration. "Should I say me or I?"

Before he could step forward and offer help, Maeve heaved the book at the wall.

Startled but amused, Charles came close to choking and revealing his presence. Maeve's determination to overcome her lack of education in certain areas was admirable. Although she might struggle with the language, he'd quickly come to realize his wife possessed a quick, intelligent mind. If she could just control her temper, Charles would feel better about her future.

A part of him hoped she would never lose the melodic lilt to her speech. The sound of her voice was like a song to his ears.

He cleared his throat. "Me. It's me."

Maeve spun around.

"Did I frighten you?"

Her head shot up. "No."

"I didn't mean to frighten you."

With a toss of her head, Maeve stepped away from the mirror. A rosy red blush heightened the color of her cheeks. "Sure'n I've never been frightened by a man."

"Why am I not surprised?"

"I did not hear ye . . . you come in."

"I knocked, but you were busy."

"Practicing my manners."

"Your manners are fine," Charles assured her. "You acquitted yourself perfectly last evening."

"I did not speak a word."

"You didn't have to say a thing. Your beauty spoke for you."

Dear God, what was he saying?

Maeve's luscious cherry-red lips parted in a hesitant smile. "Sure'n you've kissed the Blarney stone."

"No," he said softly. He'd spoken the truth.

His wife's beauty radiated from the inside, from her heart or soul—he wasn't sure which—and was captured in her glorious smile. Her real beauty, a pure beauty, shone from within. "Charles?"

Damn. He'd slipped into some sort of odd trance.

Charles made a great business of clearing his throat. "My cousin informed me today that you are now the woman of mystery in town."

Her eyes grew wide. "What?"

"By saying so little last night, you aroused the curiosity of our guests. They assume you to be a woman of great mystery."

"I did not mean to arouse curiosity. It was Stella's party so I—"

"You outshone the guest of honor indisputably," he interrupted, feeling an astonishing satisfaction.

"Oh, no!"

"I am afraid so."

"Saints above."

"You might want the saints below—by your side this evening."

"Why?"

"We have been invited to dine with my mother and Stella. My mother regrets she has been unable to spend time with you up until now."

" 'Tis only been two days. She need not worry over me."

"Dinner is at seven o'clock. Meet me in my study and we shall go into the dining room together."

Heaving a wistful sigh, Maeve again attempted to beg off. "But tonight I feel so weary and thought to have me . . . my meal right here in the sitting room."

Charles refused to let her off the hook. He was not going to dinner without Maeve. "And what did you do today to bring on such exhaustion?"

"I paid a visit to my father and cooked his favorite potato soup. Then I went off to find Shea but never did. When I returned I worked on my knitting and then me . . . my manners."

Before preying on her sympathies, he remained silent for a moment as if he might actually be considering her excuses. "In my humble opinion, you should have enough strength to join us for dinner, Maeve. Would you leave me alone to such a fate? Would you have me dining with Mother and Stella by myself?''

Wary eyes fixed on his. ''You really want me—''

''Yes,'' Charles replied quickly. ''Please. Do this for me.''

Knowing the dinner would not go well, he felt like a traitor of sorts. But the only way for Maeve to learn how far apart their worlds were was to make her a part of his at every opportunity. A world that served lobster bisque instead of potato soup.

''I suppose, for you, I shall manage to muddle through,'' she acquiesced quietly. Her sweet berry lips parted in a faint, uncertain smile.

Struck by the melancholy of her smile, Charles knew he could not put Maeve through what promised to be a punishing ordeal without rewarding her in some way. As much as he, the girl was an innocent victim of circumstance.

Her luminous eyes reflected absolute trust as they met his.

In that silent moment an unseen, powerful hand reached inside and gripped Charles's heart, melting his defenses like a red-hot seal on wax.

Maeve touched him as he'd never been touched before. She caused him to say things he'd never said before. And he seemed unable to stop himself from saying more. ''After dinner I shall take you for a sleigh ride if you like.''

Maeve's glowing smile warmed Charles to the marrow. ''Oh, Charles, I should like a sleigh ride very much.''

The depth of her delight set his heart to beating in a new, swift-thumping rhythm. An alarming excitement took hold of him, infusing Charles with a great burst of energy. All at once, he felt like a small boy on his way to a parade.

''Then let us consider dinner a duty that we will dispense with as soon as possible,'' he suggested to Maeve with all the equanimity he could muster. "A sleigh ride will follow as our just reward."

Her light, melodic laughter filled his senses with the same dizzying effect of having drunk too much French champagne. The music of Maeve's laughter struck Charles's heart anew and drew an unabashed grin from him. Although he hadn't planned a sleigh ride for tonight, he'd accidentally hit on a good idea for himself as well as his temporary wife. A change of routine with a quiet, intimate ride might prove just the thing.

Normally, Charles relaxed alone in his study following a particularly trying day as this had been. During the first appointment of the morning he hired Herbert Lynch to recover the stolen sketch of St. Nick. The private investigator could have been more encouraging concerning the chances of finding the lost art. But he wasn't, mumbling that too much time had elapsed and the trail was cold.

In a later meeting with Martin, Charles argued again with his cousin about the future course of Rycroft Publishing. Martin could never win—and could never stop feeling sorry for himself.

When Charles became head of the company, he resolved to make Rycroft even more successful than when his father had been at the helm. Conrad had never expressed faith in his abilities, preferring to disparage Charles at every opportunity. Although his father had been dead for three years, Charles still felt driven by the need to prove he could operate a successful business enterprise. He meant to take the publishing business to heights Conrad Rycroft never dreamed of.

Martin could not be expected to understand.

Finally, toward the end of the day, Charles worked out his increasing restlessness by fencing with Spencer Wellington.

When tension stretched him to his limit, Charles could usually find relief by fencing with his friend. Today, however, the match had not eased the edginess coiled in the pit of his stomach like a snake ready to strike. He wondered at that.

"Will you read your book on our sleigh ride?" Maeve asked, stirring Charles from his uncomfortable reverie.

He looked down in surprise. He'd entirely forgotten the book he'd brought home for her. "It's for you. A novel called *Around the World in Eighty Days,* by Jules Verne. I thought perhaps you might not have read it yet as it was just published last year."

Maeve smiled up at him, a sweet, reverent smile that made him feel like the hero in a dime novel. "I shall read it as soon as I finish the manuscript you brought last evening. Thank you, Charles."

She spoke slowly, once again lapsing into a practice of her speech. A bittersweet sadness settled over Charles. He felt a loss of something intangible. It did not seem right for Maeve to curb her natural exuberance. At the same time, he understood her desire to achieve the restraint and manners of his class. The fiery little bit of a woman did not wish to stand out in his circle of friends. She wanted to be like everyone else.

In his heart, Charles knew she would never be like everyone else.

Maeve displayed unquestionable courage, working diligently to fit into a world which in reality she could never become a part of. Somehow he must find a way to ease the shame of their inevitable divorce for her.

"I shall keep you well supplied with books," he promised before turning to leave.

"You have been sent to me by my faerie princess."

Dear God, she was back to the faeries.

"I'll see you in an hour for dinner."

"Dinner." Maeve repeated the word as if it were a death sentence and she were headed toward the gallows.

As he left her chamber, she began to hum. He recognized the tune. Now, if he could just remember what it was.

* * *

One lamp burned in the small, dark room where he paced impatiently. A man distraught. No matter what he attempted something always went awry. It was the story of his life. The best of his plans seemed destined to sink like leaky boats. Including his current undertaking. It was going down fast. Only desperate action would save his skin. Samson he was not.

The original plan did not call for Charles Rycroft to be killed. He'd depended on the elements to finish Rycroft, but then Charles was found and rescued before the cold could claim him. Another case of bad luck.

At last the rear door opened and his brawny accomplice lumbered through. Shoulders hunched and jaw set, the scowling amazon grunted an indiscernible greeting.

Bill "Spit" O'Brien.

The jagged scar above Bill's right eye gave him an ominous appearance, even in the full light of day. By the light of one flickering lamp, he looked truly terrifying.

"Do you know what Rycroft has done now?"

Bill shook his head.

"He's hired a private investigator. The man was here today asking questions."

Bill just stared.

"Why is this happening to me?"

Bill shook his head.

"In just a few weeks I will be able to leave the country with no questions asked. In the meantime something must be done about Rycroft. I refuse to be constantly looking over my shoulder. It's not expected for a man in my position."

Unfazed by his scolding, Bill "Spit" O'Brien merely shrugged.

"I paid you to do a job and I expect you to finish it. I don't want to see you again until it's done."

The ferocious-looking giant simply nodded.

"Do you understand?" he barked, irked beyond endurance. If he'd had the funds to hire a true professional at the beginning, he wouldn't now have to deal with this slow excuse for a man. He just had no luck at all.

Bill nodded again.

Samson could not fully trust a man of so few words.

"Send me a message when you've completed your task. We can't risk meeting here with a private investigator lurking about. I'll meet you at the footbridge in the public gardens."

Again, Bill nodded. His dull blue eyes seemed to have no life nor comprehension behind them.

He feared the worst. A repeat of past calamities. He asked once again, "Do I make myself clear, Bill?"

Chapter Eight

Maeve entered the dining room on Charles's arm. She held her head high even as her knees threatened to buckle out from under her. Hopefully, neither Beatrice Rycroft nor Stella Hampton could detect the nervous trembling of her lower lip. The moment they'd crossed the threshold, Maeve felt as if she were on trial. Rules of etiquette swirled in her brain.

Always use your napkin before and after drinking. Never cut your bread with a knife, break it by hand. Use your napkin before and after drinking. Never make a display of your napkin.

A display of your napkin. Whatever did that mean?

The seating arrangements had Charles at the head of the table, his mother and Stella to his right, and Maeve to his left. Beatrice Rycroft and the pale widow sans dog were already seated.

Swathed in dusty rose satin and diamonds, Beatrice appeared every inch the grand dame. Despite the deepening lines fanning her eyes and framing her mouth, traces of the beauty she'd once been were evident. Charles's mother possessed magnificent high cheekbones and perfect bowed lips, rouged to an apple-red.

Unlike Maeve, she moved in fluid, elegant grace and spoke in soft, modulated tones.

With barely a flicker of an eyelash, she appraised a quaking Maeve from the top of her head to the hem of her dress. When Beatrice completed her perusal, neither approval nor disapproval registered in her bland expression.

Although Maeve had dressed with care and presented herself with nary a hair out of place, she knew her mother-in-law must disapprove of her, beyond what the eye could see. With her stomach churning like a storm-tossed sea, Maeve did not hope to swallow a bite of the meal. Instead, she meant to win a small piece of her mother-in-law's regard.

"Good evening, Maeve," Beatrice greeted her with a cool nod before bestowing a brilliant smile on her son. "Charles dear, you look exhausted."

"Not quite, Mother." He held Maeve's chair before seating himself.

"I don't see why you must work. Martin can handle the firm."

"I work because I enjoy it."

"And you do it so well," Stella put in. "Even with all the New York publishing houses, Rycroft is as well known in the city as any that are headquartered there."

"You may overstate the case."

"Oh, no," Stella protested. "But have you ever thought of moving the company to New York City?"

"Never. My father founded Rycroft in Boston not long after Little, Brown and Company."

"But publishing flourishes in New York City," Stella insisted, smiling all the while. When she spoke to Charles, her dark cocoa eyes never left his.

"Rycroft flourishes here."

Unlike the amiable man who had come to her rooms, Charles appeared aloof and conversed in short, curt sentences. Maeve thought there must be something she could say to soothe the conversation. She just could not think what.

Stella had again chosen a dress with a neckline that amply displayed her cleavage. The azure blue silk pongee with wide lace trim and flounces heightened her delicate appearance. But Maeve feared that if the merry widow sneezed, she would shatter like glass and her mighty bosom would burst from her gown. Maeve had taken to thinking of Stella as the merry widow.

Having no luck with Charles, Stella turned to Maeve. "You must convince Charles to move, Maeve. In my experience a wife exercises astonishing influence over her husband."

Maeve demurred softly. "Charles is a most intelligent man. I respect his business decisions."

From the corner of her eye, she caught Charles's grin. She loved the great, warm grin that transformed his features from aloof to affable. She wished he'd smile more often. As Charlie, he had.

"Where is your dog this evening?" he asked Stella.

"She isn't just a dog, Charles. Babe's a purebred Pomeranian." The pale woman tilted her head and sighed. "Unfortunately, she's feeling poorly. Perhaps due to the change in the climate."

Maeve wondered if it was too much to hope that the repulsive wee dog's illness might be more serious.

In her rather high-pitched tones, Beatrice demanded Maeve's attention to completely alter the course of the conversation. "Tell me, dear, do you believe in the afterlife?"

Taken aback, Maeve could only stare.

"The spirit world," Beatrice added.

"My mother is attempting to communicate with my father," Charles explained. "Although he died several years ago."

Beatrice's gaze moved slowly around the room as if her deceased husband might be hovering. "Be careful what you say, Charles."

"Mother, you didn't communicate with Father while he was alive. Therefore, it's difficult for me to understand why you wish to do so now."

"I might have said some things in the heat of anger . . . not knowing he was about to pass . . . that perhaps I should not have said."

"You're feeling guilty, are you? Looking for forgiveness?"

"Heavens, no. You may not believe as I do, but you need not be rude. Whatever will Maeve think?"

Maeve thought her mother-in-law daft. The very idea that Beatrice believed in ghosts amazed her. Until another thought occurred: perhaps the matriarch played some sort of game, subtly ridiculing Maeve's lack of worldly knowledge.

"And what *do* you think, Maeve?" A silver light danced in Charles's eyes as they locked on hers.

"I think . . . I think we should keep an open mind."

"There, you see!" Beatrice cried in triumph.

Charles rolled his eyes.

"You shall attend our seance," the older woman declared. "When the moon and stars are properly aligned, Helen Foster, who is a world-renowned medium, has agreed to communicate with Conrad right here in his home."

Maeve forced a smile. A seance. "Thank you. How . . . how kind of you."

Without heed to the rules of etiquette—not one of which she could remember at the moment—she lifted the gold-trimmed goblet at her place and sipped the fruity wine.

Until she put the goblet down, she didn't notice that everyone was watching her. Her insides withered. She couldn't swallow.

"Maeve is our heroine," Charles remarked dryly. "First she saved my life, and now she's saved my mother's."

"You exaggerate the matter," Beatrice objected.

"Forgive my curiosity, but did you marry Maeve only because she saved your life?" Stella asked with a sweetness that belied the cruelty of the question.

This could not be in Beadle's etiquette book! How dare Stella Hampton talk about Maeve as if she were not present? Fixing an angry gaze on the wicked woman, Maeve struggled to control her temper. One horrid hot spot burned in her belly. Hoping the wine would put out the fire, she took another long swallow.

"Of course not," Charles snapped, slicing his beef with undue vigor.

"Then just what was it, dear?" his mother asked.

Charles raised his head and met Maeve's gaze. If she was not mistaken, a dash of humor glinted in his soft gray eyes. "It was an arranged marriage . . . so to speak."

"I intend to make your son a good wife in all ways, Mrs. Rycroft."

"Yes . . . well, you certainly are attractive, dear."

"Thank you. And you . . . you are . . . beautiful."

Beatrice gave a trill of pleasure. "Well, perhaps twenty years ago."

"Maeve, is your family among those I shall meet while I am in Boston?" Stella inquired, quickly dashing the moment of good will between Maeve and her mother-in-law.

"I shall be glad to introduce you to—"

Charles interrupted hurriedly. "Maeve's father and brother came by the other night. Did we neglect to introduce you?"

"Your mother was near collapse. I was needed at her side," Stella explained softly before turning on Maeve once again. "Your family name . . . is it one I would know?"

"Have you ever met an O'Malley?"

"No. I don't believe so. O'Malley. It's an Irish name, is it not?"

"Aye. And you would remember if you had met an O'Malley before I . . . me. Before." A silent scream tore through Maeve. She couldn't allow this woman to fluster her! She took another hurried sip of the burgundy wine.

Because of her father's disturbing fondness for the stuff, Maeve never touched alcohol. She'd never tasted wine before tonight but discovered she liked the flavor. The more she sipped, the more she enjoyed it. Without the wine, she might have fled from the table.

In a brazen attempt to claim Charles's attention, Maeve noticed the cool New York guest played with the beads that fell over her cleavage. Her long, eloquent fingers picked up the beads, twined them, twirled them, and made circles around them.

But she wasn't finished with Maeve yet. "How do you enjoy passing time? Do you play the piano, or do needlepoint, perhaps?"

Maeve shook her head.

"I am seeking to find common ground," Stella explained to Charles. She cast him a smile that appeared less than genuine to Maeve, but one a man might find beguiling. "I should like to discover that your wife and I share some interests, or friends, owing we are near the same age."

"Maeve is only nineteen years old."

For an instant, in a tightening of her lips and a sharp flash in her eyes, Stella revealed her displeasure. "I am not so much older, sir."

"Indeed, Stella is at the age where the impulsiveness of youth has passed," Beatrice offered in her friend's behalf. "Which is to be admired."

"What charity do you attend, Maeve?" Stella, obviously anxious to depart from the conversation on age, abruptly resumed her questioning.

Maeve did not understand the question, but knew it was another designed to belittle her. Hoping it would help, she took another long sip of wine. It didn't.

She burned to give Stella a piece of her mind, a lash of her Irish tongue that would not soon be forgotten. In the face of the pale beauty's lack of manners, Maeve's blood ran hot. If she held her temper another moment, she surely would explode.

"Maeve has been much too busy to engage in charity work," Charles replied for her.

"Except for the orphanage."

Charles, Beatrice, and Stella stared at her.

"I knit garments for the children at the Essex Orphanage. Sometimes I go by to play with them. It's a hard life they have."

Charles gave her a lopsided smile that made Maeve's heart skip and thump. His light charcoal eyes shone with what appeared to be delight, or pride ... or perhaps both. For an infinitesimal moment, she could not catch her breath. For one frozen moment in time no one else existed at the table for Maeve but Charles. Locked in his gaze, she was alone with him.

"You don't knit in public do you, dear?"

The moment passed.

"No, Mrs. Rycroft. I should never knit in public."

Charles chuckled aloud.

His mother's eyes narrowed on him. "Did I miss something humorous?"

"Not at all. Maeve is the model of propriety, Mother. You need not worry about what she shall do in public."

Maeve almost giggled aloud. Instead she covered her amusement by sipping more wine. Her glass seemed always full. She supposed one of the servants filled it when she was not looking.

Dinner was just slightly less sumptuous than the feast offered at Stella's party the night before. Maeve wondered how four people could consume the courses of partridge pie with truffles, boiled codfish with oyster sauce, tenderloin of beef, boiled potatoes, and stewed tomatoes. She knew many families, including the children at the orphanage, who had never seen this much food on one table. She felt guilty not eating. Even though the wine she'd sipped through dinner had relaxed her a bit, Maeve almost applauded when dessert was served. Dinner was coming to an end.

Feeling somewhat dizzy, Maeve declined servings of chocolate cake, fruit, and hot apple pudding. From the start of this extraordinarily long dinner, in deference to an unsettled stomach, she'd simply been pushing the food around on her plate.

"Do you have a problem with your weight?" Stella asked *sotto voce*. With a coy, sidelong glance at Charles, she added, "Forgive us just a moment of women talk."

Maeve would rather have died on the spot than admit she would like to be thinner. But then, looking as bony as Beatrice Rycroft, or as pale and slender as Stella, did not appeal to her either.

"Weight problem? Not at all. My husband likes me just the way I am . . . don't you, my love?"

Charles appeared momentarily stunned. But he recovered nicely, although his lip twitched slightly. "I should weep if you ever change."

Stella's lips were so tight they'd turned white.

Maeve swallowed hard. What had made her make such a brazen statement? It must have been the wicked fairy again—or the wine.

"Tea, perhaps?" Beatrice asked.

"No, thank you." Maeve daintily wiped her lips with the soft linen napkin. *Always use your napkin before and immediately after drinking.* "We must be off now. Charles and I are going for a sleigh ride."

"How wonderful!" Stella declared, making a remarkable rally. "It's a perfect night. I should love to go for a sleigh ride, too!"

"You don't mind taking our guest along with you, do you, Charles dear?"

Charles sat wedged between Maeve and Stella in the open sleigh like a stiff-spined, scholarly text between two soft leather-bound first editions. Damned uncomfortable. The two women could not see each other without bending forward to peer around his body—which was the better part of the arrangement.

A light snow blanketed the moonlit night. The bite of the winter breeze and the wet sting of snowflakes as they nipped at his skin were not to blame for Charles's discomfort. Although a good reason eluded him, Charles resented Stella's intrusion.

The snow warden would be out soon, but for now the sleigh bells jangled merrily as the high-stepping Andalusian carriage horses pulled the Rycroft sleigh smoothly down the snowpacked street. Pine garlands and red bows decorated the gaslight poles on Beacon Hill. As he watched the snow fall gently under the golden light, Charles regretted the loss of a ride alone with Maeve.

She'd behaved in a far more civilized manner during dinner than either his mother or Stella.

To his right, Maeve slouched, silently fuming. Every so often she would let loose a petulant sigh. Each time, due to the cold, a small cloud issued from her mouth reminding Charles of a tiny dragon breathing fire and smoke. He had little doubt Stella's presence displeased her. It displeased him. But Charles had to credit Maeve for keeping her anger at bay as the sleigh slid through the snowy streets.

On his left, Stella's teeth chattered. Cold as a cod, his mother's friend.

This isn't what Charles had planned.

After discovering Maeve's love of books, he was interested in knowing more about what types of books she read and what she enjoyed. He hoped he hadn't made a mistake with the Jules Verne book. His small companion's strange beliefs tickled Charles's curiosity as well. Why did a young woman of seeming intelligence believe in faeries? And Charles wanted to know how Maeve felt when forced to marry him, a complete stranger?

There were many things about this beguiling creature

who was his wife that he did not know and that somehow had become important for him to know.

The sweet scent of violets drifted up from Maeve. Charles breathed deeply of her. She promised spring in the midst of winter. To his relief, her heated sighs lessened as she took an interest in the passing scenery.

Another fragrance assaulted him—the thick, spicy perfume of Stella's, which threatened to clog Charles's throat. She looked up at him, her dark brown eyes all dewy and dreamy. What had his mother been telling her guest about him?

Actually, he didn't want to know.

"It's cold, isn't it?" she asked.

"Aye!" Maeve chuckled. " 'Tis always cold on a December night."

Ignoring Maeve for the moment, Charles turned to Stella. "Would you like to return?" he asked hopefully.

"Oh, no. But how is a girl to stay warm?" Finding her own answer, Stella snuggled closer to him.

"Let's just pull the blanket up higher," Charles suggested, sliding more of the wool sleigh blanket Stella's way and shifting toward Maeve.

Maeve wiggled away from him.

Damn.

He did not understand the little Irish beauty at all. She did not feel his glare. Her gaze never wavered from the passing buildings. In profile, her nose turned up at the tip in a quite enchanting way. Charles felt an involuntary, almost overwhelming urge to kiss the dainty tip of Maeve's nose, reddening quickly from the cold.

But he practiced self-restraint. Charles prided himself on his ability to be dispassionate when other men grew angry or anxious or frightened.

At least Maeve looked warm in the new coat Mrs. Potts had fashioned for her. The dark meadow green color complemented her fair complexion. Both the cape of the coat and hem were trimmed in gleaming sable. Her hands were warmed within a thick sable muff instead of scratchy half-mittens. Charles especially liked her saucy green hat. Trimmed with the same rich sable, the small wool hat covered her ears and tied under her chin at a rakish angle. The way she looked tonight, Maeve could pass as a young woman born and bred on the Hill.

Stella, in her navy blue, only managed to look like death in an open sleigh.

"Do give us a tour, Charles," the widow pleaded. "Where are we now? Are those government buildings?"

"That's the state house to the right."

"I do so favor Gothic architecture. Don't you, Maeve?"

Maeve giggled. "No."

Charles experienced a sinking feeling in his gut.

"What do you like then?" Stella pressed.

"I like . . . no, I love the wide blue sky above my head. I want to feel the green, green shamrocks beneath my feet. I loathe walls!" she cried passionately. "I love the sea and the mountains and . . ." Maeve's voice trailed off and she simply stared into space.

The sleigh bells jangled crisply in the sudden silence. *Dear God, she was tipsy!*

She'd gone from seething to silence to snickering in less than thirty minutes. Clearly, Maeve had sipped too much wine at dinner. The idea of an inebriated Irish woman beside him gave Charles an anxious pang in his midsection and a keen desire to end this sleigh ride.

"May we ride to the Common, Charles?" Stella asked as if nothing uncommon had passed. The New York socialite obviously did not concern herself with anything Maeve did or said. There could be no doubt, the two women did not circulate on the same plane.

Charles had little choice but to direct Stuart to drive to the Common.

"Once around, Stuart." *Quickly.*

Boston Common offered fifty acres of open space and

during the winter became a popular spot for sleigh rides, ice skating, and sledding.

Charles looked upon the passing sleighs with a certain asperity. Courting couples who had escaped from prying eyes were wrapped in each other's arms. Their laughter floated with the snowflakes on the frigid evening air. He felt an unaccustomed envy spiraling through him, leaving a bitter taste in his mouth, a taste similar to kerosene.

"Oh, this is wonderful!" Stella exclaimed. "Nature in all of her beauty! Do you like nature, Maeve?"

Charles looked to Maeve. Busy catching snowflakes on her tongue, she hadn't heard Stella.

His heart gave a strange lurch and he smiled down at her. Maeve amused him. She was a woman-child, a complex combination of intelligence and superstition, of unfailing kindness and uncomely frankness. Charles came alive when he was with her.

If possible, Maeve was even more beautiful with cheeks glowing from the cold. Her blue eyes twinkled and her delicious cherry lips were parted to catch the falling snowflakes on the tip of her tongue. His gaze fastened on her tongue, pink and sweet.

A powerful need to gather Maeve into his arms assailed Charles. All he could think of, all he wanted, was to cover her lips with his and feel her cold tongue grow warm in his mouth. His need sparked an alarming heat in his loins.

If Stella weren't here . . .

Dear God! If only Stella weren't here.

"Look at the skaters, Charles!" the oblivious widow exclaimed. "We must go ice skating. Do you like to skate, Maeve?"

She shook her head in an exaggerated motion. "No."

"What a shame." Stella actually tsked like an old woman.

"Going around in circles holds no interest for me," Maeve remarked.

"Then you wouldn't mind terribly if I asked Charles to take me skating?"

"Nooooo." Her head continued to wag slowly back and forth.

"Don't you think you should give skating a try, Maeve?" Charles asked gently. "You might like it."

"Sure'n if the good Lord meant for us to skate, we would have been born with wee blades instead of toes."

Stella arched a scornful brow. "Do you even own skates?"

"No."

"I will purchase skates for you tomorrow," Charles said to Maeve.

"An' how do ye plan to keep me upright?"

"Surely you're not afraid," Stella taunted with a hard-edged smile.

"Aye and I'm not afraid! It's just that I'd rather be dancing a jig by a warm fire than circling a frozen pond on cold feet."

Charles laughed aloud.

Stella shot him a tight little smile. "Good. Then it's settled. We'll plan a skating party."

Apparently, the only way he could be alone with Maeve lay in kidnaping her. But not tonight. On the way home from the Common she fell asleep or, more likely, passed out.

Charles carried Maeve from the carriage into the house.

In the foyer, Stella stopped him with a hand pressed to his back. "Would you join me for a glass of mulled wine after you've deposited your sleeping bride?"

"I'm afraid not. I must tuck the . . . little woman into bed."

What little color remained in Stella's face, drained.

Although Charles felt shameless for using Maeve as a shield to thwart the widow's advances, he also felt grateful at the moment to be married.

Slightly astonished by how little she weighed, how

light she felt in his arms, Charles carried Maeve to her bed, lowering her carefully.

With painstaking patience and no small amount of imagination, he managed to remove Maeve's coat, shoes, and hat. He'd never undressed a sleeping woman before; she felt like a limp rag doll who moaned occasionally.

Dolly bustled in just as Charles was removing the pins from Maeve's hair, a task he'd looked forward to completing.

After the housekeeper had recovered from her initial shock, Dolly had taken a shine to Maeve. "I'll take care of the miss now, sir. Sorry to keep you waiting."

But Charles wasn't sorry. He'd enjoyed the intimate moments with Maeve. "Call me when you've finished. I'll wait in the sitting room."

He heard Maeve groan in her sleeping state several times but mostly silence prevailed until Dolly reported she'd finished. Dismissing his housekeeper, Charles returned to Maeve's bedchamber.

Her dark hair fanned the pillow like waves of a shining ebony sea. She possessed an enchanting, ethereal beauty. For a long moment Charles could only stare, breathing in her loveliness. Dressed in a white silk shift trimmed with yards of lace at collar and cuff, she resembled sleeping royalty.

But it wasn't Maeve.

After a hasty search Charles found her red nightshirt folded neatly in the back of a bottom drawer. Slowly and with great care, he removed the silk and lace shift. Afraid to wake and startle her with an untoward touch, he could only allow himself a lingering gaze. He contemplated Maeve as he would a precious work of art. But even Barnabas in his best hour could not have captured her beauty. From her long, graceful neck to her full breasts and creamy thighs, she was perfection. His blood grew hot.

Dear God, he wanted her.

He studied his wife's small body, a gentle swirl of curves and pastels that made his heart roar like a wild beast. Maeve was a gift of nature, as much as the warm whisper of the wind or the haunting song of a lark.

Summoning his willpower, Charles moved stiffly as he redressed the ravishing woman in his arms. Holding one arm around her back to brace the sleeping beauty, he slipped the red nightshirt over her head.

Her head slumped. She groaned.

Tenderly, he eased Maeve's limp body down and smoothed the flaming red nightshirt down around her. The ache in his loins became a pulsating pain.

Charles pulled the comforter up to Maeve's chin. If she hadn't passed out tonight he might have been tempted to make love to her. The desire to remember how it felt making love to Maeve had become an urgent need, a need he should not act upon.

Charles had no one but himself to blame for Maeve's current condition. He knew she was anxious, and if he'd been paying attention he would have noticed she'd turned to the wine to ease her anxieties. He just hoped she didn't feel too badly in the morning.

He bent to blow out the candle but caught himself. Although she hadn't admitted it, Maeve feared the dark. Why, he wondered? He wanted to know. He left the candle burning for her.

Gazing down at the petite woman who had no right to be his wife, Charles's heart thumped heavily against his chest. His dry throat scraped when he swallowed. Leaning down, he brushed his lips against her forehead.

"Good night, Little Bit," he whispered. And then, in a husky voice, he promised, "I will hold you again."

Chapter Nine

Maeve woke the next day with a dull, throbbing headache and the awful feeling that on the previous evening she might have drunk more wine than recommended by any etiquette book. She fervently hoped she'd said or done nothing to humiliate Charles or herself during their sleigh ride with Stella. But if she had said anything untoward, Maeve hoped at least she'd spoken in soft, dulcet tones. She was full of hope.

As soon as Maeve consumed the hot cocoa and biscuits brought to her rooms by Dolly, she slipped from the house . . . anxious to avoid Beatrice and Stella. While her headache had eased, she wasn't quite up to dealing with either one of the widowed ladies this morning.

Braving the blustery weather, she hurried to the docks again in search of Shea. Her search proved futile and confirmed Maeve's fears that her brother was secretly preparing for another boxing bout. She had made no secret of her distaste for the sport. Risking his life for a few dollars seemed a horrid gamble. In the past, Maeve's pain was greater than Shea's when she tended his bloodied and battered body. Even when he emerged victorious, as he did after the last match of twenty-two rounds, the extent of his bruises unsettled her stomach.

Although it was frowned upon for a woman to be on the piers, it was a grievous breach for a female to cross the portals of the A Street Boxing Hall. Maeve had visited both places often. The men did tease her and carry on, but save for a blush or two she'd never come to harm. However, as Charles Rycroft's wife, Maeve knew she should behave in a manner beyond reproach which did not include paying calls on the docks or in the boxing hall.

But Charles was the very reason she wished to find her brother. She rationalized that her desire to help Charles forced her to places where proper ladies did not venture. If it was a boxer who had struck Charles down, Shea could help her find the man. And once she'd found the man, Maeve felt sure she could then recover the missing sketch of St. Nick.

She could only imagine the surprise on Charles's face when he opened her Christmas gift. He owned everything a man could want. All he lacked was what had been taken from him, the one thing he cherished most of all—the sketch of St. Nick. It was the only gift she was certain would please him. Although she wasn't certain why. The reason was not important. All that mattered to Maeve was Charles's happiness.

A light snow fell as she made her way through the narrow cobblestone streets of Boston, melting as it touched the ground, turning to a murky, slate-colored slush.

Maeve planned to walk through the Common back to Beacon Hill and the Rycroft residence as she had no money to hire a coach or sleigh. 'Twas a silly oversight. Even when working she'd sometimes forgot to keep a few coins in her pocket.

The cold air nipped at her cheeks and nose. The snowflakes melted on her lips and weighed on her eyelashes for a fleeting moment. She seemed to recall catching snowflakes on her tongue riding through the park last night. No. She couldn't have done that. She wouldn't have done such a childish thing, not in front of Stella. Not in front of her intractable husband. But a niggling voice inside her head whispered she had indeed.

When she groaned aloud, the passing gentleman turned her way.

Maeve smiled and hurried along, stopping on the corner of Tremont Street to let several coaches pass by. Before she could cross, a familiar-looking carriage veered from the center of the street, pulling up to where she stood.

"Maeve?"

"Charles?"

Charles opened the door and jumped from his coach. Wearing a long cloak with a full beaver cape, he cut an imposing figure. His shoulders appeared twice as broad and his top hat added a good foot to his height. He smiled as if he hesitated to reveal his pleasure in meeting her, but was unable to contain his delight. Despite the cold, Maeve felt her heart melt like butter on a hot potato.

"What a fortuitous meeting," he said. "We at last have the opportunity to be alone." Clasping her arm, Charles guided Maeve through the doors of the Parker House. "There's an excellent tearoom here," he explained.

While Maeve had passed the magnificent hotel many times and had on two occasions pressed her face against the glass, she'd never been inside. The aroma of fresh-baked bread and pastries filled the air. She inhaled deeply, savoring the delicious yeasty scent and welcoming the return of her sense of smell, temporarily numbed by the frigid outside air.

Trusting Charles to steer her in the proper direction, Maeve took in the lobby with undisguised awe. They were soon seated by a window in the intimate tearoom and warmed by a roaring fire. Charles ordered tea and cakes while Maeve silently admired the dark mahogany paneling and crown molding, the plush upholstered chairs, crystal chandeliers, and gaslight sconces. She wondered if she would ever become accustomed to such luxurious surroundings, if she would ever fit into this wonderful world.

Because humming softly comforted her, she began to hum. She hummed so faintly only a powerful faerie could hear her. And perhaps Charles.

He'd angled his head, regarding her with a puzzled frown. She stopped.

"Why were you walking by yourself on a day like this?" he asked.

"I . . . I was on an errand. And you?"

"I also had an errand. There are ice skates for you in the carriage."

"Skates?"

"Do you not remember our conversation last evening?"

"Oh, yes!" *She did not. Her mind spun frantically for something safe to say.* "Thank you."

Charles frowned. His dark brows met at the bridge of his nose in a suspicious angle. "Why did you not hire a coach or sleigh?"

She refused to confess she'd spent most of what little money she had when Charles whisked her from her dad's flat. And those few dollars were tucked safely forgotten under her mattress in her bedchamber.

"It's a fine day for walking," she bluffed. "A bit brisk but beautiful in the Common."

"Yes. Exceedingly . . . beautiful."

But Charles wasn't looking at the Common across the street. He couldn't see the public space from where he sat. His gaze was locked on hers, and Maeve could not drag her eyes away from his soft, smoky-gray contemplation. She swallowed, hoping to dislodge the lump that had risen in her throat, causing her to take only slight, shallow breaths.

Their waiter broke the impasse, serving a mouth-watering assortment of biscuits, cakes, marzipan candy, and steaming amber tea in delicate china cups.

Once alone again, Charles turned to Maeve. "I did not intend for Stella to ride with us last night."

"She did quite a bit of talking," Maeve ventured, eyeing a cake that would add ten pounds to her hips if she contemplated the sweet much longer—actually eating the chocolate confection was out of the question.

"The woman did not stop!" Charles exclaimed.

"Aye, still, the ride was fun."

"We shall have our ride together. Tonight after dinner, you will slip out the back door and meet me."

A clandestine meeting? With her own husband? Maeve did not know what to think. "I'm afraid not tonight. Your mother has asked me to attend her seance."

With a quirk of his lips, Charles hiked a brow. "Going to meet my father, are you?"

To keep from grinning, Maeve bit down on her lip. "Your mother is . . . is graciously includin' me in her activities."

"Believe me, Maeve, my father will not be in attendance. Which is a good thing. You should probably not like him much if he were."

"Will you be speaking ill of the dead now?"

"Are you shocked?"

"Yes." Even when her father drank too much alcohol, Maeve respected and loved her dear dad with all her heart.

"Don't be. I have good reason for feeling as I do."

A darkening shadow, a faraway look, fell across Charles's face. The muscles in his jaw tightened perceptibly.

"Yes?" Maeve inquired quietly.

"Do you know why I am so eager to recover the sketch of St. Nick?"

She shook her head. Anticipating an answer at last to the question she'd asked many times of late, Maeve's pulse beat a little faster.

"Because the artist only created a total of twelve paintings and sketches in his lifetime," Charles pronounced flatly.

"He must have lived a short life . . . or became an artist at an old age," Maeve speculated.

Charles pushed his plate away but seemed to study the untouched biscuit. "The artist lived a short life. Too short a life."

Without commenting, Maeve poured her husband more tea.

"Through the years I have been able to track down and purchase all of his work except the sketch of St. Nick," Charles told her, his tone terse and laced with bitterness. "I'd almost given up when Edgar Dines, the art dealer I've been working through these past years, discovered the sketch at auction in Philadelphia."

"You must admire this artist very much."

"More than any other."

"And what would his name be?"

"Barnabas. Conrad Barnabas Rycroft."

"Barnabas Rycroft?"

Charles's eyes met Maeve's in a steady, unflinching gaze. "My brother."

Maeve gasped in surprise. "I did not know you had a brother."

"Barnabas is not spoken about. Mother only shakes her head if his name is mentioned."

"Why?"

"He committed the worst sin of all—he disgraced the family." Charles's mouth twisted into a hard, sardonic smile. Drumming his knuckles softly on the table, he continued. "My brother was older than I by twelve years.

I did not have the opportunity to really know him. Yet, I worshiped him. Odd?"

She didn't think it odd at all. She worshiped her older brother. Maeve shook her head vigorously and felt a top curl fall.

"When my father decided it was time for Barnabas to join the firm, he rebelled. He considered himself an artist. He lived to sketch and paint. Instead of understanding, our father considered him simply lazy."

"Saints above," Maeve murmured.

"My father expected my brother to join him in the publishing firm, but Barnabas had other ideas. He disappeared for days . . . to work at his art. He was forbidden to sketch or paint at home."

"The poor man," Maeve whispered. Her heart tightened, touched by Barnabas's plight and Charles's obvious pain.

Charles clenched his jaw and nodded. For the first time, Maeve clearly perceived the deep sadness etched into the planes of his face.

"Running off only made matters worse. My father committed Barnabas to an asylum in New Hampshire where the wealthy hide their deranged—or disobedient—sons and daughters. My brother didn't belong there. He might have been rebellious . . . but he was not insane."

Maeve could not hold back the trail of slow, hot tears that seared her cheeks. "Sure'n I'm sorry."

But Charles did not see her tears. He gazed over her shoulder into space, a dark place where painful memories were locked away. Out of sight. But not out of mind. "Barnabas tried to escape one night and was shot. In the dark, a guard mistook him for a prowler."

"Oh, no!" Maeve cried. A painful spasm, sharp as a knife, slashed through her heart. She reached across the table and squeezed Charles's hand.

She understood. Charles looked anew at the woman sitting across from him. Sweet compassion filled her wide, blue eyes to the brim. He had never told this story to anyone before. It remained his family's secret, buried more deeply through the years. Charles didn't really know why he had shared the secret and his sorrow with Maeve. Perhaps he knew instinctively that she would understand what so many in his family, and in their social sphere, seemed unable to comprehend. His brother existed for his art. Barnabas could not breathe, could not live without his canvases, brushes, and pencils.

Although only a young boy at the time, Charles had understood. But his father never had, nor his mother. The rest of the family, including Martin, were baffled by Barnabas's refusal to conform.

And after his brother died, it was as if he had never lived. The family never spoke of him. Barnabas lived only through his paintings and sketches, legacies Charles treasured as remarkable evidence of his brother's life.

"My brother risked death for his art."

"How difficult it must have been for you."

Charles nodded. With time, the pain had eased, but a hollowness remained in his heart. A heart he had guarded zealously since Barnabas's death. A heart that had been shattered with the loss of the big brother he had loved and admired.

Enfolding Maeve's small, rough hand in his, he forced a smile. "Little Bit, I did not mean to sadden you. Rycrofts are expected to do the right thing. My brother simply could not."

"He did what was right for him."

Charles took a deep breath and swiped a hand through his hair. "At a dear price."

"Aye, but one your dear brother must have been willing to pay."

"Perhaps." The acid gnawing in the pit of his stomach ebbed away. She was right. Unlike Barnabas, Charles had never loved anything or anyone with such intensity that he willingly would sacrifice his life.

"You shall recover the sketch. I know you shall, Charles."

"I hope so. It was one of the few whimsical pieces my brother created. His mood was not often light."

"My eye will be open and I will be looking—"

Charles raised a hand and gave her a stern warning. "Don't even think about getting involved. You found me, you healed my bruises, and so you know the ruffian who stole the sketch is not to be taken lightly."

"But—"

"No buts."

Maeve lowered her eyes without comment. Charles took her evasion as an ominous sign. But he had no time to press his argument further. Glancing at his pocket watch, he pushed back his chair. "We must leave now. I have an appointment in my office shortly."

She raised her soulful blue eyes to his. "Thank you for the tea and cakes . . . and for telling me about Barnabas."

During the past hour Charles lost some of the restless, edgy feeling plaguing him of late. Plainly, Maeve proved superior to fencing as a method of easing his disquiet. "It's fortunate that I came upon you," he said. "You would still be walking, frozen through and through."

She acknowledged his insight with a small, captivating smile.

"I would be forced to warm you."

"You have done that very well in the past," she declared. The impish sparkle in her eyes suggested intimacies between them that teased Charles's mind and tested his patience.

Chuckling, he held the Irish vixen's coat. "No more walking in the winter."

"I shall do my best to remember."

A disconcerting thought struck him. "Do you have money to hire a coach?"

"Money is not something I think of often and I am not used to riding—"

"Never leave home without proper funds. I shall see to it that you have enough to hire a carriage when needed and for any Christmas shopping you might like to do."

"I am used to making Christmas gifts."

"This year I urge you to shop for them. You might like it. My mother and Stella seem to be keeping themselves happily occupied with shopping."

The glow of Maeve's smile set Charles's blood afire. But he knew enough not to be misled by wondrous blue eyes and an enchanting smile.

Would the strong-willed Irish lass heed his warning? Would she put to rest any ideas of searching for Barnabas's sketch of St. Nick?

On the pretense of a shopping expedition with Pansy, Maeve left the Rycroft residence shortly after Charles dropped her there. At last she understood the somber, rigid demeanor of her husband. He had lost the brother he loved under horrible circumstances. His father, disappointed in his firstborn son, then settled on his second son, driving and belittling Charles at every turn. It was clear to Maeve that even now, several years after his father's death, Charles still attempted to prove his worth as a son and as a businessman.

His overbearing and arrogant manner had been cultivated to please his father. Charles strove to be the son his father wanted him to be. But Maeve knew the Charles behind the stiff facade. She'd had a glimpse of him during his brief bout with amnesia. He was the man she'd called Charlie. Her heart ached for Charlie. She meant to free him from the ghost of his father.

Pansy had been waiting in Maeve's rooms to help with her elocution and had begged to go along to the docks. Why a highborn miss like Pansy wanted to do such a thing was beyond Maeve, but her friend courted scandal on a regular basis. Harriet Deakins would serve Maeve's head on a platter if she ever discovered this afternoon's adventure.

For the first time in her life, Maeve carried a considerable amount of money in her pocket. But money wouldn't buy what she wanted most—Barnabas's sketch of St. Nicholas. This time, with Pansy close on her heels, she did not intend to leave the docks until she found her brother.

She was vastly relieved when she found Shea on pier four. Even though her brother possessed the strength of two men, the day work was grueling. However, it was good work for an Irish man and Shea never complained. Each day he went to the docks looking for a job. It was a good day when he was hired. Maeve fancied her brother dreamed of stowing away as he loaded the ships sailing east and south on the Atlantic. But he would never leave Dad to fend for himself.

Maeve waved both arms in the air and when Shea spotted her, he handed over the barrel in his arms to another stevedore.

"Is that your brother?" Pansy whispered.

Maeve adored her older brother. " 'Tis Shea Michael O'Malley, himself," she declared proudly.

Taking long, confident strides, Shea quickly reached Maeve and Pansy. The beginning depressions of a frown wrinkled his broad, sun-darkened forehead. For years she'd known her older brother worried first and asked questions later. From the time of their mother's death, he'd taken on more responsibility for Maeve's health and welfare than Dad.

With a brief, curious glance at Pansy, he removed his cap. His frown grew deeper as he focused on Maeve with a hard squint. "What brings ye here, Maeve?"

"I have been trying to talk to you for days now."

"But ye know ye shouldn't come down to the docks."

"If you are never at home, what should I do?" Without waiting for his reply, Maeve turned to Pansy. "This is my friend, Pansy Deakins. My brother, Shea."

Pansy extended her hand, gazing up at Shea with a soft, sweet smile. Maeve had never seen her friend smile that way before, like a simpering miss.

"I am exceedingly pleased to meet you, Shea."

Shea shot Pansy a disarming Irish grin, the one he usually saved for the girls at Rosie's Saloon. "The pleasure is all mine. Me sister has talked of you often enough. I thank you for yer many kindnesses to 'er."

To Maeve's horror, Pansy's eyes grew dewy, locking on Shea's steady, twinkling gaze. She watched with mounting apprehension as Shea and Pansy regarded each other in silent admiration. Her brother and best friend no longer knew Maeve existed. It was as if the faeries had raised a Fe-fiada around her, rendering her invisible to mortals.

Pansy finally spoke. "Your sister has become a dear friend," she said in a breathless tone.

"Which is the only reason Pansy is with me today," Maeve explained hastily. "She insisted that I bring her along."

"Aye, I see she has a weapon aimed at your back."

"Don't be teasin' now, Shea. I'm here on serious business."

Shea did not take his eyes from Pansy. "Is your husband mistreatin' you?"

"No. As a matter of fact, I think I may be growing on him."

"Charles is a good man," Pansy offered. "He would never knowingly harm Maeve . . . or anyone. His only sin is stuffiness."

Shea laughed at that, and Pansy as well.

But Maeve took umbrage. She dug her fists into her

hips, a difficult maneuver when one is couched in a muff. "My husband is misunderstood!"

"Don't turn your temper on me," Shea chuckled. "I believe you. And as much as I'd like to spend the day chatting, if I don't get back to work, I'll lose me job."

"Wait. I'm bound to find the sketch stolen from Charles the night we found him."

"How do you suppose to do that?" her brother asked, giving Maeve his full attention at last.

"You said at the time he appeared to have been beaten by a professional. I'd like you to look for any among your boxer friends who may have more money than he should."

"Do you think me friends go round beating and stealing from innocent men?"

"No, but it may be that your acquaintances do. If you will just look around when you're sparring or such."

Shea took a step back, narrowing his eyes. "What makes ye think I'm sparring?"

"Dad says you're not home much of late. And you're not drinkin' at Rosie's either. That says to me you're getting ready to box."

"Yer dreamin', sister o' mine."

"You promised me you wouldn't box any more after I left," she reminded him. "You said with one less mouth to feed, fightin' wouldn't be necessary."

Shea inclined his head. "Darlin', I can't for the life of me recall sayin' such a thing."

"Shea—"

"I've got to get back to work. If I hear anything, I'll let ye know."

Maeve gave an annoyed puff. But it was all she could ask—for now.

"Miss Pansy . . ." His voice trailed off as if he would say more but thought better of it. Instead he winked and cocked his head. "Good day to you."

"I hope we meet again, Shea O'Malley," Pansy blurted.

Maeve nudged her red-haired companion with her elbow.

Shea just grinned. Jamming his cap back atop his curls, he strode away whistling.

Pansy spun on Maeve. "You never told me your brother was such a handsome man."

"You never asked. And it matters not." Maeve had a new worry now.

Something had passed between Shea and Pansy. It was nothing Maeve could put her finger on, but she knew something had happened. Her earlier misgiving about allowing Pansy to accompany her to the docks had been correct. A woman who believed in Victoria Woodhull's philosophy of free love did not belong anywhere near Shea O'Malley.

Maeve hustled her friend away from the docks and hired a coach to take them into the heart of Boston.

She did have some shopping to do and Pansy's opinion would help.

Charles met in his office with Herbert Lynch. The private investigator he'd hired to find his brother's sketch of St. Nick was a small, dour man who smelled of stale tobacco. His fingers were yellow from constantly holding a cigar, lit or unlit.

"What have you to report, Mr. Lynch?"

Lynch pointed the ragged, unlit stub of his cigar at Charles. "Very little. The trail is cold."

"You mentioned that when I hired you."

"I'm doing my best."

The tension that had drained from Charles while having tea with Maeve snaked through him again—a spiraling, squeezing sensation that caused his whole body to become as rigid as a walking stick. "Are you telling me you have nothing to report?"

"No. I've something. Something. Did you know your

cousin, Martin Rycroft, is in financial straits? Bad financial straits?"

"I did not."

"His wife is expecting their first child and the house she made him buy a few months ago is more than he can manage. More than he can manage."

"Are you suggesting Martin is the thief?"

"Does he know the value of your sketch?"

"Yes." Charles wondered if Martin's unceasing proposal for a monthly magazine could be attributed to his cousin's poor financial status. Martin would win an increase in his salary if he were to head such a project. "My cousin would never steal from me."

"In most cases it's someone close, someone who you'd never suspect. Never suspect. Someone close."

The investigator's habit of repeating himself aggravated Charles's gut-wrenching tension. "Mr. Lynch, I advise you to dig deeper. Report back when you have more."

Lynch shook his head and shuffled to the door.

An hour later, Charles still battled his consuming tension. He could send a message to Spencer and arrange another fencing match, or he could do something quite out of character, something quite impulsive. Against all accounting, he did the latter.

Charles strode past his startled assistant's desk. "I'm leaving for the day."

Was there anything better than a shopping spree? Although Maeve had never enjoyed one before this afternoon, now that she had, she could not imagine anything more pleasant. Pansy guided her with the skill of a practiced shopper. At times, they giggled like schoolgirls, marveling at their purchases.

They had just emerged from the toy shoppe when Maeve heard Charles shout.

"Maeve!"

She spun around. "Charles!"

He'd come upon her twice in the same day. Was her husband following her?

"Get in the sleigh—you're coming with me."

Maeve would have felt better about complying if Charles had been smiling.

Chapter Ten

A little dazed and more than a bit wary, Maeve settled into the sleigh and pulled the warm carriage blanket over her. She'd only been on the docks a short time. No one that she knew of had seen her. She didn't deserve to be banished from the city of Boston—if that's what Charles had in mind.

"I hadn't expected to find you so easily," he said. His mouth turned up in a satisfied, almost smug, smile.

"Where are we going?"

"To the country, to Sycamore Falls."

Maeve had never heard of Sycamore Falls. But she knew there was a town west of Boston where they'd burned witches at the stake in bygone days. Her doubts resurfaced. She knew last evening would come back to haunt her.

While Charles had been a gentleman at tea earlier and not mentioned her indiscretion, he knew as well as she that Maeve had not been especially judicious with the dinner wine. Each time she turned away, her goblet had been refilled, causing Maeve to sorely misjudge the amount she drank. If truth be faced, she might have been a trifle intoxicated during the sleigh ride.

Perhaps Charles had mentioned this trip to the country while Maeve's mind was not functioning as well as it should.

"How far away is Sycamore Falls?" she asked.

"About an hour's ride. Our country house is there: Ashton Pond."

"A country house?"

"If it were possible, I'd live at Ashton Pond all year long. It's where my mother was raised. I suppose that's why she prefers city life today—she is ill-suited to the isolation of the country. Beatrice hasn't been to Ashton Pond since I was a boy."

"I see." But she didn't. For the life of her, Maeve could not understand why anyone would prefer noisy, crowded city life to the peaceful serenity of the country. "Will we be back in Boston in time for your mother's seance?"

"If we act swiftly."

Act swiftly? Maeve had no patience for mystery. She had been encouraged when Charles confided in her over tea this morning. Her hope of forming a true love match with him had been rekindled. But now—now, she was leery. Had it all been a ploy?

Could Charles have decided to become a single man again by some notorious manner? Maeve was not entirely an innocent. She'd heard stories, listened to rumors. Wives had been known to disappear, or worse, die in terrible accidents at the hands of their husbands. Was Maeve about to have an accident on a lonely country road?

"What . . . what are your plans?" she asked as casually as possible. If Charles's scheme sounded the least bit suspicious, she planned to leap from the carriage before losing sight of Boston.

"I require your help to select our Christmas tree.

Mother has charged me with this grave responsibility. And you know what a difficult woman she is to please."

"Charles, you make momentous decisions every day at business. Why do you need my help to select a Christmas tree?"

"There are a great many trees on the farm—I require a woman's opinion."

Maeve's pulse spurted into an unsettling beat even as her heart swelled to twice its normal size. Charles valued her opinion—over Stella's, the merry widow. How silly Maeve had been to think for one moment Charles would harm her. She couldn't have wished for anything better. Alone with Charles, she would have the opportunity to win his heart.

The journey took over an hour through winding country roads lined by thick evergreen forests dusted with snow. Maeve worried as the sky grew darker, threatening a storm. Would they have time to find the perfect tree and return to Beacon Hill before nightfall? They certainly couldn't traverse dark country roads during a blizzard. As Charles did not appear worried, Maeve took heart.

She huddled beside her laconic husband, content to bask in the warmth of his solid heat. To stave off boredom, she launched into a rousing, slightly off-key rendition of "We Wish You a Merry Christmas." To Maeve's surprise, Charles soon joined in, adding his deep baritone voice. When the song ended he started another: "Hark the Herald Angels Sing."

Maeve and Charles sang in unison to the hoary sky, to the majestic snow-tipped trees, and to the winding road. Charles sang out loudly, with twinkling eyes and a wide, happy grin. Maeve could not remember seeing him look so at ease and content. She kept their duet alive with one song after another until at last the sleigh passed through the gates of Ashton Pond.

On either side of the long, curving drive, the branches of pine and elm dipped with the weight of snow. The snowy sentinels appeared to be bowing as the carriage passed. They passed a fair-sized pond iced over and empty: Ashton Pond, sprawled in the front acre of Charles's country house.

At first sight of the spacious gingerbread house, Maeve caught her breath. Icicles resembling long, knobby fingers dripped from beneath the eaves. With its dark green shutters and gabled second floor windows, the charming home on Ashton Pond appeared to be a storybook illustration. Snow drifted against the porch steps and the welcoming glow of candlelight shone in every window. Here was a real home, a haven that instantly captured Maeve's heart.

"Do you see the wooded area behind the house?" Charles asked. "It's the Rycrofts' own Christmas tree farm."

"It's lovely," she replied, marveling.

"Let's choose our tree first and then we'll head for the house and get warm."

"Sure'n we'll find a grand tree," she said as Charles helped her from the carriage.

Maeve took in her surroundings with light-headed wonder. This was another whole new world, one promising comfort, one where she might feel a sense of belonging.

The snow-encrusted ground crunched beneath their feet as Charles took Maeve's gloved hand and led her out into the woods. In order to keep up with her tall, long-legged husband, she took three steps for every one of his.

A soft snowfall began as they reached the edge of the woods. But Maeve didn't mind. Nothing could dampen her spirits. She breathed deeply, inhaling with relish the thick fir scent of the small forest. Her body buzzed with anticipation. A vague sense of unbridled joy washed through her. With only the slightest encouragement, Maeve would have danced a jig right then and there in the snow.

She meant to treasure each moment alone with Charles in this glorious place. He seemed less intense, even lighthearted. Somewhere along the way, Charles had undergone a transformation. He'd become Charlie again, the man she had married.

He led Maeve deeper into the copse. Fragrant pine and fir trees shared space with ancient oak, sycamore, old maples, and elm. There were any number of trees to choose from, for almost any purpose.

Pursing his lips and studying several candidates, Charles made a great show of the tree selection. "Remember, we must bring the perfect tree back to Boston."

Maeve shook the snow from a branch on a large fir to her right. "This one is full and green."

"Too short."

"This one?"

"Too tall. But what do you think of this?" he asked, gesturing to the tree just ahead.

Listing precariously and misshapen about its bottom, the pine stood well over twelve feet. Maeve had never seen Charles dwarfed before. But no tree could diminish her husband's towering form, the striking silver gleam in his eye. His strong, broad shoulders were wide enough to carry the entire Emerald Isle. Sheer masculine power shimmered from his compelling figure.

A hard, hot shudder swept through Maeve.

Taking a deep breath to steady herself, she shook her head. "Much too skinny."

"Are you an expert?" he asked. His normally unreadable silver gray eyes shone with amusement.

"I've had but one Christmas tree and Shea found it," she laughed. "The poor scrawny fir had been discarded."

"If you've had but only one tree, we must make this year's tree the largest possible."

"Like this?" she asked. Maeve stared up at the fullest, greenest, tallest tree in the forest.

Take 4 FREE Books!

We created our convenient Home Subscription Service so you'll be sure to have the hottest new romances delivered each month right to your doorstep — usually before they are available in book stores. Just to show you how convenient Zebra Home Subscription Service is, we would like to send you 4 Kensington Choice Historical Romance as a FREE gift. You receive a gift worth up to $24.96 — absolutely FREE. There's no extra charge for shipping and handling. There's no obligation to buy anything - ever!

Save Up To 32% On Home Delivery!

Accept your FREE gift and each month we'll deliver 4 brand new titles as soon as they are published. They'll be yours to examine FREE for 10 days. Then if you decide to keep the books, you'll pay the preferred subscriber's price of just $4.20 per title. That's $16.80 for all 4 books for a savings of up to 32% off the cover price! Just add $1.50 to offset the cost of shipping and handling. Remember, you are under no obligation to buy any of these books at any time. If you are not delighted with them, simply return them and owe nothing. But if you enjoy Kensington Choice Historical Romances as much as we think you will, pay the special preferred subscriber rate of only $16.80 each month and save over $8.00 off the bookstore price!

We have 4 FREE BOOKS for you as your introduction to KENSINGTON CHOICE!

To get your FREE BOOKS,
worth up to $24.96, mail the card below
or call TOLL-FREE 1-888-345-BOOK
Visit our website at www.kensingtonbooks.com.

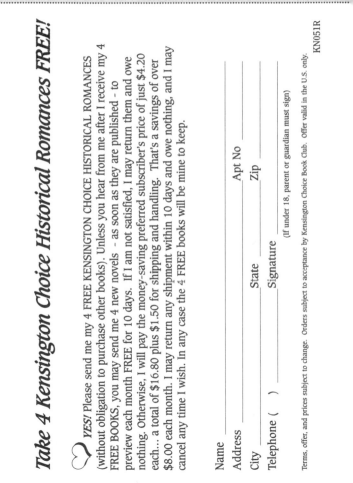

Take 4 Kensington Choice Historical Romances FREE!

YES! Please send me my 4 FREE KENSINGTON CHOICE HISTORICAL ROMANCES (without obligation to purchase other books). Unless you hear from me after I receive my 4 FREE BOOKS, you may send me 4 new novels – as soon as they are published – to preview each month FREE for 10 days. If I am not satisfied, I may return them and owe nothing. Otherwise, I will pay the money-saving preferred subscriber's price of just $4.20 each... a total of $16.80 plus $1.50 for shipping and handling. That's a savings of over $8.00 each month. I may return any shipment within 10 days and owe nothing, and I may cancel any time I wish. In any case the 4 FREE books will be mine to keep.

KN051R

Name _____

Address _____ Apt No _____

City _____ State _____ Zip _____

Telephone ( ) _____ Signature _____

(If under 18, parent or guardian must sign)

Terms, offer, and prices subject to change. Orders subject to acceptance by Kensington Book Club. Offer valid in the U.S. only.

4 FREE

Kensington
Choice
Historical
Romances
are waiting
for you to
claim them!

(worth up
to $24.96)

See details
inside....

‖‖‖‖‖‖‖‖‖‖‖‖‖‖‖‖‖‖‖‖‖‖‖‖‖‖‖‖‖

KENSINGTON CHOICE
Zebra Home Subscription Service, Inc.
P.O. Box 5214
Clifton NJ 07015-5214

"Perfect."

"Then let it stay. We can't chop down such a beautiful tree."

"What?" he winced.

"We'll take the skinny, misshapen one back to Boston and tell Beatrice it was the best of the lot. We shall claim that it's a very bad year for trees. How will she know?"

A grin spread slowly across his face. "She won't."

"We'll cover the tree's . . . slight imperfections with decorations."

"You are an extremely clever woman. Has anyone ever told you so before?"

"Yes, many times," she teased. "But never by you."

Standing not three feet away, Charles's gaze fixed on hers. He cast a spell Maeve could not readily break free from. She felt certain his smoky eyes carried a silent message meant for her heart. What Charles could not put into words was reflected in his eyes. Was it love?

Here in the woods where their voices echoed, they were the only two people in the world. This beautiful wintery snowscape was their very own faerie land, their own Tir Nan Og. Beyond the snow, Maeve envisioned an ice castle where she and Charles could live without the interference of his world—and hers.

Abruptly, Charles's gaze fell to the rope in his hand. "We should go inside before we freeze to death," he said, turning to wrap the rope around the tree as a tag.

The spell had been broken.

The snow fell faster. "If you freeze to death, your mother will put the blame on me as your dreadfully unsuitable wife."

Charles chuckled and gave Maeve a lopsided grin that caused her heart to fly.

"Let's go," he said. "Our caretaker, George, will chop the tree down for us."

"Shouldn't the country house have a Christmas tree as well?" Maeve asked, hugging herself to ward off the cold seeping through her once again. "This would be the most wonderful place to spend Christmas."

Charles agreed. "I've only spent one Christmas at Ashton Pond but it was a memorable one."

"Aye. I'm certain."

Perhaps the best, he thought.

"My mother came to Boston especially for the Christmas socializing," Charles interrupted quickly, anticipating Maeve's question. "Beatrice would not miss the Cabots' Snow Ball for the world and I'm afraid she will not allow me to miss it. In other words, Christmas at Ashton Pond is impossible."

"Oh." Her disappointment showed in the fleeting shadow that fell across her eyes, the quick press of her full cherry lips.

"But before we go in, I think you should pick one more tree, for the country house," Charles said in an effort to ease Maeve's disappointment. "George and Hilda won't mind."

Casting him a heart-spinning grin, Maeve closed her eyes and twirled awkwardly around until she was dizzy. "I choose . . . this one." After pointing, she opened her eyes.

It was a small, bushy tree not over four feet. Charles let Maeve tag it with a short loop of rope before grasping her hand and hurrying back toward the house.

"Wait!" She stopped suddenly, jerked her hand free from his, and bent low to the ground.

Charles watched in bewilderment as she scooped up the snow. Before he realized what Maeve was doing, she'd made a snowball, tossed it and hit him on the shoulder. A grown woman hurling snowballs, playing as if she were a girl again!

When Charles reached out for her, Maeve scampered away, grinning mischievously. He stopped to make a snowball of his own but as he righted himself she tossed another that landed in his midsection. He hadn't thrown a snowball in years, not since he was a boy. Charles threw his ball badly and it missed its mark, sending Maeve into peals of laughter.

Once again, Charles gave chase and just as he was about to reach her, his snowball opponent stumbled in the snow and fell flat on her face.

"Maeve!" He ran to her, falling on his knees beside her. "Maeve, are you all right?"

She was making some sort of gurgling sound.

Dear God. He'd killed her.

But in the next moment, with only a little help from Charles, Maeve pushed herself to her knees. Wiping the snow from her face, she began to laugh once more.

She was obviously delirious.

Framing her face with one hand, Charles helped her wipe the snow from her cheek and from her lips. And then all he could see were her lips, blue and wet with snow. He gently covered Maeve's wet, cold lips with his.

Soon she'd wrapped her arms around his neck and he held her close, drinking the laughter from her full, sweet mouth. The snow whirled around them, kicked up by a sudden breeze, but Charles was warm, very warm. Very alive. Completely unable to tear his lips from Maeve's.

She moaned, a soft and passionate sound that caused an unnatural spurt of his pulse. A powerful white heat sparked deep in his loins.

Dear God, he could take her on this blanket of snow. He wanted her that desperately.

The realization of what he was willing to do to have Maeve brought Charles up short. The fire within him died. He'd lost his mind. For the past weeks one unexpected event had followed another, apparently taking a toll on him. Why else would he consider making love in a blizzard? Those were not the thoughts of a rational man.

Charles dragged his mouth from Maeve's. Carefully

regaining his footing, he pulled Maeve up. "Forgive me. If you suffer frostbite, I will be to blame."

"Is it cold? I hadn't noticed," she said and dissolved into laughter.

Caught up in the infectious music of Maeve's laughter, Charles found himself laughing as well. He didn't know himself any longer. Shaking his head, he scooped Maeve's beguiling body into his arms and carried her into the house. She weighed no more than a snowflake. She felt light and right in his arms. A rocking, searing desire swept through him. Despite the cold he grew hot and hard, aroused beyond endurance. Charles groaned inwardly as Maeve settled snugly into his embrace . . . as if she was meant to be there.

"Hilda! My wife needs a warm bath immediately," he shouted as he marched through the front door.

What made him say that? He'd said the word aloud again— wife. He hadn't been thinking.

"And so do you!" Maeve exclaimed.

Ignoring her impudence, Charles continued delivering cheerful orders to the unseen Hilda. "And then we shall require supper and a warm fire in the parlor."

Maeve started to protest. "But—"

"I'm afraid there's no going back to Boston now. It's a bad northeaster blowing out there."

"We're snowbound?"

"We'll have to make the best of it."

"I can do that."

"I was hoping you wouldn't be too . . . distressed."

She beamed. "I shall overcome the inconvenience."

He grinned. "You are an uncommon woman, Maeve O'Malley."

"But my clothes are soaked through."

"Since mother never comes to Ashton Pond, I'm afraid there are no women's clothes about. You shall have to wear something of mine. Do you think you can find something for this little woman, Hilda?"

The broad-hipped caretaker's wife shot him a strange little smile. "That I will, sir."

"Did I say something humorous?"

"No, sir. It's just that except for Mr. Wellington, you've never brought anyone to the country before. And now, here you come all smiles and fit to burst with a wife. It's . . . a miracle."

"A miracle?" Charles repeated, feeling a bit wounded.

Maeve giggled.

"Yes, sir. I never thought I'd see the day."

"I didn't mean to shock you. And I understand it's an imposition arriving without notice and requesting food and clothes—"

"Mr. Rycroft, the mister and me wish you would spend more time with us. I'll get the baths now." With that, Hilda gave a no-nonsense nod and waddled from the room.

None of the ornate furnishings and luxurious fabrics of the Beacon Hill house were in evidence at Ashton Pond. No modern bathroom had been installed as yet. Simplicity and warmth reigned within the cozy, rambling structure.

Hilda quickly prepared adjoining rooms on the second floor and Maeve settled into a bath by the fireplace in her room. The furnishings were old but comfortable, crafted of sturdy maple by New England furniture makers. A bright blue-and-yellow quilt covered the four-poster bed and lace curtains graced the windows.

During her bath, Maeve pondered the significance of Charles bringing her to Ashton Pond when, according to Hilda, he'd not brought anyone else to this house. She took it as a positive sign.

The clothes Hilda appropriated for Maeve consisted of a pair of dark trousers that Maeve rolled up to her ankles and a white linen shirt with full sleeves. Several other petite persons could have helped Maeve fill Charles's trousers and she felt swamped by the hopelessly large shirt. She made do by rolling up the sleeves and leaving the top buttons undone. The caretaker's wife supplied one of her own magenta scarves for Maeve to wrap around her waist. As a means to hold the trousers up, the scarf succeeded. A pair of Charles's dark socks completed her outlandish costume.

Maeve unleashed her hair from its pins and brushed the blue-black mane until it gleamed. Still, a quick glance in the mirror told her she looked misbegotten, a little woman drowning in a man's clothes. She tilted her head, pressing the side of her face against the shirt-sleeve. The musky, masculine scent of Charles clung to the fabric. A warm tingle of pleasure trickled down Maeve's spine.

Curious to see if her husband had gone downstairs, she opened the connecting door and peeked into his room. He sat in the copper tub, long legs bent awkwardly at the knee. He appeared uncomfortable; nevertheless, Maeve thought he looked magnificent. The dark curls peppering Charles's broad chest and muscular legs glistened with beads of water and sparkled like jewels. With his wet, dark hair slicked back, his handsome features became more prominent, even more appealing.

Temporarily immobilized by the lusty allure of her husband, Maeve could not imagine even the great faerie lord, Fin Bheara, looking quite so splendid. She could not tear her eyes away. She could not catch a complete breath of air. Actually, she felt quite feverish.

"Maeve!"

Saints above, she'd shocked him again. He must think her a brazen hussy. "Please, I did not mean to . . . to disturb you."

Frowning, Charles hurriedly pulled his knees almost up to his chin and wrapped his arms about his legs.

Although she admired his attempt at modesty, Maeve bit her lip in order not to smile. "If you recall, I've seen you . . . like this before."

"Oh?" A disconcerted scowl flickered across his face. "Oh."

And if she dared breathe the truth to Charles—which she didn't—Maeve looked forward to seeing her husband buck naked again soon. "I'll wait for you downstairs."

Flashing a distracted smile, she spun on her heel and, humming happily, sailed from the room. The sight of Charles in all his naked glory filled her with longing. She yearned for the days when he had been a man with no memory of what was proper and what was not. The man she married would have invited her into his bath.

Those were the days. Too few and too brief.

Maeve entered the parlor in a wistful mood. Hilda had set a lovely candlelit table by the fireplace. The ragged, unadorned Christmas tree Maeve had selected earlier sat on a nearby table. Its heady pine fragrance mingled with the scent of cinnamon and apple already perfuming the air.

Hilda carried a tray to the table piled high with cheese and apples, steaming barley soup, hot bread, and chocolate cake. Maeve declined the wine.

"Thank you, Hilda. Your timing is impeccable," Charles said as he strode into the room refreshed and feeling in especially good humor.

He sat across from Maeve at the small table. While he felt the heat of the fireplace, Charles knew another fire simmered within him. A fire that intensified as he met Maeve's upturned eyes. "Are you comfortable in my trousers, Maeve?"

She tilted her chin and gave him a sassy smile. "I have never been so comfortable, Charles. A woman should always wear pants."

Enveloped in his country clothes, Maeve resembled a small waif. When she moved, the gaping neck of Charles's open shirt revealed her creamy shoulders and the deep, sweet valley of her cleavage.

The ache in his loins neared the point of pain. Charles

raised his gaze to Maeve's sloe-black hair tumbling in a glossy mass of curls cascading past her shoulders. He drew in a deep breath and exhaled slowly, searching for calm and strength of will. He required the will to overcome an involuntary, but overwhelming, need to bury his fingers in her silky mane.

Charles wasn't sure he could eat.

Distraction might be the answer. "Maeve, this will be a different Christmas for you. I'm quite certain that the Rycrofts' traditions are different from the O'Malleys'."

"Of that there can be no doubt."

"Tell me about your finest Christmas."

Inclining her head, she teased her bottom lip. His gaze focused on her moist, highly desirable lips.

"I . . . I can't think of when that might have been."

Attempting to forget Maeve's lips, Charles studied his soup, pushed his spoon through the thick stuff, and posed another question. "Can you remember a special toy you received from Santa when you were a child?"

Frowning, she shook her head. With the slight movement, a thick midnight lock brushed against the bare porcelain skin of Maeve's shoulder. A shower of hot sparks prickled down Charles's spine.

She appeared deep in thought. She had no idea what she was doing to him.

"Maeve?"

"Santa never brought me a toy."

He was astounded. "Never? Not one?"

"No."

"Not even a doll?"

"No." A rueful smile played at the corners of her sweet cherry lips. "But I do remember yearning for a beautiful doll of my own."

A quick, jabbing pain pierced Charles's heart. "You never owned a doll?" he repeated again in disbelief.

"Not as I can remember. We had no money," Maeve replied in a matter-of-fact tone. "Poor Irish children were happy with a piece of rock candy or a shiny apple."

"Maeve—"

She interrupted Charles by leaving the table in a swift, abrupt movement. "Dad did whatever he could."

With her head held high and her shoulders straight and proud, Maeve shielded herself from any pity he might be about to express.

"Of course." Charles could not explain the heaviness in his heart, the consuming need to hold Maeve in his arms.

"Since coming to America we've been able to observe Blackfast on Christmas Eve."

"What is Blackfast?"

"A dinner of boiled salt cod and potatoes followed by Christmas cakes. 'Tis a feast."

Charles grimaced. "Boiled cod?"

Maeve grinned. "It's an acquired taste."

"By some, perhaps." He left the table to join her.

Her generous hips undulated slowly, softly beneath his trousers as she wandered toward the small, barren Christmas tree. His throat felt dry, dry as book dust.

"And do you remember a special toy delivered by old St. Nick that struck your fancy?" she asked.

Her deep blue eyes sparkled with challenge as they met his, locked on his, took him prisoner. Lost in the mysterious ocean-blue depths of Maeve's eyes, Charles's mind became a blank slate. Stripped of all cognitive ability, he could not determine right from wrong, impulse from procrastination. He felt suspended in time.

Seconds that felt more like hours slipped by until at last a faded image appeared in Charles's mind. The red toy replica of a tall ship. "My special toy was a ship and I sailed it on the Common ponds. When I was young I dreamed of being an explorer," he added unnecessarily.

Dear God, he babbled like a schoolboy!

"Have you seen the world?" she asked, in a voice as

soft and melodic as a lullaby. A voice that could soothe and comfort a man until he grew too old to hear.

"No." Carrying on a conversation became more difficult with each minute. The ache deep within Charles had become a painful throbbing. And each time he looked into Maeve's eyes, or allowed his gaze to drift down her delicate form, his pulse pounded so loudly he feared she would hear.

He cleared his dry, scratchy throat. An explanation was in order. "I've a publishing company to run."

"Ah, yes."

Maeve's gentle smile struck at Charles's heart like a mallet against a bass drum. A series of tingling vibrations shot through him. If he didn't regain his composure quickly, the woman would drive him to ravishing her here and now. Surely, if he asked a serious question, the answer would take his mind off of Maeve's warm lips, her full, inviting hips, the whimsical light in her eyes, her seductive smile. Surely.

"What did you dream of when you lived in Ireland?" he asked. "What did you hope America held for you?"

Maeve gave a little shrug, displacing the oversized shirt to reveal one exquisite shoulder. A satin shoulder Charles's lips longed to savor.

"I didn't know what I would find here," she admitted, obviously unaware of his physical distress. "But I wanted to be a teacher. It seemed to me that if a man or a woman knew something besides how to grow potatoes, life would be better for them. I wanted to learn, and pass on whatever knowledge I gleaned to the children who came after me."

Charles could barely hold himself together. Every ounce of his rigid self-control seemed to be seeping from his body. "But you became a maid."

"And studied at night."

"You're quite a woman." The words fell from his mouth without warning, a whisper of honest admiration.

She gave him a hapless smile. "Not at all like the

ladies you are accustomed to. The ladies who have been to finishing school and who play the piano without missing a note."

"You are unique."

"Is that a good thing or a bad thing?"

"It's good." Charles had lost perspective again. His focus had returned to Maeve's lips, her sweet tempting, tasty lips. "Very good."

"And do you find me . . ." she paused, taking a breath before continuing quietly, hesitantly. "Do you find me . . . the least bit attractive?"

Charles's heart crashed against his chest. "You . . . you aren't just attractive. You are a beautiful woman, Maeve."

"Even like this?" She looked down at her borrowed clothes.

"You are more beautiful tonight than I've ever seen you."

"Then why . . . why . . ." Maeve's voice trailed off, her gaze fell to the scarf at her waist which she twisted nervously.

"Why what?"

Using the tip of his finger, Charles gently lifted Maeve's chin until her eyes, misty blue pools swimming with unshed tears, met his. She spoke in a jagged, barely audible voice. "You . . . you have not come to my bed since your memory returned. I'm your wife. Do you . . . do you not want me any longer? Have you forgotten what we shared?"

"I want you."

Dear God, he wanted her.

A tear slid down her cheek.

"But Maeve, I must confess, I don't recall what passed between us before."

She took his hand.

His heart stopped.

"Tonight . . . if you, if you make love to me in this

special place perhaps . . . pleasant memories will return to you."

There was nothing in the world Charles would rather do than make love to Maeve. He could not speak. His throat felt raw. His heart drummed.

Her eyes, as big and round as a blue moon, fixed on his. "Charles, will you make love to me?"

Chapter Eleven

Dear God, she had asked him to make love to her! Brazen hussy, Irish tart ... remarkable, extraordinary, heavenly woman!

At that moment Charles could not remember wanting to make love to any woman more fervently in his life. He'd done everything in his power to resist Maeve's charms. The last thing in the world he wanted to do was take advantage of an innocent. But the dark-haired beauty had just requested that he make love to her. What hot-blooded, sane man could refuse?

The thought of claiming her with his memory intact gave Charles goosebumps. A surge of unprecedented energy swept through his body. Charles felt as if he could fly, that his feet would never touch the ground again.

How could one night of love that they would *both* remember cause any harm? They were secreted away at Ashton Pond and no one need ever know what passed between them.

Charles was no martyr, nor was he deceiving himself. Fulfilling Maeve's request would be for his benefit as much as for the captivating little woman in his arms. He fully expected making love to Maeve would relieve the painful ache plaguing him almost constantly of late. Perhaps the restless, edgy feelings he'd been suffering since she came into his life might cease as well. He could only hope.

And, after all was said and done, Maeve was his wife.

Without another word, he scooped her into his arms and carried his beaming bride upstairs to his bed.

The winter storm had worsened to blizzard proportions. Icy snow tapped sharply against the windowpanes. The frigid wind slapped against the house, howling like an angry demon. But in his room a roaring fire blazed in the fireplace and the big four-poster canopied bed had been warmed. Gaslight sconces cast dancing shadows across the room. Carefully, Charles set Maeve down on the soft, thick bearskin rug spread before the fireplace.

Overwhelmed by her own audacity, she lowered her eyes and clasped her trembling hands. Cold shivers spiked down her spine. She'd been shamelessly impertinent in asking Charles to make love to her. It simply wasn't done by women in general and wives in particular. Maeve's very proper Beacon Hill husband must think the worst of her for certain now. How could he respect a woman who behaved like a bold Irish Jezebel? She dared not meet his gaze. So she hummed, softly.

Maeve excused her unseemly request as the act of a desperate woman. For the first time since their hastily exchanged vows, she and Charles were alone together. There might never be another opportunity to feel the warmth and strength of his arms enfolding her again, or know the toe-curling thrill of his kiss once more. If Beatrice Rycroft had her way, Charles would shortly be quickly and quietly divorced from Maeve.

Maeve meant to fight for her husband, but if she should lose, she would have this night for all time. A time she would remember for the rest of her life, and one she hoped Charles would never forget. Understanding that Charles had undoubtedly agreed to make love to her out of pity or some sense of obligation did not lessen Maeve's resolve.

When she finally summoned the courage to raise her eyes, she found her husband's gaze sweeping her body in a languid, burning perusal. A small, enigmatic smile played on his lips. Maeve's heart reacted like a wild thing, instantly fluttering.

"Do you have any idea how arousing a woman dressed in a man's clothing can be?" Charles asked.

The husky timbre of his voice ignited delicious chills and aching warmth within Maeve simultaneously.

"Am I . . . arousing you then?" she whispered.

The corners of his mouth turned up in a bemused smile as Charles gently cradled Maeve's face between his hands. Slowly he brought his mouth down on hers. He kissed her tenderly. He kissed her fiercely. He kissed her with an intensity that caused her heart to race and her knees to weaken.

Her lips parted beneath his, welcoming the soft, intimate plunge of Charles's tongue. He filled her mouth, exploring, tasting, savoring. Maeve's pulse pounded in a spurt of dizzying speed.

He gathered her in his arms and within his warm, sheltering embrace, Maeve became more than a poor Irish maid; she became a queen who possessed all she could possibly desire. She ruled from a gilded fairy palace and her heart beat for only one man. The pine and musky masculine scent of Charles invaded her senses as she reached for his cheek and felt the prickly stubble of his jaw. Humming with core-deep pleasure, she ran her fingertips into his thick, dark hair.

Through the light-headed haze of her desire, Maeve became aware of Charles unbuttoning her shirt; his fiery touch brushed her skin and set her flesh to tingling. With the barest contact he'd kindled a simmering heat within her. When all the buttons were undone and the linen garment parted, Charles gently eased Maeve's arms from the oversized shirt. His gaze fell to her breasts. Maeve drew a deep, quivering breath. Her heart swelled to twice its size; milk and honey flowed through her veins, moist and warm.

Charles's eyes darkened with desire, dove-gray deepened to granite shot through with silver light. Maeve's heart crashed against her chest. Her throat closed. Her mouth watered.

Charles raised his burning gaze to hers. He tore impatiently at his vest and shirt, tossing them aside. Maeve ripped off the scarf holding Charles's trousers about her small waist, and wiggled free from his pants. Since her warming bath before dinner, she'd worn nothing beneath the trousers.

The flash of fire in Charles's eyes revealed his sudden understanding. He sucked in his breath. Exhaled heavily.

She smiled.

Maeve lay on the bearskin exposed and vulnerable, prepared to abandon not only her wildly beating heart to Charles, but her soul as well.

Charles stood. At his full height, he towered above her like a magnificent mountain, dark and mysterious. Galvanizing. His intense gaze never left hers as he hurriedly removed his trousers and undergarments and kicked them away. Before Maeve could appreciate the power and perfection of his sculpted-steel body, he fell to his knees beside her. Pulling her up to him, Charles crushed Maeve against the thick muscular wall of his chest and the hardness of his manhood. She held her breath. He wound his fingers through her hair, sprinkled kisses at the throbbing hollow of her neck, the soft sensuous inner core of her ear.

The lusty essence of Charles sent an exquisite white heat spiraling though Maeve. A slow, sultry burn.

And then he eased her down again onto the soft bearskin rug. She rested on her back, waiting, unable to draw a single, steady breath for the excitement, the unbearable anticipation careening through her.

At last Charles's mouth came down on Maeve's, smothering her with kisses both fierce and tender. She splayed her hands against the crisp, curly mat of his chest as the pads of his thumbs brushed gently against her nipples. A river of fire surged up from the feminine core of her.

Lifting his mouth from hers, Charles turned his attention to the taut buds of her breasts. Maeve gasped as he sucked one and then the other until the glorious sensations of heat and light, of bittersweet delight, caused her to moan with an aching pleasure she could not articulate.

She was unwilling for him to stop, and yet her moist, eager body demanded much more from her lover. Her heart yearned to be one with him, the man she loved more than the moon, the sun, and the stars. She loved him with all the love she had to give.

When Charles raised his mouth from her swollen breasts to cup them in the palms of his hands, she thought she would cry. His smoky eyes smoldered with passion as they met hers. And then he braced himself beside her and softly stroked Maeve's arm. His gaze flickered over her body as if she were the most beautiful woman in the world. His world?

"You are even lovelier than I dreamed, Little Bit. Lovelier than a man can fathom."

Before she could reply, he leaned in to kiss her. Hot sparks skipped down Maeve's spine, between her thighs to the tips of her toes. While his fingertips traced every curve from her waist to her calves and back, Charles's sensuous lips remained fastened on hers. He devoured her like a starving man who could not be filled. She wondered that her heart didn't explode.

Soon his lips traveled the length of her. His tongue circled her belly button, his palm caressed her flat, fluttering stomach. When Charles's mouth returned to hers, his palm lingered to softly massage the soft sensuous area of Maeve's inner thighs.

She felt as if her body was dissolving like sugar in a sun shower. A puddle of aching need would soon be all that was left of her. Her hips shifted impatiently, her back arched, her mind spun in light-headed exhilaration.

The truest happiness she had ever known began with her blueblood husband's touch. Like the great faerie lord, Fin Bheara, Charles possessed the power to transport Maeve to a magical place, to Tir Nan Og, the land of eternal spring, the land of eternal youth. He was the only one who could take her to the mythical kingdom where peace, happiness, and beauty prevailed. The uncharted destination could be seen by mortals through a silvery sea mist, but few ever gained admittance.

"Charles," she pleaded breathlessly, "come to me, be one with me, my love."

He needed no further urging. Rising above her, his smoldering silver-gray gaze met Maeve's. The desire she saw in his eyes ignited a flood of warmth that cascaded through her, leaving her breathless. She curled her arms around his neck. Her heart overflowed with happiness.

With a gentle nudge, Charles parted her legs. A sigh of elation escaped Maeve as her husband buried himself in her, filling her with the strength of his manhood. Slowly, his hips ground against hers as he plunged deeper within her. Now her body itself hummed.

Breathing heavily, hotly against her cheek, Charles submerged himself in Maeve. Each deep thrust carried her higher, until she abandoned herself to a passionate frenzy and unspeakable bliss.

With every breath Maeve inhaled the tantalizing blend of musky male and deep pine forest. She inhaled him. Savored him. The more Charles gave of himself, the more she craved. She pulled him into her. Deeper. Stronger. One with Charles, she soared higher and higher.

Deeper, stronger, higher.

A loving thrust. A soul explosion. Colors of the rainbow splintered in jewels, in kaleidoscope form. Maeve cried out in joy.

A great peace settled over her. The sun circled her heart. It had been like the first time Charles had made love to her . . . only better. Much better.

Maeve felt the shudder that rocked his body. She heard his soft groan before he eased his body down onto hers and buried his face in her hair.

"Dear God," he said, when at last he lifted his head. "How could I have not had memory of this?"

Charles wasn't as priggish as she'd first thought.

The morning sun blazed through the window; the fire had gone out but the woman in his arms warmed him. And for a moment, he mused upon the eerie sense of *déjà vu*.

His own stamina amazed him. His desire for Maeve astonished him. Instead of being satiated, he craved more. She excited him as no other woman ever had. If possible, she was even more beautiful with her skin aglow with the soft pink flush from making love. He could not run his hands over her silky, opalescent skin enough. He could not tear his gaze from Maeve's dark, dewy eyes that held him mesmerized. He could not live without the lilting laughter that made his heart thump.

He came alive under her spell.

Unable to let Maeve go, Charles made love to her for hours. He thought his heart would burst when she made love to him, tentatively at first, sweetly, and then a little wildly. She indulged him, explored him, cradled him, and when he thought he would burst into flame, Maeve settled herself upon him and brought Charles to a body-shattering, blinding summit he'd never reached before, never known existed. He roared like a jungle cat. His heart thundered. When at last he could catch his breath, he reached up to bring Maeve's sweet lips down on his, to taste once again the delicious peppermint taste of her. When they were too spent to move, she nestled against him and he fell asleep holding his wife.

He'd hated to wake Maeve but had no choice. He nibbled at her ear, enjoying the salty sweet morning taste of her.

Maeve groaned and moved her head.

"It's time to wake up, Little Bit. The sun is shining." He nuzzled her throat for good measure.

She whimpered. Her sweeping dark lashes curled against her cheeks, a slightly giddy smile teased her lips. Lips . . .

Dear God, he could not start again.

"The blizzard is over and there are people in Boston worried about us no doubt," he said in a firmer tone.

She shook her head, wiggling in his arms to face him. "I don't want to go. Please, can't we stay here?"

Charles found it difficult to deny the tousled, charming woman sharing his bed. Maeve's moist, swollen lips invited his and the haze of passion lingering in her eyes beckoned him. "No, we cannot stay," he said, summoning resolve. "Life waits for us in Boston."

"Isn't this life?" she teased.

The luster of her ebony curls as they brushed against her gleaming ivory shoulders just about took his breath away. Charles bent to kiss a lock of her hair.

"This is paradise," he agreed hoarsely.

"All the more reason to stay."

"I wish we could." He could feel his resolve weakening as he bent to kiss one rosy nipple. "I could make love to you all day."

"Oh, do!"

And then the other.

"Ooooh. Do."

Charles lifted his head and braced himself beside his astonishing bride. "Maeve, you are breaking my heart." And tempting him unbearably.

"I want to be your Lhiannon Sidhe."

"What is that?" he asked warily.

"Lhiannon Sidhe is a powerful fairy mistress who seeks the love of mortal men. If a man refuses her, she becomes his slave, if he consents, he becomes hers for all time. The Lhiannon Sidhe creates such desire in her mortal man he will overcome all obstacles just to embrace her."

"I would just as soon not dally with a fairy who enslaves men, Maeve." Lying beside him, Charles could easily envision Maeve as his faerie mistress. Not that he would admit to such fantasies.

"Every woman, mortal or not, yearns to be so loved by a man."

He wasn't surprised. And he wished she didn't believe in fairy tales. Clinging to Irish legends could not be healthy. "From what I have observed, but only in Boston, mind you, such a love is extremely rare."

Plainly, Charles had disappointed her. A flicker of sadness clouded the sprite's eyes. Damn. He didn't mean to do it, felt badly about it. But talk of love, obstacles, and slaves made him nervous. He moved to leave the bed. "I shall get a fire started now and have Hilda bring you your clothes. They should be dry."

One small hand reached out to him. "Were you happy last night? Truly happy?"

"A man could not be any happier than I . . . even now . . . but we still must return to Boston. We'll start immediately after breakfast."

"Could one more day in the country make a difference?"

"Maeve, the publishing firm needs my attention and I must keep after the private investigator I've hired to find Barnabas's sketch of St. Nick."

"I see."

Leaving the warmth and temptation of his bed for the icy room, Charles snatched up his dressing gown draped on a nearby chair. "Besides, I expect you have much to do with Christmas a few weeks away."

"Aye." She nodded her head. "I have a dance lesson with Mr. Raymond."

Glancing down at her, Maeve's small body looked lost and waiflike in a sea of white silk sheets and the thick down quilt. Someone as lovely and delicate as Maeve deserved a man to protect her from the ills and evils of the world.

Charles wondered how he could divorce her. Although she had her saucy moments, they made her more interesting than most women of his acquaintance. But for the most part Maeve was sweet and smart, and she made his body soar without wings. She freed his spirit . . . if only for a time. He felt different this morning. The edgy, restless feeling haunting him of late seemingly had slipped away as he slept.

Maeve made Charles feel alive. There was a new lightness in his step.

If he was not the heir to Rycroft Publishing, Charles might be persuaded to follow his present inclination and remain married to the sprite. But Beatrice insisted on Charles acquiring a thoroughbred wife, just as his father would have. A Rycroft always does the right thing.

To further complicate matters, his cousin Martin's wife was already pregnant. A Rycroft heir would be produced shortly.

For a fleeting moment, Charles wondered if Maeve would settle for being his mistress after being his wife. Divorcing her now after their splendid night at Ashton Pond would be more difficult than before. Instead of dwelling on that dim future, Charles decided to make the most of the time they had left together. He meant to make this the best Christmas Maeve ever had. A holiday to remember for all time. One the Lhiannon Sidhe would approve.

An unexpected pall overtook Charles as he helped Maeve into the sleigh later that morning. Smiling, she waved to Hilda and George before sitting down. George would be bringing the Christmas tree they'd selected to Boston the next day.

Charles tucked the carriage blanket securely around Maeve's lap to ward off the chill. He hadn't planned to bring her to Sycamore Falls. Selfishly, he'd never brought anyone to the country house before. It was his secret harbor, a shelter when life became too stormy. He never expected anyone would appreciate it as much as he did, but Maeve had. And there was something more, more important.

Here at Ashton Pond Charles and Maeve were equals. Alone together it didn't matter where they were born, to whom they were born, or how they were raised. At Ashton Pond, Maeve and Charles existed in one world. Here they were simply a man and woman who took pleasure in each other.

Yes, he had taken a great deal of pleasure in Maeve.

With a snap of the reins, Charles signaled the horses and the sleigh glided forward.

Maeve and Charles arrived back in Boston mid-afternoon. He immediately departed for his office, and Maeve did not miss a step of her dance lesson with Mr. Raymond.

They met again at dinner. To their surprise and Maeve's dismay, they were joined by Beatrice and Stella.

"We canceled our previous plans," Beatrice explained. "Poor Helen fell ill, so the seance was postponed until this evening. I am so pleased you didn't miss it, Maeve."

A motion much like a somersault took hold in Maeve's belly. She forced her reply through a tight smile. "I am pleased as well."

"I am certain that Conrad will have something to say to you."

Maeve's worst fear was confirmed.

"Father must be delighted knowing you wish a word with him, Mother."

Beatrice turned to her son. "Charles, I think perhaps you should not attend the seance. As much as this pains me to say it, dear, you often irritated your father."

"That's true, Mother. My father held neither of us in great esteem."

Mrs. Rycroft reared back, eyes large, hand to throat. "My dear! Your father showed me every respect. He never denied me my slightest desire."

"Of course not. He wished you to be happy and well occupied at all times."

"Beneath his gruff exterior lay a generous heart," Beatrice countered primly.

Maeve just knew she would leave the table with indigestion.

Charles could not resist goading his tradition-bound mother. Although he knew he should rein in his remarks, the short journey to Ashton Pond had invigorated him. He felt a bit devilish.

"The devotion your mother and father shared cannot go unrewarded," Stella offered in a placating manner. Her pointy-nosed dog snarled at Charles.

He suppressed the urge to snarl back, turning his attention to Stella.

The pale houseguest had rouged her lips to a bright crimson, apparently to match her dress. The daring, low-cut neckline did not claim Charles's attention as much as her lips. They stood out, bowed and pouty in fishlike fashion.

On the other hand, he could barely keep his eyes off Maeve. Dressed in another of Ilona Potts's confections of deep blue velvet and lace, she looked delicious. With only a slight effort and long reach, he could pull the pearl combs from her hair and watch the magnificent midnight tumble.

"Conrad will give me a sign tonight," Beatrice declared. She was relentless.

"Perhaps he'll be home for Christmas," Charles replied in droll tones.

"To mock your own mother is unforgivable. I must attribute it to the influence of that woman!"

"What woman?" he demanded, feeling an unusual and swift burst of anger. To have his mother insult the only person in the room who had given him an ounce of happiness irritated Charles immensely. "The woman seated opposite you? Maeve O'Malley? That woman?"

His mother appeared momentarily paralyzed. She paled.

Maeve's cheeks burned, but she did not cry or flee the room. She lifted her chin in a most regal manner. "I would be so pleased, Mrs. Rycroft, if you did not speak of me as if I were not present."

"Indeed." The blood began to flow through his mother's veins again as she recovered herself with a stilted apology. "Forgive me. I can only blame my son for my lack of manners. His behavior of late puzzles me. I do not know what has overcome him since I last visited Boston."

"Charles is a good man," Maeve said. "You are to be praised for raising a fine, intelligent, honest son."

Smiling prettily, Stella hastily added, "I must agree with Maeve."

Beatrice looked utterly confused. The lines in her forehead doubled in depth. One hand fluttered over her heart. "Yes, quite. But I cannot approve of last evening's episode. If word gets out, such an escapade will ruin Maeve. Imagine! Spending the night at Ashton Pond, just the two of you without a chaperone."

"But Charles is my husband."

"Had you forgotten, Mother?" Charles asked with a quirk of his lips.

His pride in how Maeve was handling this difficult encounter knew no bounds.

"Oh, dear. You haven't done—" Beatrice stopped mid-sentence, her cheeks and neck flushed.

Charles arched an eyebrow. "Mother."

"No one . . . no one knows you are married."

"And no one knows we were snowbound at Ashton Pond. No one but you and Stella."

And Stella appeared quite appalled. Her dog bared his teeth.

"Is our secret safe?"

"Your father won't like this at all."

"Then don't tell him." Charles pushed back his chair.

"Where are you going?" Beatrice asked with alarm. "Helen isn't scheduled to arrive for another thirty minutes or so. I thought we might adjourn to the parlor and discuss . . . the future."

"Please convey my good wishes to both Helen and Father," he said, crossing with two purposeful strides to his Irish bride. "But Maeve has a terrible headache and I have an important manuscript to read."

Maeve's eyes widened in surprise, but she did not object.

"I'll help you to your room." Placing his hand in the small of her back he guided her to the hall. Once they were out of earshot, he whispered, "I'll come to you tonight as soon as the house is asleep."

Chapter Twelve

The flickering mass of candles cast a fanciful dancing light tripping across the cabbage rose wall covering. A warming fire crackled and burned in the fireplace.

Maeve donned one of her beautiful new silk and lace negligees. The pale blue fabric was like the shifting shade of a late summer sky. It's silky softness caressed her flesh, making her feel like a *femme fatale*.

But where was Charles?

To put an end to her fidgeting, Maeve sat down at the rosewood dressing table and brushed her hair to a coal-black sheen. She hummed as she brushed, a Christmas carol she especially liked, one she found comforting in both melody and lyric—"God Rest Ye Merry Gentlemen." Sometimes she hummed it slowly and sometimes she gave the carol a more spirited rendition.

Tonight humming did not help to soothe her nervousness. With each moment that passed, Maeve's excitement and anticipation doubled. She sprinkled violet water behind her ears, at her pulse points . . . and beneath her breasts. And waited.

She checked her appearance in the mirror. And waited.

Charles promised to come to Maeve's rooms after everyone was asleep. Inherent in his promise was the thrill of being in his arms before the clock struck midnight. Charles wanted her! He might even be falling in love with her. Maeve's heart beat a feathery tattoo. Expectation bubbled up within her like a warm, foamy surf. She could barely contain herself, was completely unaware as the volume of her humming increased.

If Charles did not care for her, he would not have saved her from attending the seance, a sentence just short of death. Further, if he had no feelings for Maeve, why would he risk his mother's wrath by sneaking to her rooms?

Winning Charles's heart meant everything to Maeve. With the support of his love, she could brave whatever insults came her way from a society which frowned on their marriage. Every lesson she took, every rule of etiquette she learned, every move Maeve made, was directed to becoming a part of her husband's world. Ultimately, she sought to become accepted by Boston society.

Maeve lived for the day when she would hear Charles say I love you.

Tonight, a fire of hope burned brightly within her, along with another, smoldering fire. 'Twas the heated passion Charles stirred and drew from the very depths of her being.

Since she had heard Stella's door close nearly an hour ago. Maeve felt safe in opening hers a crack, leaving it ajar for Charles in welcoming invitation. She wondered how his afternoon had passed, if he thought of her as much as she thought of him.

Maeve could hardly wait to stroke her fingertips through the crisp dark curls of his chest and feel the steady, strong beat of his heart. She craved the taste of him, the pressure of his lips on hers. She yearned to dive into the enveloping warmth of his smoky gray gaze. A rocking shudder swept Maeve's body. The humming stopped. Gasping for breath, she bolted up from the dressing table.

A sound in the corridor sent Maeve rushing to the opening of her door. She peered through. Across the hall, Stella's door opened. Holding a fully lit, blazing candelabra high above her head, the New York widow stepped out into the corridor. Close behind, yapping ferociously at her heels, Stella's wee imitation of a dog jumped up and down like a marionette on a string. Not much bigger than a rat, Stella's pet could not defend her mistress from a tomcat.

Maeve regarded the pale woman with growing irritation. Why wasn't she asleep? Although she hated to admit it, Stella looked quite lovely. Her blond hair tumbled beyond her shoulders in thick sausage curls. Locks gone astray fell clear to her cleavage and brushed against her soft green satin dressing gown. A gown trimmed with feathers. Feathers enough to cover three grown peacocks edged the collar, cuff, and hem of Stella's gown.

Stella's large doe eyes widened. "Charles, is it you?"

"Ah, yes. Yes, it is I, Stella."

Maeve watched through the crack as Charles sauntered toward Stella. Elegantly dressed in a burgundy-and-gold dressing grown, he carried a wooden bowl filled with grapes. He must have dropped the bowl. Where had he found grapes? And what did he intend to do with them? Maeve's heart raced faster than hummingbird wings.

"May I ask what you are doing on the guest floor?" Stella asked in a soft, singsong tone. Before he could answer, she gasped as if the answer quite suddenly had come to her. She wrinkled her nose. "You came to see me, did you not? We haven't had the opportunity to speak alone, to be alone, for that matter."

And if Maeve had her way there would never be any such opportunity for the merry widow.

"No, we haven't," Charles agreed. "We must make time to do that."

"I have time now." Stella stepped back and gestured to her open door. Babe, the vicious Pomeranian, barked nonstop.

"My wife has her rooms on this floor as well."

"If she were truly your wife, she would share your chamber, Charles. Why keep up this pretense with me?"

Maeve's heart palpitated wildly, furiously. Stella was attempting to seduce her husband! The cream of New York society knew Charles was a married man! How could she offer such a wicked invitation to a man whose wife's door lay only a few yards away?

Charles hedged. He sounded uncomfortable, as if something large and bitter lodged in his throat. "Well, actually, I, ah, came to make sure Maeve had gotten over her headache."

Maeve breathed easier as Charles gently rejected the merry widow's proposition. Her husband owned an honest heart. He possessed a full measure of integrity, unlike Stella, who Maeve suspected of being spawned by Satan.

"I'm certain Maeve sleeps," Stella told him, *sotto voce.* "I've not heard a sound from her rooms since I retired. She'll never know if you pay me a visit."

"She will. She's . . . she's Irish, you know," he offered in a hapless explanation.

Indeed she was Irish! And Maeve's Irish temper presently teetered on the brink of an all-out explosion. In a grave effort to suppress her rage, she gritted her teeth and agitatedly fanned herself with an open hand. It did no good; angry thoughts spun in Maeve's head as her temperature rose.

Stella did not mean to give up. "She's Irish and I . . . I am . . . starved."

"I beg your pardon?" Charles dipped his head as if he hadn't heard correctly.

Maeve apparently wasn't the only one who did not understand Stella's hunger. She'd witnessed the woman enjoying a full dinner just hours ago.

Lowering her eyes and purring like a feline in heat, Stella took the role of coquette to greater heights. "I'm a widow, starved for affection," she explained in a husky voice. "If you would come to my rooms for just a short time, I would appreciate your kindness, Charles. And I would be certain you left a happy, satisfied man."

Saints above! Maeve's heart slammed against her chest. The nerve of the woman! Stella was no better than the dreaded vampire faerie. Once a vampire faerie attached herself to a mortal man, the unfortunate male could not bear to be touched by another woman.

Maeve could barely restrain herself from leaping out into the hall and pulling Charles to the safety of her room.

Charles's dark brows gathered in a deep frown at the bridge of his nose. "You flatter me, Stella. But you forget I'm a married man."

"Why do you keep up the sham? All who live beneath this roof know that your marriage was an unfortunate accident. You were a victim of circumstance. Do you believe your mother will allow such an unsuitable match to last much longer? Come into my rooms and see what is in store for you at the end of your so-called marriage."

The end of his so-called marriage? Incensed beyond the risk of revealing herself as an eavesdropper, Maeve called out as sweetly as possible—under the circumstances. "Charles? Is that you?"

"Ah, Maeve is awake," Charles remarked quite cheerfully. To Maeve's great satisfaction, he sounded relieved to be rescued from the claws of the female predator.

"Yes," Stella sighed.

He thrust the bowl of grapes into Stella's free hand. "And may be . . . in pain."

Maeve was definitely awake and quite definitely in pain. With hands on hips and toes tapping, she waited.

Her mortified husband backed away from Stella toward her door. "If you'll excuse me . . . ah . . . thank you again for your . . . kind offer."

Charles burst through the door, slammed it shut, and pulled Maeve into his arms. He brought his mouth down on hers with a fierceness he could barely control. But the sweetness and softness of her comforted him, calmed him. His bruising kiss dissolved into a tender meeting of lovers' lips.

His body ached for her, had been aching for her since this morning when he left the bed they'd shared at Ashton Pond. And there had never been a day so long as this one.

Throughout the day Charles's thoughts returned again and again to Maeve. While engaged in yet another argument with Martin, he pictured Maeve's blond instructor holding her, whirling her round in a romantic waltz. While he sought to put his own mark upon the company his father had built, another man danced with his wife. She had passed the day without Charles . . . doing what? Had the hours passed pleasantly or in turmoil? His mind seemed never without a thought of her.

But now Maeve was in his arms and all felt right with the world.

His heart hammered with the force of a runaway locomotive. Even when Charles raised his lips from Maeve's, his heart continued to fly on wings of its own. He looked down into her eyes. The sparkling light had died. Their lovely blue color had darkened to a purple hue. A small, worried frown wrinkled her porcelain brow.

"What is it?" he asked, more disturbed by her apparent distress than he cared to be.

"Your mother. What do you suppose your mother plans to do about our marriage?"

He shook his head. "What can she do? My marriage is none of her concern." Tamping down an uneasy feeling in his gut, Charles guided Maeve toward the bed. "It's not something I wish to think about at the moment."

Maeve teased her lip. "Beatrice feels that you deserve a . . . a better wife. I know she does."

"Who could be better than you?"

"Please be serious."

To Charles's great consternation, Maeve's eyes misted. "Should I allow my mother to direct my life?" he asked.

"Like your father attempted to do?"

Dear God. Did this little bit miss nothing? Her bluntness chafed.

Charles rubbed his forehead, looking over her shoulder as Maeve blinked back her tears. Her bed lay in his direct line of sight. The covers had been turned down in invitation.

This was no time to be discussing marriage or his mother. It was definitely not what he came to do. Gathering Maeve into his arms, Charles spoke softly into her ear. "Mother will do nothing until after the holiday season."

"And after, what can she do?"

"We shall worry about that later." Grinning, he tweaked Maeve's nose, attempting to shift the atmosphere from leaden to light. And take her mind off of what mattered not at the present. "At the moment I am bent on taking you to bed and ending your suffering."

"Suffering?" Maeve stepped out of his arms.

"Needless worry is a form of suffering."

" 'Tis not needless worry. Stella wants you," Maeve said with what appeared to be a pout.

"But *I* do not want Stella," Charles assured her. What use had he for a pale matron of polite society when he had the colorful Maeve within his arms?

She smiled then. A sliver of light crept into the dark blue of her eyes. "How do you intend to end my suffering?"

"By making love to you until dawn."

"What if Stella is counting the minutes you pass with me?"

"Then let us hope for her sake that counting minutes is like counting sheep, and she will soon find herself fast asleep."

With a light peal of laughter that sent tingling waves of warmth skittering through him, Maeve led Charles to her bed. Gone was the red flannel nightshirt and in its place a blue gown that hinted of every alluring curve beneath its silky folds. The near-transparent fabric softly draped against Maeve's full, firm breasts and generous hips. With each move she made, his excitement grew. His body heat intensified.

Charles drew an unsteady breath.

Maeve came to a stop beside the bed and turned to him. With a secretive smile on her lips and a mischievous glint in her eyes, she pulled the sash of his dressing gown.

He'd never seen a woman's eyes reflect the undisguised pleasure he saw in Maeve's as her gaze drifted from his eyes, to his chest, to the hard evidence of his manhood. Charles's heart felt afire, his body aflame with desire. It was all he could do to stand still.

"You are a feast to a woman's eyes, my love. My Charles."

Dear God, she had no shame! He loved it!

Maeve's murmured statement sent Charles's body into turmoil. His heart drummed. The aching heat in his loins nearly doubled him over. The bottom dropped from the pit of his stomach and his pulse pounded like a madman's.

He crushed Maeve against him. Her breasts, soft and pliant, pressed against his chest, creating rippling tremors of fire. She circled her arms around his neck, grinding her hips against him. In a blurry haze of passion, Charles fell to the bed with Maeve. He tasted her, relishing the delicious, tart peppermint flavor of her. Driven by a fever he couldn't control, Charles devoured the rosy buds of Maeve's breasts as she held him, stroked him, cradled him. All thoughts of languid lovemaking were lost to a frenzy of desire. He could no more stop the passion that fired him than leap to the moon. And when Charles buried himself inside Maeve's deep, moist warmth, he spilled his seed and cried her name.

He was a new man.

"Charles," Maeve whispered minutes later. "What were the grapes for?"

The following evening, not long after dark, five sleighs filled with holly, jangling with a cacophony of bells and piled with young, laughing, and singing bodies, carried Spencer Wellington's party from his Beacon Hill home to the ice-covered pond in the Common.

During the brief sleigh ride, Maeve had joined in the chorus of hearty voices singing "The Holly and the Ivy." Due to the crowded conditions of the sleigh, Maeve was forced to sit halfway upon her husband's lap, an inconvenience she found delightful.

Although it was a cold night, there was no wind nor falling snow. The area around the pond was well lit with gaslights, their bases wound with fresh holly and tied beneath the light with big, red bows. Even the benches scattered round the pond were decorated with crimson bows. Wellington's servants stood by with jugs of hot cocoa and eggnog.

Minutes after they arrived, Maeve sat on a bench as Charles knelt before her, tying the new skates he'd purchased especially for her.

She leaned forward, close to him. "I think I should just like to watch for awhile," she said in a hushed, confidential tone.

"You cannot learn by watching, Maeve." He stood up, towering over her, and held out his hand.

Charles towered over most of Spencer's guests. But

it was not only his height that made him so compelling; his patrician features, so finely hewn, were a riveting factor. His broad, solid frame appeared even more striking in his long, fur-lined coat. Early on, he'd discarded his hat. His hair, thick and dark, gleamed beneath the flickering light. The tips of his ears were red, and his dazzling smile as white as fresh snow.

Maeve would do anything for Charles—she would even attempt to skate. She took his hand.

Charles pulled her up to his side and wrapped a supportive arm about her waist. Her ankles wobbled. Her heart sank.

"Easy now," Charles cautioned. "We're going to skate onto the ice now. It will feel different, but I'll be holding onto you until you gain speed."

"Speed?" *Saints above!*

In the center of the ice Stella, dressed in her navy coat and ermine muff, twirled once and began to skate backward. The show-off! Maeve wouldn't be standing if it weren't for Charles's arm around her. The solid strength of him gave her courage. And she needed courage for this unnatural act.

"Speed gives us balance," Charles told her. "You'll see."

Determined to master the sport for Charles's sake, Maeve was hampered by ankles that kept buckling inward. All around her, his friends skated with ease. Young men and women glided by, hand in hand. Some of the fellows raced and all obviously were enjoying themselves—but Maeve.

She had to skate. She had to fit into this group of Charles's friends. A knot formed in the base of her belly. What was she thinking? How could she ever be accepted by the cream of Boston society?

Charles had maneuvered them to a rather frightening speed but surprisingly, Maeve felt stronger on her feet, more secure on two thin blades than she ever imagined. The sting of the cold nipped at her face, an exhilarating sensation that made her laugh. Or maybe she was laughing because she was skating. Charles released her with a gentle push and she skated solo. Triumphant! Straight ankles and on her feet.

Maeve raised her arms and screamed in delight.

Boom. And then, somehow she was on her bottom, sliding across the pond.

Charles skated to her side and helped her up, encouraging her with his great, hypnotic grin and rallying words. "You've got the idea!"

She fell three times more.

Charles showed no sympathy, only laughing and coaxing her to try once more. "This is the way everyone learns to skate, Little Bit."

Her husband's support strengthened Maeve's determination. He never strayed from her side . . . and she loved hearing his laughter. Each day it seemed Charles laughed more often, more easily. Each day she loved him more.

After an hour of spills and shaky starts, Maeve finally skated on her own. Many of those who'd watched her final victory glided up to congratulate her. She accepted their smiles and friendly words as genuine. But as soon as Charles went off to race with Spencer, she collapsed on the nearest bench.

Pansy, a longtime member of the young society crowd, had come to the party as well. She brought a steaming mug of hot cocoa to Maeve and sat down on the cold bench beside her.

"You're a fast learner, Maeve. It took me weeks to learn how to skate."

"I don't believe you. More likely you mastered the skill in little more than a minute."

Pansy laughed. Dressed warmly in a nut-brown coat and matching hat, she looked different somehow. Her eyes shone brighter, her cheeks glowed and her tight, rusty-red curls brushed against her coat in splendid contrast. "All right. It was less than weeks and more than a minute."

Maeve grinned. She was so grateful for Pansy's friendship. Pansy Deakins might have strange ideas, but she had accepted Maeve as an equal even when Maeve had served as her maid. If it were not for her hazel-eyed friend, who would have spoken with her at Beatrice's party or sat with her tonight?

"I fear it will take me weeks before I feel comfortable," Maeve sighed.

"Well, you certainly earned the respect of this group tonight."

"Do you think so?"

"I know so. It takes courage to learn to skate before twenty or more people."

Maeve basked in the ray of hope Pansy had just offered as her friend sipped at her cocoa.

"Maeve, have you seen your brother recently?" she asked after a moment of silence.

Maeve's gaze was on Charles, skating in sure, swift strides around the pond with his friend. "No, but I will have to chase after him soon."

"Do you think he has the information you need?"

"If anyone can discover who attacked Charles, it will be Shea. I have more confidence in him than in the private investigator Charles has hired."

"Shea is intelligent?"

"Of course. He's an O'Malley," Maeve teased. But then, seeing the dreamy look in her friend's eyes, she became serious quickly. "Don't be getting any ideas about Shea," she warned. "You're a friend of mine and I shall be frank with you. My brother has a roving eye."

"Perhaps because he has not found the right woman."

"Perhaps, but you know your parents would not approve of a man like Shea. They expect you to marry a man like Spencer Wellington."

"I have known Spencer Wellington all of my life."
Pansy made the remark as if their long acquaintance
alone made Spencer ineligible as a mate.

"Please, Pansy, do not spend time thinking about
Shea. It can come to naught. And if your mother even
suspects that you're mooning over an Irish boxer, she'll
send you clear out of the state."

"I want to see him box."

"What?" The thought horrified Maeve.

"I have been a good friend to you, Maeve. Please
arrange this one thing for me. If you do, I shall never ask
another favor and I shall never ask about Shea again."

Maeve's misgivings weighed like a boulder tied to her
heart. If she were thrown in the ocean at the moment,
Maeve would sink like a brick. But how could she refuse
the first time Pansy ever had asked anything of her?

"We shall see Shea box together," she agreed quietly.

"Oh. Oh."

"What?"

"Stella is headed our way."

Maeve's evening was rapidly falling apart. She had
managed to avoid Stella by remaining in her rooms
most of the day, busy with her lessons and finishing the
knitting of Shea's Christmas sweater.

Stifling an inward groan, she greeted Stella with a
smile and a kindness. "You are an accomplished skater.
I admire your skill."

"Thank you, Maeve. Hello, Pansy."

Pansy said nothing in reply, only inclining her head
as if she were waiting for a shoe to fall.

And it did.

"I should like to have a woman-to-woman chat with
you at your earliest convenience, Maeve."

Stella's wooden smile did not distract from the bright,
cold gleam in her eyes.

Maeve suppressed the urge to run.

* * *

The man who preferred to think of himself as Samson prepared to leave for the night. He was deep in thought when he heard the soft rap and then the jingle of the bell as the door opened. He hurried from his back office to find his accomplice.

The big man's patched jacket appeared to be two sizes too small. The dirt-brown wool stretched across his wide frame and the sleeves fell inches short of his thick wrists. He held a knit cap in his hands.

"What are you doing here, O'Brien? I warned you never to come here again."

The oafish man nervously shifted his weight from foot to foot. "Had to."

"No. You could have sent a message and I would have met you in the Common as we agreed. Or don't you recall?" He was as impatient with himself as with the boxer. He should have known better than to hire a man who'd had his brain knocked about. Bill "Spit" O'Brien.

"This couldn't wait."

Hope leaped in his heart. "Has Charles Rycroft met with an accident?"

The big man shook his head. "No. Ah'm needin' more money."

Samson slapped the heel of his hand against his forehead. "You fool."

"I never did in a man before ... on purpose," O'Brien said.

Speechless, he could only stare at the only human link to his crime. How had he, a respected businessman, been reduced to keeping such company? What began as a simple plan several weeks ago had taken on unforeseen complications. Now he felt as if he lived in another man's body, and that body was quickly being pulled under by a sucking quagmire of quicksand.

A shudder ripped through him and he shook the black thoughts away. If he could keep his head up for a few more weeks, he would be out of the country and all of this unpleasantness would be behind him. Everything would be fine.

Stroking the waxed end of his mustache, he narrowed his eyes on the nervous hulk standing before him like a misbehaved child. "What do you want?"

"Ten dollars."

"Ten dollars," he repeated. Throwing his shoulders back, he tugged at his waistcoat. Unwilling to show his relief, he scowled. O'Brien could have demanded more and he would have had no choice but to pay. "Five."

"No, ten."

"Agreed then," he said with a huff of annoyance. "But it's the last money you will see from me. Do not think to blackmail me."

The big fellow nodded. "It's a big job."

"What did you have in mind for Rycroft?"

"A runaway sleigh."

This time it was he who nodded. "It happens. It's common. A man can't be too careful with all of the snow and ice we've been having. Do the job and report to me directly with your . . . success. I emphasize *success*. I shall walk in the public gardens every afternoon before tea."

"Aye."

"But I warn you, stay away from my place of business. Do not come here again."

"Aye."

He watched O'Brien lumber out the door and into the cold. After locking the door, he returned to the back office. The big lout revolted him, irritated him. Stroking his mustache, he deplored the state of the work force. It was impossible to find good help anymore.

But he could hardly scuffle with Charles Rycroft himself, could he?

He hadn't the stomach for it.

Chapter Thirteen

"That was a close call, Cousin."

Charles was shaken but not hurt as he walked through the doors of Rycroft Publishing with Martin the following morning. If it hadn't been for Martin, the runaway coach, which veered off the street and toward the Rycroft building, most certainly would have hit him.

After leaving his coach, Charles had sauntered across the street with his head in the clouds. Martin, who had been briskly approaching the Rycroft Building from the opposite direction, saw the coach bearing down on Charles and rushed to shove him aside.

Apart from some bruises and dirt, neither of the men emerged the worse for wear. Although Martin's favorite felt bowler was blown away.

"You might have saved my life this morning," Charles said as he led the way into his office.

Downplaying his heroics, Martin undertook a rather pompous preening, straightening the bow of his narrow tie. "Of course I saved your life. Who would I argue with if you were gone?"

"Rycroft Publishing would be yours," Charles said

flatly, falling into the leather chair behind his immense mahogany desk.

"I have no desire to run the business by myself, Charles."

"But you have been campaigning relentlessly for a monthly magazine."

"A different matter entirely." Martin finger-combed his hair and smoothed his beard and side whiskers as he spoke. "Rycroft Publishing must expand beyond books, and I see a monthly magazine as a viable, profitable way. You know very well that several of our competitors have already launched monthlies."

Charles knew. He also knew Rycroft profits had diminished over the past year. The idea of taking funds from the slim profit margin to invest in a risky venture had put him off from the first. His father never would have taken such a risk.

Steepling his fingers, Charles studied his tall, heavyset cousin, who now brushed unseen lint from his tweed jacket. "If you undertook such a major project, Martin, you would certainly be entitled to a substantial increase in salary."

Martin raised both bushy eyebrows. "A substantial increase would be welcome. With a new home and a baby on the way, I find myself forced to practice a . . . certain frugality for the first time in my life."

"Quite understandable." Charles leaned back in his chair, folding one long leg across the other. If Martin had been behind the theft of his St. Nick sketch, his cousin would not be experiencing financial difficulties.

And if the big man really wished to take over Rycroft Publishing, he would not have saved Charles moments ago from what easily might have been a fatal accident. While Martin often drove Charles to distraction with his overbearing ways, he was not a criminal.

Charles had to ask himself why he had been resisting launching a monthly magazine. Because the venture had been Martin's idea? Or was it because after years of his father insisting Charles had neither the creative nor business head to lead Rycroft Publishing into a new era, he had to prove his father wrong by succeeding alone? Charles had committed himself to single-handed success even if it meant he had no life other than publishing. He was leading his father's life.

He still allowed his father to influence him . . . a man who had been dead for three years. Maeve was right. As all thoughts eventually did of late, his thoughts had led to Maeve.

If Martin were given more responsibility in the business, Charles would have time for other things. He and Maeve could spend time at Ashton Pond. He and Maeve would have more time together—until the day came when they would go their separate ways.

Soon it would be Christmas and the New Year. Charles had promised his mother he would provide Maeve with a generous settlement and quietly set her free after the first of the year. He found it interesting that Beatrice would rather brave the scandal of divorce than see Charles married to a woman she considered beneath him.

"Charles?"

Charles started. Absorbed in his thoughts, he had forgotten Martin.

From across the desk, his cousin engaged in a frowning examination of him, apparently searching for head or facial bumps. "When I knocked you down, did your head hit the ground?"

"No, Martin. No, I'm fine. Just thinking. As you know, I don't come to decisions easily. It's not in my nature to be impulsive." He smiled then, knowing that in the last several days he had acted impulsively a number of times.

Martin's eyes fastened on the half-empty inkwell sitting on Charles's desk. "As much as I am loath to admit it, Rycroft Publishing has done well under your . . . thoughtful . . . direction," he said.

Amused at his cousin's attempt at diplomacy, Charles chuckled. He stood up. "At the first of the new year I would like you to begin the planning and production of a Rycroft monthly publication."

Martin's gaze shot up to Charles, even as his brow deepened into a dark, skeptical frown. He pulled at his ear as if his hearing may have deceived him. "Do you mean it?"

Charles arched a brow. "Do I ever jest about the business?"

"Never."

"Congratulations, Martin," he said, extending his hand to his cousin.

Martin vigorously pumped Charles's hand. "I'll make you proud."

How many times had Charles said that same thing to his father? How many times had his father laughed in response? Innumerable.

"I know you will, Martin. We'll set up regular weekly meetings. I'll expect to be informed every step of the way." With his hand on Martin's shoulder, Charles walked him to the door.

"You will know every move I make, Charles. And I, ah, I might get started before the new year."

Laughing, Charles closed the door after his cousin. They might have just shared their finest moment together.

But from that point on, Martin popped into his office on an hourly basis. Apparently, ideas for a monthly had been stewing for months in Martin's brain and his cousin meant to share all of them in one day.

Charles did not even look up when his door opened for what must have been the thirteenth time. Until he heard the swish of silk and the delicate sigh.

"Mother!" Charles jumped to his feet. "What are you doing here?"

She gave him a withering look.

"Have a seat." He rushed to hold a chair for Beatrice.

Swathed in yards of mink, his mother's tall, thin frame appeared especially fragile. She wore a tall, boxy mink hat and carried a mink muff the size of Rhode Island. His mother looked as if she'd been swallowed by a mammoth mink.

She perched primly on the edge of the chair. "Thank you, dear."

Her exceedingly formal demeanor told Charles he was in trouble. "You've taken me by surprise, Mother. To what do I owe this honor?"

"I so seldom see you at home," she said, giving a limp flick of her wrist. "After coming all this way to spend the holiday season with you, I find you are rarely available to me . . . and our guest."

"It has been unusually busy at the firm."

"You do not appear busy, all alone in this great big office."

"I'm figuring the Christmas bonus for our employees . . . which does not require a great deal of physical activity," he said, retreating behind his desk.

Her charcoal eyes met his in cold accusation. "Your father spent a great deal of time here, too."

Charles could not deny it. His father had spent most of his waking hours at the publishing house, albeit for different reasons. "Speaking of Father, how did your meeting go with him the other night?"

"He did not appear."

"No!"

"But he did appear to Helen Foster and told her quite clearly that I should follow my own desires."

"Do you have proof Father appeared to your medium?"

"Of course." Beatrice pressed a hand over her heart. "I saw the drapes move. And both Stella and I felt the table shake."

"Definite signs."

But his caustic comment was lost on his mother as she warmed to her tale. "Conrad asked Helen to convey his message to me. Your father wanted me to know that he always considered me an intelligent woman." A tear sprung to her eye and she fished in her muff for a handkerchief.

"Father said all that, did he?"

"What's more, he conveyed his regrets that he had rather ignored me during his lifetime." Beatrice dabbed at her eyes with the lacy cloth.

It was all Charles could do to suppress his laughter. "So, Father came to all this understanding in the afterlife, did he?"

"Apparently Conrad is happy in the spirit world."

"Good. Did he give any other messages to Helen?"

"No." His mother sighed and tucked her hanky away. "Although he did tell Helen that I should not feel guilty for any untoward remark I might have made to him . . . or about him, just before he passed away."

"Then all is forgiven. You must feel much better."

"Oh yes, I do, dear. But your father requested that I allow him to rest in peace. So I shall no longer be attempting to reach him in the spirit world."

"Just as well, Mother."

"But now my mama is to make contact with me through Helen."

"Apparently Helen is well connected in the spirit world."

"I daresay! And all she asks in return is a small donation for her efforts."

In an effort to suppress his frustration, Charles closed his eyes. "Mother, the dead do not return."

Beatrice raised her head in a most regal manner. "I did not come here to discuss the spiritual world with you," she replied in a clipped, frosty tone. "You brought it up."

"So I did." He opened his eyes. "What is it you wish to speak to me about?"

"That woman."

She could only mean one. "Maeve?"

His mother launched into her scold mode. "You are spending entirely too much time with a woman you shall discard soon, and not near enough time with Stella."

"In your opinion."

"And my opinion should be important to you," she snapped, and then sat back in her chair, regaining her composure. "Stella feels slighted. When I tore her away from family and friends in New York, I promised to see that she enjoyed a festive holiday."

"I believe Stella has been included in all of our holiday activities."

"Not in the manner I had anticipated. Charles, I expect you to perform as Stella's escort at the Cabots' Snow Ball."

"Mother, I shall do my best, but dividing my attention between two women is not always easy."

"That is what concerns me. You have yet to divide your attention equally. You hardly converse with Stella—your eye is always on the Irish maid."

"Maeve interests me."

"She is only a novelty. A novelty you will soon weary of and be sending on her way. And then what?"

"And then I shall concentrate on business. While I appreciate your efforts to find me a bride, Mother, I am not attracted to Stella."

Giving a small, shrill hoot, Beatrice bounced in her chair. "I was not attracted to your dear departed father, either, and yet we had a long marriage."

"Duration is not what I seek."

With a glare that would freeze the sun, Beatrice rose. "I expect to see the last of Maeve O'Malley come the new year. If I don't, I will feel compelled to take matters into my own hands."

"Don't fret, Mother. I will take care of Maeve."

"See that you do." Beatrice sailed to the door and stopped. She glanced back over her shoulder at Charles. "I've arranged for a small group of family and close friends to join us tomorrow evening for a light supper and the trimming of our Christmas tree. I expect you to be there, Charles."

"I believe I'm free."

"And I expect you to be attentive to Stella. Remember, *she's* one of us."

The following afternoon Maeve arrived at Rycroft Publishing on a mission. She carried a large package and hummed a new tune. The fact that Charles came to her rooms every night and made love to her with great enthusiasm encouraged Maeve to believe he would help her.

She pleaded and cajoled, smiled and batted her lashes in mock flirtation until finally Charles agreed to leave the building wearing the outfit she'd brought for him.

A hush fell over the first floor offices of Rycroft Publishing as Charles's employees stared in dumfounded disbelief.

"I've never played Santa Claus before," he grumbled beneath his breath.

" 'Tis a shame," Maeve said cheerily. "You look splendid in your Santa suit."

"I don't look splendid. The pillows feel awkward and the beard itches."

"Bah humbug!" she laughed.

"How did you talk me into this?" he demanded as he helped her into the coach.

"You're doing it for the children," she said, settling back on the bench opposite him. "Santa Claus has never paid a visit to the Essex Orphanage before."

Charles plopped down across from Maeve. "What must I do again?"

"You will wish every child a Merry Christmas, give them a toy from the sack I have brought . . . and try to be jolly."

"Jolly?"

"Laugh if you can." She demonstrated for him. "Ho ho ho."

"Where have the toys come from that I shall be distributing?"

"You."

"Me?"

"The funds you gave me for Christmas shopping enabled me to buy many wonderful toys. You'll find dolls and toy trains in your bag along with tops and wagons—"

"You bought toys for orphans?"

"Yes. Thanks to your generosity."

"Did you not purchase anything for yourself?"

"Well, yes. I bought a lovely warm jacket for my dad and a lovely fringed parasol for Pansy. Too much sun darkens her freckles, you know."

Charles leaned forward as much as his newly acquired girth would allow. "I repeat, did you not purchase anything for yourself?"

"Christmas is about giving, Charles."

"I know, but—"

"You'll see how wonderful you feel when you give out the toys."

Maeve felt as if she would burst with excitement. She could hardly wait to see the expressions on the children's faces. No matter how embarrassed Charles might feel about his appearance, she knew he would be warmed by the experience as well.

As they pulled up to the orphanage, Maeve squeezed into the space beside Charles and plumped the pillows beneath his red velvet jacket. "I wonder if I could give Santa Claus a kiss?"

"If you don't, Santa isn't getting out of the coach."

Maeve raised her lips to his. A gentle buss became a fierce, warming kiss. Charles ground his mouth against hers, sending sparks shooting though Maeve's every limb. She moaned softly.

"Have you ever made love in a coach?" Charles whispered.

"Never. But I should enjoy the challenge," Maeve replied breathlessly. "At another time."

When his driver opened the door, Maeve swallowed hard and did her best to collect herself. Slanting Charles what she hoped was a dazzling smile, she took his hand and led him into the Essex Orphanage.

The children waited in the hall where they took their meals. Immediately as Maeve and Charles entered the large, unadorned room, Elsie Dunn led the children in singing "We Wish You a Merry Christmas." Pansy played the brand-new piano she'd donated.

Charles stopped in his tracks.

Pansy grinned.

Maeve squeezed his hand. "The children won't bite. On the contrary, they are oh, so happy to see you."

In the two days since the skating party, Maeve had been busy preparing for this party. Much to her dad's delight, she'd baked dozens of gingerbread and sugar cookies in her old flat—leaving him and Shea a good supply. This morning she had come early to the orphanage with Shea to build a small platform for Santa's rocking chair and sack.

Charles followed Maeve to the chair, smiling and waving to the children. He sat down a bit tenuously.

"They love you. You're doing fine," Maeve assured him in a whisper, before sitting on the floor beside her reluctant Santa Claus. She spread her lavender silk skirts about her. Wearing one of her favorite new dresses, trimmed with wide strips of ruching and fringe about the overskirt and bustle, she felt almost as if they were posing for an artist who drew Christmas cards.

Stuart stood behind her, sporting a silly grin. Together they would help Charles distribute the toys to the children while Pansy continued to play Christmas carols and songs. When Pansy first discovered Maeve's work at the orphanage, she'd insisted on helping, too.

In just a matter of minutes the boys and girls, ranging from four to twelve years of age, approached. Some advanced shyly, and others grinned and giggled as they stood before Santa. All eyes sparkled with joy.

Charles quickly fell into the spirit of the occasion as Maeve had felt certain he would. The delighted smiles of the children proved contagious. Soon everyone was smiling and laughing. Maeve's heart swelled with love, a love that spilled through her, warming her thoroughly.

When they finished, and every toy had been given out, the hall rang with music and the excited laughter of the children.

Maeve looked up at Charles to find him regarding her with a gaze that made her heart stop. It almost looked like love shining in his eyes. For her. Just for her.

"Did you have a good time?" she asked, knowing the answer.

"I have never enjoyed myself more."

Charles learned that afternoon that the little Irish maid, Maeve O'Malley, was a far better person than he. What had he done for anyone other than himself lately?

His father, his brother, his mother—none of his immediate family had set a generous example. Father donated to the church, but that was to salve his conscience and bring good will, Charles suspected.

Elsie Dunn, a middle-aged widow who had started the orphanage by taking one child and then another off the streets, thanked them with tears in her eyes. Charles felt humbled.

Pansy parted from them at the door. "I shall see you tonight for the tree trimming," she said, giving Maeve a brief embrace and a peck on the cheek.

Charles did not miss the relief in Maeve's answering smile. He knew Pansy's presence helped Maeve through each holiday festivity, more than he ever did. A quick, sharp stab of pain pierced his heart. A heart that expanded and softened, day by day.

"What will you do now?" he asked Maeve when they were once again inside the town coach.

"I planned to visit Dad, practice with old friends who will be caroling on Christmas Eve, and then purchase some mistletoe."

"You do not spend much time at home, do you?"

"Only when I have lessons."

It did not require genius to understand that Maeve avoided Stella and his mother by being out and about. Charles couldn't blame her. "Come with me," he urged. "After I discard this Santa suit I must go shopping and find a Christmas gift for my mother . . . and Stella. I would be most appreciative of your womanly opinions and assistance."

A small smile danced at the corner of Maeve's berry lips. "I think you should find a husband for Stella."

"Oh, that I could. I would wrap and bow-tie Spencer but he's asked to be seated far from her at supper tonight."

Instead of laughing, as he'd meant for her to do, Maeve grew serious. "If Spencer feels that way about Stella, how does he feel about me?"

"He quite likes you, Maeve. He thought you were a game girl, learning to skate with all eyes upon you."

"Does he know we are married?"

Charles shook his head slowly. "No."

"You haven't told even your best friend?"

"No," he confessed reluctantly. "It's not come up."

"Pansy knows."

"Men don't discuss personal matters as women are wont to do. Before long the new year will be here, Stella will be gone, and the entire city of Boston will know what we have done."

"You say it as if we'd done something criminal."

"Look!" he exclaimed, pointing out the window. "Barclay's, an exceedingly fashionable shoppe. We'll shop there."

A twinge of guilt grabbed at his stomach. Charles

knew he continued to disappoint Maeve by keeping their marriage secret, but what else could he do? He would make it up by giving her the best Christmas she'd ever had.

Maeve and Charles returned to Barclay's within the hour. Smudges of charcoal clouds dotted the winter sky and a raw wind whipped through the downtown streets, but Charles hardly noticed the cold. Shed of his Santa suit, he felt in especially good humor.

Barclay's provided an assortment of fine and expensive gifts.

Maeve held up a blue bottle. "This is called Romance, a perfume from Paris. Do you think Beatrice would like it? It's the fragrance of camellias."

Charles sniffed at the bottle. "It has a cloying scent. I prefer yours. The scent of violets is so much more refreshing."

Maeve shot him a disarming smile but did not reply.

He ambled on, stopping at a glass case. "Ah, look. What do you think of these pearl earrings?"

"They're very beautiful," she said with genuine admiration.

"The set shall be our gift to my mother then." From the corner of his eye, Charles spotted delicate diamond stud earrings that would look quite excellent in Maeve's small ears. He sent her to the opposite side of the store and directed the shopkeeper to deliver the diamonds to his home. He added a matching necklace as an afterthought.

Charles had promised himself that he would give Maeve the most memorable Christmas ever, and he intended to do just that. His gaze roamed to a case containing rings, exquisite diamond and sapphire gems that far outshone the ring Maeve so stubbornly wore round her neck. If he were to remain married to the little bit, she would have one. Married or not, she should have a ring that matched the sparkle in her eye. He

ordered the largest ring in the shoppe and then joined
Maeve on the far side of the store.

She looked at a chessboard and figures made of
marble.

"Do you know how to play chess?" he asked.

"No, but I should like to learn."

"Very well. I will teach you."

Maeve shot him a radiant smile. Charles felt his bones
melt.

Dear God, had he no resistance left?

"I promise to be an eager student," she said.

With her quick intelligence, Charles had no doubt
Maeve would pick up the game immediately. At last he
would have someone to challenge other than a reluctant
Spencer.

His stomach tightened. A short time with Maeve as
his opponent would be better than no time at all, he
told himself.

"Why not one of your books as a gift for Stella?" she
suggested.

"Have you ever seen her read?"

"Well, no."

"But of course, the right book might encourage her
to become a reader."

Maeve agreed. "In time, Stella might even support
Rycroft Publishing with her voracious reading appetite."

"Parkens Booksellers, next stop." Charles guided
Maeve round the corner to the old bookstore, musty
and fragrant with the scent of leather.

Before long, Charles picked up a small, leather-bound
volume. "Here is the perfect book."

Maeve read the title aloud. *"A Widow's Life.* Do you
dare, Charles? A Rycroft does the right thing."

"Very well. This will do, won't it?" He held up a book
by Walt Whitman. Charles didn't care to spend much
time shopping for Stella. But in a quick scan of the
books, he had found something perfect for Maeve. After

dispatching her to the biography section, Charles ordered another book and directed the bookseller to deliver the purchases to his home.

Charles had never had such a pleasant time purchasing gifts. His spirits were almost as high as if he'd been sipping brandy all day. He liked the feeling. He enjoyed Maeve's ready laughter and brilliant smile.

In short order, he and his small companion came upon a stand selling holiday items on the corner of Tremont Street.

Charles held up a mistletoe ball. "Do you like this one?"

"It's so large, Charles."

"That's good—it promises more kisses."

Maeve grinned. This afternoon with Charles had been more wonderful than she'd expected. He'd surprised her by leaving the office to shop, but she fully enjoyed his company. "If with each kiss a berry is removed, how long do you suppose that mistletoe ball will last?" she asked.

"A month?" He shook his head. "Not long enough. Perhaps we should purchase two."

"Are you planning to kiss a lot of ladies under the mistletoe?"

"Only one. You."

The warmth that trickled through Maeve threatened to undo her. If she could, she would have thrown herself into Charles's arms and kissed him soundly right in the middle of Tremont Street. With her thoughts on Charles rather than what she was about, Maeve did not see the woman heading her way and jostled her by accident.

"Oh! I'm so sorry . . . Mrs. Deakins."

Pansy's mother held tight to the patrician alignment of her features. Either unaware or unconcerned, Charles was close by and might overhear what she spat out beneath her breath. "Don't think I don't know where my daughter's strange ideas come from. You have been a dreadful influence on Pansy. After I opened my home to you and treated you with all kindness, you betrayed me and my family. No matter what airs you may put on, you were once my maid. And no one shall forget it, Maeve O'Malley.''

Chapter Fourteen

On the way home, Charles attempted to comfort Maeve—to no avail. She could not be consoled. Harriet Deakins was right. No matter what Maeve did, no matter how adept she became at using the proper fork or turning her toes outward when she walked, she would always be the Irish maid to Charles's friends and family. Harriet didn't even know Maeve was married to the Rycroft heir. Being seen in Charles's company too often had been enough to earn the dowager's displeasure. That, and leaving her employ without notice, if Maeve knew anything at all about Harriet Deakins.

Pleading exhaustion, she fled to her rooms as soon as she and Charles crossed the Rycroft threshold. Charles followed, offering, with a teasing grin, to banish her weariness or simply hold her through the night. After much persuasion he finally left Maeve to nurse her wounded pride in solitude.

Ever since her unexpected encounter with Harriet Deakins, a seemingly permanent lump lodged in Maeve's throat, making it impossible to take a normal, deep breath. Her lovely balmorals had become iron-soled shoes that weighted her every step.

Maeve stayed to her rooms, moving about like a sleepwalker, caring little whether she ate or slept, searching for an answer to her dilemma.

Conflicting emotions contributed to the turmoil simmering in her belly. Should she stay on Beacon Hill and fight for her husband and a place in his world? Or should she return to her family and the community where love and acceptance abounded for her?

Maeve pleaded a headache in order to avoid Beatrice's Christmas tree trimming party. She was convinced that Beatrice only included her out of necessity—and for the opportunity of observing her. Maeve had the distinct feeling that any breach of etiquette was duly noted and reported to Charles. With the possible exception of Pansy, no one approved of Maeve's relationship with Charles.

The lovely golden dress she'd intended to wear to the party, before her spirits had been crushed, hung on the open door of the armoire. Maeve sat by the fireplace, knitting. The needles clicked in a furious rhythm while she hummed a comforting carol, attempting to forget the fun she might be missing. At least Shea's Christmas sweater would be finished before the night was over.

"Maeve?"

Charles.

She went to the door, opening it only a crack. Charles grinned down at her. The irresistible, heart-melting smile momentarily immobilized Maeve's ability to breathe. When had he learned to do that? While her wondering gaze locked on Charles, the distant sounds of piano music and laughter drifted upstairs. The party had been underway for an hour. She felt a foolish sense of longing. Dad always said an O'Malley must live up to the tradition that called upon the Irish to be the first to arrive at a party and the last to leave.

"How is your headache?" Charles asked, planting his foot in the open door.

"Painful." Maeve demonstrated her suffering by raising the back of her hand to her forehead.

"I have brought you something that might help. May I come in?" Without waiting for an answer, he strode through the door, forcing Maeve back.

She felt like a small, insignificant twig standing next to a powerful, towering oak. Dressed in dark frock coat and trousers with a deep holly green satin waistcoat edged with gold, her husband cut a dashing, patrician figure. Caught in the gleaming light of Charles's eyes, Maeve allowed herself a moment to admire the man she'd married without knowing who he might be, or where he had come from.

From his slick, dark hair curling ever so slightly at the nape of his neck to his clean-shaven jaw and down his long, muscular body, Charles manifested raw masculinity. Fine tailoring and a restrictive code of conduct could not disguise his virility. He owned a lusty appetite and Maeve knew it. She knew it well. And the knowledge made her weak in the knees.

He gave her a crooked smile. Her heart fluttered wildly.

"Charles, I really don't think anything can help ease my pain."

"Harriet Deakins is to blame. Don't think you can hide the truth from me. That inane woman wounded you and she shall never step foot in my house again."

"Charles, she is a friend of your mother's. You cannot ban her from the house. Besides, I would not like it if you did."

"You have a more forgiving nature than mine."

"Harriet Deakins is not a bad person, only conventional. And I expect she is not alone in her thinking."

"Are you going to allow such a woman to prevent you from enjoying yourself this evening? That is not the Maeve O'Malley I've come to know."

The Maeve O'Malley he'd come to know did not belong at Beatrice's party. She wasn't welcome, only tolerated. Charles knew it but his heart refused to admit it.

"The Maeve you've come to know is being held captive by a throbbing head."

Charles ignored her excuse, ambling toward the armoire. "Ah, what a beautiful gown. Did you plan to wear it this evening?"

"Yes."

"Mrs. Potts outdid herself. Would you mind putting the gown on for me, since I will not have the pleasure of seeing you wearing it downstairs tonight?"

"Oh, Charles, my head—"

He promptly cut off Maeve's objection. "It will only take a minute," he coaxed with a devastating twist of his lips. "And I'll be only too happy to help you."

He helped. Sprinkling kisses along her bare back and nuzzling her neck and the soft, sensuous spot behind her ear. Wave after wave of delicious chills swept through Maeve. Laughter bubbled in her throat.

"Charles . . ."

"Hush, I am chasing your headache away. Call me Doctor Rycroft." He nibbled at her ear.

She'd gone soft inside like bread-and-butter pudding, warmed too long on the iron stove. "Charles . . ."

Engulfed in his soft kisses and pine forest fragrance, feigning a headache became exceedingly difficult. The ache Maeve felt pulsated from between her thighs.

She did not know how much time passed but at last Charles secured the back of her dress and turned her to him. Her knees wobbled so that she could barely stand.

"You look ravishing." A smoldering silver light burned in his ashen eyes. His keen gaze traveled the length of her in unabashed admiration.

Her sumptuous gown featured an overskirt of champagne beige-and-ivory silk stripes swept from front to a small natural bustle in the back. Delicate golden silk roses were gathered at the bustle and bordered the deep square neckline and hem of her dress. Maeve felt regal in the golden gown, and Charles's obvious appreciation boosted her spirits.

Returning his gaze to hers, he applauded.

Could it be possible that her husband had come to truly care for his Irish maid of a wife? Just as soon as she thought it, Maeve dismissed the idea as wishful thinking. "And *you* have a silver tongue."

But Charles paid no heed to her. Grinning, he drew out a box from his jacket. "I'd intended to give you these as a Christmas gift, but I cannot wait."

"Christmas is but days away."

"Much too long." He opened the black velvet-lined box.

Maeve gasped. Diamonds. The box contained a necklace of beautiful sparkling diamonds and matching earrings.

"Charles!"

"Don't you think these diamonds would look elegant with your dress?" But once again, he answered his own question before she could form a reply. "Let's try them on."

Maeve stood transfixed as Charles placed the necklace round her neck and then stared in bewilderment at her ears. "I require help."

Grinning, she showed him how to fasten the diamonds in her ears. The merest brush of his fingertips set her skin aflame. Maeve stood back to regard her reflection in the mirror with amazement. The diamonds did indeed transform her appearance . . . from plain to princess.

The sparkling gems caught the gold of her dress in their light.

Maeve fingered the necklace. "Charles, I cannot accept such a gift."

"Nonsense—you are . . . you are my wife. You deserve diamonds and more."

Tears burned in her eyes.

Charles clasped Maeve's hand firmly in his. "Come downstairs with me so that I can show you off. Come for just a few moments," he coaxed. "I promise not to leave your side."

"Show me off? But no one knows I am your wife."

"They know I have showed a preference for your company in public."

"And they whisper. How long can you ignore the whispers?"

"Come. We will observe and whisper about our guests after they have gone."

She relented. ". . . But only for a few moments."

The downstairs rooms were full with not only the friends of Charles but his mother's as well. Her devotion to promoting Stella among their Boston friends could not be questioned. On the other hand, she treated Maeve with polite indifference.

If it were not against the law, Charles would have dispatched Harriet Deakins to an unknown afterlife with his own hands this afternoon. But all he could legally do was comfort Maeve.

Charles proudly escorted Maeve down the stairs. Although he could feel her hand trembling on his arm, and hear her soft humming, she held her head high. When they reached the parlor, she smiled and greeted the guests as if she were born to the manor.

Spencer Wellington approached them as they made their way to where Robert Raymond entertained at the piano. "I see you were successful in retrieving the beautiful Maeve," he said to Charles, but his gaze focused on Maeve. Smiling, Spencer raised her hand to his lips.

"Charles! Where did you disappear to?" Beatrice sailed up to her son's side, dipping her head in swift acknowledgment to Spencer and Maeve. But something caught her eye and her head snapped back. She stared quite openly at Maeve's diamond necklace before recovering herself with a nervous twitter. "My, my."

"Did you miss me, Mother?"

"We have guests who have been asking about you. Come with me, dear, please. The Wards have friends visiting from Philadelphia who want to meet you. Their son is a writer."

"Couldn't this wait?" He'd promised Maeve he wouldn't leave her side.

"It will only take a few moments. Can you spare my son, Maeve?"

"Certainly." She flashed a forced smile as Charles was led away to what he felt would be certain slaughter. Everyone knew a writer with a novel in dire need of a publisher.

The scents of orange and clove and evergreen permeated the parlor. Beaded and satin-bowed ornaments brought by several guests filled a small table to the side. None of the dozen or so people conversing over eggnog were familiar to Maeve. But all of them seemed to be enjoying themselves. The ladies were dressed elegantly in dresses especially made for them from the finest satin, silk, and velvet. The male guests vied for sartorial recognition in the choice of their waistcoats. It was a beautiful gathering.

Spencer guided Maeve to one of the tufted settees. While she liked Charles's friend, she felt uncomfortable with him nonetheless. She feared committing a breach of etiquette that might reflect poorly on Charles.

"At last I have you to myself," Spencer said, pushing back a thick lock of black hair that had fallen to his forehead.

"But there seem to be several young women looking your way," Maeve noted. She wished to make a good impression but her palms were already perspiring from nervousness and her gaze kept drifting to Spencer's protruding Adam's apple.

"No glances I wish to return."

She wondered if it were really so. Maeve thought him a nice-looking young man; however, he had no strong feature to recommend him.

"You are too modest."

Slanting her a trace of a smile, Spencer shook his head. "I'm afraid not." His amber eyes met hers. "There's something I need to know and only you can satisfy my curiosity."

Saints above! She was in for it now. If Spencer Wellington asked her a question she could not answer, Maeve would lose her hard-won poise. Her old manner of speaking would tumble from her in an uncontrollable stream and she would humiliate Charles and Beatrice. More than likely, Stella as well. But that she would not mind so much.

Maeve drew in a deep, bracing breath. "I hope I can help."

Spencer leaned forward in a conspiratorial manner. "It astounds me how Beatrice found two such different houseguests. You are so unlike Stella."

"It's . . . it's true," she stammered. "Stella and I do not seem to have a great deal in common."

"Do the Irish fare better in New York?"

He thought Maeve was visiting from New York like Stella! How had he gotten that idea? And then she knew. Spencer's information came only from one person. Charles. Her beloved husband was so ashamed of her that he had purposefully misled his best friend.

"It is the same everywhere for the Irish," she answered vaguely. Her spirits dipped lower than the bottom bough of the Christmas tree.

"I must tell you, Maeve. You have been excellent for Charles, the change in him has been extraordinary. A closed door has opened."

"You . . . you believe I—"

"I've known Charles since we wore short pants. I have never seen him smile or laugh as much. And thanks to you, he does not require me to fence with him until I am half dead just so that he can release all his inner demons. You have chased his demons away."

Maeve could hardly believe she had made such a change in Charles's life, but she fervently hoped Spencer was right. Voices raised in laughter thwarted the luxury of mulling this new information over.

An impromptu game had begun. Each guest in the parlor contributed knowledge on how Christmas was celebrated in different countries around the world. Pansy appeared just in time to save Spencer, whose expression betrayed his complete lack of knowledge.

"In Spain, festivities are held on Christmas Eve, called *Noche Buena,*" the redhead announced.

Maeve grinned at her friend, but her heart twisted painfully. If she had not already done so, Harriet Deakins would forbid Pansy to associate with Maeve.

"And how do they celebrate in your part of town, Maeve?" Stella asked in a voice sweet as sugarplums.

"I beg your pardon?" Maeve's calm question belied her racing heart.

"How do the Irish celebrate Christmas?" Spencer repeated the question.

Maeve bit down on her lip, determined not to show her anger. Although she was certain that Spencer had asked the question in all innocence, Stella had meant to humiliate her. She would not allow it.

"Very similar to the way you do," Maeve answered, with a defiant tilt of her chin. "We eat, drink, sing, and dance."

"Do you do the jig?"

The question came from Martin Rycroft, who sat off by himself in a corner.

"Yes."

"Show us!"

"Pansy!" She couldn't believe her friend had made such a request.

"Do. Show us," Spencer urged.

"Oh, I couldn't."

"Surely, you are not ashamed?" Stella asked.

Where was Charles when she needed him? Maeve's anger shot through her like a wildfire. She fully expected flames to leap from her nose and ears momentarily.

"On the contrary, I am proud to be Irish and will be delighted to dance a jig for you. As it happens, Robert has accompanied me before." She cast Mr. Raymond's son a smile.

Robert's eyes twinkled as Maeve stood up.

"Clear a space for me now."

The center of the room cleared.

"The jig is a side step dance," she told the gathering, as Robert played softly. "We keep our arms and hands flat against our sides, like so. As I hop on my left foot, I bring my right foot up in front, with a pointed toe."

"We cannot see the step," Martin complained.

Maeve picked up her skirts. "I shall do it again."

The third time she demonstrated, Robert loudly played the only Irish jig he knew, the one he'd played for Maeve before.

Giving herself up to the music, Maeve danced with her heart and soul, lost to those who watched her. She might have been dancing alone on a shamrock-filled meadow. But before long, Spencer had joined her and then Pansy and Martin. Soon half the young people in the room had joined hands in a circle and danced the rousing jig with Maeve.

Charles appeared in the doorway with his mother. For a moment he only stared, and Maeve thought her heart might break. But after a moment, he did the unexpected. He joined the circle and danced.

Stella vanished.

Beatrice appeared to be in the throes of apoplexy. Fortunately for Maeve's sake, Charles's mother recovered quickly when she realized her guests were having the time of their lives.

When the dance was done, Maeve enjoyed a new

popularity. For the remainder of the evening she found herself dodging the mistletoe—strategically placed in every doorway.

At all previous social occasions she'd been quiet and retiring, her unnatural demeanor designed to prevent potentially embarrassing moments for the Rycrofts. Tonight she'd become a success by being herself and dancing a rather wild jig. Who would have imagined?

The guests still talked about the new dance they'd learned as they trimmed the tree. Maeve was awed by the elaborate ornaments owned by the Rycrofts. Covered with pink satin, Beatrice's favorite color, the decorations were beaded with pearls and sparkling gems and bedecked with ribbons.

At the end of the evening, Maeve was chosen to climb the ladder and place the star on top of the tree. Charles assisted her. He held her hand as she reached to the top with the other. Looking down upon him, his eyes shone with pride and something else . . . something she had not seen before in his smoky gaze.

The next morning Maeve chose to breakfast in her sitting room. Although tired, she still felt a tingle of triumph. Perhaps she could overcome Harriet Deakins's opinion.

"Maeve!" Stella's voice snapped like a bullwhip on a quiet morning. A sharp rap at Maeve's door followed.

She could not think of a worse way to start the day; nonetheless, Maeve opened the door for the pale widow.

"I caught you!" Wrinkling her nose, Stella swept through the door, carrying her ugly dog in her arms. As she sashayed into Maeve's sitting room, Babe began growling. Ignoring the Pomeranian, Stella continued. "At last we can have a chat. You dash out quite early in the day, usually before I am awake."

"Yes—"

"I suppose as a servant you were used to getting an early start."

"I find morning the best part of the day."

Stella sank into a chair. Three feathers from her dressing gown floated to the floor. "Just another point we disagree upon."

Maeve told herself to tread carefully as she perched on the edge of the chair opposite Stella. "Is there something I can do for you?"

Wrinkling her nose again in her annoying manner, she forced a smile. "I wish to speak frankly to you. Before it is too late."

"Too late?"

Babe stood on her mistress's lap and barked at Maeve.

"On a night like last night with everyone dancing your . . . your Irish jig, you might have the impression that you have been accepted into Boston's society."

When Maeve did not respond, Stella went on. "But that is far from accurate. Maeve, I do not mean to be unkind, but someone must tell you the truth. You are an oddity, providing temporary distraction."

Saints above! The woman had been sent to torture her—as if the yapping dog alone could not do it.

"I beg your pardon?"

Stella pushed Babe down into her lap and stroked the angry animal. "Beatrice hoped her son would be attracted to me, and me to him. Her tales of Charles intrigued me. But it did not take long before I understood that he and I would not make a good match. And for entirely different reasons, neither are you a suitable match for Charles."

"Why are you telling me this?"

"Because, despite what you may think, I do have a heart. You must not delude yourself. Take it from one more experienced in these matters. Dismiss any thoughts you may entertain of remaining married to Charles."

Maeve's heart felt as if it had stopped. The blood in her veins froze. "Charles cares for me."

"Charles takes advantage of your so-called marriage bed, but he cannot long be wed to the former maid of a neighbor. Word will get out. It just isn't done. Think of his reputation and his role in Boston society. He is from a distinguished family."

"I . . . I know that." Maeve felt like one of the icicles dripping outside her window, numb and frozen.

Babe quieted.

"As his wife, you shall only make him the subject of ridicule. He will no longer be invited to Boston's finest social events. Like you, he will become an outsider."

"No." The word caught in Maeve's throat.

Stella stood. "If Charles's happiness means anything to you, Maeve, you will agree to the divorce."

The hard ache in Maeve's chest took her breath away. She rasped out the words. "My . . . my husband has said nothing about a divorce."

"He will. He promised Beatrice that after the first of the year he would free himself."

Although her knees trembled and her stomach tossed, Maeve pushed herself up. "How do you know this?"

Stella started toward the door. "Beatrice confided in me from the first. Charles feels indebted to you because you saved his life. And, of course, he pities you for the poor life you've led."

Maeve moved in a shrouded haze of pain. Her heart shattered like colored glass dispersing thousands of sharp, piercing shards to every part of her body. She rubbed her chest but the pain only intensified.

"No . . ."

"I have come to you in confidence, Maeve. The truth is difficult to face but you have a certain intelligence and I felt it was my duty as a woman. Do not betray me."

With another forced smile, and a single yap from her insufferable dog, Stella turned and left.

Maeve fell back against the door, blinking back her tears until she heard Stella's door close. And then she sobbed.

Charles paced his office. Herbert Long had just left after reporting no progress. The private investigator insisted he'd scoured every art gallery and questioned every artist in the area without success. No one had seen anything or heard of the St. Nick sketch becoming suddenly available for sale. Charles was growing impatient. Not only had Long made no progress on finding his stolen sketch, the investigator had been dead wrong when he implied Martin might be involved in the theft.

Pulling out his watch fob, Charles glanced at the time. He decided to leave the office early and pick up a gift for Maeve to acknowledge her triumph at last evening's party.

In polite society, awkward questions were not asked and she continued to be known as one of his mother's houseguests, a mystery woman. But a new dimension had been added; the gossips suspected her of being an Irish princess.

Charles's friends and acquaintances were charmed by her beauty and lyrical accent. Last night enough of his male friends had maneuvered Maeve beneath the mistletoe to set his blood to boiling.

But today she would be waiting at home just for him.

Charles called for his coach.

When he arrived home an hour later, he carried an armful of flowers, including a bouquet each for Stella and his mother. The other four were for Maeve.

"How sweet, dear. Where did you find flowers in December?"

"The Rawlings greenhouse." The Rawlings were thought to be eccentric when they'd constructed their greenhouse. The ability to provide flowers throughout the year eventually dispelled the notion.

Stella wrinkled her nose at him. "You are the sweetest man."

Charles winced. He'd never been described as sweet, nor wanted to be.

His mother tucked her arm through his. "You must come with us to the ballet tonight, dear."

During the journey home, Charles dreamed of spending the evening with Maeve curled beside the fire. "I really don't feel up to it. Difficult day at the firm."

"You have not accompanied your mother anywhere," Beatrice cried. "I feel quite neglected."

"I'll see you before you leave," he promised. "But now I must take Maeve her flowers."

"Maeve is not here, my dear."

The ricochet of sharp disappointment that shot through him took Charles by surprise. "Where is she?"

Beatrice wore a pained expression as she shrugged. "There's no telling when the little Irish girl will return. She went to visit her father. She said he's ill."

Chapter Fifteen

"I'm a sick man," Mick O'Malley groaned, rubbing his bloodshot eyes.

"Oh, Dad. You just had a wee bit too much ale last night. You ought to be ashamed of yourself, drinkin' all of your pay away."

Maeve made her father comfortable on the Deakineses' cast-off sofa and set the kettle to boil on the old iron stove.

"I felt all right at the time I was doin' it. Must be a sickness goin' round."

"Aye, the leprechauns are playin' with ye to be sure, Daddy," she said with a chuckle. "It's a good thing I happened by."

It felt good to be home. This damp, cramped flat had been the center of Maeve's world since coming to America. She felt safe and secure within its peeling walls. And on the streets of South Boston, everyone knew and respected Maeve O'Malley. She wielded influence in the immigrant Irish community. This is where she belonged. Or did she?

"And did ye just happen by now?" her ailing father asked.

"Aye. An sure'n it's a good thing. You've got to stop your drinkin', Dad. I can't bear the thought of you bein' as drunk as a piper and no one here to care for you."

Maeve could not yet bear to speak of it, to confess she'd come to mend her broken heart. If ever it would mend, if ever the pain would end. Instinct told her what Stella had said was true. Charles pitied Maeve and felt obligated to her for saving his life. He made love to her because he could, not because he loved Maeve. He'd never told her he loved her.

"Ye are a good daughter to come to yer old daddy, showin' mercy and understandin'."

"And listening to your blarney?" she asked, hands on hips. "I told you I would be comin' by from time to time. It seems you cannot be trusted to refuse the second mug of ale. Or the third or fourth."

" 'Tis a sad Irish affliction that a woman is not meant to understand. But I'll not be goin' to work at Rosie Grady's tonight."

"Oh, I understand all right about you and your ale. 'Tis Shea I can't understand."

"Every boxin' match yer brother wins brings him closer to ownin' a fishin' boat," Mick said, quickly taking up his son's defense.

"Even when Shea wins, he leaves the ring bloody and bruised."

"Marks of honor to a pu . . . pugilist."

"I think I shall stay the night," Maeve said flatly. When her father defended her brother so readily, using a three-syllable word at that, it was a sure sign they were both in trouble.

"What?" Mick bolted upright on the sofa and immediately grabbed his head with both hands. "Ow!"

"Do not move too suddenly or your head will explode," she warned him with a grin.

Her father settled back on the down pillow that Maeve

had slipped beneath his head when she'd found him earlier. He opened one eye, regarding her warily. "Do ye mean to stay the night, or longer?"

"Longer."

"Have ye had a lover's spat with yer husband then?"

"I don't belong on Beacon Hill, Dad. I never will."

"Aye, you've had a lover's spat."

"Sure'n I speak softly now, and I've learned to pronounce my words clearly and without a trace of County Armagh. I know the difference between a salad fork and a calling card, but it is not enough. A person must be born into Boston society to be accepted."

"Are ye sayin' you're not happy?"

"I'm wretched."

"And that fine upper-crust husband of yours doesn't ease the way for ye with his people?"

"He pities me."

"What?" Again Mick bolted upright, grabbed his head and fell back. "Holy—ow!"

For once, Maeve's pain took precedence over her father's as she struggled to hold back her tears. The empty space where her heart once had been, burned. "Charles has been kind to me because he feels obligated," she explained. "He believes I saved his life and therefore he must be generous with me."

"And what's wrong with him bein' generous with ye?"

"Dad, I want a husband who loves me."

"Aye, and he will soon enough. You're a loveable lass."

"I thought he might come round, too, but 'twas only wishful thinking. To this day, Charles has told none of his friends we are married—that's how ashamed he is of me."

"Society-born are peculiar ducks. Not all of 'em right in the head. If yer husband was in his right mind, he would not be ashamed of ye, me cailin. Feel for 'im. Yer a compassionate lass."

"Not at the moment."

"Ye can stay the night. One night."

"Thank you, Dad."

"And do ye think I might have a wee bit of whisky in that tea yer makin' for me?"

"No."

"I feared not. One night and then ye must return to your husband."

Maeve did not argue, but she had no intention of returning to the Rycroft residence. She went to the window and lit the candle. Traditionally, during Christmas a lighted candle remained in the window day and night to guide the way for travelers looking for shelter.

Folding her arms beneath her breasts, Maeve looked out over the weathered brick buildings and the tenement maze seemingly connected by a tangle of stiff, icy clotheslines. A dreary, gray blanket swept the sky. Cold air seeped through the windowsill. The dark afternoon matched her mood.

Maeve felt certain the sun would never again shine for her. A swift, cold shudder rocked her body. Her future looked as bleak as the back alleys. Harriet Deakins would never hire her back again. But perhaps she could find work in Rosie Grady's Saloon. At least she'd be able to keep an eye on her father if she served in the saloon.

She fingered the lump beneath her dress. 'Twas her mother's wedding ring dangling over her heart. Ever since Maeve had married Charles, she'd worn the ring somewhere on her person. But now the legend of the Claddaugh mocked her. What a fool she'd been to believe someday her husband would come to love her. She would be a fool no more. With one swift tug, Maeve yanked the chain holding the precious ring from round her neck.

"Do ye think you could put more coal in the stove?" Mick asked.

"Aye." But first Maeve slipped the Claddaugh ring into her coat pocket. Her beautiful new coat hanging

on the kitchen peg. She wouldn't be wearing the ring
again, and in all conscience should not wear the coat
either.

With the little money she had left over after purchasing a coat for Dad's Christmas and toys for the orphans,
Maeve had bought coal for the flat's stove, its sole heat
source. She'd also purchased food for her father and
brother's stomachs and a small fir Christmas tree for
their souls. Broken heart or no, she and her family
would celebrate the season of love.

After scooping coal into the stove and pouring Dad
his tea, Maeve sat down to string cranberries. The O'Malley tree would not boast beaded pink ornaments and
silver bows like the Rycrofts' tall pine. But it would be
the finest the O'Malleys had ever had. Maeve planned
to drape the green needle branches with garlands of
cranberry and popcorn and tie bright red bows on every
limb. She would clip small candles to the boughs and
hang colorful penny candy.

Was it just last night that she had trimmed the Rycroft
tree, danced a jig, and made what she thought at the
time were new friends? Hours ago, she had been giddy
and lighthearted. Now, she felt like an empty shell in
which her thoughts echoed. Now, she knew the new
friends she'd thought she made had only humored her.
In all likelihood they snickered behind her back. But
she could not think of it. Thinking of it brought tears.

The knock on the door jolted Maeve from her reverie
and woke her snoring father. Putting the half-strung
garland aside, she crossed the small room. Only Stella
and Beatrice knew she was here and Maeve expected
they would keep her whereabouts to themselves. She
assumed when she opened the door she would find no
one she knew. But she did.

"Pansy?" she blinked in surprise.

"Maeve?" Pansy's eyes rounded.

"What are you doing here?"

"I might ask the same," her redhead friend replied

with a grin. Bundled up in a fur-lined navy cloak with matching hat and muff, Pansy's freckled cheeks glowed crimson from the cold. "What brings you home?"

"I . . . my dad's sick."

"No, I ain't."

Pansy looked from Mick to Maeve.

Maeve turned up her palms. "You can see for yourself."

Their unexpected guest nodded knowingly.

"And what brings you to South Boston?"

"I brought a plum pudding." Pansy held out a box to Maeve.

"You made a plum pudding?" Maeve took the box, regarding it as if it had wings.

"Several, in fact. This one appears to have turned out better than the others. So I expect it's eatable."

"Come in."

"Who is it?" Mick groaned, peering at the newcomer through narrowed eyes.

" 'Tis a friend of mine, Pansy Deakins."

"Not one of your uppity friends?"

"No, one of my mad friends!" Maeve dragged Pansy into the room which used to be hers but now belonged to Shea. Signs of him were scattered about the room. The unmade bed, a torn shirt, and hole-ridden socks lay on the floor.

Apparently fascinated, Pansy surveyed the room slowly.

"May I ask why you brought a plum pudding to my father and Shea? You hardly know them."

"It's the season of giving."

"And?"

"I hoped to find Shea at home. Frankly, Maeve, you are the last person I expected to see."

Shaking her head, Maeve took her friend by the forearms. "Pansy, you must not see Shea. Not today, not ever. Your mother would disown you if she found out you'd come to South Boston in search of an Irish boxer.

And that would be nothing compared to what she would do to me."

"It's none of her affair."

Maeve's stomach somersaulted—several times. "But 'tis mine. Shea is my brother and I forbid you to chase after him like some dreamy, wanton adolescent."

"I am not a dreamy adolescent, only a woman who has been looking for a real man for some time and never thought to find him. I was prepared to devote myself to the women's rights cause until I met Shea."

"But it's Spencer Wellington who looks at you as if you were the Queen of Beacon Hill."

"Spencer is a good friend, but tell me what is exciting about him?"

"There are many ways a man can be exciting, not all of them evident."

"Shea's very presence lends excitement to a room."

Not in Maeve's experience. Heaving a sigh of frustration, she took her friend's hands in hers. "Oh, Pansy. Does Shea know you are interested in him?"

"I don't think so. That's why I decided to take matters into my own hands—"

"And baked something for the first time in your life?"

Pansy's hazel eyes twinkled. "They say a way to a man's heart is through his stomach."

"Saints above! You might kill him first." Pansy barely knew salt from pepper. To Maeve's knowledge she'd never stepped inside the Deakins kitchen—until now, if she indeed had prepared the plum pudding.

"Maeve, let me stay until Shea comes home and then you and I will hire a coach and return to Beacon Hill. We'll say we were shopping together."

"It's not right." Maeve knew that what Pansy wanted could only lead to a broken heart. Suffering keenly from a broken heart herself, she could not knowingly inflict such pain on her friend.

"Please, Maeve."

"No."

"Just an hour. We'll have tea."

In the light of Pansy's beseeching eyes, Maeve felt her resistance give way. Her rebellious friend had done much to help and protect her over the past few weeks. And more than likely this infatuation with Shea was just another small act of rebellion. "All right," Maeve said, relenting. "We shall stay for dinner."

The doorbell jangled—an odd, echoing sound— when Charles entered the stark gallery. With Maeve off visiting her father, he'd decided to take advantage of the unexpected time to pay a visit himself to Edgar Dines, the art dealer. But if he'd stayed at home, his mother would have badgered him into accompanying her and Stella to the ballet later, the last thing he wished to do.

He hadn't visited the gallery since the purchase of Barnabas's sketch and the subsequent beating and theft. The place felt eerie.

Charles had dealt with Dines for a number of years. Edgar had found several of Barnabas's sketches for him before the St. Nick, which he'd charged a pretty penny for. As Charles studied a new, quite interesting oil on the wall, Dines bustled from the back office.

A small man with sloping shoulders, he reminded Charles of a feeding bird by the way he carried his head forward. Round spectacles perched on the bridge of Dines's rather broad nose. He parted his thin, brown hair down the center and always dressed in dark, well-pressed trousers and jacket.

"Mr. Rycroft." Dines flashed his quick, birdlike smile. "To what do I owe this honor?"

"Just in the neighborhood, Edgar." Charles extended his hand in greeting. "So, I thought I would stop in."

"It's always a pleasure to see you." Dines nodded his head and stroked the wax tip of his mustache.

Charles gestured to the wall behind him. "I see you

have acquired some interesting new art since I was in last."

Dines nodded. "Every week I add to my gallery."

"Have you heard anything further about the St. Nick sketch?"

The little man frowned and adjusted his spectacles. "No, I am sorry to say. I would have sent word to you immediately if I had."

"Of course."

"However, I did have another inquiry last week."

"The private investigator I hired?"

"I shall tell you what I told him. If the thieves knew what a valuable piece of art they had in their possession, it's long gone. I believe Barnabas's sketch of St. Nick has made its way to San Francisco, or possibly Chicago by now."

"Then I will broaden my search."

"On the other hand, the sketch may be hanging in a South Boston tenement. Though I shudder to think."

Charles was getting nowhere with Dines and could hardly conceal his disappointment that the art dealer had no better news. "You are saying that the sketch could be anywhere from South Boston to San Francisco?"

"Anywhere."

"Then it might be overseas as well. London or Paris?"

"Anything is possible with a fine work of art," the dealer allowed.

"Do you suppose increasing the reward would help recover my sketch?"

"If the thieves know its value and the reward is enough. How much were you thinking?"

"Twenty-five thousand dollars."

Edgar Dines's eyes bulged. "But that's more than the sketch is worth."

"Not considering the sentimental factor, Dines. My brother's only holiday sketch is priceless to me. I mean to recover St. Nick at any cost."

"No questions asked?"

"Oh, there may be a few questions." Charles gave him a wry smile. "But I may keep them to myself if that's what it takes to recover St. Nick."

"Of course," Dines replied. "I shall be happy to post a notice for you if you decide to increase the reward."

Charles pulled on his gloves. "Thank you."

"And if I should hear anything, I will contact you immediately." The small sparrow of an art dealer accompanied Charles to the door, once again stroking the tip of his mustache. "Let me know what you decide to do—about the reward, I mean."

"I shall."

A cold blast of air hit Charles as he left the gallery, adding to his irritation. He'd hoped for some encouraging news from Dines and had heard none. Further, Charles realized he should have increased the reward much earlier. His annoyance extended to himself.

He directed Stuart to take him home. Maeve would have returned by now. A quiet dinner with his spirited wife would soothe his distress. And after dinner, he would curl up with Maeve by the fire and make love to her. His plans worked to cause Charles to feel a great deal better by the time he reached Louisburg Square.

But the house was unusually quiet.

Stella and his mother were busy dressing for the ballet and Dolly reported that Maeve had not returned.

Once again, Charles felt the crushing weight of disappointment bearing down upon him. But this was worse than what he felt leaving Edgar Dines's establishment. The spark of anticipation, the light-headed excitement he'd felt as he bounded up the steps moments ago, drained away.

He wandered lethargically into his study and poured himself a brandy. Sinking into a chair by the fireplace, Charles gazed into the low-burning fire.

Although he'd spent many nights sipping brandy by the fire in his study, he'd enjoyed the solitude. He'd never required companionship as he read or indulged in idle speculation. Charles had never experienced the bone-deep ache of loneliness . . . as he did now. Maeve's presence made a difference.

As the grandfather clock in the corner struck eight, Charles searched his mind for reasons why his unsuitable but exceedingly desirable wife hadn't yet returned. Perhaps Mick O'Malley was dying. Unlikely. Maeve's father struck him as a tough old bird. The old Irishman would never die. He was pickled.

More likely, Maeve had forgotten to take money along with her again. The charming Little Bit might even now be walking from her father's flat in South Boston back to Beacon Hill in the cold, dark night. She would freeze before she made it home.

Charles shot up from his chair, splashing brandy about. Striding to the door, he called for Stuart to have the coach brought round. He would either meet Maeve along the way or find her at her father's flat. Either way, he meant to bring his wife home.

As soon as his town coach pulled up at the South Boston address, Charles jumped out and took the rickety stairs of the neglected building two at a time until he reached the O'Malleys' fifth-floor flat.

Mick answered the door. The old man held his head with one hand. He looked like hell.

"Good evening, Mr. O'Malley."

Mick squinted his eyes as if he couldn't clearly see Charles. "Rycroft?"

"Is Maeve here?"

The grizzly old man with a bright red bulb of a nose smiled and opened the door for Charles. "Aye."

Charles quickly scanned the small area that served as both kitchen and parlor. Signs of Christmas were evident. A garland of holly swagged above the window and a scraggly, three-foot fir tree bedecked with a string of cranberries nestled in one corner. Along with a smattering of candles, a single oil lantern lit the small room.

Charles's stomach growled in response to the pungent aroma of corned beef and cabbage issuing from a large pot simmering on the stove. But his attention was diverted as the opposite doorway opened and Maeve peeked out. Pansy's head bobbed up behind her.

Taken by surprise, Charles momentarily forgot his manners. Harriet Deakins would fall into a dangerous swoon if she knew her daughter was in a South Boston tenement. "Pansy! What are you doing here?"

"I came to visit . . . Maeve."

"Who came by to visit her old sick dad," Mick put in.

Charles turned to the old man. "My deepest sympathies on your illness."

"Sure'n I nipped a bit too much whisky," Mick explained without shame as he scratched the back of his head.

"I see." Charles cleared his throat. Maeve still stood behind the door to the room he recognized as being the one he had shared with her. The room where he had been Charlie, the room where he had regained his memory. "Are you ready to come home, Maeve?"

She shook her head. Her eyes looked misty.

"When shall you be ready?"

She shook her head again.

Charles's stomach rolled over. His spine stiffened. He had a bad, bad feeling.

Apparently, Pansy did as well. The Deakins girl slipped out from behind Maeve and marched into the small living area. She wore a forced, over-bright smile. "I believe I'll join you for tea, Mr. O'Malley."

Mick O'Malley grimaced as if Pansy had promised him castor oil.

Charles slowly crossed the room toward Maeve. "Is there something wrong?"

Maeve nodded her head and silently stepped back for him to pass.

Charles entered the room where he'd spent his wedding night with a bit of trepidation. His heart beat quickly, and out of time, skipping erratically. There seemed no place to sit except the unmade bed. Charles stood. Tension spiraled through the room as thick as mill smoke. He thought he might choke.

Maeve shut the door.

"What is it, Maeve?" he asked softly. "What's wrong?"

He could see no sparkle in her lovely lapis eyes. Instead, her gaze appeared misty and as dark as night. Teasing her lip, she clasped her hands tightly together and lowered her head.

"I do not feel at home on Beacon Hill."

"You will in good time."

"I don't think so."

A nasty suspicion struck Charles. "Has my mother said something to offend you?"

"No. Though Beatrice has made no secret of her dislike for me."

"My mother's feelings have nothing to do with mine. You cannot blame me for something my mother has said or done."

"I don't."

"In any event, Beatrice will be returning to New York with Stella after the first of the year. You shall not have to deal with her much longer." He held out his hand. "Come home with me."

Although Charles felt he had put Maeve's mind at rest, she did not move. She still stared at the floor.

He dropped his hand. In one stride he was at her side. Gathering her small, warm body into his arms, he breathed in her sweet violet fragrance, rested his check against her silky curls.

"Come home with me now," he pleaded in a voice strangely husky.

"I cannot," she whispered. She stood as stiffly in his embrace as an ice-slicked lamppost.

If it wasn't his mother who had hurt Maeve, it must have been Stella, he reasoned. "Stella . . . has Stella wounded you?"

"No."

Charles didn't believe her. Clasping Maeve's hands in his, he stepped back. She stubbornly refused to meet his gaze. "Tell me what has happened. I shall make it right, whatever it is."

"You cannot make it right. 'Tis an accident of birth."

Charles bit back his rising panic. "What are you talking about? What do you mean?"

Maeve raised her eyes to his, eyes glistening with tears. "We are not suited."

"What makes you think that?"

"Everything."

"Everything?"

Pulling her hands from his, Maeve spun about, marching toward the door. "You were not in your right mind when you married me."

Dear God, she was going to make him leave. She wasn't going home with him.

Alarm charged through Charles like a rocky landslide, pain tore at his insides. He clenched his jaw to keep from crying out.

"I have my wits about me now."

While tears glistened in her eyes, Charles saw a flash of anger as well. Maeve's little fists dug into her hips. "And I suppose you are going to say ye ardently wish to remain wed to the likes of me?"

"The likes of you?"

"An Irish maid."

"I do."

She rolled her eyes . . . to one of her saints above?

"I do," he repeated resoundingly.

Charles thought for a moment Maeve would spit fire.

Instead, with her gaze glued to the floor, she took several deep, calming breaths.

When at last she raised her eyes to his and spoke, she made her request in a soft, resigned tone. "I want a divorce . . . now."

Chapter Sixteen

Maeve did not expect an argument from Charles. She'd used every ounce of strength to tell him she wanted a divorce. Her parched throat swelled, her voice broke on the word . . . *divorce.*

Saints above, she was bound for Hell! She would be struck dead on the spot. She raised her eyes to the ceiling, eyes swimming with hot tears.

If her dad knew what she'd asked for—a divorce— he'd be calling on Father Thom for an exorcism.

To Maeve's surprise, instead of being relieved, Charles appeared stunned. Stiff and unmoving, he stared at her as if she had spoken to him in a language he did not understand.

"What have I done to make you feel you want to be rid of me?" he asked quietly.

Unable to face him, look into his eyes, Maeve bowed her head, focusing on the hem of her dress. " 'Tis nothing you've done. You have been generous and kind to me."

And when he made love to Maeve, Charles made her

body sing and her spirits soar. He made her happier than a woman had a right to be.

"Then why do you wish a divorce?"

" 'Tis just the way of the matter. We come from two different worlds, we do. Look around you. This is my world, my life. I will never belong in yours. I will never be accepted or feel comfortable on Beacon Hill."

"Pansy would be lost if you left. Spencer and Martin—"

"It has been weeks since we were married and no one except for Pansy knows I am your wife," she interrupted a bit too sharply. "And your mother and Stella, who manage to keep the secret well for their own interests."

"Haven't I said all along that after—"

Once again Maeve interrupted, spurred by a spark of anger. "Our secret has been so well kept, we can be divorced and no one will be the wiser."

Charles took a step toward her. "Stay with me until Christmas, until the holiday is over."

Maeve stepped back. For one brief moment she entertained the idea that Charles hadn't been planning to divorce her. In an attempt to save her own pride, had she wounded Charles? No, the thought was ludicrous. Her husband was a good man trying to save face. He wasn't saying the words she longed to hear. He wasn't vowing his love for her and declaring that his heart would shatter if Maeve was no longer his wife.

"Time cannot change how dissimilar our lives have been," she insisted. "Time will not make a difference."

"Until Christmas," he coaxed, in a hoarse timbre. "Come home with me until Christmas."

What had happened to his voice? What had happened to his heart? Charles could not feel his heart beating. His lungs refused air. He felt as if he'd been turned to stone by one of Maeve's evil Irish fairies. A granite knot sat squarely in his midsection.

A Rycroft did the right thing, he reminded himself.

Begging was not among the right things in life and not at all in Charles's nature nor experience.

Dear God, she wanted a divorce!

Maeve had handed Charles a way out of this highly unsuitable marriage on a silver platter.

Indisputably unacceptable.

He'd been waiting to divorce his Irish wife quietly and without a scandal ever since he first woke up in this room after regaining his memory. And now, to his utter amazement, Charles did not want to divorce Maeve. She'd become an integral part of his life. He wanted to keep her by his side always.

Nothing in his experience had prepared him for a moment like this. He and Maeve had reached a crossroads, and Charles dared not veer off onto the wrong path. He did not know what to say or do to convince her that divorce would not answer. He only knew Maeve must come with him. Her laughter must continue to fill the corridors of his house, her violet scent must remain to sweeten each room.

"This is my home, Charles. And what good would it do to come to Beacon Hill with you until Christmas? It's just days away—what difference can a few days make?"

"Perhaps all the difference in the world."

Tears shone in Maeve's extraordinary eyes and her chin trembled when she raised her gaze to his. "I thought you would be relieved when I asked for a divorce, Charles."

"Why would you think that?"

Because he was supposed to feel relief.

Now Charles could not bear the thought of never seeing Maeve again.

Dear God, she'd cast some kind of fairy curse upon him!

Her lips quivered in a rueful smile. "I would think so because I know my behavior has been an embarrassment to you upon occasion."

He slowly shook his head, denying the truth. "On the contrary, Maeve. You've made me proud to know you." The stilted tone of his voice disturbed Charles. How could he hope to convince his doubting wife if he sounded subhuman? A Rycroft never revealed his emotions, however. He had learned that lesson well.

Yet, the firestorm of feelings thundering through Charles threatened his composure. If he wasn't careful the passions he held at his heart's core would burst in a flood of words and action he would never be able to retract.

Maeve inclined her head. The quizzical purse of her lips, along with her clearly skeptical expression, challenged Charles as no mere words could have done.

"You showed great courage learning to skate in front of a party of critics waiting to pounce on your lack of performance," he began. "But you showed them otherwise. And if you weren't a plucky, proud woman, my friends and I would have missed a rousing lesson in the Irish jig the other evening."

The corner of Maeve's luscious mouth turned up in a tentative smile. "That did turn out well, didn't it?"

"Yes, it did." Charles could not tear his gaze away from her lips. He could not throw off the longing to make her his, here and now. The unmade bed beckoned to him. The knowledge that he'd once made love to Maeve on that same bed set his pulse spinning. He could do it again, make love to Maeve on her bed, and this time he would remember every kiss, every sigh, every soaring sensation.

"Charles? Are you all right?"

He made a great show of clearing his throat; in reality he cleared his mind of tantalizing visions. "Yes. Quite."

No, dammit. I am not all right.

"Furthermore," he continued. "I have never experienced the unselfishness you demonstrated by giving the Essex Orphanage a Christmas party with the funds I meant for you."

"Having the ability to give the children a party was a dream come true—and actually your doing, Charles."

He dismissed her claim with a shake of his head. "And . . . and just how many women do you think I would allow to talk me into putting on a Santa Claus costume?"

"You were very good," she grinned. With the memory, the sparkle returned to her blue, blue eyes. "You possess a natural talent for portraying Santa. I think you should repeat your role every year."

Charles jumped on her proposal. "I will. I'll play Santa Claus again tomorrow if you will just come home with me tonight."

The smile on Maeve's lips, the sparkle in her eyes faded. "Returning will just prolong—"

"I expected to escort you to the Cabot's Snow Ball. Do you know what my fate will be if I cannot?"

"No."

"Mother will insist I escort Stella alone."

"Saints above! 'Tis a dire fate," Maeve exclaimed with a mocking wag of her head.

"If you grant me these few short days I promise I shall respect your privacy. I will not come to your rooms, nor . . ."

Dear God, what was he promising?

"Nor?"

"Nor pressure you in any way to stay beyond the holiday. It will be your choice if you wish to be with me. I would never force myself upon you."

A strained silence fell over the cold, unkempt room. Maeve could hear a teacup clink against its saucer in the next room. She could hear her heart beat, a slow thump . . . thump.

Charles hammered at Maeve's resolve with his earnest promises and soft persuasion. He wore her down with the troubled light in his deep ash eyes, his compelling magnetism and masculinity. Charles was like the jaguar, sleek and strong, prowling, circling her. How could she resist him? How could she turn a deaf ear to the eagerness in his voice to please her? With Christmas less than a week away, she doubted anything could happen in such a short period of time to change her mind about the divorce.

Maeve knew she would always love Charles. But there was only one way she could stay with him. If he loved her and told her so, told her over and over again.

If the wee people or Santa Claus could make a wish come true, she would wish for only one. She would wish for her husband's love. With Charles to love her, Maeve could survive the society snubs and gossiping tongues. She could survive anything at all. Charles's love would be the grandest Christmas gift of all.

But she knew by now that wasn't to be.

"Please, Maeve. Say yes," Charles coaxed. "Come home with me."

Her heart skipped in an ominous rhythm as Maeve gazed up at the man who towered over her. His forehead folded into a dark frown and his firm-set lips pressed tightly together as he waited for her answer.

How could she deny Charles anything? It was only a matter of days and he'd promised not to pressure her. Besides, if what Stella had said was true, Charles had been planning all along to set her free following the holidays.

Maeve's stomach lurched and her hands trembled like an old woman with palsy. Undaunted by these unsettling physical signs, she forced a smile and sealed the pact. "Yes, Charles. I'll come with you"

The following day Charles placed Martin in charge and left his office at Rycroft Publishing shortly after luncheon. Of late, he worked less and enjoyed Martin's help more. Except for Maeve, he felt a new sense of control over his life.

Maeve was another matter. While they had enjoyed a quiet dinner in his study the night before, she'd left him immediately following to retire. After arguing for her return, Charles had hoped she would give him the pleasure of her company. Instead he paced his study, attempting to sort his feelings, his duty against his desire. The long, lonely evening resulted in no resolution.

But this was another day, another opportunity for Charles to come to terms with his own needs and determine just what it was he wanted of Maeve. The answer would certainly come. A Rycroft did the right thing.

Charles left the *Boston Globe* after placing a full-page advertisement announcing the increase in reward for the return of Barnabas's irreplaceable sketch of St. Nick. It was his last hope. The erstwhile investigator Herbert Long still had not uncovered any new information. To ease his mind, Charles chose to believe he'd been attacked by a poor fellow who didn't know the value of the sketch and used it to decorate a tenement wall. He reasoned the news of such a large reward would get around and soon the sketch would be returned.

Because he hadn't been fencing with Spencer of late, Charles walked for the exercise rather than ride. By prior arrangement, his driver would pick him up in the town coach in just over an hour. Charles had Christmas purchases to make for Maeve. He had vowed to make this the best Christmas the Irish sprite had ever known and he was determined to do just that.

Charles went into several shoppes before he noticed a tall, brawny fellow appeared to be following him. While he told himself the likelihood of being ambushed and robbed again was improbable, Charles decided to exercise caution. He stopped to gaze into the dry goods emporium of Mr. Jordan and Mr. Marsh. The window display featured an array of colorful toys. From the corner of his eye, he noticed the brawny fellow had stopped as well. Wearing a knit cap and dark jacket outgrown years ago, the ominous figure leaned against a lightpost, ostensibly picking at the dirt beneath his nails.

What attracted ruffians and thieves to him? Charles wondered, with no small amount of annoyance. He considered confronting the man until, with another surreptitious glance, he noticed a glint of metal against the black post. A knife? Was the fellow carrying a knife?

A hasty survey of the street told Charles there were no mounted patrolmen in sight. At times like this there never was. He decided to take refuge in the emporium until the bully tired of waiting for him and fixed on some other poor soul.

Sleighbells on a strap attached to the door jangled noisily when Charles strode purposefully into the dry goods store. After greeting Mr. Jordan, he browsed through the toys. He discussed the workmanship of every toy boat and porcelain doll as if he had a dozen children waiting for him at home.

If he had children with Maeve, Charles hoped they would have her sparkling jeweled eyes and fair skin. But not her Irish temper.

Dear God! Children! What was he thinking now?

Charles dallied a full hour before the thug who had followed him finally gave up and went away.

"If you will wrap my purchases and deliver them to my home I shall be much obliged." With those brief instructions and a perfunctory smile, he left the emporium, eager to return home and be with Maeve.

"Your mother will have my head," Maeve declared, hurrying along beside Pansy as the two young women headed for South Boston.

Even wrapped in her heavy coat, hands burrowed deep inside the warmth of her muff, the chilling cold wind still managed to penetrate her clothing, sending icy shivers down Maeve's spine. The frigid air of early afternoon stung her cheeks and numbed the tip of her nose.

"My mother will never know," Pansy assured her. "If Charles hadn't led you away, and me along as well, before Shea came home last evening this visit would not be necessary."

"This visit is not necessary in any case," Maeve huffed.

She only agreed to accompany Pansy because she needed to speak to her brother. Maeve still meant to recover Barnabas's sketch of St. Nick for Charles. Although she'd given it much thought, Maeve could not think of a better gift, nor one that could possibly make him happier—but time was running out.

"It is necessary," Pansy snapped. "I would like to know if he enjoyed the plum pudding I made."

"I can tell you—Shea enjoys food of any kind."

"I want to hear it from him."

"Society's elite do not go to gymnasiums."

"This one does. I am most curious."

"Shea will not have anything to do with a blueblood lady like you, if that's what is on your mind." And Maeve knew that it was.

"If he doesn't, it won't be because I didn't try."

Maeve recognized an obstinate kindred spirit when she saw one. For a moment she felt tempted to confess her imminent divorce, the only end for people from two different worlds. Maybe then Pansy would understand why she must stay away from Shea.

After supper last night Maeve had fled to her rooms. She feared being with her husband in the intimate atmosphere of his study. She feared succumbing to her attraction for Charles, an attraction that grew instead of lessened. Leaving him when the time came would be difficult enough. Maeve had only days to shore her resolve and keep her wits about her.

"We will only stay five minutes at the boxing hall," she warned Pansy. "No more."

"Yes, Maeve. Only five minutes and then I shall hire a coach to take us home."

"You are asking for trouble by doing this," Maeve muttered.

"Like the kind of trouble you have?"

"I would not warn you if you were not a friend."

"If Shea would look at me for just one moment the way Charles looks at you, I should be content."

Maeve stopped in her tracks. "What way does Charles look at me?"

"Adoringly. He adores you. And you know it."

"Adoringly?" The wind whipped about, parting her coat with a cold slap and whooshing up her skirt. Loose tendrils of hair lashed into her near-frozen face. True to his word, Charles had observed every propriety from the moment Maeve agreed to return to Beacon Hill with him. Rigid with form, he'd acted the perfect gentleman, treating Maeve as if she were made of crystal. She repeated the word again, this time not questioning its truth. "Adoringly."

She started off again with a lighter step and a smile upon her face, unprepared for the blast of wind that hit Pansy and her as they turned the corner. The frosty rush of air took Maeve's breath away. Hunched over, head down, she hurriedly led the way down the short block and into the boxing hall.

Once used as a stable, the cavernous building held four makeshift practice rings. A large, open loft held shabby equipment and medical supplies. It was almost as cold inside the gymnasium as it was outside. The dank smell of sweat, alcohol, and stale tobacco assaulted the senses. Fully dressed boxers sparred in two of the rings; several groups of trainers, boxers, and hangers-ons engaged in heated conversations.

"Isn't this exciting?" Pansy gushed.

"No," Maeve replied flatly.

"I would wager my life that none of the other Beacon Hill ladies have ever been to a gymnasium. Certainly no one I know has ever met a pugilist."

"Which is to be desired."

"But our men regularly attend boxing matches and horseraces."

" 'Tis a man's sport," Maeve said, as she scanned the room in search of her brother.

"They even wager on clam digs," Pansy added on a sulky note.

Maeve spotted Shea in the far boxing ring, talking with a man who appeared to be his sparring partner.

"I see him!" Pansy announced seconds later. "I see Shea."

Shea's thick biceps strained beneath his long john undershirt. Maeve conceded that her brother's dark, rugged features and thick, black curls had turned many an unsuspecting woman's head. She could not deny that her brother was a handsome man. But he wasn't meant for the likes of Pansy, just as Maeve wasn't meant to be with Charles.

Pansy appeared positively thrilled at the prospect of a clandestine meeting in a forbidden place with a man Harriet Deakins would consider unfit—as suitable for her daughter as P.T. Barnum. In fact, Mama Deakins would probably prefer P.T.

Determined to return Pansy to the safety of Beacon Hill at once, Maeve marched toward her brother, waving her hand above her head. Pansy kept pace.

Grinning, Shea slipped through the ropes and jumped to the ground to give Maeve a hearty embrace. "What are ye doin' here, sister of mine? Dad has warned ye against comin' to the gymnasium."

"Do you and Dad think if I do not see you practicing, that I will not know you are getting ready for a match?"

"We've never been able to fool ye," he chuckled.

"My friend Pansy came along with me."

Shea turned his smile on Pansy.

The rebellious redhead regarded Shea as if she'd just met Hercules himself. "You are like the mightiest gladiator," she greeted him breathlessly.

He grinned. "Tomorrow night I will fight like one."

"Tomorrow night?" Maeve asked.

Flashing a most mischievous smile, Shea turned to her. "I'll make enough to put a big, fat goose on the table this Christmas."

"And who'll be cookin' your goose?" she demanded with hands on hips.

"Mrs. Gilhooly."

"Oh."

"You told us to call on Grace Gilhooly if we needed anything. She's been a darlin' help."

"I see." Maeve's heart sank. Her family didn't need her anymore. She would not be missed on her first Christmas away from home. The life force drained from her. Heat and energy ebbed away as she realized the sad truth. Maeve no longer belonged anywhere.

"May I come to the match?" Pansy asked, reminding Maeve that her friend had forced this rendezvous. "I would like to see you box."

Shea shook his head. " 'Tis not a pretty sight for a woman, especially one like you."

Surprisingly, Pansy blushed.

"Can I not stop you, Shea?" Maeve pleaded. "Must you fight?"

"Maeve, me darlin', as soon as I've earned enough for me boat, I promise ye never to lift a fist again."

"With each fight you run the risk of hurting yourself so that you will be unable to fish, boat or no," Maeve argued.

"Me sister tries to frighten me at every match," Shea said to Pansy. "She cannot see the good sport of it. 'Tis far better than street brawlin'."

With her eyes locked on Shea's, Pansy nodded. She appeared to be in some sort of trance, smiling insipidly.

Maeve felt her anger rising. Shea flirted shamelessly, without regard to consequences. It was up to her to protect her freckle-faced companion. "Pansy and I must get back before we're missed."

"I'm not in a rush," Pansy objected.

Maeve ignored her. "Have you done what I asked, Shea?"

"Aye. Do you see that big fellow over there?" he asked, gesturing with his head.

"Yes." The man her brother pointed out was of giant proportions and bore frightening scars. A chill skipped down Maeve's spine.

"Bill 'Spit' O'Brien he is. Called Spit because he . . . he—"

"I understand," Maeve interrupted. "Go on."

"Spit's been sparrin' here every afternoon for as long as anyone can remember. But he hasn't won a match in years. Not long ago the big lad began betting. Unless he met a leprechaun and found the pot o' gold at the end of the rainbow, it's a mystery where his money is comin' from. He's not winnin' as much as he's losin'."

"You say he spars here every afternoon?"

"Aye. Every afternoon."

A bubble of hope, a bolt of excitement, shot through Maeve.

Bill 'Spit' O'Brien. At last a likely suspect. This could be the man who attacked Charles and stole the precious St. Nick sketch by Barnabas. There was only one way to find out.

"Thank you, me beautiful brother." Maeve stood on tiptoes to kiss Shea good-bye.

Pansy extended her hand to Shea. "I wish you luck tomorrow night."

"Thank ye, me lady." Shea's blue eyes danced with delight as he gazed at Pansy.

Maeve couldn't be sure but she thought she detected her brother squeezing Pansy's hand. He fancied himself a ladies' man. Sure'n he'd be wearing a hat size larger now that a fair, society-born miss had paid him a visit. Shea knew well enough Pansy Deakins didn't belong in the A Street Gymnasium.

For a moment, Maeve considered throwing herself between her cocky brother and headstrong friend.

"And I look forward to seeing you again." Pansy's hazel eyes glowed with a dangerous light.

"Don't you worry now, lass. I'll be beggin' me sister to bring you by."

Maeve seized Pansy's hand. Whirling on her heel, she practically flew from the gymnasium, pulling the improper Miss Deakins behind her.

Once outside in the bitter-cold air, Maeve did not stop. Nor did she notice the man who followed them.

Chapter Seventeen

The night of the Cabots' Snow Ball at last arrived, anticipated by Beacon Hill society, dreaded by Maeve. As she dressed for the evening ahead, her mind raced in review of every point of etiquette she'd ever read.

When walking, a lady keeps her toes pointing slightly outward.

"And under no circumstances," Maeve warned her corseted reflection in the mirror, "do not slip back into your South Boston brogue! If you do, the gossips will be talking about you from now until they raise their flags on the Fourth of July."

During the past few weeks Maeve had acquired a proper Bostonian accent—with a slight Irish lilt. But when she grew tired or especially nervous, the Irish in her erupted—which pleased her father but no one else.

Keeping her mind on the ball proved difficult. She'd been filled with excitement since leaving Shea this afternoon. Her brother had given her hope along with the name and face of Bill "Spit" O'Brien. While O'Brien possessed a truly fearsome appearance, it was an aversion she must overcome. The boxer might well lead her to the sketch of St. Nick. To recover the last outstanding piece of Barnabas's work for Charles, Maeve would follow the burly man wherever he might lead her. Starting tomorrow morning, O'Brien would not make a move without Maeve close on his heels.

The thought of finding the sketch before long sent a tingling rush of warmth from her head right down to her toes. St. Nick, just in time for Christmas!

If Maeve had her druthers, she would rather be on O'Brien's trail than be dancing with Charles Rycroft tonight. The danger of dancing with Charles caused Maeve more anxiety than the thought of any physical harm done to her by a ruffian boxer called Spit.

To feel Charles's strong, protective arms around her always caused her to go weak in the knees . . . and almost everywhere else. Perfectly sturdy, healthy limbs dissolved to the consistency of a meringue cloud. The very scent of him, masculine and woodsy, melted her heart. And should Charles give her one of his devastating crooked smiles at the same moment his soft pewter gaze met hers, Maeve would be rendered defenseless. Speechless. Breathless. She risked capitulation.

Enfolded in her magnificent husband's arms, Maeve became as vulnerable as a chicken courted by a fox. She became as pliable as fresh, warm taffy. Charles possessed the power to turn her heart.

Maeve could not risk a dance with him.

Her idle musings were brought to a halt with a sharp rap on the door as it opened. Dolly bustled in to help Maeve finish dressing, a task not included in the housekeeper's regular duties. The experienced lady's maids in the Rycroft household were devoted to Stella and Beatrice looking their finest tonight.

Maeve appreciated Dolly's help. What the housekeeper lacked in fashion sense, she made up for in enthusiasm. When, an hour later, Dolly had completed her administrations, Maeve stared at her reflection in stunned disbelief.

"I do believe you are my fairy princess."

Rotund Dolly looked less like a fairy than anyone could. But her ruddy face lit up like the summer sun at Maeve's compliment. " 'Tis you who looks like a princess tonight."

"I hardly recognize myself. You have made a miracle."

"The miracle is you and what you have done for Mister Rycroft."

"Oh, Dolly. You have been so kind to me." Maeve reached out to clutch Dolly's hand. She would miss the efficient housekeeper who had been so kind to her. Although the brusque woman had made no secret of her disapproval when Maeve first arrived, within days she had taken to helping her whenever possible.

"It's been my pleasure." Dolly dipped into an awkward curtsey. "I'll let Mr. Rycroft know you are ready."

"Thank you."

Long after she heard the door close behind the Rycroft housekeeper, Maeve continued to stare at her reflection. Who was that woman?

Charles paced the foyer. He felt in no mood for the Cabots' Snow Ball. Even though, on the Boston social scale, the Snow Ball ranked in the top five activities of the season. A tug of war played inside him. What Charles wanted was contrary to what was right, Rycroft right. What his heart craved, his mind rejected.

"Maeve O'Malley will be down shortly, sir."

He looked up at Dolly, beaming from ear to ear like a cat who'd got into the cream. Unusual for the no-nonsense woman.

"Thank you."

Tonight he would escort Maeve, his mother, and Stella to the Cabots' Snow Ball, but only Maeve's pleasure interested him. It was true they came from two different worlds but he'd begun to consider the possibility of creating their own world. One world.

Dear God! He'd never been so tormented by a dilemma.

If Maeve did not enjoy herself tonight socializing with the cream of Boston society, how would he convince her to stay? His wife. An Irish maid. His father must be rolling over in his grave. In all likelihood, even now the earth of the Granary Burying Ground was shaking with the ghost of Conrad Rycroft's rage.

Charles weighed the special characteristics of Maeve O'Malley: an incomparable beauty, tenement-raised, intelligent and generous, fiery temper. His friends and acquaintances would find her imminently unsuitable.

"Charles."

He looked to the stair landing where the sound of Maeve's voice had come from.

And his heart stopped.

"Maeve."

A shimmering vision in red velvet stood before him. When she smiled, Charles's heart swelled to twice the size it was meant to be. He could not catch his breath or tear his marveling eyes away from her as she slowly descended the long stairs.

Her midnight hair, swept up from the sides, was held at the top with a delicate posy of mistletoe and red velvet ribbon. Strands of the red ribbon intertwined in her lustrous curls as they cascaded down her back. Maeve's full, delicious lips were parted slightly in excitement or expectation—he did not know which.

He forced his gaze lower to her long, graceful neck, to the contrast of her silky alabaster shoulders caressed by crimson velvet. A deep border of delicate lace skirted the low, round neckline of her gown and peeked flirtatiously from along the hem. The tight bodice emphasized Maeve's tiny waist, and beneath the full bustle a hint of the lush comfort of her hips. Charles wanted the lady wrapped in red beneath his Christmas tree. He could think of no better Christmas gift. He would open her carefully, tenderly . . . although the tightening of his loins suggested another approach.

The only jewelry Maeve wore were the diamond earrings and the necklace he had given her as an early Christmas gift. But her beauty outshone even the bright white, sparkling stones.

Charles greeted her on the third step, taking her hand and leading her down to the foyer. "You will be the most beautiful woman at the ball."

"If it is true, I have Dolly to thank."

More than ever, Charles regretted having to attend the ball. He would rather stay home and make love to this lovely vision. But he had made a bargain. He would not force his attentions. If Maeve wanted his kiss, his caress, she must come to him. Unless he could melt her resolve.

Soon Stella made her entrance, but Charles only had eyes for Maeve. He was barely aware of the pale widow sashaying down the stairs in a rustle of emerald taffeta and gold fringe. Beatrice was the last to leave her rooms. She wore a swirl of white crape and silk festooned with pink and red silk roses. Rubies glittered in her hair, in her ears, and around her neck.

Charles dutifully complimented his mother and Stella on their appearance, but knew in his heart that Maeve would outshine them at the ball. The knowledge brought a proud smile to his lips.

"Is that mistletoe in your hair?" Stella asked.

"Yes, it is." Maeve grinned mischievously.

"I don't believe I've ever seen mistletoe worn before." The young widow adjusted the gold combs in her hair as if to make a subtle point.

"It's a new style I wish to introduce. And should there be a lovely boy at the ball I wish to kiss," she paused to grin. ". . . I am very well prepared."

Shock registered on the faces of Beatrice and Stella.

Charles chuckled. But his heart constricted with a painful squeeze. Why would she want to kiss any other man but him?

Each year the Snow Ball took place at the Cabots'

mansion. The thirty-room edifice, overlooking the Charles River, was the closest thing to a palace that Boston could boast.

While the Cabots' estate was not far from the Rycroft residence, the carriage ride proved slow. Although the streets had been flattened by the snow warden, they remained icy and picturesque. Snow-feathered tree branches bowed gently along the route and soft powder snowdrifts lined the way. The ethereal beauty of the glistening winter landscape inhibited conversation during the ride.

Maeve climbed the mansion steps, humming softly. Passing through the marble hall arches, it was all she could do to suppress her awe and plant a complacent smile upon her lips. Exerting a supreme effort, she pretended the appointments of this magical place were as familiar to her as her South Boston flat.

Earlier this evening, in a last-minute decision before she left her rooms, Maeve decided for better or worse to be herself tonight. She had nothing to lose and meant to enjoy her last society appearance. She would speak quietly and correctly, but she would say whatever came to mind—as long as it was not unkind. She would not dance the Irish jig but she would fill her dance card.

Charles escorted his mother on his arm as they entered the main ballroom. Fearing association with riffraff perhaps, Stella followed the Rycrofts, sailing out half a step ahead of Maeve.

Lifting her chin and straightening her shoulders, Maeve assumed perfect posture—according to all the etiquette books—and made her own regal entrance into the glittering ballroom. She could see heads turn as she passed, feel eyes following her. Men's eyes, women's eyes, all eyes were upon her. The unexpected attention stirred a startling, uncomfortable feeling. Maeve attempted to ease her anxiety by reminding herself the ball was merely a large party, and no one knew how to enjoy a party more than the Irish.

Still, she found it difficult to conceal her astonishment with the grandeur of the gilded ballroom. Beatrice Rycroft and Stella observed the dancing couples while whispering behind their painted ivory fans. Charles, in the role of gallant, supplied the ladies with crystal cups of thick, foamy eggnog spiced with fresh ground nutmeg. Maeve slowly sipped at her drink while taking stock of her luxurious surroundings in unabashed wonder.

Blazing gold sconces adorned every wall. She could almost see her reflection in the gleaming marble floor. Hand-painted mythical figures floated on the ceiling above ornate, carved mahogany molding. Deep mulberry velvet drapes framed frosty, ten-foot windows which stretched along the entire length of one wall. Braided loops embellished with golden tassels held the rich window coverings back.

An ensemble of musicians played from a balcony above. Recognizing the music of Mozart and Strauss for the first time gave Maeve great satisfaction. She was learning. She hummed along with "The Blue Danube."

Before she had time to finish her eggnog, Spencer Wellington was at her side requesting a dance. When she looked to Charles for approval, he dipped his head and flashed a toe-curling grin.

One dance followed another. Maeve danced with men she knew slightly from the Rycrofts' circle, and those she had never met. She danced with tall men, short men, young men, and those old enough to be her father. Each dance partner proved to be exceedingly polite and friendly as they whirled her beneath immense crystal chandeliers casting a golden shower of light.

After over an hour of dancing, she repaired to the ladies' powder room just to catch her breath. And there, to her delight, discovered Pansy.

"You have set Boston society on its heels," her red-haired friend announced gleefully, embracing Maeve. "Did I not tell you weeks ago that you would be the belle of the Snow Ball?"

"But I hardly credited it."

"The women are jealous of you and the men want you. How perfect!"

"Perfect?"

"Your husband has not taken his eyes off of you all night. And I have seen his lips pressed tightly. With Charles, tight white lips are a certain sign that he is severely peeved." With a wide grin, Pansy leaned toward Maeve and whispered confidentially, "I don't think he enjoys having a room full of men coveting his wife."

"No one knows I am his—"

"Charles knows. And he is the only one of importance in this room."

"Yes, but—"

"There is something I must tell you," Pansy interrupted. Excitement sparkled in her eyes as she seized both of Maeve's hands in hers and led her to a small corner settee. "My mother is sending me to Europe."

"What?"

With a grin as wide as the Charles River, Pansy giggled. "She feels I will benefit from a year on the continent."

"And how do you feel?"

"I think I shall have a wonderful time out from under Mother's eye!"

Maeve breathed an inner sigh of relief. Although she would miss her friend dreadfully, there would be no unfortunate romance with Shea for Pansy.

"Of course, the journey is just a ruse to remove me from your wicked influence!"

"You have been the wicked influence on me!" Maeve protested. "Before I came to work as your maid I knew nothing about free love, wearing bloomers, or women like Elizabeth Cady Stanton."

"You have had the benefit of a liberal education," Pansy boasted, obviously pleased with herself. But in the next instant she became serious, emitting a brief, sorrowful sigh. "I had looked forward to becoming more closely acquainted with your brother, but I shall write to him."

"I'm sure Shea will welcome your letters," Maeve replied. Just as she had suspected, Pansy's interest in Shea had been little more than a respite from boredom.

"I hope he does. Now, let us go find your handsome husband before he sends his mother after us—or worse, my mother!"

Maeve and Pansy were only midway to their destination when Pansy came to an abrupt halt and gasped. "Uh-oh. Martin Rycroft is headed our way. I think I shall be off to the refreshment area."

"Wait—"

But Pansy had disappeared in the crowd and Maeve faced Charles's stout, whiskered cousin by herself.

Martin led her onto the dance floor. "I must say, Maeve, that you are the loveliest woman at the ball tonight."

"Thank you, Martin. I do hope your wife is feeling better."

"Sally is showing signs of recovery. She is only ill in the mornings now, but she's still weak."

"I look forward to meeting her soon."

"Speaking of meetings, where again did Charles find you?"

"A back alley in South Boston."

Martin gave a low, rumbling hoot. "No. Really. Where did he find you?"

"In a back alley. If you remember, I found Charles after he'd been robbed and beaten."

He nodded his head and stepped on her foot. Maeve bit her tongue to keep from yelping.

Deep in thought, Martin seemed completely unaware of his misstep. "It's a shame about the sketch being stolen."

"Hopefully it will be recovered."

"Yes. But I have come to think that rescuing him

from freezing in the alley was just one of the ways in which you saved my cousin's life.''

"What do you mean?"

"He's a different man. He's not bound to his desk at the publishing house any longer.'' Martin lowered his voice and whispered gravely in Maeve's ear. "Between you and me, since you've been a guest in his home, Charles has given me increased responsibility and an increase in salary.''

"He must be pleased with you, Martin. Your good fortune does not have anything to do with me.''

"I'm not so certain. I've witnessed definite changes in my cousin.''

"Perhaps you are seeing the man he is and always was instead of the man his father wanted him to be?''

Martin considered her question. "Maybe so,'' he said at length. "Conrad could be quite terrifying. I kept my distance.''

Before Maeve could reply, Spencer Wellington appeared behind Martin and tapped his shoulder.

Martin regarded him with resignation. "I suppose I must relinquish the lady.''

Spencer nodded.

"Charles has always been a fortunate man,'' Martin said, turning back to Maeve and bowing graciously. "No more so than now.''

If he only knew.

More than halfway through the evening, everyone but Charles had danced with his wife. It was difficult to dance with anyone else and keep an eye on Maeve. He was relieved to come upon her in the spacious hall adjoining the ballroom that was set aside for rest and refreshments.

"I have not had a moment with you all evening,'' he complained. "The next dance is mine.''

Maeve peered at the dance card looped to her wrist

and then raised a seemingly stricken gaze to his. "My dance card is filled, Charles. I am so sorry."

"How could you have forgotten to save a dance for me?"

"I lost track."

"I'm your husband!" he protested, hissing in her ear.

"Yes, Charles, but you have not approached me all evening."

"Because I had to execute my obligations to my mother and Stella."

"They have kept you very busy."

"Tell one of these selfish men that you can't dance with him." He glanced at her dance card quickly. "Ah, look. Spencer. You have already danced with him twice."

"The rules of etiquette neglected to mention that I may be rude to another upon my husband's bidding."

Before Charles could argue this point, a strapping blond fellow he recognized from Spencer's law firm sidled up to them. "Miss O'Malley, I believe this dance is mine."

Maeve gave the young man a bright smile, handed Charles her empty goblet, and bestowed a dainty wave before being swept out onto the dance floor once more.

Charles strode directly to Spencer's side and went straight to the point. "You are scheduled on Maeve's dance card for the last dance."

"Yes. I'm looking forward to another waltz round the floor. She is wonderful, as light as the proverbial feather in my arms."

"I have yet to dance with Maeve. And her dance card is full."

Spencer smiled and shrugged. "Sorry, old man."

Charles scowled. It was not the answer he'd expected from his friend. "I would like to have your dance."

"No." Spencer swiped an unruly black lock from his forehead.

"What?" The shock stunned Charles. It was as if he

had been doused with a bucket of icy ocean water. "But . . . but you're my best friend," he blurted.

"I am. But I'm not giving up my dance."

"Damn it, Spencer. She's my wife!"

Dear God, what had he said?

This time it was Spencer's turn to be shocked. "What?"

Charles could hardly believe he'd lost his composure and barked the truth without thinking, without care of repercussions.

"My wife," he repeated softly.

Spencer's amber eyes were as round and large and bright as Charles had ever seen them. "You lucky dog!"

Charles wasn't sure that he'd heard correctly. "I beg your pardon?"

"For God's sake, how did you win the Irish beauty? And when? And why the secret?"

"She's not one of us."

"Hell no, Maeve's a hundred times more interesting."

"Yes," Charles agreed. "She is rather fascinating."

"Our proper Boston women are the most boring beings on earth. With the possible exception of—"

"Which is why I remained a bachelor for so long," Charles interrupted, suddenly feeling righteous and wishing to make a point.

"Does Maeve have any sisters?"

"No. And if you will not give me your dance, Spencer, I will take it."

"You sound like a desperate man." His friend gave him a lopsided grin.

"I am not desperate."

"Equally incredulous then . . . you are a man in love with his wife."

Dear God! Love?

"Spencer, I would appreciate it if you would keep our little secret to yourself until I am able to . . . to make the formal announcement of my betrothal to Maeve."

"Your secret is safe with me." Spencer winked in a plainly conspiratorial manner. "And now that I fully understand the extent of your infatuation with your wife, I will give you the last dance with her."

As the evening neared its end, the dance floor was less crowded, the music sweet and mellow. The excited buzz of the ball guests heard at the beginning of the evening had given way to a soft murmur of sound.

When Charles came to Maeve in Spencer's place, her heart flew beyond all bounds. No one held her just as Charles did, no one looked quite as splendid in his formal black suit with bow tie and pearly white shirt.

Maeve came alive in her husband's arms, in the lusty power radiating from the length and breadth of him. A fresh surge of energy infused her body and her feet floated above the dance floor as if they had wings.

There was no need for small talk. An unspoken harmony flowed between Maeve and Charles, too delicate to disturb with unimportant observations. They danced as one, moving in unison as if they'd been dancing together all of their lives. Maeve felt as if even their hearts beat as one.

Charles held her inches apart from him. To her amazement, pride shone in his eyes as he gazed down upon her . . . and something else. But she wasn't certain what.

Maeve had observed Charles watching her throughout the night, scrutinizing each of her dance partners. Could it be that Charles Rycroft was jealous? The idea stunned her, made her smile.

When she was back in the flat with Dad and Shea, she would remember this night as the most glorious of her life.

"I am going to pluck the mistletoe from your hair when we get home," Charles whispered in her ear.

"And then what?"

"I shall kiss you soundly."

"If you are dangling mistletoe above my head, I suppose I must allow a kiss,'' Maeve replied with a feigned sigh as her body warmed.

"If you are not careful, I will dangle the mistletoe above you through the night,'' Charles warned in a raspy, seductive tone.

Her heart careened wildly. "I shall not be careful then.''

Maeve wanted her husband tonight. She had done her best to stay apart from him but their time together was swiftly running out. One more night. Tonight. A sultry heat sparked deep inside her and slowly spread silky fingers of warmth until Maeve's entire body was afire.

Beatrice and Stella left the ball at midnight, Cinderella widows. Stella claimed she was not feeling at all well. Although it appeared the pale New Yorker had captivated more than one older man, she seemed to be in a constant snit. Beatrice had worn the cloak of a martyr as she left Boston's social event of the winter season with her guest.

It was almost two o'clock in the morning when Maeve and Charles arrived back at the Rycroft brownstone. Intoxicated with her success—she'd made not one breach of etiquette—Maeve felt as if she could have danced until dawn. Charles entertained better ideas.

Helping Maeve out of her coat, he cautioned his little bit of a wife to be quiet. He hoped his mother and Stella were fast asleep but if not he did not care to risk an unwanted encounter. It had been a tortuous night for him and he intended to end the evening quite differently.

Charles contrived to slip into Maeve's chamber, take down her hair, and put the sprig of mistletoe to good use. After endless nights of having her door closed to him, she'd not protested his suggestion that he come to her tonight.

Beatrice called to him just as he started up the steps with Maeve.

"Charles, dear. May I have a word with you in the drawing room?"

Chapter Eighteen

Charles recognized an invitation he could not refuse. Beatrice beckoned from the drawing room doorway. His heart sank. What was his mother doing up at this hour?

Maeve gave him a melancholy smile. "Good night, Charles."

"Good night . . . Little Bit."

Charles watched as Maeve climbed the stairs alone, her hips gently swaying beneath the bustle of her red gown, a seductive summons. His spirits sank lower than the tidal flats. He'd had such high expectations.

Resigned to a fate only slightly better than death by discussion, Charles followed his mother into the drawing room. Settling into the elegant Queen Anne sofa, Beatrice smoothed her skirts. "I would so much enjoy a sherry, dear."

Charles poured a small amount of sherry for his mother and a goodly quantity of brandy for himself.

"Maeve afforded a tolerable accounting of herself tonight," Beatrice noted begrudgingly. "Observing her from a distance, no one would guess she was not society-born."

"Maeve triumphed. She was an unqualified success, Mother."

"In her own way, perhaps." Beatrice gave a dismissive flick of her wrist. "But I have a matter of more importance to discuss with you."

Nothing could be more important than Maeve. Dear God, was that true?

Charles sauntered to the fireplace. Picking up the poker, he attempted to stir a fire from the low-glowing embers. "What is it, Mother?"

"Stella has not felt quite herself for the past few days."

"I'm not surprised," he replied rather smartly. "She's extremely pale. I thought so from the first."

Charles could barely disguise his annoyance. It was ridiculous—no, it was sinful to be discussing the state of Stella's health when he could be tasting Maeve's warm, moist lips, dipping his tongue into the sweet secret valley between her full, lush breasts.

"Stella is always pale, dear." The deep lines in his mother's forehead folded into a disapproving frown. "As most intelligent women do, Stella uses vinegar to whiten her complexion."

"Really? She does so on purpose?" He could not imagine Maeve applying vinegar to her face.

His mother exhaled wearily. "I'm afraid you know so little about women. My fault, to be sure. Stella takes care to protect her delicate complexion from the sun and other harsh elements—which evidently Maeve has not learned to do as yet. The Irish girl is always out and about in the worst of weather."

Beatrice's criticism pricked beneath Charles's rather thick skin. "But you did not wish to discuss Maeve."

"No. No, I don't, dear. It's Stella. Stella wishes to return home at once."

"Now?" he asked, unable to hide his surprise. "Christmas is but days away."

"We will take the train to New York in the morning."

"We? Are you going as well, Mother?" Charles could barely suppress the swirl of excitement that warmed his blood and lifted the clouds of his distress. To be alone with Maeve on Christmas was more than he dared hope.

"Well, yes. After all, I brought Stella to Boston as my guest. I can hardly send her on her way alone. And now that your father has forgiven me, I may spend the holiday with Mr. Van Zutoon."

"Father forgave you?"

"Have you forgotten the seance?"

"No." Charles swallowed a great gulp of brandy, sacrificing enjoyment for expediency. "How could I?"

"As you may recall, Conrad spoke through Helen Foster to reassure me."

"As I recall, Father's strong suit was never reassurance."

"One changes in the spirit world," Beatrice admonished.

Dear God, Charles hoped so.

"Knowing that Conrad does not hold my words against me—words spoken in a moment of anger, I might add—frees me."

"Frees you?" Charles never had an easy time following his mother.

Beatrice's fingers skimmed over the silk roses bordering the neckline of her gown. "Without Conrad's blessing I did not feel I should encourage Harold Van Zutoon's suit."

"You have a . . . gentlemen friend, Mother?"

"He's a Dutch merchant whom I met at the opera several months ago."

A wealthy Dutch merchant, if Charles didn't miss his guess. "Father blessed your . . . association with Mr. Van—?"

"Zutoon." Beatrice finished for him. "Yes, your father gave his approval. In a manner of speaking."

"I'm speechless."

His mother heaved another overwrought sigh as if dealing with Charles was a tiring ordeal. "But more than a companion of my own, I do so want grandchildren. I thought Stella might be a credible match for you but I was sadly mistaken. You need a more . . . lively woman. Someone like Pansy Deakins."

"Pansy believes in free love—"

"Heavens!" Beatrice bolted upright.

"And I have it from a reliable source that her mother is shipping Pansy off to Europe."

"Poor Harriet."

"Pansy will be fine . . . eventually." Charles drained his snifter of brandy. "But I regret that you and I shall not be spending Christmas together."

"As do I, dear." Beatrice rose, tilting her head, eyeing Charles as if to gauge his true feelings. "You won't be too upset, will you?"

"No, Mother," he answered honestly.

"It isn't as if you haven't spent other holidays by yourself," she reminded him.

"No, it isn't." Although he knew Beatrice loved him in her own way, he'd spent too little time with his mother through the years. Even when she was in residence in Boston. And his mother could not take all the blame. He had spent too much time by himself in the past, buried in his books, in his work, while life passed him by.

"I shall make this holiday up to you," she vowed as she had so many times before.

"Mother, you have nothing to make up to me. I promise you I will not be upset, nor alone."

She arched a brow. "Maeve will celebrate with you?"

"I will celebrate with Maeve."

Beatrice nodded and with a slight lift of her chin glided to the door. With her hand on the knob, she stopped and turned. His mother's soft, pearly gray eyes met his with ominous intensity. "Do remember what your dear departed father always said, Charles A. Rycroft always does the right thing."

Dear God! His tyrannical father had now become a saint.

"How can I forget? Don't be concerned, Mother, I shall do the right thing. I will do the right thing . . . for me," he repeated beneath his breath.

The morning following the Cabots' Snow Ball, Edgar Dines opened his gallery on Warren Street and made ready for business as he did every morning, six days a week. In the privacy of his back office he sat in a worn leather chair beside the wood-burning stove and opened the *Boston Globe*. He hadn't been reading long before he yelped and shot up from the comfortable old chair.

Just as he had promised, Charles Rycroft offered an increased reward for Barnabas's sketch of St. Nick. The full-page advertisement offered a reward three times more than what the sketch was worth, with no questions asked. No art dealer, Dines included, could ever hope to sell the sketch for more. The expenses Edgar would incur traveling to Europe to sell the sketch, as was his original plan, would only eat further into his profits. He immediately decided to abandon his original plan and claim the reward.

When the other Boston and New York art dealers were buying Winslow Homer, Edgar had purchased the watercolors of Jonathan Box. When his colleagues raved about Turner, he saw more merit in the work of Ely Sykes. He'd spent a fortune buying the abstract oils of an unknown French artist with great promise, while eschewing Whistler. Not long ago the French artist jumped off a bridge.

Edgar had failed bitterly in his attempts to establish himself in the art world as a dealer of great repute. He had not been a particularly successful art dealer—nor crook. Now, with this one sketch by Barnabas, he could recoup the monies he'd lost in the past. He would not have to risk a journey abroad, nor deal with the underworld.

All he had to do was send the Irish boxer to Charles Rycroft. O'Brien would tell Rycroft he had found the sketch of St. Nick and arrange to exchange the sketch for the reward in a public place. The Old North Church would do. Edgar could wait across the street in the Symthe's Olde Book Store until the exchange had been made. O'Brien would bring him the reward. Edgar would give the Irishman a bill for his trouble and send him on his way.

The simple scheme gave Edgar more happiness than he'd experienced in weeks. His tiny laughter echoed in the gallery. Light headed and muttering with relief, he danced by himself around the sputtering stove. Not only would he have more money than he bargained for by collecting the reward, he would retain Charles Rycroft as a loyal client! He felt like Samson after all. He was a man to be reckoned with . . . strong and powerful.

Edgar dashed to his desk. Trembling with excitement, he stroked the tip of his mustache with the fingers of one hand while scribbling a hurried note with the other. The whole messy business would be concluded by Christmas. There was no longer a reason for Charles Rycroft to meet with an accident. Within the hour a runner had been dispatched with Edgar's simple message: *Come at once.*

On Beacon Hill Maeve awoke to the sounds of doors slamming, high-pitched, nonstop doggie yapping, footsteps running on the stairs, and servants whispering in the corridor. The floor creaked and groaned as if shifting beneath great weight.

What now? Leaving the warmth of her bed, she padded quickly across the cold floor. Opening the door a crack, she peeked out. Stuart and Charles's coach driver carried a sizable and obviously heavy trunk from Stella's rooms.

Maeve closed the door and leaned back against it. The pale widow and pointy-nosed dog were departing! It was too much to hope for. Scolding herself for indulging in wishful thinking, she quickly dressed and ventured across the hall. Stella's door was ajar. Maeve pushed it opened and strolled inside. The merry widow was nowhere in sight, but her maid was busy packing.

"Is Miss Hampton leaving?" Maeve asked.

"Yes, ma'am. Miss Hampton and Mrs. Rycroft are returning to New York on the morning train."

Both ladies were leaving! Maeve's heart drummed with excitement until another thought occurred. She would soon be alone in the house with Charles.

If it hadn't been for Beatrice's intervention last night, Maeve certainly would have surrendered to her husband's plentiful charms and welcomed him to her bed ... for one last time. Alone in the house with Charles, she faced a severe test of her resolve. Could she hold fast?

Maeve paced in her rooms, humming fiercely. Instead of embarking on her pursuit of St. Nick as she had meant to do, she was forced to wait until Beatrice and Stella departed. When the time arrived, she joined the widows in the foyer and expressed her regret that they were leaving. Giving each a polite, light embrace, Maeve bid the ladies a safe journey.

Stella's cold lips pressed against Maeve's cheek before the tall, pale woman stood back and softly issued a final warning. "Remember what I told you. Do not think because I am leaving for a richer hunting ground your marriage will continue. It is quite impossible. Quite unacceptable. Think of Charles."

"I always think of Charles."

Babe, the wee Pomeranian, bared her teeth and growled.

Maeve was thankful she had no reason to accompany

the ladies to the railway station. Although Charles had gone to his office early, she learned from Beatrice that he'd made plans to meet her and Stella before their departure for a final farewell.

Just before leaving the brownstone, Charles's mother drew Maeve aside. "I must apologize if I have offended you, Maeve O'Malley. You are an intelligent and beautiful young woman. Nevertheless, you are not one of us. And although you have much to recommend you, a woman of your background does not belong here."

Maeve tilted her chin and attempted to smile, even as tears gathered behind her eyes and a landslide of fieldstones rained down inside her body, crushing her, pushing the air from her lungs.

The lean widow leveled a gaze as cold and flat as winter storm clouds. "I warn you not to mistake my son's gratitude for love."

All Maeve could manage was a slight dip of her head. Swallowing the hurt she'd been handed, she raised her head proudly, defiantly. And hummed the national anthem.

Maeve waved from the porch as Beatrice and Stella departed in a parade of coaches. She wished the ladies well, but wished them their wellness as far away as possible. Although Maeve knew she would not be a part of Charles's life much longer, she also knew he would do extremely well without the interference of his mother or Stella.

With the ladies away, the time had come for Maeve to put her plan into action. She intended to leave Charles with something he would always remember her by . . . St. Nick by Barnabas.

Her plan began with following Bill "Spit" O'Brien until he led her to his home or to whoever his thieving boss might be. He might work alone, or he might be working under the direction of another nefarious character. There was much she didn't know and little time to find answers. Once Maeve discovered where the boxer lived, she would contrive to "visit" while O'Brien was away from home. With any luck, she would then find the precious sketch of St. Nick and return it to its rightful owner.

If, however, the brute led her to a mastermind who directed his villainy, Maeve would report the scoundrel to the authorities, who would take him prisoner and restore the sketch to Charles. It all seemed quite simple.

Fancying that a woman could be as keen a private investigator as the man Charles had hired, Maeve set out on foot. A mottled gray sky, holding promise of more snow, greeted her. Thin, crusty layers of soot settled over melting snowdrifts. Stepping around mounds of slush, she walked briskly to ward off the biting cold that wrapped about the city like an icy muffler.

Less than an hour later, Maeve marched into the A Street Gymnasium. On the pretext of searching for her brother, she looked for Bill "Spit" O'Brien. She'd tracked Shea down so often, the regulars were used to seeing Maeve in the boxing hall and paid no mind to her presence. But neither her brother nor the suspect boxer were at the hall.

Refusing to give up, Maeve decided to bide her time. Leaving the gymnasium, she hurried to the flat in hopes of finding her father. But no one was home. Exasperated, Maeve's tension mounted. Her insides felt fluttery one moment and tighter than a fiddle string the next. In a vain effort to calm herself, Maeve stopped at Mrs. Gilhooly's for a spot of tea before returning to the boxing hall. The withered old widow confided in Maeve that she'd taken a shine to Mick O'Malley. Not knowing whether she should laugh or cry, Maeve returned to the boxing hall.

It was late in the afternoon when she took a seat in a corner of the A Street Gymnasium. Pretending impatience while waiting for her brother, she studied the sparring boxers in each ring. New fighters had arrived during her absence and it did not take long to spot O'Brien, the man Shea had pointed out to her when last she visited—with Pansy Deakins.

The Irishman boxed in the middle ring with a young fighter who was not quite as tall or beefy. O'Brien's alarming countenance caused Maeve to reconsider her plan for a moment. Should Spit suspect her interest in him and waylay her as he had Charles, she could find herself in a world of trouble. Maeve considered alternative plans as she watched.

Bill "Spit" O'Brien did not do well in the sparring match. After boxing thirty minutes or so, his young opponent landed a blow that knocked O'Brien to the canvas. Maeve winced and covered her eyes. After being splashed with a bucket of water, the big, lumbering man dragged himself up and staggered about the ring for another thirty minutes before the young fighter called an end to the practice match.

A sweating O'Brien shrugged into his sweater and jacket, withdrew a scrap of paper from his jacket pocket, and stuffed it back inside. Drawing a knit cap over his addled head, he ambled out of the gymnasium.

Maeve followed.

He headed back to Boston on foot. Maeve thought it highly unlikely the giant boxer lived in the city, nor was it probable he had friends there. For all she knew he could be up to no good, like picking pockets or some other notorious activity. She followed at what seemed a safe distance.

O'Brien did not appear to be in any hurry as Maeve trailed him down narrow streets. The gray light of day deepened to a purple haze. She jumped and stopped in her tracks when from the corner of her eye she caught the flash of a dark shadow across a dirty snowdrift. The downy hairs on the nape of her neck stood on end. She took several deep breaths before pressing on. Humming softly.

In the past, Maeve had always avoided being out alone after dark, but on this day she had little choice. Maeve offered up a silent request to the wee people who granted wishes. She did not care to be on a wild goose chase. Please, let O'Brien be the one who was even now leading her to the stolen sketch of St. Nick.

With her gaze glued to the fighter and her fearful heart thudding against her chest, Maeve was not aware of the man keeping to the shadows, following her every move.

O'Brien turned on Warren Street. Maeve's heart began to beat a bit faster. The chill that swept through her had more to do with fright than the weather. She had never been particularly courageous.

Although she'd never had reason to be on the street, Maeve knew it boasted many exclusive shoppes. Perhaps Bill O'Brien had come to rob one! Only a handful of shoppers bustled along the street against the cold. There was not a coach in sight. If need be, who would she call upon for help?

The big boxer stopped.

Maeve ducked into the small portico of a fabric shoppe and peered around the edge of the building. Her quarry had paused, looking both ways down the street. To determine if he'd been followed? If that wasn't the sign of a guilty man, she didn't know what was. Afraid to be seen, she pulled back and counted to ten. When she next dared peek, O'Brien had disappeared.

Her pulse raced at an alarming speed. Tension gnawed at the pit of her stomach. She could taste the bitter bile of her fear.

Saints above, she must be out of her mind.

But she could appear as if she were in full possession of her wits. She could appear calm. Maeve headed to the spot where she'd last seen O'Brien. She walked slowly, spine stiff, head high, fearing she might lose Mrs. Gilhooly's tea and cakes at any minute.

Maeve stopped at the shoppe approximate to where she had last seen the Irish fighter. And sucked in her

breath. The lettering painted on the glass door read:
EDGAR DINES, ART GALLERY.

How odd.

She stepped up to the glass door and peered inside. The gallery was dark. She was afraid of the dark. Only one low-burning lantern shed any light. Her belly constricted into a tight little burning ball. It felt as if her legs were bound in lead gaiters. She couldn't go into the darkened gallery. Her feet refused to move.

Maeve knew she had come too far to go back now—she was too close to recovering the sketch. Bill O'Brien's presence at Mr. Dines's gallery meant only one thing. For whatever reason, Edgar Dines had sold Charles the sketch of St. Nick and then had the fighter steal it back. Bill O'Brien obviously worked for the art dealer. Why else would the muddle-headed boxer come to a business like this? Maeve felt safe in assuming the big man was no art connoisseur.

Another thought occurred to her. If she had guessed their scheme, perhaps Edgar Dines hoped to sell the sketch again to someone else. Or already had!

The fear she might be too late to recover the sketch of St. Nick temporarily overpowered her fear of the dark. Maeve opened the door and hurried inside the gallery. The jangle of the doorbell gave her a start that resulted in a squeak—a sound she'd never made before. Her throat felt as dry as her daddy's empty flask. With wobbling knees, she closed the door behind her.

"Hello!"

No one returned her greeting.

"Merry Christmas," she called out cheerily.

A rather high-pitched man's voice came from the back, beyond a black velvet curtain. "Patience. I will be with you momentarily."

Maeve waited. She tapped her toe and entertained truly alarming thoughts and grave doubts. Perhaps she shouldn't have come by herself. Perhaps she should have asked Shea to accompany her or told Charles what she'd learned about O'Brien. One dire thought led to another as she shivered in the gallery, barely aware of the art.

Would Charles mourn her if she died here? Would he miss her at all? Would he know why she'd come? Would he understand how deeply she loved him?

She hummed. "Bring a Torch, Jeanette, Isabella" came immediately to mind.

At last a small man wearing round spectacles and an annoyed frown scurried from the back room. He seemed unduly disturbed to have a customer.

"How may I help you, Miss?"

Maeve's lips quivered as she forced a smile. "I'm looking for a special gift."

"Miss, I do not mean to be rude but it's late and I was just about to close the gallery."

"But I should like to purchase a painting or sketch of St. Nick."

The man frowned, peering at her over his round spectacles. "Look around you. Do you see such a thing?"

"No, but it's Christmas and I thought you might have one . . . perhaps in the back?"

"No," he replied with a fierce scowl. "I don't."

Maeve played the little witless woman. "I am certain I once saw a sketch of Santa Claus in your gallery."

With his shrewd eyes narrowed on her, Edgar Dines stroked his mustache. "You haven't been in my gallery before."

"Oh, but I have."

"Who are you?"

"Maeve O'Malley."

At that moment, Bill "Spit" O'Brien pulled aside the curtain separating the gallery from what appeared to be a back room. "Ain't ye Shea O'Malley's sister?" he asked.

"Yes, I am." Maeve's pulse raced erratically. Her stomach spun round like a carousel.

Spit grunted. "I seen you at the hall."

She forced a bright, warm smile. "And I've seen you."

O'Brien kept his squinty eyes on her as he ambled to Edgar Dines's side. "She's the interferin' lass who pulled Rycroft from the alley."

Maeve whirled on her heel and marched toward the door. "I'll come back another day."

But the big boxer beat her to it.

Edgar Dines locked the door.

She hadn't counted on this.

"Take her into the back room and tie her up," Dines snapped at O'Brien.

O'Brien spit toward a corner brass spittoon and grabbed her arm.

"Why would you want to tie me up?" Maeve asked in a trembling voice. "I'll just leave quietly and come back another day if you don't have what I—"

"You think I have Rycroft's sketch, don't you?" Dines demanded.

She blinked. "What sketch?"

The skinny, bespectacled leprechaun stepped up to her until he was within inches of her face. "Did Rycroft send you?"

His breath smelled of onion. "No. No, he doesn't know I'm here."

As soon as the words were out of her mouth, Maeve knew she'd said the wrong thing.

"Take her to the back."

Maeve dug in her heels but O'Brien put his big hand over her mouth to keep her from screaming and easily yanked her back through the black curtain.

She found herself in a small, cold room. The fire in the wood-burning stove was close to dying. And maybe she was as well. A deep, hard shudder rocked her body as the fighter tied her to a straight-backed chair.

"Please let me go. I won't say a thing . . . and you know," she lowered her voice to an ominous pitch . . . "if I am harmed in any way my brother will kill you."

O'Brien turned out to be a man of few words. He

grunted as he tied a red wool scarf around her head and tightly against Maeve's mouth. She gagged. Standing back to check his work, O'Brien gave an abrupt nod and strode out of the room.

Maeve looked around her. The fire would soon go out and only drops remained in the kerosene lantern. Soon she would be alone in pitch blackness, the prisoner of two ruthless men.

Chapter Nineteen

Charles took the stairs two by two. He could swim the Atlantic, sail round the world single-handedly, run to Stockbridge and back. Filled to overflowing with a sense of liberation, Charles burst into Maeve's rooms without bothering to knock. Alone at last with his Irish bride! Alive with anticipation, his heart fairly sang.

"Maeve?" She was not in the sitting room. "Maeve?" Nor did he find her in the bedroom.

His exuberance burst like a bubble pricked by a pin. He ran downstairs. "Dolly, where's Maeve?"

The ruddy-faced housekeeper offered a hapless twist of her lips and shrugged her shoulders. "I can't say, Mr. Rycroft. She left the house shortly after your mother and Miss Hampton departed this morning."

Damn.

Charles glanced at his pocket watch and then to the window. It would soon be dark. The lamplighters were already at work. Maeve did not stay out after dark. He knew she would be home soon.

"I'll be in my study," he told Dolly.

Disappointed and somewhat disgruntled, Charles

poured a brandy, lit a cigar, and settled in his favorite wing-back chair to read a long-neglected manuscript. He'd been spending more time with Maeve or thinking about Maeve and very little time attending to business.

Although he could not have imagined feeling this way mere months ago, Charles felt fortunate to have Martin heavily involved in the publishing company. While they didn't always agree, they had reached a meeting of minds and forged a foundation that promised success.

It seemed eerily quiet in the house with all of the women gone. Charles found the silence discomfiting. Yet he had enjoyed the very same solitude—or thought he had—until Maeve came into his life. The little bit of Irish heaven had been followed quickly by the arrival of his mother, Stella Hampton, and her snarly pet. His big brownstone had suddenly seemed smaller and indisputably noisier. But this was no time for reflection—he had a manuscript to read.

Some thirty minutes later, sorely pressed to concentrate on his work, the sound of the door knocker brought Charles to his feet. Maeve!

But why would she be knocking?

He sat down again.

Less than a minute later came a soft rap on his study door.

"Yes?"

Charles's butler opened the door. "There is a Mr. Lynch to see you, sir. Do you wish to speak with him?"

Charles tossed the manuscript aside. "By all means."

Other than Maeve coming home, the only news that could possibly give him any solace would be word of his stolen sketch.

"Mr. Rycroft."

He rose to greet the intense, ever-frowning private investigator. "Mr. Lynch, have you news?"

"Yes, indeed. Yes, indeed. I've been working long and hard on this case." He paused to scratch his rather billowy, untrimmed side whiskers. "My original suspicions have been recently confirmed. Confirmed."

"How is that?"

"I have been shadowing Maeve O'Malley."

"You've been following my wife?"

Dear God, he'd said it again. Wife.

"Your wife?" Lynch repeated in a rasp.

Outraged, Charles bellowed, "What sort of private investigator are you? You did not even know Maeve was my wife?"

Lynch smacked his lips. His deep frown brought his bushy brows together at the bridge of his nose to form one furry line. "No, Mr. Rycroft, I didn't know. You never mentioned it."

"And you are supposed to be an investigator."

"Well, I know she's the woman who saved you from freezing to death in the alley after you were beaten. After you were beaten."

"And so?"

"Suspicious coincidence," he whispered, nodding his head sagely. "Suspicious coincidence."

"I beg your pardon?"

"That she should just happen along."

"My wife did not attack me and steal my sketch, if that's what you're implying." Charles took a menacing step toward his investigator.

The Civil War veteran backed up. "I didn't say that, didn't say that. Before I knew the lady was your wife I suspected she might be an accomplice."

Charles turned away and slammed his fist against the mantel. "If you knew anything about Maeve O'Malley you could never suggest her as an accomplice to any illegal or unkind act."

"Yes, sir."

"While engaged in following my wife, have you discovered anything of significance?" Charles asked caustically as he turned to face his inept investigator once again.

Lynch did not reply immediately; he looked thought-

ful as if he were weighing the effect of his answer. "Just
an hour ago I saw Miss O' Ma . . . Mrs. Rycroft go into
Edgar Dines's gallery. Edgar Dines."

"What?"

"I'm hating to say this in light of the fact she's your
wife but all along I thought the two might be working
together."

"Are you mad?"

"I may . . . I may be wrong."

"You are fired."

Charles strode to the door and held it open.

Herbert Lynch stood his ground. "How was I to know
the O'Malley woman was your wife without you giving
me all the facts? All the facts. Now that I know, I'll
investigate another avenue. Another avenue."

"No, Mr. Lynch. You are off the case."

"Just one more chance," he pleaded in a voice that
croaked like a frog soprano. "One more."

Charles could barely contain the anger shooting
through his blood in a red-hot stream. "I'm holding
the door for a reason. This is the way out."

"She stayed in Dines's gallery a long time. A long
time."

"You can pick up your payment at my office."

"She may still be there. Still there. I watched for an
hour and Miss O'Malley . . . Rycroft, didn't come out."

Lynch's words hit Charles like a fist to the stomach.
"What?"

"Your wife is with Edgar Dines. Dines."

"Impossible." Charles turned on his heel and strode
to the window. He peered out into the dark, expecting
her to bound up the steps, out of breath and eager to
reach the warmth and safety of Rycroft House.

But no one raced to the door. The street was deserted
save for the light, powdery snow falling from the dark
night sky. He clenched his jaw and drew a deep breath.
The only thing the Irish vixen feared in this world was
being alone in the dark.

What had Maeve got herself into? Why had she gone to Dines's gallery and why hadn't she come home yet?

Charles turned back to the investigator. "Are you carrying any kind of weapon?"

"A small pistol, sir, hidden on my person. My person."

"Come with me," Charles commanded. "We're going to pay a call on Edgar Dines."

Herbert Lynch's frown lifted.

Charles instructed Stuart to bring the town coach around and called for Dolly. "On the chance that Maeve returns before I do, sit on her if you must, but do not let her leave the house until I come back."

"Yes, sir."

Charles did not miss the amused twinkle in the housekeeper's eye. Dolly believed Maeve led him a merry chase. And she was right. Except in this instance, it was not so merry. He was sick with worry, a new and exceedingly unpleasant feeling.

"We will devise a plan on our way, Lynch," Charles said, as he donned his cloak. "More than likely Dines has closed his gallery by now."

The private investigator gave a smug, twisted smile. "I'm skilled in the art of forced entry, sir. Skilled in the art."

Charles felt heartened to hear the man was skilled at something.

As he marched out the door and down the steps to his coach, a steady pain burned within Charles's chest. His pulse throbbed hard and fast as if he'd been galloping for miles astride a runaway horse.

It seemed improbable that the bespectacled art dealer was behind all this. But if he was and if he had harmed Maeve in any way, the sparrow man would pay. Edgar Dines could steal from Charles, attack him, even kill him. But if he hurt so much as a hair on Maeve's head, Charles would see that he spent the rest of his life behind bars.

* * *

She'd put up a good fight, but Maeve was no match for "Spit" O'Brien. She'd kicked and flailed to no avail. The brawny giant quickly overpowered her. Maeve found his laughter especially mortifying.

Alone in the dark with tears streaming down her cold cheeks, she said prayers and lashed out at the wee people, blaming them for her present distressing predicament. She hummed every Christmas carol she knew in a futile attempt to gather the threads of her composure.

Sour-faced and unsympathetic, O'Brien had bound Maeve tightly to a wooden chair centered in the back room. Her hands were tied behind the chair and her feet lashed together at her ankles. The back spindles of the chair dug into her and she shivered with the cold. Second only to the frightening blackness was the numbing cold. After the last log in the wood stove burned out, the already chilly room became an igloo. Maeve could barely feel her toes.

Her heart crashed against her chest again and again, like the waves of a storm against the craggy rocks along the shore. Tension gripped her body in its tight, powerful fist until she could barely breathe. The soggy woolen muffler stuffed in her mouth tasted like an old fuzzy boot.

Maeve had been left to die.

Although, before he left her to die, Dines had written a ransom note which might mean he intended for her to live. The art dealer did not strike Maeve as a man with the heart of a killer. He might be arrogant, smug, and sly, but he wasn't a killer. He might be dull-witted, but she doubted if he was deranged.

Dines seemed almost childlike when he confided that the ransom note offered the return of Maeve and the sketch of St. Nick both, for only a thousand dollars more than Rycroft's reward. Greedy man.

Maeve was not at all certain Charles would pay for

her return when he planned to divorce her in a matter of days. But she did not share her concern with Edgar Dines.

Stroking his mustache and grinning rather wickedly, Dines dispatched his boxer henchman to carry the note to Rycroft Publishing. "Rycroft works well into the night. Leave it, but don't let him see you leave it."

"Aye."

After O'Brien left the gallery, Dines shared his plan with Maeve as if he were used to talking to himself. "Now, Miss O'Malley. In my ransom request I have informed Mr. Rycroft that the sketch he wishes, and you, are safely hidden where he will never find either one. He has been instructed to leave the ransom money in a satchel at the base of the George Washington statue in the public gardens at dawn tomorrow."

Dines appeared quite lighthearted as he put on his hat and cloak. "I shall visit my mistress, Lydia, now and make arrangements for you to spend the night with my lady. Under the circumstances, I am certain she will be glad to see me again, and only too happy to accommodate us in this small matter. She does so enjoy a rich man . . . which I am soon to be."

Maeve pleaded with her eyes and a smothered burbling sound for the little man not to leave her.

"In the meantime, you'll be safe here. Forgive me for not leaving a light burning but since the great fire of last year it would not be the thing. Further, a light might intrigue any passersby."

Maeve blasted him in a muffled manner.

"I should have liked the time to plan this better, but one must seize the opportunity when it occurs, Miss O'Malley." His smirk reminded Maeve of a cat stalking a canary. "Don't go away now." He pointed a finger and chuckled. "I will be back for you within the hour."

It seemed as if two hours had passed since he'd left her to the mercies of the dark, cold night.

In the stillness Maeve heard the hands of a clock

tick—and the rustle of rats. She feared she would swoon from pure terror before Dines returned. Attempting to free her hands only made matters worse as the rope cut deeper. She'd rubbed her throat raw with strangled cries that evidently no one could hear.

In the deadly dark, Maeve struggled to control her anxiety. She'd come so close to obtaining the sketch of St. Nick. She was so close to it now. Maeve had no doubt the stolen sketch resided in the safe beside Dines's desk, only a few yards away.

Rushing headlong through the night, Charles's town coach came to a hurried stop in front of Edgar Dines's gallery.

"There's no light, no sign of anyone in the gallery," he barked at Lynch. "Are you certain Maeve was here?"

"Certain, sir. Certain."

Charles jumped out of the coach, hoping against hope that his private investigator was right about something. Although he'd kept his eye on the street during the drive, he'd not seen many people walking, and no women who resembled Maeve in size or stride.

"Well? What are you waiting for?"

"I'm waiting for you to authorize a break-in."

"Do your best," Charles growled. No authorization from him would make what Lynch was about legal.

Hunched in a stealthy manner, much like a mole approaching his burrow, the investigator scurried to the door and fumbled at the lock for a full minute before Charles heard the door give.

Stepping in front of Lynch, Charles pushed the door open. A soft creak gave way to a jangle of bells. He closed the door quickly.

"Can't see a thing," Lynch hissed.

"Did you hear something?" Charles asked.

"Bells. Bells."

Charles carried a box of cigar matches in his coat

pocket. Groping in the darkness, he found the box and using his fingers to guide him, as a blind man might, he struck a match against the side of the box. The illumination was enough to see a kerosene lamp set on a table in the center of the gallery. He burned his finger before he reached the table. But on the second match he was able to light the lamp.

"Doesn't appear to be anyone here now," Lynch whispered, hovering behind Charles.

"Do you hear that?" Charles cocked his head, straining to hear the sound.

"What?"

"Humming."

"Humming?" Lynch looked at him as if he were mad.

"Humming, coming from the back. Let's go."

Holding the lamp up with one hand, Charles pushed the dividing curtain aside.

"Dear God!" His heart slammed against his chest. "Maeve!"

The humming abruptly stopped.

Bound and gagged, her beautiful blue eyes wild with fright, Maeve brightened with relief when she realized it was Charles. To his horror her little body trembled involuntarily, in fits and starts. Tears spilled down her cheeks, pale as the snow on the window ledge. Her gleaming raven curls tumbled in total disarray about her shoulders, and her jaunty, holly-green hat sat at a precarious angle.

Shoving the lamp at Lynch, Charles rushed to her side and tore at the ropes holding Maeve and then loosed the muffler covering her mouth. Within seconds he pulled her up from the chair and gathered her into his arms. Charles crushed her against him, silently vowing never to let her go.

Maeve cried out his name on the ragged edge of belly-deep sobs. "Oh, Charles! Charles!"

At length he stepped back. Holding her by her forearms, Charles scrutinized her anguished face and skirted his gaze down her cold body, looking for signs of physical harm. "Are you all right? Have you been hurt?"

"No . . . no, I'm, I'm fine," she stammered.

Thankful to find his brave little wife in one still-perfect piece, Charles's heart overflowed with happiness. If anything had happened to Maeve, life would never have been the same for him.

Dear God, he did love her!

Maeve's sobs subsided. Still clinging to Charles, she wiggled in his arms to point behind her. "The sketch of St. Nick is in Dines's safe. I'm certain you'll find it there."

"Is that why you came here?"

She lowered her eyes. "I wanted to recover the sketch and give it to you on Christmas. I couldn't think of anything you would like more. Dines must have had O'Brien steal the sketch from you so that he might sell St. Nick again. I'd hoped that was the case and that he would sell the sketch to me."

Charles felt his heart melt in that moment, honey-thick and hot, pouring over carefully constructed walls that once protected him from this very thing. Caring, loving. Needing.

He gently lifted Maeve's chin between his thumb and forefinger until her eyes met his. "But there is something I want more than Barnabas's sketch, my wild Irish lady."

Appearing crestfallen, Maeve frowned. "There is?"

"You. I want you by my side for the rest of my life. You are the one work of art I cannot, will not, live without."

Dear God! It was true. He wanted Maeve desperately . . . for a lifetime.

Her lips trembled as they slowly turned up into a blinding, dizzying smile. Mesmerized, Charles dipped his head, focusing on the delicious lips he meant to kiss.

But Lynch, still crouched behind Charles, made his presence known. "The door!"

Charles's head snapped up. Newly alert, he listened. A key turned in the back door lock. Clasping Maeve's hand, he motioned Lynch to stand on one side of the door while he quickly strode to the other.

Positioning Maeve flat against the wall, Charles poised to spring on whoever walked through the door in the next second.

Edgar Dines.

Charles jumped the villain while Lynch slammed the door shut behind him.

Dines passed out from fright.

It took several minutes to revive the art dealer and by then Lynch held him fast.

"Rycroft!"

"I understand you sent me a ransom note," Charles said—calmly, he thought, for wanting to rip Dines's heart out.

"Who told you that?"

Maeve stepped forward. "I did."

While he burned to pummel the birdlike man with his bare fists, Charles instead kept a grip on his emotions. He spoke quietly and distinctly. "And now I'd like you to open the safe, Edgar."

Dines grimaced and gave a great put-upon sigh. "Why does nothing ever go right for me?"

"Open the safe quickly or Mr. Lynch will help you," Charles threatened sharply, abandoning all pretense of manners.

"Nothing, nothing has gone my way for years," the art dealer mumbled as he worked the lock on the safe.

"A man who cheats and steals cannot expect things to go his way," Maeve told him, apparently restored.

After the art dealer opened his safe, Lynch bound him with the same rope used to tie Maeve. Charles sat on his heels to inspect the contents of the safe. Maeve stood behind him, the sweet violet scent of her softening the hard, thick tension engulfing the room.

His pulse quickened at the sight of the package resting alone inside the safe. He withdrew it carefully and stood to tear away the brown paper wrapping.

Barnabas's sketch of St. Nick.

Unable to contain his delight, a grinning Charles held the sketch for Maeve to view.

"Saints above! It's the merriest, sweetest Santa Claus I have ever set eyes upon."

"And we shall enjoy it this Christmas, thanks to you," he said, kissing her lightly on the forehead.

"What are we going to do with Dines?" Lynch asked.

"We're going to hand him over to the authorities and find his accomplice."

Maeve supplied the accomplice's name. "Bill 'Spit' O'Brien."

"Spit?" Charles repeated.

"Terrible habit the man has," she said with a rueful wag of her head.

"I see. Do you know where O'Brien can be found, Edgar?"

"I don't know."

"Would you like me to set my man Lynch upon you?"

"No, I would not. Not one opportunity have I had in this life," the miserable man grumbled before grinding out the information between his teeth. "You might look for O'Brien at a boxing match."

"Aye!" Maeve's hands went to her mouth. " 'Tis Shea O'Malley he's going to see! My brother is boxing tonight!"

Men from all over the Boston area packed the A Street Gymnasium. Thick with cigar smoke and shoulder-to-shoulder bodies jostling for a better position, the hall felt overly warm and stuffy. The noise of a high-ceilinged hall filled with men rooting for the boxers, jeering in some cases and just being rowdy in others, was enough to make a woman deaf.

After what she'd just been through, Maeve was in no mood.

Charles found a small, empty space to stand in the back of the hall. His height allowed him to see the boxing ring but Maeve stared at a sea of backs, male backs of all sizes and shapes.

"You shouldn't be here, Maeve," Charles's shouted over the din.

"It's my brother who's boxing. Of course I belong here. I've never missed a match yet." Standing on tiptoe, Maeve stretched her neck, attempting to see the ring. The results of her efforts yielded nothing but a crop of heads, the hairy backs of heads. Was everyone in the world taller than she?

"Can you see what's happening?" she asked Charles.

"Your brother is pounding his opponent into the ropes."

"Oh, dear!"

"It's better than the other way around."

A loud roar went up from the crowd.

"What was that?" A spasm of anxiety gripped Maeve's stomach.

"Shea stepped back. An impressive, sporting gesture."

"Do you see my father?"

"Yes, he's standing alongside the ring. Looks as if he's coaching your brother. He's smiling."

"A bit too much of the ale." Her father always primed himself before one of Shea's matches. "Is Shea bleeding?"

"Not much."

"Saints above!"

"Hmmmm—"

"What?" Maeve's heart collided with her chest.

"Spencer Wellington is here . . ."

Maeve breathed a sigh of relief.

"And I think that's Pansy I see with him."

"Pansy at a boxing match! Her mother will have my head for certain now!"

"Why? Pansy is with Spencer, not you."

"Harriet Deakins blames me for Pansy's strong-willed ways."

"I can't blame her."

"Charles!" Maeve protested.

"In any event, Pansy appears pleased."

"She must have persuaded Spencer to bring her to watch my brother box. It's certain she knew that I would not."

"To see your brother?" Charles arched a skeptical brow. "At present, Spencer and Pansy only have eyes for each other. Our friends may not even be fully aware that they are in a boxing hall and a match is in progress."

"What?" Maeve bounced up on her toes once again in a vain attempt to see Pansy, Spencer, Shea—anyone or anything.

She was about to ask Charles to give her a hand when the crowd gave a resounding cheer. Whistles, applause, and shouts of approval all rang out as the bell sounded. Pure pandemonium broke out in the hall.

"Is my brother on his feet?" Maeve shouted.

"Yes." Charles bent his head down and hollered so that she could hear. "Shea's arms are raised above his head and he's grinning from ear to ear. Apparently your brother has won the bout."

"Heaven be praised."

"And if I'm not mistaken, over near the other corner of the ring Spit O'Brien has just been arrested."

"It's a sad thing but only right."

Taking Maeve by the arm, Charles guided her quickly from the hall. "Don't be sad, he might have killed you."

"But not without a fight." Maeve smiled, tickled with the memory. "Before the big bully tied me up, I did manage a good swift kick in the chins that made him yelp," she confessed. "Mr. Spit O'Brien ranted a bit with words that should never be spoken in the presence of a lady."

Charles rubbed his forehead as if it ached. "Maeve, you must promise me you won't do anything to put yourself in danger ever again."

"I can promise to try." And she would. The thought of repeating such a draining day of drama as this had been gave her goosebumps. Not a good faerie to help her anywhere, all of the day.

Charles chuckled as he led her out of the hall. Icy needles of air stung Maeve's cheeks, almost taking her breath away. But the cold night could not touch the glowing warmth within her. Shea was safe and at last Charles had what he wanted. She could not be happier.

"Would you like me to ask your brother and father to join us for Christmas Day?" Charles asked when they were settled inside his coach.

She *could* be happier! "I would like that more than anything."

His eyes, the soft hazy gray of morning fog, met hers. "I want this to be the best Christmas of your life."

Maeve didn't doubt it would be. It was what the new year held that worried her.

Chapter Twenty

On the drive home from the boxing match, Maeve fell asleep in Charles's arms. She did not attempt to see her father and brother after the fight as both men had been instantly surrounded by a wild surge of cheering Irishmen.

It had been a long, emotionally trying day and Charles hesitated to disturb his sleeping beauty once they arrived home. He carried Maeve to his room and to his bed, where he carefully removed her coat, hat, and shoes. Half-awake, half-asleep, his groggy wife allowed Charles the liberty of undressing her without protest. Although she moaned occasionally.

Uncertain if Maeve could sleep comfortably in a corset, Charles still could not bring himself to fully awaken her in order to undertake that particular task—as much as he would have enjoyed freeing her.

After removing the pins from her hair, he settled her under the down cover. An extraordinary tightening gripped his chest as Charles stood over Maeve, watching her sleep. The warm tide of summer flowed gently through his body, from the soles of his feet to the tip of his head. He tingled.

He knew of no artist with talent enough to duplicate her beauty to canvas. But he would never forget the way she looked at this moment, at peace and content. Maeve's lustrous midnight mane fanned the snowy white pillow in startling contrast. Her long, black lashes curled along high, silky alabaster cheekbones. And her cherry lips, slightly parted, puffed small breaths of air as she gently exhaled.

Charles bent to kiss the tip of Maeve's nose, to feel her warm breath against his cheek, to inhale her sweetness. Straightening, he forced himself to turn away. After almost losing her, he could not bare to be parted from her. Undressing with more haste than usual, Charles slipped into bed, careful not to wake his sleeping wife. Gathering Maeve's small, voluptuous body into his arms, he held her close to his heart through the night.

Much to his chagrin, Maeve woke earlier than he the next day and was gone when he woke. Somewhat belatedly, Charles joined her at the breakfast table. His lovely little wife shot him a somewhat hesitant, shy smile. Was she nervous to be alone with him? He dismissed the thought as preposterous. Nothing ruffled Maeve O'Malley Rycroft.

He dipped to kiss her cheek before taking a seat across from her. "Good morning. You look lovely, and none the worse for our alarming adventure last evening."

"Good morning." She eyed him warily.

He didn't understand her edginess but persevered with his plan. "How would you like to spend Christmas at Ashton Pond?" he asked.

Maeve underwent an instantaneous transformation. Her guarded expression gave way to one of pure joy. Her smile outdazzled the sun on the brightest summer day. "That would be glorious!"

Charles's heart beat in triple time, his body warmed

in the glow of Maeve's radiance. He found himself unable to speak.

"Do you mean it, Charles?"

"I'm closing the company at midday," he told her, unprepared for the husky timbre of his voice. The gut-wrenching desire swamping him was not the sort a man admitted to feeling at breakfast. "Can you be ready to leave when I return?"

Maeve clapped her hands together in delight. "Sure'n I can be ready to leave now—but I shall wait."

It was all Charles could do to leave her even for such a short time. He made her swear not to leave the house while he was away. But he did not intend to be gone long. He was closing Rycroft Publishing after only half a day's work. But it was a special day, Christmas Eve day, and for the first time he realized that more than likely his employees wanted to be with their families as much as he longed to be with Maeve.

Cousin Martin did not bother concealing his astonishment but heartily approved, slapping Charles on the back and wishing him a happy holiday. The two men had resolved their differences to mutual satisfaction. In the new year, the *Rycroft Monthly* would make its debut featuring a story discovered by Maeve from the manuscripts Charles had brought home to her.

Conrad Rycroft would never have allowed his employees to work only half a day. Paying men for time they had not worked would be unthinkable. But Charles wasn't his father and never could be.

He felt especially pleased that at last he understood, accepted, and took pride in the difference. Since his revelation came about recently, he suspected it had something to do with Maeve but wasn't quite certain. The one thing Charles was certain of, was that he must dissuade Maeve from seeking a divorce. Ashton Pond provided the perfect setting for seduction.

He was fairly bursting with excitement when at last he bundled Maeve into the sleigh beside him for the ride to Ashton Pond. Ralph, his driver, assured him that the journey would be cold but free from snow.

Maeve kept a tight rein on her emotions, afraid to hope her handsome husband had experienced a change of heart. If she was wrong, the letdown would be too shattering. But there was reason to believe. She could always find reason to believe.

Charles had appeared happy to find her alive at Edgar Dines's gallery, albeit tied and bound like a piglet on its way to market. He'd whisked her away to Shea's boxing match with only mild protest and now he was taking her to her favorite spot.

On the other hand, he'd vowed to give Maeve the best Christmas of her life. He hadn't vowed to give her the best life . . . a life shared with him.

Maeve spotted the chimney smoke before the sleigh rounded the bend at Ashton Pond. The flickering light of candles burning in every window of the house offered a cheerful welcome. Her heart loop-de-looped with delight. Charles squeezed her closer. She'd been cradled in the strength of his arms and the warmth of his body heat for the entire journey. With every breath she'd inhaled his lusty male scent, held it within her, savored the essence of Charles. By the time the sleigh came to a stop in front of the country house, Maeve wanted her husband quite desperately.

Hilda and George greeted them at the door, bustled them into the cozy warmth of the country house, and helped them off with their hats and coats. Maeve felt as if more than a heavy coat had been removed from her shoulders. Her intangible burden also lifted. She truly felt at home here, at peace within the comforting walls of the rambling cottage.

"Look, our little Christmas tree is still bare," Charles pointed out as he strode into the parlor, heading for the fireplace. "After supper we must see to its decorations."

Maeve followed, briskly rubbing her hands together.

"We shall make it the loveliest tree in New England," she promised.

"Perhaps the loveliest tree in Ashton Pond," he grinned. "I've sent Ralph back to Boston. He'll bring your father and Shea to Ashton Pond tomorrow."

A sweet heat rose up inside of Maeve as she met Charles's smiling eyes. "You are most kind."

He frowned. "Is there something wrong?"

"No."

"You're certain."

"Certain." She rubbed her hands together, smooth and ivory white now.

Charles angled his head, regarding her warily. "You are unusually circumspect."

Maeve lowered her eyes, away from the face she longed to touch, the lips she yearned to kiss. "A lady is expected to be discreet and ... judicious in your world."

"We're in *our* world now, Maeve. And I favor your usual, ah ... spontaneity."

"Truly?" Maeve remained skeptical.

"Truly. And we are free to be ourselves here. We can howl at the moon if we like, dance a jig or ... make love all day."

Her smile came straight from her heart.

"I will demonstrate love-all-day as soon as possible," Charles assured her with a wry twist of his lips.

Maeve's heart thumped a bit too hard and a bit too swiftly in response. Hoping to calm the upheaval, she pressed a hand against the runaway spot within her chest.

"If that's all right with you," Charles added.

They had not made love in many days, and Maeve's longing for him had grown almost unbearable. But before she could answer, Hilda announced supper.

Over steaming bowls of creamy oyster chowder, Charles's gaze locked on hers. Maeve's throat went stone dry. Undisguised desire burned in his dark ash eyes.

"You know oysters are an aphrodisiac, don't you?" he asked, rather thickly.

"No . . . I . . . did not."

"Be warned." His lopsided smile held a promise of passion that took her breath away.

In order to finish her meal without throwing herself into his arms, Maeve avoided her husband's eyes, did not venture a glance at his sensuous lips. Instead, she devoured the delicious hot meal of chowder and biscuits, stewed tomatoes, and macaroons. Once, she stopped long enough to look beyond Charles's broad shoulder to the window.

A steady snow fell through the velvet black night. The bright white crystal flakes created a fresh new cover of snow that glistened beneath the scant rays of fluttering candlelight.

Love and desire curled through her like a tunneling cloud, leaving an exquisite ache in its wake. Being within arm's reach of the man Maeve loved more than life itself gave her more happiness than she'd ever known. Determined to live for the moment, she refused to think of what lay ahead, after the holiday had passed.

Alone in the intimate room, a deep river of magnetism flowed between Maeve and Charles. A tumbling current of unspoken need. His dusky gaze held hers. Her body trembled.

Pine cones snapped in the fireplace, leaping flames crackled. Charles made no move to retire for a cigar and brandy as was his custom after dinner in Beacon Hill.

"Hilda has set out decorations to hang on our tree," he said, breaking the heavy silence. "But first let's hang Barnabas's sketch of St. Nick."

Maeve bobbed her head in assent as Charles held her chair. Clasping her hand in his, he led her into the parlor. The warmth of his touch sheared through her. She slipped from his grasp, stepping up to the wall.

"I think we should place it there beside the tree,

where the Frederick Church painting hangs now. Every guest will see St. Nick immediately upon entering the house," Maeve pointed out, pretending a self-possession she did not feel. She felt afire.

"You don't know how many times I'd feared this sketch was lost forever," Charles said, replacing Church with the work of his brother Barnabas.

"But you believed."

"Because you believed. A woman who believes in faeries and in Santa Claus is a mighty force. Your great and wonderful capacity for believing kept me hoping somehow."

Words caught in her throat.

Charles retrieved a package from under the tree. "This is for you."

"But . . . but it's not Christmas."

He gestured toward the jolly likeness of St. Nick hanging on the wall. "I have my Christmas gift to enjoy—it's only right you should have yours now, too."

Sinking into a nearby ottoman, Maeve opened the package adorned with paper cherubs and golden ribbon. Her fingers shook when she opened the box. "Oh, Charles!"

She could say no more. The most beautiful porcelain doll Maeve had' ever seen rested on a bed of cotton. The delicate figure possessed large pansy-blue eyes and perfectly bowed ruby lips. Dark sausage curls fell from under a velvet bonnet and skimmed the shoulders of a hunter green coat, just like Maeve's.

Her first doll.

"Do you like her?" Charles asked.

"Saints above! She's the most beautiful doll in the world."

"Not quite." His lips turned up in a small, crooked smile as his eyes met hers.

Maeve rose to give him what she meant to be a kiss on the cheek but somehow Charles turned his head in time for his lips to claim hers. Within a heartbeat, he'd wrapped his arms around both Maeve and the doll. As her lips parted beneath his, her knees wobbled and a deep, moist yearning swirled inside of her.

It seemed a very long time before Charles raised his mouth from hers and spoke. "I saw the doll in a shoppe window and she reminded me of you, Little Bit."

"I shall treasure her forever. And I . . . I shall call her Charlotte." Hugging the doll to her, Maeve wheeled from Charles's embrace. She didn't want him to see the tears in her eyes again.

While regaining her composure, she stared out at the snowy night, shimmering flakes dancing in slender ribbons of golden light. It was almost as if Maeve and Charles had done the impossible and slipped through the Great Mist into the faerie land of Tir Nan Og, a magical place of love and happiness. They had traded two different worlds for one magical world.

"Maeve?" Charles sounded worried.

"I should like to stay here forever," she murmured.

He came up behind Maeve then and held her, pressing her back against the hot, steely wall of his chest. "I think we can manage to spend a good deal of time at Ashton Pond. It's a splendid place to raise children."

Her precious doll dropped to the floor. Maeve whirled around. "Children?"

"Wouldn't you like to have children, Maeve?"

"Aye . . . yes, but—" Lowering her eyes, Maeve stooped to reclaim her doll.

"But what?"

"Di . . ." Her throat closed. Taking a deep breath, she tried once again. "But . . . the divorce."

She held her breath, waiting to be struck down dead for saying the word aloud on Christmas Eve! Charles took the doll from her and laid it on the marble-topped tea table.

Taking both of her hands in his, he looked into Maeve's eyes. "I don't want a divorce."

"You don't?"

"I've never been as happy as I've been these past few weeks. And I can think of only one reason. You. I cannot imagine living without you. I cannot conceive of living without your laughter, or sleeping without you beside me."

"But you are from Beacon Hill and I come from—"

"We are both besot with Ashton Pond. This is common ground for us."

"But we cannot live here. Your business is in Boston." She shook her head in dismay. "And I shall never belong in Boston society."

"I need you in my world, Maeve. You have the power to open eyes and hearts. You've already done so. Do you think Spencer, Pansy, or my mother ever thought they'd be dancing the Irish jig?"

Maeve could not help but laugh at the picture the memory conjured. "No. I expect not!"

"I know it won't be easy, but I promise to support you and care for you so dearly that no one will dare hurt you."

Charles was begging her to stay. Maeve could hardly believe she was not dreaming. But she loved him too much to cause him the loss of his friends. She loved him too much to cause him any pain at all. So, she raised still another obstacle to their happiness. "Your mother does not approve of me."

"My mother will come around. Did you know she complimented your triumph at the Cabots' Snow Ball?"

"No."

"Besides, Beatrice advised me at the last to do the right thing."

"The Rycroft right thing."

He nodded. His lips turned up in a gentle smile. "For me the right thing is being married to you, Maeve."

Maeve could hardly credit what she was hearing. She thought to pinch herself. "Are you . . . are you asking me to be your wife forever?"

"Forever." Charles lifted her hands to his lips and brushed her palms with a soft breeze of a kiss.

Maeve tingled from her fingertips to her toes. Her body flooded with startling warmth.

"Forever yours," she murmured.

"And if you do not allow me to make love to you immediately," he said quite earnestly, "I will be forced to run outside and roll in the snow until my hot body freezes over."

Maeve grinned. "I should dislike it if you took a chill on my account."

Without another word, Charles scooped her into his arms and carried his laughing wife upstairs to his bed. He made love to Maeve with reverence. With each tender caress he brought her closer to the land of legends. She lay in a lush green meadow of shamrocks, where the beautiful wee people sipped nectar from flower petals and an azure sky glimmered with specks of silver faerie dust. In precious moments Maeve reached the place of her heart, the magical splendor of Tir Nan Og. Ever-young. Spring eternal. Love forever. It was all hers, all found in Charles's arms.

Charles could not stop loving her. He filled his palms with the lush, soft mounds of her breasts, the full, silken curves of her hips. Bittersweet pain rippled through his body from the throbbing ache in his loins. His mouth covered her ear, and then a dusky, taut nipple. She tasted pleasantly salty. She tasted like peppermint. She smelled like violets in the spring . . . a whole bouquet of sweetness. When he could not bear the pain of being apart from her, Charles buried himself deep inside the welcoming warmth of Maeve's body, thrusting wildly, loving her recklessly. Too soon, his hammering heart shattered and his seed spilled in a hot rush of delicious release.

Dear God, he loved this woman!

The grandfather clock in the hall chimed the midnight hour. The fire in the fireplace burned dangerously low and the candle on the bedside table was about to flicker out.

"It's Christmas," Maeve whispered. "Merry Christmas, my love. My love."

Chuckling, Charles kissed his saucy Irish wife and then grew serious. Bracing himself on one arm above her, he looked into the mystical shining blue irises of Maeve's eyes. He knew it was time to confess what he'd known from the start, but could not reconcile. "I love you, Little Bit. Do you know how much I love you?"

Her eyes widened. Her lips, swollen from his kisses, parted in wonder.

"If I have never told you how much I love you and how dear you are to me, I am telling you now. I love you."

She turned her ear toward him as if she might not have heard him. "Did you say you loved me?"

He chuckled again and nuzzled her ear, sprinkled bite-sized kisses along the porcelain column of her neck. "I love you more than I thought it possible to love a woman. If I had the words of a great poet, you would know with utmost clarity the love that fills my heart. And I need you," he confessed thickly. "You give life to my soul. Will you be my wife?"

"I will be your wife," she whispered. And then Maeve's arms curled around Charles's neck and brought his lips down on hers.

Mouth-watering aromas filled the country house on Christmas Day. Roasting turkey, fresh-baked apple pie, cinnamon, and bubbling cranberries mingled in the air.

Maeve wore one of her new silk dresses, a green-and-white striped confection with a soft bustle in the back. Charles thought the light in her eyes bright enough to guide whaling ships from far Nantucket to the Boston harbor. Happiness radiated from her as tangible as the toy soldiers dangling from the Christmas tree. They'd belatedly decorated the tree this morning.

At the sound of distant sleighbells, Maeve ran to the door. She greeted her father and Shea—who looked none the worse for wear after his boxing match—with great hugs.

"Merry Christmas!"

Charles stood at her side, greeting each of her family with a hearty handshake. "Father Thom?"

Father Thom stepped from behind Shea.

"Father Thom!" Maeve exclaimed, bewildered. "What a pleasant surprise."

"Merry Christmas to ye, Maeve."

She could not imagine who invited the good father— Dad or Shea—but she was always happy to see the priest.

"Father Thom has come to marry us," Charles said.

Startled, Maeve turned to her husband. "But he has already done so."

"Not so that I can remember. The best, very nearly the only, right thing I've ever done in my life is to marry you. But I have not one memory of it." He gave her a wide grin that caused her heart to fly. "Do not expect me to live without the memory of marrying you, Maeve."

Within the hour, Father Thom married a grinning Charles and a beaming Maeve. At the conclusion of the brief ceremony, Shea passed Charles a small velvet box. When he opened it, the gleaming gold of two rings winked at Maeve. Irish Claddaugh rings. Heart, hands, and crown intertwined on the bands symbolizing love, loyalty, friendship, fidelity, and faith.

"But this isn't my Mam's ring," she said.

"No. It's yours. Shea will give your Mam's ring to his bride one day."

"Oh, Charles!" Maeve threw herself at her husband and, risking his embarrassment, kissed him soundly in front of the others.

The wedding party celebrated with Christmas dinner. Maeve wished everyone at the table could feel the same happiness she felt. But that was not within her power. Near the end of the meal, she leaned toward her brother. "I hate to bear bad news," she said, laying a gentle hand on his arm, "but I think my friend Pansy has proved to be fickle. She's discovered another man."

Shea broke into a wide smile. "Not bad news, me Maeve. That is good news to me ears. Sure'n I found her red hair bonny, but wondered just the same how not to hurt a friend of yours. I'm not ready to settle yet, Maeve, my darlin'. I've got a fishing business to build."

"Did I hear *fishing business?*" Charles asked.

"Aye."

Charles arched a brow. "What an astonishing coincidence. One of the investments I've been considering for the new year is a fishing enterprise. Tell me, do you have a boat?"

"Not yet."

"I think I can help with that."

To Maeve's absolute delight, the proof of Charles's love continued to blossom around her, reaching out and touching the ones she loved.

When the small group pushed themselves from the table, Hilda served plum pudding drenched in sweet hard sauce as they opened gifts around the Christmas tree.

Dad took to his new jacket immediately and Shea looked amazingly handsome in the heavy cable sweater Maeve knit for him.

Charles whooped with laughter when he opened the package from Maeve. She'd made him a Santa Claus suit in hopes he would entertain the children at the orphanage again next year.

True to his word, Charles had given her the best Christmas of her life. But she knew there would be many more. The sweet Charlie she'd married weeks ago had become one with the Beacon Hill blue blood, a combination one could only love.

Later, after everyone had retired for the night, Maeve

waited in bed, propped against a small mountain of feather pillows. She waited for her lover. Her husband. One small candle burned at her bedside.

At last she heard a soft rap on her door, the rap she'd been waiting for.

She called softly, "Come in."

She wasn't expecting the man who walked through the door.

Santa Claus, wearing a full red velvet suit and fluffy white cotton beard, strode toward her bed. His dove-gray eyes twinkled and he wore a silly grin upon his face.

"Ho . . . ho . . . ho!"

Maeve squiggled down in the bed, giggling.

Santa greeted her in a deep, rumbling voice. "Merry Christmas, Little Bit!"

"Oh, no!" she cried, tears of laughter streaming down her face.

"Oh, yes," Santa declared, before lowering his voice to a seductive rumble. "I brought more love for you."

"A woman can never have too much love," Maeve gasped between giggles. Reaching up, she pulled Santa into her bed.

But Charles was enjoying his charade. "Ho . . . ho . . . ho! Merry Christmas to all . . . and to all a good night."

There seemed only one way for Maeve to silence him.

She blew out the candle.

She had nothing to fear in the dark.